ᐠᕮᏒᑎᏳᑎᐧᐠᐠᐱᏒᑢᑎᐁᏕᏗᏒᏒᐞ

Runasarre'afeithen

Between Starfalls

Book One of Children of the Nexus

by S. Kaeth

This is a work of fiction. Names, characters, places, and incidents either are the product of the author's imagination or are used fictitiously. Any resemblance to actual persons, living or dead, events, or locales is entirely coincidental.

Published by:
Hakea Media
350 W 6th St #932
Dubuque, IA 52004
hakeamedia@gmail.com
www.hakeamedia.com

In association with Teacup Dragon Co-op

Print ISBN: 978-1-955220-01-9
Ebook ISBN: 978-1-7333281-4-2
Library of Congress Control Number: 2020903061
First Edition

Cover by Dave Brasgalla
https://www.davidbrasgalla.art

Author's website: www.skaeth.com

Content Warning:
Includes descriptions of combat, drugging, imprisonment, mutilation, ableism, domestic abuse, children in peril, and animals in peril.

A Map of Rinara

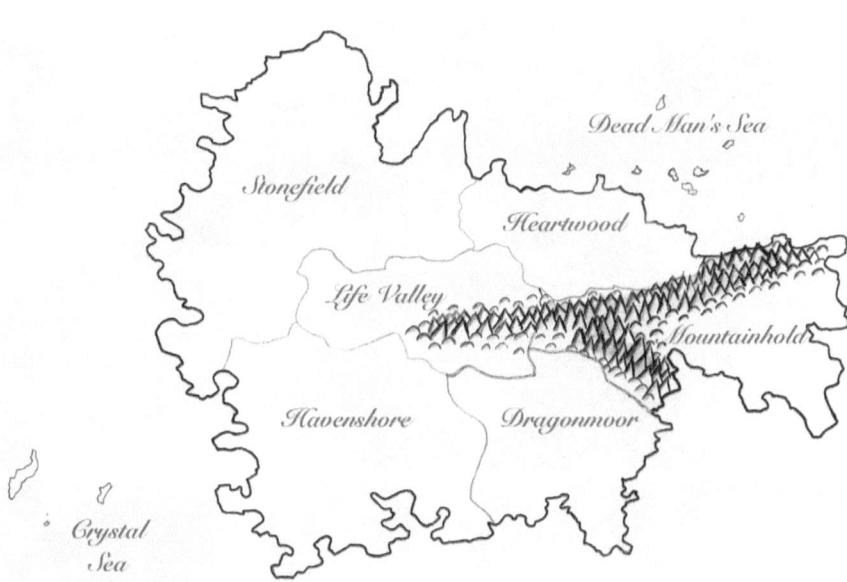

Dead Man's Sea

Stonefield

Heartwood

Life Valley

Mountainhold

Havenshore

Dragonmoor

Crystal
Sea

To my boys. Never let the world dim your light.

Chapter One

The Rinaryns believe they were created by the smallest spirit during a contest of creative ability. According to their legends, this event also produced such wildlife as toelfas, tserworas, zeriys, and tailosaes; such sentient races as the fae, elves, and of course the viperous dragons; and the mythical Kamalti beneath the mountains, which the Rinaryns refer to as their brother race.

While their true origins are undoubtedly a great deal more mundane than creation-by-spirit, the Rinaryns themselves are less than extraordinary overall. They are bipeds, a little smaller on average than humans, and a great deal lighter in build (I expect they have hollow bones). They have round faces and brown skin, and their hair tends to be black or brown, although children can have golden-blond hair that often darkens as they age. Their eyes are typically brown but can also be blue or grey. Their one extraordinary detail is that a small percentage of them have wings, resulting in six limbs rather than four. I would love to study them further, but the aeneshenon, as they call the winged Rinaryns, are quite rare and very seldom am I fortunate enough to encounter them. According to their legends, when the Rinaryns were created, all had wings.

—journal excerpt

Rain beaded off Kaemada's nose and dripped onto the sodden leaves littering the forest floor. Straining her ears, she moved forward, careful to prevent even a single leaf movement from betraying her presence.

"Where is he?" Ra'ael muttered ahead of her.

"Quiet," hissed Takiyah. "Do you want him to hear us?"

Kaemada grimaced. Yet another argument, and she lacked the patience to deal with it. It didn't help that they were soaked through. They'd all grown snappish through the morning's challenge, and the typical verbal battles between Takiyah and Ra'ael had become nearly constant. As she twisted her foot to avoid a fallen branch in her path, her big toe throbbed in protest. She'd jammed it tripping over her son's wooden wagon toy while leaving in the grey dawn light, still sleepy from being up half the night helping her cousin soothe a colicky baby. Stifling a yawn, she breathed deep, as if she could pull more alertness from the forest around her. It seemed the spirits planned a difficult tune for her today.

At least the rain, which had fallen all morning, had slowed. Kaemada glanced to her right, meeting a pair of yellow eyes. Tannevar shook out his fur and trotted ahead, a grey shadow in the wood.

The three women crept through the underbrush, their steps as silent as the wolf's. The trees surrounded them, muting sounds while displaying every shade of yellow, orange, and red imaginable. Rowoods, cha'awoods, píewoods, elderwoods, and broadleafs stretched for the autumn sun. The lofty treetops drew her heart, but no matter how hard she worked, her story seemed destined to remain one of the ferns sprawling across the forest floor. She needed to either grow or leave the team to avoid tripping them up. Tears stung her eyes, and she blinked them back before either of the other women could notice.

Birds flitted about their business, and tailosaen hung from branches, scolding the women's intrusion with shrill chitters as they stepped between the mist-shrouded trunks. Kaemada shot the furry creatures a glare. So easily, their presence could be given away. Every Rinaryn in the Heartwood region learned how to move through the forest without leaving a sound or trace from the time they could take their first steps. Still, few could pass the tailosaen without triggering their sharp alarm cries. Another picked up the call.

"We will be at the edge of the trees soon, near Seven Times Ridge," Takiyah murmured.

Ra'ael nodded, taking a moment to squeeze water out of her securely confined black hair. "We go there, then, and use it as a lookout. Maybe we can see some sign of him."

Kaemada nodded. If they could find the hermit before he found them, she'd be happy. Having proven her worth, she'd stay with the team, and no one would need to know she'd thought of leaving them.

"More likely he will find us, out in the open like that." Boredom oozed from Takiyah's voice.

Ra'ael bristled. "Fine. We will endure a scolding—"

"Or bruises from those ripples he throws," Takiyah interjected again, and Ra'ael fixed her with a menacing stare.

"And then, we will have finished training for the day. I have other duties to tend to."

"In that case, just leave now." Takiyah's eyes flickered down at Ra'ael and then back to scanning the landscape.

"I cannot do that!"

Kaemada tuned them out as they bickered yet again, reaching out to Tannevar through the bond she shared with him. A flood of scents engulfed her, and she stumbled into an elderwood tree. Shaking her head, she placed a hand on the trunk to steady herself before continuing, once again firmly in her own body with her limited sense of smell. "Galod isn't up ahead."

"How do you know?" Ra'ael asked.

"Tannevar does not smell him. The breeze is blowing this way, so if he were ahead, Tannevar would know."

"You use your psionics too much," Ra'ael growled.

Takiyah shook her head, her red hair lashing. "We must draw on all our skills to succeed, even those frowned upon. Taunos would already have found him."

Kaemada's brother would certainly be waiting for them with Galod, ready to laugh at their tardiness. Would be, that is, if he were around. Kaemada crept out onto the rocky outcropping. This time, they'd win the challenge, proving she was right to continue training. Otherwise... The dread of their disappointment only flared her own.

Seven Times Ridge afforded a view of a great expanse of Heartwood, though they would have to stay low or risk Galod spotting them. Kaemada swept her gaze carefully across the land while Takiyah and Ra'ael slithered up next to her.

"Who's that?" Takiyah peered intently at someone in the distance.

Kaemada leaned toward her, sighting along her finger. Locking her gaze on the lone figure, she leaned toward Ra'ael on her other side, pointing. Only the barest gesture was needed before Ra'ael bumped her shoulder in acknowledgement. Kaemada squinted as the figure strode through a meadow.

"They're heading toward Torkae," Takiyah whispered. "I cannot make out who it is, though."

"It cannot be Neven or Farel. They're already back from their yah," Ra'ael said.

Kaemada nodded. The celebration for the boys' completion of the ritual would be tonight.

Ra'ael leaned forward. "They do not move like Galod, although that does not necessarily mean anything."

"At this pace, it will take, what, till midday for whoever this is to reach Torkae?" Kaemada guessed. Her son was in Torkae.

Takiyah nodded.

Was this a Dark scout, left over from the attack a couple of days ago on a neighboring kaetal? Or perhaps a fae? People travelling alone were uncommon in Rinara—hunters typically travelled in groups or at least pairs. Kaemada frowned. If they meant harm to her son, no old battle wound would keep her back.

Kaemada reached out to the birds. A telepathic link with animals was not so hard, once she adjusted to the vast differences in ways of thinking. Still, telepathy worked best at very short ranges. Birds, however, were everywhere, always alert, and they passed messages between themselves with marvelous speed, unlike tailosaen, who kept their knowledge strictly within family groups. Between the bird network and Tannevar's nose, she often had a pretty accurate idea of what dangers lurked nearby.

She shook her head after a moment. "I cannot get a clear sense. Although there is danger to the northwest, the birds say. Watch for it while I go farther."

"Be careful." Worry filled Ra'ael's voice.

Kaemada smiled at her, then closed her eyes and laid her head on her folded hands. She dreamwalked, leaving her body in between her friends while Tannevar crept forward to cover her, to keep her body warm. A thin link extended from her to him, preventing her from drifting aimlessly as she swam out like a fish in a creek. She headed for the spirit-songs of a flock of migratory birds flying north above the figure.

Riding the waves of that song, she touched one of the birds' minds and looked out of its eyes, trying unsuccessfully to convince it to fly lower. Even at such a height, its vision was sufficient for her to see that the man was, indeed, a stranger. His clothes were Rinaryn and appeared to be in decent shape; he looked clean and well-groomed, at least from the distance. Not a Dark nor fae, then.

With a dissonant chord, the bird ejected her, thrusting her into the dreamscape where she drifted, disoriented. Her bond with Tannevar was her lifeline. The warmth and wildness of his spirit's song twined inseparably with her own, drawing her back to her body.

Smashed between Ra'ael and Takiyah, with Tannevar smothering her, she couldn't breathe, couldn't move. She had to get out, had to gain room. A strangled cry escaped her as she burst upward. Ra'ael and Takiyah reached for her, but she shook them off.

An orb-shaped ripple shot toward her from the northwest. The orbs Galod threw bent the light as if there was a pool of water in midair, defying the senses. She stared at it, overwhelmed and disoriented, but Takiyah yanked her sideways. The orb flashed past, into the forest. Kaemada landed hard on her knee, and Tannevar yelped with the pain that flashed up her leg.

"What happened?" Takiyah demanded.

"The bird got tired of sharing," Kaemada gasped. "It's a stranger,

4

possibly a messenger."

"The bird is a stranger?"

"The person!" Kaemada scowled, rubbing her knee.

"You must be careful. You could easily end up as No-mind," Ra'ael said. Kaemada suppressed a shudder.

Ra'ael drew in a deep breath and sighed it out, staring toward the northwest. "We failed... again. Better not lose the sparring. Let's go."

Now that he'd found them, Galod would be coming, just like a Dark scout would. They backed toward the shelter of the misty brambles, pain piercing through Kaemada's bad knee with every step. She'd caused them to fail, just as she'd feared. Her injury still held her back, and in one moment of weakness, she'd betrayed their location. Pain soured her song —not the ache of her knee, but that of being unable to help protect the people she loved.

Once among the brush, Ra'ael led them around in an arc toward Galod's hiding place. Ra'ael drew her short sword and dagger. Takiyah held her metal staff close to her side as she crouched low, scanning the forest. Together, they moved through the trees, swift and sure.

If she had to leave them, would she grow jealous watching them gather all the glory they deserved? The very thought caused her chest to tighten. She didn't want to be jealous—she just wanted to be equal to them once more. She couldn't let them see the turmoil inside her. If they knew she considered leaving them, she'd never hear the end of it, and already the very thought dragged her low.

Kaemada struggled to avoid snapping twigs and rustling leaves with her limping. She reached into the oiled pouch in her belt for her bowstring, but rainwater had managed to get in at the corners. Her string was soaked, her bow useless. Nothing today was going as she'd hoped it would.

Her scouting skills hadn't been enough, and now she couldn't use her bow. Psionics was all she had left. A splash of water tumbled from the leaves above to coat her. She closed her eyes and focused hard on the sounds of the forest, trying to force her song to a tune of hope, or at least resilience. Rain, limp, and useless bow or not, she couldn't give up.

Ra'ael glanced back and gestured westward. Kaemada nodded and turned, creeping along a low barrier of prickleberry bushes, against the protests of her knee, until Ra'ael signalled again. They waited, Kaemada's every sense alert for danger on any side, checking in often with Tannevar and the bird network.

A tailosae chittered and threw fruit at Takiyah's ambush site. Kaemada reached out to try to soothe its territorial wrath, but then the whole forest erupted in alarm cries.

A cloud of dust and wind swirled in their direction, and the hairs on the back of Kaemada's neck prickled. Tannevar slunk away. He'd been interested in finding the hermit, but now that he was found, the wolf preferred to keep his distance.

Kaemada watched Ra'ael for the signal, and when Ra'ael nodded, she pushed at a nearby log both telekinetically and physically, sending it tumbling downhill. Another log rolled toward hers, pushed by Ra'ael. Takiyah leapt up, in line with where the logs would collide, and released her flames. A mighty, swirling windstorm obscured their teacher, yet four orbs, one right after another, came shimmering toward Kaemada. She dropped to the ground.

You use your psionics too much.

That was all she had left. Kaemada advanced, throwing large sticks at the back of the whirlwind with telekinetic boosts of power. Takiyah and Ra'ael would be able to box him in if she could drive the old hermit close enough. Maybe, just maybe, if she could help them best Galod, she could stay with them, stay part of the team they'd grown into the last twenty summers. After all, the goal was to protect her people from attack.

Takiyah stood before the storm, her long hair whipping behind her as she struck and parried. Fire flowed from her hands down the length of her long grey staff. Around her, Ra'ael ducked and flitted, slashing at Galod with her sword and striking precise hits whenever Takiyah created an opening.

Between one heartbeat and the next, the familiar rhythm of combat training faltered. Ra'ael turned on Takiyah and lashed out with her dagger. Takiyah dove away just before Ra'ael's sword slashed through the air where she'd stood.

The whirlwind disappeared to become their old teacher, his stormy eyes the hard grey of the Holy Mountains to the south. "Stop."

Ra'ael threw herself toward Galod, and Kaemada's breath caught in her throat. Her friend had slipped into the blood rage, that state when she struck at anyone and everyone in front of her. In battle, they always stayed well behind those with the blood rage. Ra'ael loathed losing control.

Three orbs in quick succession blasted Ra'ael into the ground. Kaemada shuddered, racing over as Galod crouched beside the fallen woman. Panting for breath, Takiyah leaned on her staff, pressing one hand to her upper arm. Kaemada took strips of cloth from Takiyah's belt pouch, grateful she was always prepared, and helped her bandage the cut.

"I will be fine," Takiyah said, shaking her off.

Kaemada wrinkled her nose at her, double-checking the knot of the bandage.

They both stilled, staring at Galod's vigil over Ra'ael. He wielded his ripples of power with uncanny control, but accidents were possible. It seemed the whole forest sighed with relief when Ra'ael regained her feet, rubbing her chest and head with a pained look. Kaemada embraced her, ignoring her embarrassment and the way she avoided looking at Takiyah.

"Takiyah, forgive me."

"I'm fine." Takiyah gripped Ra'ael's arm.

Galod cleared his throat, wearing a familiar frown. His black hair was streaked with grey, and his clothes draped him in a foreign style, all blue and grey. Kaemada clustered close to Ra'ael and Takiyah as they turned to face him.

"Not good enough," he shouted.

His glare pinned Kaemada like prey. "You are too slow, too cautious. You have been training for twenty summers, Kaemada, and this should be in your blood by now! You live and breathe this. When the time comes, you must surrender to it. No excuses, no avoiding imminent conflict. An enemy will not be so gentle as I."

She stared at her clenched fingers, clasping them in front of her until the skin whitened. Was it her inner turmoil that had caused her to fail, or was she still not good enough?

He turned on Ra'ael. "You must control your blood rage. Control allows the telekinesis. Its absence allows the blood rage. You must always decide when that happens. Do not be afraid of the risk, but do not allow a slip from lack of control, either!"

"You." He narrowed his eyes at Takiyah. "Finesse, Takiyah, finesse! Wading into the thick of battle and waiting for your friends to save you only works if you don't leave them behind. If they're not with you, don't step forward unless you want a knife in your back."

Kaemada stared at the fallen leaves around her boots. She could feel Galod glowering at them, but they each knew better than to engage him. There was no need to make a bad day worse. She bit her lip, her heart torn to pieces, engaged in a bitter battle with itself. Her gaze went to the east, where three dead trees clustered. Their roots had withered away, yet still, they were home to many creatures, and vines grew around them. For as they died, they fell together, each supporting the other, even in storms.

When they'd been younger, Taunos had laughed and named the trees for them, but Kaemada saw the truth in it. When there were only three supports, each needed to be strong. When there were many, as in a hut, the weakness of one no longer mattered so much. If she could not be strong, she would have to leave the work she'd trained so hard to do.

If only her heart could accept that.

Shaking his head, Galod waved them away. "Go now. You have a ceremony to prepare for."

How did he always know the kaetal's celebrations, though he rarely left his clearing?

Ra'ael and Takiyah nodded a formal farewell to Galod and turned to go. Kaemada quickly followed, glancing back to see the hermit striding away.

Takiyah nodded her head toward a large fern. "Torkae is that way."

Ra'ael narrowed her eyes at her. "The path is this way."

"That takes longer." Takiyah headed through the vegetation without looking back, ignoring Ra'ael's glare.

Kaemada shrugged. "The only paths we have to stay on are those through the mountains."

Grumbling, Ra'ael tromped behind them.

The trees thinned as the women descended the hill outside the kaetal. Beyond, the tall grasses of the prairie danced in the wind, where animals grazed and children played in the waning rain. The domed huts of Torkae, made from woven grasses and bent branches tied together with sinew and twine, stood in harmony with the natural surroundings, whether they be in the prairie or forest. Every home's doorway faced the central fires.

It should be enough to be a part of a hut rather than to be a tree against the storm. Kaemada lifted her face to the wind and forced a smile to veil her troubled thoughts.

A wide path swept through the middle of the kaetal at the forest's edge. At the western end, it led across the grassy field, which they were decorating for the ceremony, and then up a hill where a large wooden building with a roof of woven grasses stood—the Ellewyn. Most nights, Ra'ael supervised the unmarried youth of Torkae as they gathered there, where they could sing, dance, and mingle freely without disturbing others.

The bustle of activity filled the air. Hundreds of people went about their business in a flood of brown skin, dark eyebrows, and round faces that bore the many kisses of rain and sun and wind. Laughter and conversation created a pleasant hum that sang of life all around. As hunters returned, tools were cared for and meat butchered. Others whittled, tanned hides, or tended the smokehouse. A true smile broke on Kaemada's face upon seeing her son, Eian, playing with string alongside two other young children while one of the Elders gestured widely, telling them a story.

Groups of mostly women tended fields or clustered around the fires at the center of the kaetal. Mothers worked with babies strapped on their backs or playing nearby. They sang and talked in small groups as they mended clothing, wove fabric and grass mats, spun fibers into thread, or mixed dyes. Children ran through the kaetal, playing at races, throwing sticks through hoops sent racing down the hill, or leaping about in the trees. Older children tended the lumbering, shaggy alanshorn as they grazed, music drifting through the air from their pipes.

Turning away from her morning frustrations, Kaemada's smile grew. She met Ra'ael's gaze as the other woman retrieved her pale blue shroud of priesesshood from their house and draped it over her shoulders. Everything was just as it should be.

"It would be helpful if you three would at least gather some greens or hunt some meat while you play at war with Galod." Talaera emerged from the trees carrying a large basket of sprawling stars-of-evening, her black eyes sharp with disapproval.

Kaemada's smile vanished. Dropping her gaze to the grasses beneath her boots, she searched for harmony. She was never comfortable with the worry from her mother's cousin and tried to avoid it as much as possible, just as the words that would bring peace now evaded her.

"We cannot train and bring back food at the same time, as we have discussed before," Ra'ael said, facing Talaera's reproach for her.

"Then why not gather on the way back?"

Ra'ael's eyebrows raised. "We each have our tasks, and you seem to have this one well in hand."

Talaera frowned, matching their pace as they wound their way toward the center of the kaetal. "Why set yourselves apart so? Other kaetaln would be quite alarmed, seeing psions together and idle. Especially students of Galod."

"Pay no mind to the shrieking of tailosaen, for it is only gossip and of no consequence." Saimahkae Maeren, the Great Mother of Torkae, waved them over with a smile to soften her words. "You are ours, and we know your challenges, but also how brightly you shine."

Kaemada quickened her step and settled beside the square-faced woman with short, grey curls. While Talaera was her closest kin besides her brother, Maeren always felt more like family. "Betah teimelei, Saimahkae Maeren."

"Ah, Kaemada, so formal." Maeren laughed and reached for Takiyah with both hands. "Takiyah, come here, my daughter."

Takiyah bent down, receiving and returning Maeren's kiss. "Betah, Mother."

"I'm off to alert the Storyteller and Teros about the messenger Kaemada spotted," Ra'ael said.

Kaemada lifted a hand as she hurried away, but Ra'ael didn't acknowledge her. Her loss of control with Galod must still be troubling her.

"I must finish Alaren's dagger," Takiyah said as her mother handed her a wooden bowl of berries to sort. "I promised him it would be ready tonight."

Maeren frowned and passed the bowl to Kaemada instead. "Go well. I have enough help in Lína's daughter."

Thankful for the work to display her contributions to the kaetal, Kaemada sorted the berries, throwing out the odd one that had gone bad.

"I worry how others see us," Talaera said, settling on Maeren's other side.

Kaemada's stomach churned. Why couldn't Talaera let this go? But at least Maeren was there—not even Talaera could argue long with the Saimahkae. Kaemada tried, but she couldn't be what Talaera wanted. She always came up short, like this morning. She couldn't be her brother.

If she left Galod's training, Talaera at least would be happy, but certainty filled her as she tossed out another bad berry. If she didn't try to protect her people somehow, that would poison her just as surely as the bad berries rotted the rest. She wanted to contribute more than poor baking or tangled weaving. Galod's teachings had always drawn her, sure as the mists clustered by the rivers. But the only tasks she was good at brought strife.

Talaera retrieved a bowl from her basket and began separating the stems from the petals of the flowers. They would be crushed and used as a seasoning once dried. "Takiyah's forge? Psions together outside the kaetal? We must look to the rest of Rinara and be harmonious with them."

Maeren raised her eyebrows at Talaera. "I seem to hear more shrieking. Is it just these old ears?"

Kaemada hid a smile as Talaera ducked her head, her stone knife slicing furiously at the flowers, bruising the petals.

"They're not Rinaryn. These antics of yours—nursing that pegasus colt to health, the conversing with birds, this talk of training psions as a group—must end!"

Kaemada's eyes narrowed. "It would be easier to train psions as a group, as Galod trains Ra'ael, Takiyah, and me. Especially if you wish me to have more time for other tasks."

"It's not our way. You must be above any suspicions. The honor your mother gathered to herself, despite being a psion, will not protect you if you continue such ways. Please, Kaemada, for your own sake, please. Do not be so strange."

Why was it that her mother and her brother—even her sister—were highly honored despite choosing tasks her people thought unusual, yet Kaemada couldn't manage the same? Wilting, she scowled at the berries. "I only wish to help, not bring disharmony."

"Why do we allow Galod to stay, Saimahkae?" Talaera asked. "Why do we allow his students to go outside our laws for training? Not all are easy with Galod, nor with us because of him."

Maeren raised her eyebrows again. "What is the uneasiness of others against the defense of our kaetal? And, unlike many Rinaryn, Galod has been happy to help in this way."

"Some worry Galod may muddy our song. We should be harmonious with other Rinaryn," argued Talaera.

Heat rose to Kaemada's cheeks. The hermit's teachings helped her keep her son safe. She didn't want more disharmony, but she couldn't sit back while Talaera attacked Galod. The words came out before Kaemada could stop them. "And so we sent supplies to Tanelwith when the Darks attacked."

Talaera fixed Kaemada with a piercing stare. "You should not have sent those two wagons of supplies."

That sparked a fire in Kaemada. "The attack decimated Tanelwith. They were afraid and needy, and I helped them. Is that not part of the harmony you spoke of?"

Talaera drew in a deep breath as if settling herself. "I know your father had family there."

Kaemada dropped her gaze, shifting. She'd been avoiding thinking of that.

When Talaera continued, her tone was hard. "That does not mean we must leave ourselves open to misfortune. You act without forethought. With Tanelwith hit so hard, it will fall to us to make up for their lack of offering for the Feast. If we do not, the mutterings against us will grow louder."

Maeren shook her head, gesturing for peace. "We will make do—we always do. Remember, Talaera, harmony first within, then without. The thoughts and hearts of land spouses are elsewhere, not on the day-to-day work of the kaetal. Each of us must be free to pursue the spirits' song."

11

S. Kaeth

Kaemada dropped her gaze to the bread. If the Saimahkae saw that in her, perhaps she wasn't prideful and selfish to see it in herself. But training hadn't gone well, and if the way forward wasn't training with the others, as she'd done all her life, what was it?

Talaera's tense eyes spoke of the fear that drove her complaints.

Kaemada reached out to make peace, speaking carefully. "Our presence makes our kaetal different, and so some look askance at us. This isn't something I would have any of you suffer."

The Great Mother's gaze captured Kaemada. "Listen and understand. Gifts such as Kaemada's, Ra'ael's, and even my Takiyah's, are more and more common these days. It makes the Council of Elders nervous. Those like you initiate change and influence the future, and it can be uncomfortable, even frightening. But the Council knows that many times it all works out for the best."

The Council of Elders gathered together every planting and harvest season at the Feasts of Starfall to discuss issues and mediate disputes that were unresolved by regional Councils. Kaemada blinked in surprise.

"Surely not nervous!" Talaera objected. "The Elders are the wisest from each of the kaetaln."

Maeren laughed. "Yes, my dear, nervous. After all, they're as flawed as any."

Frowning, Kaemada considered her words as she helped Maeren spread the dough on a smooth, flat rock.

"Do not worry about it, either of you." Maeren shook her head. "Do you think Taunos will be back for the Feast of Starfall?"

"Oh!" One of the kaetal women, Taela, stopped short in passing by and twirled her hair around one finger. "Is your brother coming home?" she echoed breathlessly.

"Wait!" Shana paused with a basket of grasses ready for weaving. "Taunos is coming home?"

Kaemada laughed through the longing in her heart. It'd been moons since she'd heard her brother's booming laugh, since his jokes and pranks had lighted the kaetal. Though he spent much of his time away, still the young women competed for his attention. Perhaps the one caused the other, on and on as a cycle.

"There are many other fine men of marriageable age," Talaera said, though her smile spoke of pride in Taunos.

"Now both of you, off. I believe there are meaningful tasks to do elsewhere." Maeren shooed them away and winked at Kaemada. "You see? I will settle that brother of yours down with a marriage—likely this

12

summer even. The young women still find him desirable, and he cannot run forever."

"He still travels the realms looking for ways to protect our kaetal," Kaemada said, flicking away a stray stem from the bowl.

"He could do much good right here in Torkae, or anywhere else in Rinara. It's time for him to come home," Talaera said.

"You may try to convince him, but I also know the men have taken him aside to talk to him many times. He always replies that his work is out there, to learn, and to watch, and to keep our people safe." Kaemada focused on mashing the berries. "It seems no amount of talking can quell his wanderlust."

"Oh, Kaemada." Maeren rested a hand on her shoulder. "I know you miss him."

Kaemada forced a smile. "He's all Eian and I have left."

With a wooden spoon, Maeren slathered the bread with honey. "I do not see what your brother thinks he can do that your mother could not. If any could get the Darks to see reason, I think it would have been Lína. Everyone loved your mother, psion or not."

Kaemada pressed her lips together. Her heart stung at the suggestion that her brother was wasting his time and at the mention of her honored mother. Keeping silent, she spread the mashed berries on the honeyed dough. The rock it lay on would be placed among the coals so the bread could bake. She could see some women digging a place for it near the fire.

Maeren folded the bread in layers, then rose slowly, one hand pressed to her back. "Now enough chattering. Kaemada, you must practice with little Laran to control his telekinesis, so he stops throwing rocks while appearing innocent. Then I can get some rest from his mother's complaints!"

~

Kaemada made a game of tossing swatches of cloth at Laran, challenging him to push away only the blue ones. As blue cloth hit the ground over and over again, Maeren and Talaera's words rang in her mind. Talaera was her closest relative in the kaetal, in part due to so much devastation from Dark attacks over the summers. If only the work that fulfilled Kaemada didn't worry Talaera so much.

"Hah!" Laran giggled as he thrust a piece of yellow fabric in her face, dancing with glee just out of arm's reach.

She forced herself to focus on his laughter rather than her troubles and smiled at him. "Good work today, Laran, but remember: what did the rodent get for tormenting the alanshorn?"

The glee melted off him, and his shoulders sagged. "Trampled."

With a nod, she tapped him on the chin. "But what about the wolf who honed his strength?"

He swiped at the air. "He got a feast! Like tonight!"

Laughing, she nodded. "Be the wolf, Laran, yes? Not the rodent."

He scampered off, and Kaemada wound her way through the people to check on Eian, exchanging pleasantries along the way and wishing her heart weren't so troubled. Near the central fires, Takiyah's voice rang out, dripping with condescension.

"Oh, my thanks! Can you also tell the color of the sky by looking?"

Takiyah and the stranger they'd spotted before faced off, while around them, others distanced themselves from the simmering confrontation. He must be a messenger, but what could have darkened Takiyah's face with fury like a rolling thunderstorm? Kaemada hastened toward them.

The man's teeth bared in what should have been a smile if it wasn't for the malice in his eyes. "But they're not your parents. You're not one of us."

The hair on the back of her neck raised. What was the messenger insinuating? Takiyah had been adopted, but that didn't matter. After all, Kaemada had adopted Eian, and her son surely belonged, regardless of her turmoil.

She spoke carefully, searching for the peace they should be able to build together. "Shareil. Takiyah is as much one of us as I am, or as you are. She was raised here. She eats with us, sleeps in her parents' hut, and helps keep us all safe and well. Surely you're mistaken."

"Kaemada Sierso." The man spat her name like a bitter seed, but Kaemada gave a polite nod.

"No," he drawled. "No, I think you're right. She's as much Rinaryn as you are."

Her skin prickled with danger. At least Ra'ael was heading toward them again, but where was this contempt coming from?

Takiyah's tone sliced the air. "What cause have you to come here and spread your poison?"

Setting her hand on Takiyah's shoulder, Kaemada tried to mute the argument before further words were said that could not be called back. "Perhaps if you rest for some time here, you will see there's nothing to be afraid of."

As the stranger opened his mouth, Ra'ael gave them a saucy grin over his shoulder before snagging the man's sleeve with deft fingers. By the

14

time he turned to look at her, calm respect had filled her expression.

"I'm happy to welcome you." Ra'ael smiled. "Please, may I see your token? Not that you're Fallen, of course, but we must follow these traditions for the good of us all. What kaetal has sent you?"

He stared at Ra'ael for a moment before producing the carved wooden figure he'd been given from his Storyteller. He shifted his weight under the adherence to tradition so rigid it was almost—but not quite—insulting. "I bear a message from Storyteller Utalen of the kaetal of Tseril."

Ra'ael gave him a nod. "Wonderful. Please, come with me to the Ellewyn. Teros, our head priest, is expecting you, along with Storyteller Zeroun. We do not want to keep such busy people waiting."

She guided him forward by his arm, the dignified motion honoring the messenger, but as they walked away, Ra'ael turned to flash them a wide smile. Kaemada returned it as beside her, Takiyah let out a deep sigh.

Kaemada turned to her, searching her eyes to see if she was all right. "Why was he so combative with you?"

Takiyah shook her head. "I do not know. With his zeal, I expect we will find out soon enough."

Darkness lurked in her friend's eyes, and Kaemada grabbed her hand. "Forget what he said, Takiyah. You belong here as much as anyone, in this community, as part of tonight's celebration, as one of our people."

A grin answered her, and Takiyah squeezed her hand before turning to the fires, shaking coals, surely from her little forge at the edge of the kaetal, into the central fires. Kaemada watched Ra'ael and the messenger walk away. If she couldn't defend her people, if she couldn't live up to the expectations of her closest family, if she couldn't meet the task she'd set for herself, what good was she to her community? What good was she to her son, especially in the face of such hate?

As the sun went down, the scent of roasting meat mingled with the aromas of cooking vegetables and honeyed bread baking on the coals. Families gathered on the field with their instruments, breaking into impromptu songs while children laughed, danced, and played. Neven and Farel remained sequestered as they had been since their return—Farel a day ago, and Neven early that morning. They'd only been allowed contact with the Storyteller and the priests as they prepared themselves for the ceremony.

Eian ran, shrieking with laughter, around her legs, and Kaemada caught Takiyah's eye with a grin, including her in the joy. The taller woman had been tense all day, not that Kaemada blamed her. She'd kept close to Takiyah, just in case, ever since the Storyteller and Teros had finished their meeting with the messenger. Fortunately, he'd kept his distance, and Kaemada was determined to enjoy the evening.

The sound of drums began: a steady thump, thump, thump rising to the sky, calling her back from her worries. The peripheral music faded away, and conversations quieted.

"Mahkae, Mahkae, pick me up!" Eian danced around her.

She hoisted him, even though at four summers of age he was getting too big to hold for long, and perched him on her shoulder so he could see. Two priests entered the field from around the hill, beating on small hand drums, and the other two priests followed, pulling behind them a cart over which was stretched a large, tanned hide. On the hide, Ra'ael danced, striking out the rhythm with her feet. Her rattling bracelets and anklets emphasized the rhythm, gleaming in the light of the fires.

Takiyah's father, the Storyteller, came next, rattle bracelets shaking with each clap of his hands, a broad smile splitting his face. Tension melted away from her as she joined in, stomping her feet and clapping her hands. Maeren followed her husband, holding Neven and Farel's hands up high. The Naming Song was beginning, the ritual that had folded each person firmly into the community after they completed their yah. Beside her, Takiyah caught her eye, and a true grin split her face as she clapped to the ancient rhythm. They were all tied together, woven tightly into the community, regardless of how much family they had or where they were born.

The celebratory air was contagious, and Eian shrieked with laughter. Kaemada brought him back down to the ground and hushed him, kissing his dark brown curls. He promptly pushed his way through the crowd so he could see, and Kaemada peered after him, even though there were plenty of adults about to be sure he did not get into trouble.

Once they reached the fire, Neven and Farel spun to face the Storyteller. Ra'ael stomped one final beat on the drum and leapt to the ground as all the drumming stopped.

The Storyteller's voice rang out, shattering the stillness. "Tonight, we welcome back Neven and Farel, now men in their own right. They have completed their yah and harmonized their songs with those of the spirits and Eloí. They have proven they can survive alone and can live in service to the world we depend on."

The Storyteller turned and whispered in Neven's ear, then faced them again. "In the presence of his family and kaetal, Neven Anadero has been given his true-name, to share with only those he chooses."

Neven's cheeks flushed as the cheering of the kaetalyn grew to a thunderous roar. The Storyteller bent to whisper in Farel's ear, then turned once more. "In the presence of his family and kaetal, Farel Daros has been given his true-name, to share with only those he chooses."

Clapping his hands through the whooping cheers, the Storyteller shouted, "Come then, and welcome your men!"

Kaemada laughed, joining the surge forward as the crowd descended on the two young men. She caught Eian's hand and whisked him back into her arms to avoid losing him in the press.

"Congratulations!" she said as she embraced Neven and Farel, kissing each on the cheek. They stood, beaming and wide-eyed, and she remembered how full her heart had felt when she'd stood there with Ra'ael and Takiyah. The last of the tension melted, unable to stay in the face of such camaraderie, and Kaemada gave Eian a squeeze.

He giggled. "Can we eat now?"

"Yes, my dear." She laughed and followed the flow of the crowd toward the bowls, pots of meats and vegetables, and the sweet, fresh-baked breads.

Letting Eian down again, she dished out food for both of them and grabbed two wooden mugs of tea. Eian led her, skipping and twirling, to a spot on the grass, where he plunked himself down, wriggling in anticipation.

Ra'ael joined them, and then Takiyah, their bowls laden with food.

"How did the meeting go?" Takiyah asked.

Ra'ael shrugged. "The messenger seems to have a distrust for psions. He hates Galod, too, for some reason. He kept pointing him out as an outsider and a bad influence."

Takiyah grinned. "I'm surprised you did not punch him."

Her mouth full of meat and gravy, Kaemada smiled. The food was tender and perfectly seasoned, and she'd always loved stars-of-evening. Eian snuggled against her as he ate, and she threw her free arm around him, balancing her bowl on her leg.

Ra'ael shook out her long, black hair. "I have far more self-control than that." Then she grinned. "Though it took some doing. It does not matter. In a season, the fear will pass us by."

Kaemada frowned. "The Saimahkae said the Elders are nervous."

Ra'ael shrugged. "They are, but at least our Storyteller is keeping the hysteria to a minimum. It makes no sense to have such sudden terror of Dark attacks. Nothing good will come of it."

"Danger is part of life," Takiyah agreed. "Walls would be a good way to protect the kaetal from attacks."

"Walls!" Ra'ael glared at her.

Kaemada groaned as they brought up the old argument yet again. It'd been such a nice, peaceful night.

Takiyah smirked. "It's what it's called when you stack stones as a barricade—"

Ra'ael's dark eyes flashed. "You cannot go against the stories. Torkaema the Great smashed the walls of the old cities and connected us further with the spirits. Torkae was named for him. We, of all the kaetaln, should keep his ways!"

They'd had this argument countless times. Ra'ael would inevitably bring up the walls of the City of the Lost, where the Fallen went, and Takiyah would snap at the implication of lawlessness, unless Kaemada stepped in.

Kaemada gestured at them with her spoon. "You're arguing about which way to protect our people is best while forgetting we want the same thing. Better to remove the reason behind the worry."

Ra'ael shook her head. "Walls wouldn't have helped the kaetal of Tanelwith. Not with a Dark-touched betraying them."

There was a group of people who could fight the Darks, according to the stories. And with no need for walls. Perhaps the Darks could be driven off, and no other Rinaryn would ever turn traitor.

Staring at her stew, Kaemada said, "If we could get the Kamalti to help us, we might find protection against the Darks."

"Stop dreaming of legends," Ra'ael scoffed. "Why do you insist on bringing up the Kamalti?"

Takiyah nodded. "More likely Taunos has discovered some way to fight them. Not that his task is more than moving a river."

Kaemada shrugged, watching Eian turn in circles beside her. "They were our friends, back when we used terrible weapons and lived in cities. They may still have knowledge that could help us."

Ra'ael shook her head. "Why would they have preserved knowledge we lost?"

"Can I have more bread?" Eian broke in.

"You can have mine." Kaemada's stomach was knotting again, and she handed him the treat.

"Do not eat too many sweets." Ra'ael tore the bread in half, handing one part to the boy and the other back to Kaemada.

Her stomach wasn't just knotting from the conversation—wariness filled her bond from Tannevar. A strange scent tickled her nose. Leather…

and oil.

Kaemada seized Eian, pulling him down into her lap. "Something's in the woods."

Takiyah turned just as the elderly man next to her fell, an arrow piercing his chest.

"Run!" Ra'ael shouted.

Chapter Two

All psions begin training to control their gifts as soon as they're discovered, with many exercises to build up their mental walls. Children are given a fair amount of indulgence, as it is understood that their walls are weak and easily overcome by strong emotion. However, once the child has reached maturity—gone on their yah, as they say—that laxity ends. Severe penalties reign in force to persuade the psions never to use their gifts except under the direction of their leaders ("Elders"). They say this is to prevent a return to a past time when psions were hunted.

Generally, an uncontrolled psion ends up in one of two ways. Those without adequate mental walls end up as quivering masses of nerves because of the overload of other ideas and emotions (described in their story of "No-mind"). Those whose walls are stronger, but still insufficient, lose their sense of self. They bounce from the identity of one person to the next as they follow the thoughts that slip past their walls (their story of "Every-mind").

Rinaryns walk a line between encouraging young ones to practice their abilities, to build control, and discouraging those who have control from using their abilities.

—journal excerpt

Arrows rained down on them, nearly invisible against the night, and Kaemada threw herself over Eian. Shouts and screams filled the air. An arrow thrummed home in the ground next to her shoulder. Another struck the Storyteller's staff as Takiyah bellowed for her father, racing toward him. Nausea rose in Kaemada's throat. How many of those she knew and loved had just died? There was no cover here. They had to move. She forced herself to think, to account for the direction of the arrow storm and the scent of leather and oil.

"The Ellewyn!" she shouted.

"The Ellewyn! The Ellewyn! Get up the hill! Go!" Ra'ael screamed directions, shoving stunned men and women into motion.

The Darks usually launched arrows in volleys, and Kaemada suspected they had mere moments before another wave struck them. There was no way everyone would make it to safety. Clutching Eian close, Kaemada sprinted with the flood of people, her heart in her throat as she

20

gasped for breath. Eian clutched her tight, his whole body taut with panic. A woman next to her went down, and then a man just ahead of her. Kaemada dodged him and kept running, forcing down grief, terror, and guilt. She had to rescue Eian.

The cries of her people filled her ears, their pain and fear dragging at her spirit with sorrow. Anger urged her on. Eian's need sustained her in the press of the crowd, on, on, on. The feathers of another arrow brushed her hip, and her blood ran cold. A man tripped next to her. She grabbed his arm to help him regain his balance. Almost there. Blood sang in her ears as her heart pounded a song of wrath, a song of battle.

Kaemada burst inside the Ellewyn, shoving through the crowd at the entrance. "Get back! Away from the door!"

On the other side of the large room, she squeezed Eian tightly one last time. She had to go back outside, had to defend their home. Tannevar's fury howled along their bond. Taking a deep breath to steady herself, she put her son down, kissing his forehead as he clutched at her. "I will be back soon."

"Eian, come sit with me," one woman said, holding out her hand. Feet dragging, Eian went, though he watched Kaemada with big, fearful eyes. Flashing the woman a grateful smile, Kaemada turned back to her part in the larger song of the kaetal: battle.

She ran to the large box in the corner, blessing Ra'ael for her habit of never being far from a weapon. Shoving open the lid, Kaemada reached inside, only to be inundated by the hands of frightened people looking for a means of defense. Handing out daggers and bows warred with the need to get back out there and defend their home. She directed the next man she locked eyes with to take over. Grabbing a staff for Takiyah, a sword and dagger for Ra'ael, and a bow for herself, she headed back out into the night. She sidled along the wall of the building. Ra'ael and Takiyah stood at the corner, ready to leap back for cover, but there seemed to be a momentary reprieve. Able fighters clustered behind them as more streamed along behind Kaemada.

"How's your knee?" Ra'ael glanced at her as Kaemada handed her the weapons.

It was during a Dark attack just like this one three summers ago that her knee had been injured, stabbed by a former kaetalyn. A deep unease chilled her. Kaemada shifted the attention away from herself. "We need to move."

"The arrows came from the northern tree line," Ra'ael mused. "It's safe to figure they're scattered through the forest. We will split up."

Ra'ael's fingers picked out individuals with a weaver's dexterity. "You ten, defend the west side. You seven, take these bows and set up over there, under cover of the wagons. You ten-and-two are with Takiyah, and you nine are with me. Kae, take these ten-and-one over here. Come around the eastern side of the kaetal for an aerial assault after we take out the bows. We will push back the Darks to allow the healers a chance to tend the wounded and bring them to safety."

Kaemada gestured and her group fell in behind her. She motioned them low, and they ran at a crouch to the tree line. The tension in her shoulders eased with the forest she knew so well providing them cover. She wiped her sweaty hands on her pants and quickly prayed to the spirits for guidance. It was difficult to align her song with that of the spirits when her thoughts flitted to those injured and killed in the attack. Had she really seen the Storyteller with a gash on his forehead and the Saimahkae's clothes bloodied?

She focused on the smell of the trees and the soil underneath her feet to calm her heart. She had a task to complete. Ra'ael had entrusted her with five of the kaetal's precious aeneshenon, winged warriors, and she was determined to keep her whole group safe while they drove out the intruders.

Kaemada headed in the direction Ra'ael had indicated, then began the loop that would take them toward the archers. The undergrowth thickened in that direction, so they ran along a narrow wild-trail. Though all moved silently on the trails, some were less adept in the undergrowth. One stray snap of a twig would give away their location. They'd have to follow the trail to the pond and then divert to avoid a tserwora den—they had enough troubles.

How was it that the Darks were attacking tonight when they had just attacked Tanelwith? Something was wrong. Something was different now, but what?

Still moving, she cast along her link to Tannevar, and his senses engulfed her. Crisp night air, the wind blowing past as he ran. The moon Tharahel had risen full, and her sister, Anathel, was rising, providing more than enough silvery light to see by. Tannevar scented the intruders a distance upwind of him and was angling toward them.

A hand grabbed her, yanking her to the side. She jolted back to herself, staring at the pĩewood tree she'd nearly walked into. She gave her head a quick shake to get rid of the last vestiges of disorientation that accompanied deep connections with Tannevar.

"Are you all right, Kae?"

22

She nodded to Solarenn, one of the aeneshenon with her, but slowed her pace. Something was wrong, something was wrong! What was it? She frowned at the trail. Near the pond, east and north of the tserwora den, a cluster of elderwoods sprawled around a tiny clearing. Many summers ago, Tikatae had dragged her there, her last altercation with him before the Elders declared him Fallen the next day.

It was only a feeling.

Reaching along her bond, Kaemada asked Tannevar to divert to the clearing among the elderwoods.

"What's wrong?" Solarenn asked.

She shook her head. It was probably nothing, and she'd probably sent Tannevar on a useless errand. They had to follow Ra'ael's instructions and take out the archers.

"Nothing," she said. "Let's go."

They were nearly to the pond when she shivered with the force of Tannevar's rage. He passed along the scents of five more intruders he'd found. Cautioning him to be careful, she compared his position with her own. A chill ran down her spine. The extra Darks were positioned such that if they continued on the trail, they'd run right past them. She held up a hand, and her band halted.

"What is it, Kaemada? And do not say 'nothing' this time!" Solarenn growled in her ear.

She put a finger to her lips. They were too close to the ambush to risk voices carrying. Kaemada turned to the group Ra'ael had entrusted to her and held up five fingers, then pointed in the direction of the ambush. Tapping the four best hunters on their shoulders, she pointed up to the trees. They could move in silence, branch to branch, to spring onto their enemy from above. She indicated the ferns to the other two, gesturing for them to crawl through the softer undergrowth. The five aeneshenon, she motioned to come with her.

With measured, careful movements, she led them around the other side of the stand of elderwoods, the side nearest the den. Reaching out, her fingers brushed the fronds of a fern in passing. Tonight she could change the story of needing rescue in the same place where she'd once been rescued. Tonight she was needed, and she would be strong.

They crept toward the clearing, silent but achingly slow. Kaemada reached out often to Tannevar to check their progress using his heightened senses. She winced every time he heard them from his hiding place, where he waited to ambush the ambushers. They were still out of arrow range when she sent the aeneshenon up into the trees.

She wormed her way through the bushes, careful not to miss anything or give away their presence, and passed Tannevar the locations of the others. The wolf confirmed they should have the Darks surrounded, the intruders who stunk of sweat. Their scent pooled in the clearing, indicating they'd been waiting a long time. Well within arrow range, she finally saw them, moonlight gleaming on dark helmets and flashing on bared blades. She glanced upward to Solarenn, who was perched on a sturdy tree limb, and nodded.

With a roar, she rose, loosing arrows as swiftly as she could. From their hiding spots, her people attacked, crashing down on the Darks and screaming their anger. Tannevar moved in silence through the chaos, a shadow attached to flashing, white teeth. Kaemada shot a Dark that was attacking Solarenn from behind, and then another who ran at her, though her arrow bounced off his armor. She had to dodge him, cracking him in the head with her bow and a telekinetic push as he passed. Another shot, and then another, and more Darks were on the ground. One of the Darks shoved Solarenn into another man and fled.

Kaemada leapt to the chase. The undergrowth thickened ahead, so she took to the trees, running along one broad limb of an elderwood before it tapered off, forcing her to leap to another. Even as she gained on the Dark, the trees began to thin. She fired arrows, but the underbrush foiled her. She had to get him. She refused to leave a Dark out here to work only the spirits knew what mischief. They'd ruined a night of celebration, of life. They'd killed Reion. She'd seen Shana and Taela clutching each other and weeping when she'd been in the Ellewyn. Taunos, Ra'ael, Takiyah, all of them had proved their heroism time and again. She couldn't fail by letting a Dark escape, especially not one who was part of the ambush.

They were nearing the large meadow just south of Galod's clearing. Had it been only yesterday that she'd picked blueweed shoots there with Eian? Her knee shot warning pangs up her leg as she reluctantly dropped to the ground, the branches too far apart to continue using as a path. She gritted her teeth, pushing for more speed even as her knee protested in earnest. Racing through the undergrowth, she jumped onto one of the great rocky ledges that littered the forest, and leapt off. She'd lost him. No! She might catch sight of him once out of the underbrush.

She hurdled over a log and into the meadow, crashing into the Dark, who rose just as she landed. A blaze of pain shot through her as the man plunged his knife deep into her stomach. A yelp sounded from far behind —Tannevar, struck down by the same pain through their bond. She cried out wordlessly, watching in disbelief as Tikatae pulled his knife from her stomach.

Tikatae.

Her bow dropped to the grass as she pressed her hands against her wound, desperately trying to keep her insides in, even as the warm blood leaked out around her fingers. The ground crashed hard against her knees, and tears blurred her vision.

He was Fallen, cast out from her people. She'd never thought she'd see him again.

Tikatae smirked down at her. "Well, now, this was rather easy. I thought you would be more challenging prey."

"Tikatae," she gasped, fighting to breathe. She couldn't focus. She had to focus! Spirits' stories and songs, was she going to die? She couldn't leave Eian behind. She couldn't die at Tikatae's hand, so close to the grove where he'd beaten her before. It all made sense now. Too late. Tikatae was why the group of Darks knew where to ambush them. Tikatae was working with them.

She would not let him win so easily.

"Did they get your brat? I told them the first arrow should be for him."

She strained to reach the knife in her boot, wincing. Her world was pain. Tears she didn't remember crying wet her face. Gritting her teeth, she flung the knife at Tikatae, though the motion sent her face-first into the ground, pain consuming her. When next she could focus, Tikatae loomed over her, pulling her knife from his shoulder. He stepped on her arm, the new pain providing a counterpart to her stomach wound. She screamed.

"This was all for you, you see. You should feel honored. But you…" His expression twisted. "You did not spare a thought for me, did you?"

She saw his boot only moments before it struck her temple. Black sparks exploded across her vision. Her mouth filled with blood from where her tooth caught the inside of her cheek. It was the same as before. Hadn't she promised herself she wouldn't need saving? Taunos wasn't here to rescue her, anyway.

"No!" she screamed, wrenching herself away. She slammed out with her telekinesis, sending a low hanging tree branch into him.

He staggered but laughed. "Well, I thought of you. And I will finish thinking of you soon enough. Right after I bury you and burn that kaetal to the ground." He kicked her again.

Stars of light burst across the darkness that crowded her sight. "You… destroyed… yourself."

She blinked, trying to see, vaguely aware she was losing too much blood. She wasn't entirely sure where she was, but her body began to shiver. Kaemada shoved at the tree branch again, but he ducked, laughing.

"No, no, no, my dear Kae. You destroyed me when you scorned me. Then they laughed me out of the kaetal, out of my home. This is all your fault." He drew his boot back, but she curled up, and his boot hit her knee. The impact drove her skidding across the grass.

"…cannot… force love!"

"Too bad. You would have lived." He flipped his knife in the air and caught it.

Shaking with cold and terror and wrath, she gathered herself. If she could force her way past his mental defenses, she could strike at his very core, fill him with her own agony. She was losing too much focus. She had to do it on the first try. With a guttural yell, she hurled her telepathy at him like a heavy stone.

She bounced right off him as if she'd run full force into a tree trunk. Something felt wrong, broken. Lost. She vomited onto the grass, pain ringing in her head. He kicked her again, and she flipped over, coughing, struggling to breathe.

"You think I wasn't ready for you? You're pathetic. I anticipated your every move, you see? I anticipated your friends. And you, you never even thought of me. Well, think of me now!"

His knife flashed down at her. Screaming in wordless denial, she forced her battered body to move, to roll away. Too slow, too slow! She wasn't going to make it.

Orb-shaped ripples flew over her head, striking Tikatae in the center of his chest and slamming him backward. More ripples followed, streaming past like a flood until Tikatae was no more than a shimmering, quivering mass.

"Galod," she croaked.

"You, my student, would have failed this test had it been mine."

BAE
Chapter Three

It is easy to dismiss the Rinaryns as quaint savages, but as ever, this is a good way to find oneself in danger through hubris. As I have no intention of that, I have discovered some abilities in the Rinaryns that those who deal with them must be aware of. Besides the wings, some Rinaryns have psionics—either telepathy or telekinesis, but never both. These, they say, hear the song of Eloí. The more mortal danger lies in those who dance the song of Eloí—the Rinaryn healers. Both psionics and "healing" have a genetic basis, as we've seen elsewhere. Psionics show up at a young age in Rinaryns, typically at age two or three. Healing shows up much later, usually around the age of fourteen. Of course, psionics and healing never occur in the same person, and on some level, the Rinaryns have discovered the danger, for the two are forbidden to intermarry. As we've seen elsewhere, both have a risk of overuse, and if the psion or healer overextend themselves, they're unable to utilize their powers for some time.

Rinaryns allow their healers considerable leeway and treat them with nearly as much honor as they do their winged ones. Perhaps because of their history (or this may be a handy excuse), they do not treat their psions with such honor.

—journal excerpt

Vague shadows moved around Kaemada, but she was cut off from them all, wrapped in feathers and clouds. Sometimes voices surrounded her, the breeze of people passing by caressing her. Other times pain gripped her, so intense she longed for nothingness, or heat filled her, so great she dreamed she had been cast into the central fires.

"Mahkae! Mahkae! Ra'ael? Mahkae!" Eian's distress pierced her cocoon, and she tried to reach for him, to comfort him, but she couldn't move.

Cold hands chilled her forehead.

She slept or floated or time stopped spinning.

Galod's voice, shouting. She cringed instinctively from his wrath. "Get in there now, or so help me, I will bring down torment on you the likes of which you have never seen! Go, blast you, and do the one thing that justifies your existence!"

That made no sense. Galod never came to the kaetal. She must be dreaming.

27

"Galod, you must stop insulting my healers." Maeren's voice.

She tried to escape from the excessive heat, twisting in her smothering dreams. At last, she relaxed into the strangeness. There didn't seem to be anything else to do.

"Zeroun, they must heal her. They could pay Ra'ael more attention as well," Galod said.

"She refused, and healers are under Maeren's authority. You should know that, old friend."

Maeren and Zeroun were talking to Galod? What a strange dream.

"Are you going to add her to your pile of dead?"

"Do not come at us wagging that tongue like a weapon," Maeren said. "We know you too well. Now, take your own advice and let the healers look at your arm."

Galod snorted. "As if I would let them touch me."

"The wolf bit you deep. At least take the healing salve. You bandaged the wound well, right?"

"I'm fine, Maeren. I'm not the one you should be concerned about."

"I have enough concern to go around. How is it different, you not wanting healing and her not wanting healing?"

"She's not me, and I'm not dying. She is. Heal her, if only a little," Galod said.

Yes, definitely a dream. There was no way Galod would sound desperate. He was only ever angry or disappointed or, rarely, satisfied.

More shouting floated past, but feathery nothingness blocked the sound. It was too hard to pick out the words. She was so tired. Warmth suffused her. Not the cooking heat of the fire, but a gentle wash that soothed her aches. It took her a moment to understand.

They were healing her.

She thrashed and fought, though strong arms gripped her. The healers' gift was like a cup full of cool water, while the wounded were like thirsty men. There was only so much to go around. She could hold on a little longer. Her wounds were her own folly. How could she bear it if someone died because she drank? Especially Ra'ael.

Finally, her cocoon returned, soothing in its silence and peace. She slept.

Eventually, Kaemada managed to snag consciousness and hold on. She peeled open her eyes. It was all so strange; she was in her home, but everything looked different, disconnected somehow. Several others lay along the curved walls, bandages over various wounds. The rainshield had been drawn back to let the afternoon sun light the interior. She nearly leapt off her bedmats when her arm brushed against the wolf, but the movement triggered stabbing pain in her head and stomach. Tannevar. She hadn't realized he was there. She always knew where he was with just a brush of a thought. She trembled, reaching out for him. Nothing. He curled tighter into a ball, ears flattened.

She looked around herself more cautiously. Her bedmats were laid just to the left of the doorway, in Taunos's spot, with another set—Eian's—laying just beside hers. Ra'ael lay on a set of bedmats beyond Eian's. Beside her knelt Teros, though he turned to give her a withering look. Solarenn crouched among the food and medicinal supplies near the fire, seeming uninjured. Seated on an oddly carved stump between Ra'ael and Kaemada, Galod watched her with sharp grey eyes. His face seemed cut from stone, and a book lay closed in his lap, one finger marking his place.

"You're going to hurt yourself."

The beating she'd taken rushed back. Shame filled her. She had lost yet again—had needed saving yet again. Could she face Tikatae another time? He had nearly killed her. He'd nearly killed Eian. And she hadn't been able to stop him. Fear trembled through her, its grip paralyzing.

"Tikatae! Is he—"

"Dead."

Breath gusted out of her, and she shivered, wincing as the tremors awoke pain. Her odd dream came back to her, and she raised her head, squinting at him. "Galod... why are you here?"

He raised an eyebrow at her. Avoiding his gaze, she looked at Tannevar, who watched them with his nose twitching. She extended a hand to the wolf, and he let out a sigh, laying his muzzle in her hand, and closing his eyes.

"Galod?" her voice quavered, and she tried again. "Galod, I cannot feel Tannevar."

"He's lucky to be alive. You both are."

"Ra'ael! I dreamed... Is she all right?"

"She's in better shape than you are, fighting off the healers."

She stared at him. She didn't hurt nearly as bad as she should, given her injuries. Her tone lowered. "How long have I been asleep?"

"Five days."

Five days. Only two days until they left for the journey up the mountains. She should be in much more pain than she was. She fixed her gaze on Galod. "They healed me."

He nodded. She trembled. Surely others had been hurt worse than she, others who could have used the gift they'd used for her.

"No!" she shouted. "No! How many died because of me? How many could the healers have saved? I did not need healing!"

"Zero. Zero. You were dying." Galod remained impassive.

Kaemada furrowed her brow, looking from Galod to Solarenn as he came and crouched beside her with a cup of water. Tannevar grumbled as the aenesheno crowded the wolf to be farther from Galod. "No one else died?"

"Only those beyond help," Galod said.

"Who are you to decide who lives or dies?"

"I am Galod, and I am wise. Your wound became tainted and made you gravely ill. Your mind-case swelled past its bounds. I had the healers heal you slightly, twice."

Had she been that close to death? Kaemada shook her head and looked at Solarenn. "How many died?"

"Thirty-and-one." Solarenn looked down, his wings drooping with grief. "Three were aeneshenon."

"Thirty-and-one dead," she repeated. Thirty-and-one people no longer drew breath, while she who failed in combat with a single Dark survived. Three of their precious aeneshenon gone. Ra'ael sighed in her sleep and shifted, and Kaemada looked at her. With so many bandages, she must have succumbed to the blood rage.

It didn't seem right. The grief sickened her, and guilt weighed her down. Tikatae had come there for her, yet she had survived when so many others had not. And it wasn't because of any talent on her part.

She glanced down, mumbling, "You should not have had them heal me."

"One does not throw away a precious resource simply because it's damaged, not if it's within one's power to save. Would you prefer death?"

"No." What would Eian do without her?

Solarenn placed his hand on her uninjured arm. "Shareil, Kaemada. You saved our lives from the ambush, and we were able to help the others drive away the Darks."

Kaemada shook her head. "It's not enough."

Not weighed against her failure. Not weighed against the deaths of those she loved.

Solarenn squeezed her arm and offered her the cup again. "It's enough that you live. Our kaetal needs you. You helped my brother and me see sense last summer, and I owe you my thanks once again for sending those wagons to Tanelwith with my brother's children."

She took the cup and forced a smile, mostly to make him go away. But his words persisted even as he left the hut. Shoving away her sorrow and pain, she snatched for more hopeful notes for her song. Yes, they had suffered grievous losses, just like Tanelwith, but they were Rinaryn. Nothing could stop their song.

"Ameyitum." The apology dropped from her lips in a croak. How could she explain? "I failed, Galod. Again."

"What was your mistake?"

"I fell into Tikatae's trap. He knew exactly what I would do. I could not shoot him—too much cover. My psionics failed. My knee is always a liability in combat."

"You should have shot Tikatae on sight."

"I did not know it was him!"

"See, decide, act, and—"

"Face the consequences," she finished with him, closing her eyes against her shame. She took a deep breath and looked around again. "Where's Eian? Is he all right?"

"He's out playing. His manners are better than yours were at that age. You pestered me relentlessly when I sat watching over Taunos after the tserwora bit him."

Kaemada frowned, recalling the story. "I had only two summers."

The corners of his mouth pulled, almost as if he were going to smile. "Still."

"Eian is so quiet. Sometimes it worries me."

"His thoughts are elsewhere, his mind exploring worlds you can only imagine. He's too preoccupied with greater things to worry with mere words."

Kaemada knew where this conversation was heading and cut it off. "He's not to start any training yet. He has only four summers. You're much too harsh for him."

Amusement lightened Galod's expression. "You were five summers old when you started. I wasn't too hard on you."

"I cried every day!"

"Not the whole day, and each morning you came ready to train again."

Kaemada scratched Tannevar gently with the hand under his muzzle. "Did you really bite Galod?" she murmured.

"I said he was lucky to be alive."

The wolf blossomed in her mind, boasting of his ability to handle unnatural ripples in the air, should the need arrive. His head lifted, ears perking up as their link opened again, and it was like the sun had risen

31

anew.

"Tannevar!"

He wriggled closer and she wrapped her arms around him. She grinned despite the pain in her side, which faded some as Tannevar bore a share of it, just as she bore a share of his injuries. He nuzzled her chin before she buried her face in his thick fur.

Galod shifted on the stump. Of course he wouldn't sit on the ground as was proper.

Her voice was thick when she spoke. "Ameyitum, Galod. I should not have shouted at you. Thank you for everything."

The corners of his mouth twitched again—a Galod smile. With a rush, the world became alive around her. Sensations flooded her from the others around her, their wounds, the sickness in them. She knew Ra'ael's shoulder still hurt, that her left leg still ached from the breaks below her knee that the healers had mended. And Galod—

Galod's mind snapped shut against her, sending her crashing out of his thoughts just as she touched them. Her stomach turned at the look on his face and the realization of what she'd nearly done.

"Ameyitum!" she said, clutching Tannevar's neck as he stiffened.

"Your psionic abilities are returning." Something like embarrassment flickered across his face before his composure snapped back.

"I did not know. Forgive me." Her chest tightened and she apologized desperately, as if words could flow forth and cover her mistake.

The hermit's mind was even stranger than others she'd touched. Her psionic abilities must have been broken. No wonder she'd been cut off from Tannevar. She needed to rebuild her mental walls to keep her thoughts from washing out and invading the privacy of others.

Galod pinched the bridge of his nose, closing his eyes momentarily. "Only a fool consorts with psions without being sure his mental defenses are strong."

Voices approached from outside, and he stood, closing his book.

She winced. Her intrusion would drive him away. Apologies fell off her tongue like leaves at harvest. "Ameyitum, Galod. Saiameyitum."

He frowned at her and stepped out, stooping past the low doorway. Embarrassment and guilt weighed on her, and Kaemada stroked Tannevar's fur to escape them.

"There isn't enough room for supplies," Talaera was saying as she and Maeren stepped inside.

"We will manage."

"Perhaps if we had more wagons, but as it is, the wounded will fill the space." Talaera gave Kaemada a pointed look, and Kaemada lowered her gaze briefly. She didn't regret sending the wagons to Tanelwith. How could she have known?

"We can carry supplies on our backs."

"Not enough for both the journey and an offering. Everyone will be overburdened."

Maeren sighed. Meeting Kaemada's eyes, she gave a tired smile. "We will make do, Talaera. Have the healers heal as many as they can. They can ride in the wagons to sleep off their exhaustion."

Such exhaustion could injure the healers and cripple their ability, perhaps for good. Maeren knew that, which meant for her to suggest such a thing, they must be desperate. Kaemada frowned. They should be able to rest on grace extended from other kaetaln.

"With Tanelwith hit so hard, and now us, all of Heartwood will suffer. We cannot afford the disgrace! It's one thing to share with the needy, but it's another to be overly so!" Talaera lamented.

"All we can do is bring as much as we can carry. Shareil, Talaera. It will all be well."

Talaera sighed. She paused, looking at Kaemada as if she wanted to say something.

Expecting a rebuke, Kaemada looked down at her blanket, picking at the fabric, but Talaera simply moved on, ducking out the doorway.

Maeren sighed, kneeling next to her. "How are you feeling?"

"I—" She straightened and forced a smile. "I'm alive. And we will figure out a way to contribute to the Feast."

Maeren smiled wearily and patted her arm. "Worry not. There have been pegasus sightings overhead the past days. I'm taking it as a sign from the spirits. I will send someone with stew for you. You rest."

Kaemada watched Maeren make her way around to each of the people in her home, checking on bandages and making them comfortable. Outside, Eian's laughter caught her ears, and she smiled through tears pricking at her eyes. She'd nearly lost him. So easily, an arrow could have found him and she'd never hear that laugh again. Fear gripped her, but she took a deep breath. That part of her story was now over.

See, decide, act, and face the consequences.

A need filled her to do what she could to help, to lighten the darkness even a little. She tried to rise to check the other wounded, but pain halted her. She wouldn't be able to walk far without rest, just like so many others. They had goods to bring to the Feast, but no room to bring them, in part because of her. The wagons from Tanelwith wouldn't have returned yet—

she'd expected they'd get them back at the Feast. And Tikatae had attacked the kaetal to strike at her.

There had to be brightness here somewhere. She'd make some if she had to. Her story felt shaky, uncertain, so she reached out to the others her story entwined with, to strengthen their songs and thereby her own. Her fingers smoothed the blanket piled on top of her. Every thread supported the next, and woven tightly together, they were strong.

Pegasus sightings. Many summers ago, she had befriended a pegasus. They'd grown apart with time, but... She couldn't help her people in defense, nor did they wish her help with psionics. But she could help them bring supplies to the Feast if she could reach Shareilon.

She took Eian with her into the wilderness often, never with a mishap, and he was always good at following directions and staying close. But this was the sacred journey. There would be Angels to evade, though surely just two would be less enticing for the Angels than an entire kaetal. They could time their flight such that they spent only a day, maybe two, in Angel territory to reduce the danger. And the path. It would be even more important to be vigilant, to keep Eian on the sacred path. No one who left the path was ever seen again.

Kaemada breathed away her worries. She would have Tannevar and Shareilon there to help her, and she couldn't stand to have Eian out of her sight, not so soon after nearly losing him. This had to work. It was the only way to avoid serious dishonor for her kaetal, even though she would miss the sacred songs and the fellowship of the journey. But once they arrived at Talahn Valley, she could relax and enjoy the Feast of Starfall.

The Feasts were the very best parts of every summer, especially looking up at night in the crisp mountain air and watching the stars streak across the sky. If a person listened hard enough in the quiet after the starsong, they could hear them faintly whistle. According to legend, the song the stars sang as they fell used to be louder, and there used to be another song, one sung by the stars while they shone in the deep night. Over the generations, the songs had faded, and no one heard the song of the stars anymore unless they were falling.

She had to get them to the Feast with what honor they could bring. Closing her eyes, she reached out, upward, upward. Maybe if she dreamwalked, she'd have a chance at bridging the distance.

Her body was safe, guarded by Tannevar's vigilance. Her mind drifted, questing for the pegasus. She searched for the warmth of his presence, with his smell so like a horse, but mistier, his light grey coat, white mane and tail, and his white feathered wings, soft as clouds. He was the grasslands married to the sky, and his home was the foothills to the south and west.

Impossibly, he answered, a mental impression of a gentle nuzzle from that great head.

She sighed with relief, and with images and emotion, he answered her curiosity, sharing the faint, nagging pull on the part of his mind she'd bonded to. He'd come to make sure she was all right.

It must have happened when she briefly lost access to her psionics, she realized. Letting her gratitude for his care spill out, she explained the kaetal's problem.

Shareilon did not understand. He had no need for festivals, no expectations made of him regarding the bringing of food and gifts. He admonished her with a warm snort.

Kaemada strove to show how important this was to her, and Shareilon answered with bristling pride. No beast of burden was he, but a pegasus, mighty, one with the wind and clouds. A master of land and sky should not be weighed down with bags of goods like a lumbering alanshor!

Contrite, Kaemada soothed his ruffled pride with the reassurance that she appreciated his might and his spirit, and that she understood how he felt about carrying things.

With reluctance, Shareilon agreed to carry Kaemada, Eian, and only what they needed for the journey, but nothing more.

She shared her gratitude before retreating, exhausted by the effort of connecting with him.

He snorted a puff of warm wind and was gone, leaving her adrift, drawn to her bond with Tannevar. Her head pounded, and she remained laying where she was, her arms wrapped around the wolf.

She must have slept, for when next she became aware, the afternoon light had given way to evening. An empty bowl lay on its side next to her. Tannevar's lolling tongue and the wag of his tail informed her of his mischief. She grinned at him and ruffled the fur on his head, laughing when he ducked away with a disgusted look on his face. Her stomach wound protested, cutting her laugh short, but she smiled, easing herself up to sit with her back resting against the wall of her hut.

Kaemada winced. "How are you feeling, Ra'ael?"

The priestess's eyes narrowed with suspicion. "What are you planning?"

"We're planning something?" Maeren asked, her pace slow as she entered. Her face was lined with exhaustion.

"Maeren, I did not ask before. Ameyitum. Are you all right? How's

Takiyah?"

Maeren laughed. "You must be feeling better! Concerned about everyone else already, are we? We're fine, though Takiyah seems unwilling to leave her father's side."

"Kaemada!" Ra'ael snapped. "Now."

She winced, dropping her gaze to Tannevar as if he could guard her against this confrontation. It would have been easier to do this one at a time, but Ra'ael was only getting more impatient.

"We do not have enough wagons," Kaemada began.

"I told you, we will make it work," Maeren interrupted.

"Saimahkae, please. Fill my place in the wagon with goods, so at least we can contribute some to the festivities. Eian and I can ride Shareilon."

"Absolutely not!" Ra'ael shouted. "I smooth the way far too much for you already! I cannot plead tolerance for you with the priests and Elders for something like this."

"The journey to the Seeker Tree is as important as the ceremonies!" Maeren objected. "The songs, the stories, the walk itself, they tie us together."

Kaemada twisted some of Tannevar's fur between her fingers, clinging to his calm. "Let me help in this way. We need room for supplies and tents to hide from the Angels. We have supplies to share; we simply need as much wagon room as possible."

Ra'ael shook her head. "It's too dangerous. What if you fell? We're only strong together."

Maeren frowned in thought for long moments. She finally sighed. "This is highly unusual. As you said, Torkae cannot handle a disgrace."

"Saimahkae, with respect, no! She cannot! Not against tradition! Not when we're already under the scrutiny of the other kaetaln!"

"You leave the scrutiny to me, Ra'ael."

"That is why I must do this," Kaemada said, smoothing Tannevar's ears. He pushed on her leg with his paw. "The messenger, he sought out Takiyah, he sought out me. He would have sought out Galod if he could. He's intent on causing our kaetal trouble."

"You're making too much of the messenger, Kaemada." Maeren shook her head.

"Am I? Did you hear him sneer as he spoke of Galod, as he told Takiyah and me that we're not Rinaryn? Who is he to split us apart? Who is he to spit his hatred at us simply because he dislikes Galod?"

"Enough." Maeren closed her eyes, drawing a deep breath. When she opened her eyes again, she spoke with exaggerated calm. "Galod's presence is the decision of the Storyteller and me. He's not your decision, nor the messenger's. The same goes for you and Takiyah. You are ours. That's the end of it."

"That's why you must forbid this foolhardy idea!" Ra'ael broke in. "Tradition is clear! We stay on the path!"

Kaemada wrapped her arms around her legs, curling up miserably until Tannevar pushed at her again, demanding she scratch his shoulder. "The word 'on' could be translated 'above'. I will stay above the path."

"What will the others think, with you arriving separately?"

"What will they think, with us arriving with no sacrifice?"

"Both of you stop bickering!" Maeren scolded. She sighed. "The messenger lacked even the decency to stay to help us. No, we must arrive with an offering." She passed her hand over her eyes. "Kaemada, please, please be careful."

Kaemada smiled and embraced her. "Eian and I will see you at the Seeker Tree. We would never miss it."

Ra'ael sighed in surrender. "At least make sure you arrive well-groomed, lest others think you're Fallen."

Kaemada scoffed. The Fallen were banished from their kaetaln, forbidden to return to their homes and families and friends. Who would mistake her for a Fallen? The very idea was ridiculous.

Chapter Four

Every Rinaryn travels to the Holy Mountains twice a year, in the planting season and in the harvest season. Hidden in the mountains is a place they refer to as the Valley of Light, or Talahn Valley, and there grows a most interesting node. They call it the Seeker Tree—indeed, its appearance is that of a tree—and hold great reverence for it, gathering around it for their Feasts of Starfall. For seven days, they celebrate life and lives already lived, reconnect with relatives, begin courting potential spouses, and compete for apprenticeships with masters. They worship, give thanks, and sacrifice harvest bounty to Eloí.

It is not an optional journey, not even for the sick or wounded. It's considered holy and solemn, and yet at the same time, celebratory. For some, it's only during these Feasts that they visit with relatives from other parts of Rinara.

—journal excerpt

Early morning light glimmered in the thick mist. Shadows moved, their forms indistinguishable through the murky grey, as houses were dismantled. Kaemada moved toward the flaring, dancing light of the fires as the most tattered of the grass coverings from the huts were fed to the flames. Alanshorn snorted as they were harnessed to the wagons and the sledges made from the bent branches of the huts, turned upside down and covered with the woven grass coverings that were still in good shape. Firewood and tents would be carried inside them.

Each of Kaemada's movements was slow and careful, as she feared to trigger a stab of pain. Still, this was important. She knelt by the edge of the fire, scooping a handful of coals from the edge with a stick into a small clay pot. Cradling the warmth, she stood, bringing a part of the kaetal's fire with her as she left them. She'd return it when they rejoined the kaetal at the Feast, just as in harsh winters, when families split up to better survive, taking some of the kaetal's fire with them and then bringing all those flames back together in spring's bounty. Around her, other families were also collecting coals from the edges, packing them carefully in clay jars.

Orange and yellow burst across the horizon, and the mist lifted like a wave across sand, erasing the signs of their presence. No longer were homes scattered across the land. Working together, everything had been dismantled. In a moon or two, there would be no sign they'd lived there.

After the Feast, they'd build new houses and establish the central fires at a different point along the forest's edge, allowing the growth to renew where foraging and hunting and the growing of tended things had used up resources.

The forest drew Kaemada's gaze to higher aspirations. Yes, she loved the prairie, but the trees were home. They balanced the prairie with its fires. True, if a tree caught, it would burn, but together they provided a harbor for others. Their deep roots, strong trunks, and lofty branches changed the land.

"Listen to your mahkae." Ra'ael's voice drew Kaemada toward one of the wagons.

As Eian released the priestess from a massive hug, a huge grin stretched his cheeks. His eyes lit up, meeting Kaemada's, and he took her hand.

Ra'ael's dark eyes fixed on her. "We can carry both of you. You can still change your mind."

The grief and fear on Ra'ael's face pained her to see, and Kaemada forced a smile. "This is the only way. Even so, our kaetal may not have an offering. We will use much of the supplies along the way."

"I told you she wouldn't change her mind," Takiyah said, coming around the side of the wagon.

Ra'ael scowled.

Summoning all her confidence, Kaemada reached out and squeezed Ra'ael's hand. "Farewell, and safe journey."

A nod and a return squeeze was her reply, as Ra'ael's throat bobbed. The priestess always struggled when things were out of the ordinary. Kaemada forced another smile as she turned away, Eian's hand warm in hers.

"I have those satchels you had packed over here," Takiyah said, pointing as she fell in step alongside them.

"Thank you, Kiy."

A sense of awe filled her as they approached, for there stood Shareilon, waiting by the supplies. He nickered when he saw her, tossing his noble head, and she stroked his soft nose, whispering her gratitude.

She tied string around the clay pot to hold the lid on securely and then nestled it in one of the packs. With Takiyah's help, she climbed on Shareilon's back, pushing aside her worries. She and Eian would make it. There was no other option. Takiyah lifted Eian and seated him in front of Kaemada while Shareilon pranced.

Arranging the packs to evenly distribute the weight, Takiyah scolded,

"You know, you might be the worst person ever to prepare for a journey! I looked at what you packed, and it might have been enough—for a day trip!"

Kaemada frowned. She had made sure the bags would not be too heavy. "What do you mean?"

"You did not pack nearly enough food. There are two of you, and you need extra in case we take longer than usual to get to Talahn Valley. You may be waiting for us!"

Scowling, Kaemada took a deep breath. "The food was for Eian. More than enough, see? I was planning to fast on the journey. My way to atone for not journeying with the rest of you."

"You do not have to do this," Takiyah said.

Kaemada shook her head, and Takiyah grew stern again. "Well, what use will you be to Eian if you faint from fasting while injured and travelling? I packed more food, so be sure to eat it. And I put in more blankets for you. It will be cold in the mountains. And there's a knife with a sharpening stone, extra water pouches, a bowl so you two can wash, fire makers so you do not freeze to death, extra bandages because you will have to tend your wounds, extra salve, and some bitter root for pain."

"My thanks, Kiy." She'd already packed some blankets and bandages, and she had her fire makers in her belt pouch, but she didn't point that out, not wanting to fight. It was true she'd forgotten some little things—she often depended on Ra'ael and Takiyah to remember small details. She took a deep breath. She could do this.

Takiyah arranged the bags to evenly distribute the weight and handed Kaemada a length of cord. "It will be windy. Tie back your hair so you can see."

Trying not to flush further, Kaemada did as she was told.

Takiyah looked them over once more, then nodded and stepped back just as Shareilon stretched his wings and resettled them. Her expression melted into a smile, though worry shone in her green eyes. "Safe travels. And no flying lessons!"

Eian grinned and waved wildly, and Kaemada chuckled. She cast out with her mind to let Tannevar know they would soon be leaving. So bonded to the wolf was she that they could not be far apart without causing them both pain, so Tannevar also made the journey twice a summer, with them but apart at the same time. A mental thrill answered her—Tannevar, eager for the run.

Shareilon shifted restlessly as the kaetalyn moved past them: the alanshorn leaning into their harnesses, scouts on horseback riding alongside the wagons, and people on foot laden with packs. Kaemada kept the smile on her face, imagining their path. They would go westward along the winding trail up the hill and past the Ellewyn, then through the prairie of gently waving grasses taller even than the scouts on horseback. Finally, they would curve southward toward the Holy Mountains once they approached the border of Life Valley. They would have to cross the Lí Rires to get to the mountains, but by going westward first, they could cross where the river was slower and shallower.

Music swelled around them, lifting spirits like the rising sun. Adults sang, and children joined in as they remembered the ritualistic songs with their marching beat. Above them, the aeneshenon dove and spun in intricate arcs, celebrating the beginning of the journey, although they would land to walk before long. The people of Torkae filed past, no more than four abreast, until they were gone, leaving behind a line of trampled grasses in their wake.

Kaemada tangled Eian's hand in Shareilon's mane. "A pegasus ride isn't something to be taken lightly, nor ever forgotten. Drink it in well and hang on tight."

With a snort and a toss of his head, Shareilon surged into a gallop, trailed by the wolf as he came bolting from the forest after them. Shareilon stretched his wings wide and, muscles straining, forsook the ground for the sky. Kaemada tightened her arms around her son as they became suddenly, strangely, airborne. Exhilarated laughter bubbled out of her as the ground dropped away farther and farther below them.

The air was cool as they soared upward, and the wind streamed past with a force that threatened to unseat them. Any higher and it would have torn their breath from their mouths. Kaemada held tightly with her knees and pulled the edges of her cloak tighter around Eian with one hand while the other clung securely to Shareilon's mane. She could only see the side of Eian's face, but nothing could hide his beaming smile.

Tannevar soon lagged behind, though their bond thrummed with the joy of the challenge even through his exhaustion and the soreness of her stomach. Kaemada had to stop Shareilon several times as her bond with Tannevar stretched to the point of pain, like an overextended limb. Her wounds demanded frequent breaks. Still, she pushed on as quickly and for as long as she could, hoping to minimize the chance of encountering Angels. If they hurried, they could camp only that night inside the Angels' range, rather than tomorrow night as well. Their speed had brought them far beyond her people, and they landed for the evening in the shadow of the foothills.

Kaemada crouched to unpack the food while Eian explored, careful to stay on the path. The pegasus had no such qualms, grazing on the grass beside the trail.

"We will not have a fire tonight, Eian. It's too dangerous. But look, we have blankets, my cloak, and I even brought my brother's cloak. If we fold it up, it suits you," she said, wrapping the soft warm fabric around the boy as he returned to her. Eian grinned, and she smiled, tweaking his nose where it peeked out among the folds of cloth.

Kaemada's body was on fire, and she felt stretched apart with Tannevar lagging at the very edge of their bond. She gingerly sat, praying Ra'ael was faring better than she, and hoping Takiyah and Ra'ael didn't get in too many arguments. They disagreed enough during the best of times, but with Ra'ael likely irritable, those two would mix like sparks and dry grass. Hoping once again for their safety, she motioned Eian to stop exploring and come sit next to her.

"Be sure not to wander off," she murmured to him, kissing the top of his head. "You must never leave the trail. Not ever."

Eian snuggled closer. "Tell me about the Kamalti?"

"Hmm, the Kamalti. That's an interesting story choice, acha'iyih."

"'Dear little one'," mumbled Eian absently. Then he scowled. "I'm not little!"

"Why did you translate that?" Kaemada gave him a puzzled look.

He shrugged, laying his head on her shoulder. "But I'm not little."

She prodded him but got no answer, so she sighed and began the story. "Long, long ago, our people began our existence at the same time as the Kamalti. We had many disagreements and misunderstandings. Our people love light and openness, so it was natural for us to choose to live in the hills and lowlands. The Kamalti love the dark, secret places, and they chose to live here, in the Holy Mountains. Once they each found a place that suited them, our two peoples became friends, but these days, no Rinaryn has seen a Kamalti for many, many generations. Many believe they're only legends. Some think that way back in the time of Torkaema and Naran, the Kamalti were so grieved by our people fighting each other they drew back and have been hiding ever since."

"Torkae."

"Yes, our kaetal was founded by and named for Torkaema. The ideas that became our way of life came to him in Talahn Valley, the Valley of the Seeker Tree. Ideas like the Council of Elders and that no kaetal should hold greater than one thousand people."

"How did he get the ideas?"

Kaemada smiled, looking around them. "Perhaps the spirits spoke to him. Perhaps even the Kamalti had a part in his formation of these ideas. We do not know. But the Kamalti keep the paths for us, provided we never, never leave them. There are great dangers out there, from the land and from animals. Some believe the Kamalti are dangerous, with their traps and pitfalls, but I believe the Kamalti are our friends of old, upholding their end of the ancient agreement they made with our people."

As the sun sank slowly below the horizon, Tannevar caught up with them, his tongue lolling. Kaemada and Eian shared a meal of jerky, cheese, bread, and water with the wolf, while behind them, Shareilon grazed. Catching the sound of something on the wind, Kaemada put her finger to her lips. In the stillness, the songs of a multitude of people drifted to their ears from a distance, and Kaemada smiled through a pang of sadness at being separated from them.

"Tell me of the Angels," Eian said.

The sky was cloudless, ideal for the Angels. And here they were, without the support of the kaetal to join their voices for protection. She pushed her worries away. It would only be one night. "Do you not remember from the last journey? They hunt with song, weaving a tune that entices the prey to look for them. Any who look at an Angel will be frozen in place and eaten. That's why we sing the counter-song and stay behind a barrier for safety. Tonight, we will likely hear the Angels, but by tomorrow night, we should be beyond their range. You must follow directions, acha'iyih."

The sun's last rays disappeared behind the hills, leaving the sky's blanket to the two moons and the stars as they spun in their nightly dance. Shareilon raised his head, then spread his wings and took off, sending her a vague warning. Kaemada clustered their supplies together and made sure they were all on the trail.

Below, the song of their people faded away. Kaemada wrapped a blanket around herself and Eian for warmth, then covered them all with her cloak just as the haunting song of the Angels graced their ears. Melody and multiple harmonies surrounded them, wrapping them in sonorous heights and depths. The otherworldly music pulled at them to come forth and gaze upon the singers, and Kaemada fought it with the counter-tune, humming the wild music as loudly as she could.

Eian squirmed, tugging at the top of the blanket. Kaemada hugged him tightly with one arm, pulling him farther under cover as she hummed the counter-song more loudly, more desperately.

You must never look upon the face of an Angel, or you will die! she sent him mentally, breaking the boy's privacy to save his life. A shiver ran up her back as a part of her wondered how the Angels would react to such an unusual occurrence, just the three of them on their own.

The music grew nearer until it seemed the Angels surrounded them. One must be hovering near them as it sang. With her arms full with Eian and Tannevar, the blanket sagged, exposing them to the Angel's gaze. Kaemada kept her eyes downcast, watching Eian through her lashes as she belted out the counter-tune. She covered his face with one hand, her other hand over Tannevar's face. The Angel's bronze feet hovered closer, and the wind from its wingbeats tugged at her hair. Her skin tingled with the nearness of the Angel. The urge to look up was almost unbearable, even as she sang the counter-tune.

Eian pulled away, drawn to the Angel. How long could she hold him back? How long could she herself resist the call? Her arms were beginning to tremble, and Tannevar was pressing himself into her leg, though she could feel his need to look.

She called out telepathically with all her strength to the Angel. *We mean you no harm. We are not for eating.* At the same time, she kicked the blanket back over their heads.

The back of her neck prickled as Eian piped up, his words nearly lost in the Angel's wing-beats. "We mean you no harm! We are not for eating!"

She looked over at him. Her heart skipped a beat. He was staring at the Angel from around the blanket. Throwing herself over him, she knocked him to the ground and shielded him with her body.

The wing-beats moved off, the Angel rejoining its group and heading for the foothills. Kaemada rose cautiously to her knees, her body afire with pain. Behind her, Tannevar shook out his fur, pacing a circle around them.

"Eian!" she folded him into a tight embrace until he wiggled and squirmed in protest. "Eian, I told you not to look at them! You could have died!"

"I did not get frozen. I did not get dead."

"Eloí's light, Eian, I cannot explain it. No one talks to the Angels!"

"You did. You did with your mind."

Kaemada blinked. "You cannot have heard that."

Eian watched her silently. Kaemada shook her head. "It was the only thing I could think of to save you."

Eian tilted his head. "You could have used your mouth. Like I did."

Kaemada shook her head again. She shivered, looking in the direction the Angel had flown, then back at her son, who was now moving his blankets, preparing a spot to sleep. "Eian, no one speaks to the Angels," she repeated. He glanced at her, shrugged, and laid down.

Turning, Kaemada made sure Tannevar was all right, then crawled over to Eian, tucking him in as he snuggled up with the hunter doll Takiyah had made him last summer. He had talked to an Angel. Not only that, but he had survived. They both had. She felt like up had suddenly become down, like the natural order of things was twisted around. She would have to ask someone. Who would know? Storyteller Zeroun, surely. As soon as she saw them again—only three or four more days now—she'd explain everything, and he would know what to do.

"I'm so glad you're all right," she whispered, kissing Eian's forehead.

"I love you, too."

Pulling a blanket over herself, she curled around her son, while Tannevar lay at her back, providing comfort and warmth. As the stars turned in their nightly dance overhead, she dropped off to sleep.

Dawn's light woke them, but Kaemada's body was a blaze of stiffness and pain. She could barely move through the agony and bone-wearying exhaustion. The wound on her side had opened, and her legs and arms ached from holding on to Shareilon against the wind. When she told Eian they would have to stay and rest for a while, the boy's face fell. As the sun rose above them and warmed the air, Eian grew restless and complained of boredom.

"If I know Takiyah, she will have thought of this situation. Check the packs for toys," Kaemada suggested as patiently as she could. She hated feeling responsible for Eian's boredom. Even more, she shared his longing to move on. She did not want to risk another night in Angel territory.

Moments later, with a cry of delight, Eian pulled out a set of small wooden figurines complete with tiny swords. Takiyah had attached a note to them with Eian's name in flowing Rinaryn script. Kaemada smiled at Takiyah's thoughtfulness as she made use of the bitter root, bandages, and salve. After midday, she forced herself to move on, though they barely entered the mountains before having to stop for the night. At least with the evening bringing cold and rainy weather, their chances of seeing the Angels again were small.

The next morning, after breakfast and bitter root, they resumed their journey. Off the winding trail up the slopes lurked countless dangers, but going over, Kaemada reassured herself, should not be an issue. She pushed her doubt away, committed to her choice. The people of Torkae were not far behind, for they had travelled steadily. Kaemada drew in a deep breath, sorry to miss the nightly stories and companionship, but still, she urged Shareilon on. She wanted to see Talahn Valley, to see the Seeker Tree, and to rest.

Her stiff body ached all over, and the winds buffeted and dragged, cold fingers clutching at them as if to tear them from the sky and bring them back to the stony ground. It was a long, hard day of travel, and exhaustion made her clumsy when they stopped for the night. Still, Kaemada's spirits were high. They were nearly at the Valley of the Seeker Tree.

After eating, Eian yawned and cuddled next to her. "Can you tell me a story?"

Kaemada yawned as well. "Again?"

Eian nodded. "The Storyteller tells one every night."

Kaemada wished she could send him to ask Old Soren or another of Torkae's Elders instead, but out here, there was no kaetal, no backup. Only her. And Eian needed her.

She pushed aside her fatigue and smiled at him, telling the age-old tale of the Ancient Man, who travelled through the land settling disputes, imparting wisdom, and urging the people to live in harmony with each other and the land around them. At last, he walked up the Holy Mountains and found the Seeker Tree, like Torkaema before him, and there he disappeared. But according to legend, he would return in time of need.

Kaemada lay her head on the coarse fabric of her pack and listened to Eian's soft breathing. Tannevar nestled at her back. With an exhausted sigh, she snuggled the little boy close and soon dropped into a deep sleep.

When she woke, the sun was just painting the peaks with color. Tannevar hadn't moved, and Shareilon was picking at the bits of grass he'd found. Kaemada sat up, looking around. Eian was nowhere to be seen. His hunter doll lay abandoned on the ground, and she picked it up. It was cold.

"Eian?" she called. She waited a moment, then called again, more loudly. "Eian!"

She stood, shivering in the cool morning air, and pulled her cloak closer around her. The empty trail stretched before her, and she moved forward, sliding awkwardly down the steep slope that led northward, back toward Torkae. Where was her son? Had he needed to relieve himself? Why wasn't he answering?

She turned to Tannevar. "Where is Eian? Why did you not wake me?"

The wolf yawned and opened his eyes, looking around. He shook out his fur and sniffed the ground in a seemingly random pattern. Kaemada shook her head. How had Eian gotten up without Tannevar noticing? It was impossible! This couldn't be happening.

"You were supposed to wake me!" she shouted.

He shook out his fur, sending her anger, fear, and confusion. Tannevar's fear for her son only heightened her own terror, though she tried to push it away, tried to remain calm. Panic would not help.

"Eian!" she screamed, turning away.

Her voice echoed across the desolate landscape. Above her, Shareilon wheeled, circling more and more widely, and Tannevar worked his way forward, his sensitive nose working hard, whining in a high pitch all the while. Thorny bushes snagged at her clothes, and her injured side awoke with stabbing pains as she ran along the twisting path. There was no trace of Eian.

What could have attracted her little boy's attention? Where was he?

Her boots kicked up sandy dirt as she hurried forward, bent awkwardly from the pain, searching for Eian's footprints. Sweat beaded on her forehead, and she gritted her teeth against the weakness of her body.

She pushed it aside. Nothing was more important than Eian. She had to find him. How frightened he must be, alone in the wilderness! Her heart thudded in her throat, panic rising. He might be lost, or hurt, or... No, she wouldn't think it.

Why couldn't Shareilon find him? Why couldn't Tannevar track him? He kept coming back to her, sending her confusion, and then padding toward a wall of rock just off the trail.

"Stop playing, Tannevar!" she shouted, fear flashing into anger.

He sent her irritation in return, and guilt stabbed her. It wasn't Tannevar's fault. It was hers. She should have listened. She dragged her fingers down her face, closing her eyes for a moment. Desperately, she wished to turn back the spinning of time, to prevent this, to travel with the kaetal instead of with only Tannevar and Shareilon for support. She longed for it to be only a dream. Tears closed up her throat, and she gasped for breath. She squeezed Eian's doll, wishing it was him instead.

Time dragged on, and the sun ascended the sky, burning off the mists and warming the air. Kaemada screamed her throat raw calling for him. Still, she could not find Eian. Reluctantly, she returned to their camp and inspected every bit of the stony ground in a wide circle. She could find no prints. Shareilon sent her no sign of him. Tannevar could not smell him. Terror squeezed her heart until the land dipped and spun around her.

Her searching was becoming more and more chaotic, but she needed to do something, even if panic blinded her. Eian was hers to keep safe, and she had failed him.

"Why can you not find him?" she screamed at Shareilon. The pegasus snorted an admonishment, and she turned on Tannevar.

"You're a better tracker than I! Stop playing! He—" Her voice broke. Gasping for breath, she swallowed hard. The tide of tears rose in her throat. She had to push it away, had to think.

Tannevar and Shareilon both sent her irritation. Slamming past Tannevar, Kaemada tore through a clump of bushes for the fifth time.

With a growl, Tannevar stepped in her path. He lowered his head and stared at her, sending her disgust. She was acting like prey.

Offense roiled from Shareilon and the pegasus bit Tannevar, faster than the wolf could dodge.

Kaemada yelped, clapping a hand to her shoulder as Tannevar's pain echoed there. "Shareilon!"

Tannevar snarled at Shareilon, then turned toward Kaemada, teeth still bared. Shareilon stepped up beside the wolf, and they confronted her side by side.

Smell what we smell. Stop screaming. Stop panicking.

She nodded, shame heating her cheeks. A sob broke from her lips, and hot tears fell on her cheeks. She shivered, staring out across the rugged landscape. Visions of Eian's broken body lying alone, food for scavengers, haunted her. She struggled against the terror. They were right. She needed to think.

Kaemada sank to the ground, curling into a ball, clutching Eian's doll. She rocked, pressing her eyes into her knees to stem the flow of tears. She needed calm. Tannevar leaned against her side, and she reached for him, for his unique insight. Yes, fear for the pup. But no worries of tomorrow, no regrets for yesterday, although he was plotting revenge on Shareilon. A tremulous smile appeared for an instant.

Tannevar opened further to the bond. Eian tugging a stick with him. Eian tumbling backward into a tree when the stick broke, laughing. Eian running with him in the forest, scaring up rabbits. Tasty rabbits.

Her shaking subsided, though tension remained in her shoulders. Kaemada buried one hand in Tannevar's thick fur and reached along their bond. Wolf senses flooded her mind, smells thousands of times sharper than before, sounds clearer, but colors becoming wrong, less vivid. Eian's scent trail ran straight into the stone of the mountain. Right to the wall she had scolded Tannevar about. It didn't make sense. There was no way Eian could be there. But that's what the scent revealed.

Confused and defeated, she retreated to her own mind. How could she trust such an impossibility? The stone was smooth and solid. What could be behind the wall of rock? Anything? She had to see. She had to dreamwalk.

Kaemada flung her arms around Tannevar's shoulders, and Tannevar threw one large paw around her back, his comforting presence anchoring her. Closing her eyes and focusing on her task, her mind drifted out of her body and away. Immediately, her worries dampened as the calm detachment of the dreamscape crowded in. There was no sense of touch here, no smell. Only songs, strange and distorted, for distance meant nothing in the dreamscape.

The features of the land around her dimmed, blurring together. The songs of people rose around her, several of the melodies coming from behind her, but none before her. A gleaming thread, her lifeline back to reality, stretched behind her, linking her to Tannevar, humming with the unique sound of her song mingled with his. Fear whispered at her even in the detached state of the dream, but now it was easily ignored, rather than drowning her. She floated toward the wall of rock. If Eian was there, she should be able to find him. She refused to acknowledge the most likely explanation for not hearing his song. He had to be all right. He had to be alive.

Physical barriers did not matter in the dreamscape, so she tried to drift through the stone. As she approached, she slid away to the side. She tried again and slid away again. She paused. While she wasn't particularly practiced at dreamwalking, she had never encountered any barrier in the dreamscape. She tried again and then again, bringing all her will and power to bear on the task.

Abruptly, the wall gave way, overwhelming her with a moment of disorientation. Darkness spread before her, with a multitude of songs rising from below. But she barely noticed them, instead staring in awe at a pale, almost translucent form, hairless with large eyes and hardly any nose. The figure had a knobby, bare skull, adorned with a thin, gold filament that held a single jewel shaped like a teardrop, and wore a long, shimmering gown. Fury and astonishment stood out on the strange features.

Everything went black. Kaemada was shoved away from the strange place inside the mountain, back out into the open wilderness.

What had she seen? How could people be living in rock? But she'd seen a face. What was going on, and most importantly, where was Eian? Perhaps among the other people, those other songs she'd heard. She had to get to him.

Slowly, she pulled her way back to her body. Too long out of her body and her body would die, and if her body died so would her mind, and if she died, who would save Eian? Finally, she opened her eyes and then closed them again. She struggled to catch her breath, drenched in the cold sweat of overexertion. She shivered helplessly, her wounds aching as if they were freshly reopened. Tannevar whined, jabbing her in the cheek with his wet nose.

How was she to find Eian? The trail led to the rock wall, and something was beyond that wall. She focused on breathing. She couldn't panic. She had to think. How had Eian gotten through? There must be a way, and she needed to find it.

Painfully, she made her way to the wall of stone. She laid her hands on the rocks, pressing against them with her telekinesis. She gritted her teeth, grunting with the effort, straining so hard she felt she might break something in her mind—if that was even possible. Only a pitifully few small rocks fell, clattering down around her. She tried again, and nothing happened. Frustrated tears slid down her face. She wasn't strong enough.

Every moment increased the chances that Eian wouldn't survive. Takiyah, Maeren, Ra'ael—they had been right. She shouldn't have come alone. Separated from her kaetal, there was no one to fall back on for help. Why hadn't she listened? Now she was all alone and Eian was lost. She would give anything to do it over, to do it right this time. To have Eian back. Desperation, grief, rage, and terror clamored within her for release.

Dropping the walls of her mind like so many jars smashed on the ground, she screamed with every fiber in her being for help. "Eian is missing!"

The message, the urgency, flashed out of her. It drained her, and she fell back on the rocky ground, lost to time's passing.

Chapter Five

The Rinaryns call the Kamalti their "brother race" and it seems to me that they fear them as much as they respect them. The Kamalti are said to live under the Holy Mountains, and at first, I thought they were probably dwarves. However, the mountain range is also infested with dragons, making the existence of a dwarven kingdom unlikely. The Rinaryns say the Kamalti protect the mountains and keep safe ways for them to travel to and from their Feasts of Starfall, along with traps and natural disasters for those who stray from the path. I find it most likely that the Kamalti grew as an idea from the fact that the journey is treacherous and rife with dangers, as a sort of childhood monster to keep their young in line. Few Rinaryns truly believe in them, and I have found no evidence to support the existence of such a race.

—journal excerpt

Taunos strained, his fingers missing the boy's by less than a hand's width. The boy gritted his teeth and stretched, dark eyes pleading. Tears made tracks down his dirty face. Zafril had several more summers than his sister Kaemada's son. He was still too young to die alone, trapped underneath the rubble of a house.

"Just a little farther, Zafril!" Taunos shouted.

The wall had fallen across the boy's legs and pinned him down. The fighting had stopped, soldiers of both sides fleeing the arrival of the Sea Peoples. It meant there were no Dahuti around to see their apparent ally trying to rescue a citizen of the other side, but it also meant he had precious few moments before death found them. Taunos shoved at the debris, even though it was packed too tightly to move, then dove back into the hole where he could see Zafril. His phobic mind screamed at him that the sun-baked clay would collapse, that he would be trapped, that there was no air to breathe, no room to move. He'd reach him this time. He had to.

"Haari!"

Desperation choked Taunos as Zafril shouted a final plea.

The shout distorted, became a scream of anguish and terror. His sister's voice.

Taunos jerked awake. A bird perching on the grasses above his head shrieked again and took flight.

He hated that nightmare. It refused to be left behind, even now, back in his homeland. He pressed the heels of his hands to his temples as the pounding of his head chased away the last vestiges of the dream. He hadn't bedded down for the night—why had he been sleeping? His tongue felt swollen in his dry mouth, and he was soaked through with sweat, dew, and more. With a grimace, he stood, staggering as dizziness overwhelmed him. Moving carefully, he peeled off his soiled clothing for fresh clothes from his pack and gulped water from his pouch.

How long had he laid unprotected, and what had driven him to unconsciousness? He was badly dehydrated, and his stomach churned pains through his abdomen. His muscles were stiff, his limbs unsteady as he moved. He'd slept far too long to be natural. And his sister's scream at the end of the dream—that was new.

Kaemada was in trouble.

His sister was supposed to be safe. That was why he travelled the realms, so his people could live in relative peace. And now she'd gone and gotten herself in trouble.

Grabbing a hard roll and a handful of jerky, he threw his supplies back into his pack, except the water pouch. Impatience lashed him as he walked on weak, clumsy legs, following the trampled grasses left by the alanshorn-drawn wagons of his kaetal. Last he'd been aware, they were camped over the next big hill. So long as they hadn't moved, he should catch up with them by midmorning—especially once he could run.

He pushed himself into a jog as soon as his legs felt steady enough. Hopefully, he could sort out whatever had happened before the Feast. The Heartwood Elders would want to speak to him, chastise him for his failure. The most likely source of the information he needed was closed to him, had been closed to him the entire time, despite all he'd done to gain access.

Taunos shook his head and pushed himself for more speed, up the slope of the hill, his pack bouncing against his back. First, he'd get his sister out of whatever trouble she'd found herself in, then endure the inevitable meeting with the Elders. After that, there'd hopefully be time to join the contests. Eagerness filled him for some good, fierce sparring sessions, just what he needed to relieve the stress from this last mission. The competitions were the best part of the Feasts, closely followed by the music and food.

As he jogged into the circle of tents at the bottom of the hill, the back of his neck prickled. The camp was in disarray. The tents, in their bold colors, were pitched haphazardly with no regard for the normal circular pattern.

Several large, shaggy alanshorn lowed uneasily as they milled at the ends of their tethers. His people clustered in small groups with nervous, darting eyes as they worked with stone tools. Far fewer were out than he expected, and no scouts shouted his approach. Something was wrong. Faces pinched with anxiety relaxed into relieved smiles when they saw him. His gaze darted around the camp, searching for danger, looking for his sister.

Talaera, black-haired and black-eyed, rushed toward him. Her brightly dyed alanshorn wool clothing was travel-stained at the hem, and her many bracelets of bone and wood clattered as she raised her arms to embrace him. "Taunos! Thank the spirits high and low!"

"Where's my sister?"

She stepped back to look up at him. He stood a head higher than her, and she was not a short woman. "Your sister has been soft in the head again. You must find her, and quickly! With this sudden sleep and her foolishness, the Elders will meet at the first opportunity."

Find her? His gaze darted over the rest of the camp. No Kaemada, no Eian, no Ra'ael, no Takiyah. Cold dread coiled in his gut. "What happened?"

"She went off on her own with Eian. On pegasus-back, if you can believe it! Taunos, listen. Look at me!"

Taunos forced himself to meet the smaller woman's gaze. She was in a mood and wouldn't let him go until she'd had her say—he knew that from experience. His stomach twisted, seeing the fear in her sharp black eyes.

"Troubles are coming, Taunos, for Galod's students. Accusations have been made. Now, more than ever, your sister cannot stand apart. Yet she will not hear me. You must!"

He didn't have time for such foolishness. His sister and Eian were somewhere ahead, alone and in trouble. They wouldn't have left the path—his sister believed all the stories, if not the danger. He shifted, but Talaera grabbed his arm.

"You must step lightly. Make no ripples as you go. Times are not as forgiving to those who separate themselves from the kaetal as they have been in the past. For you who are set apart doubly, as Galod's students and as psions, it's even more dangerous."

Gently, he extricated himself from her grasp. "I hear you, my mother's cousin," he said, stressing their kinship to calm her. He needed to find Maeren and let her know where he was going so the kaetal wouldn't give up hope. Hopefully.

She held his gaze a moment longer before granting him a smile, pulling his head down so she could kiss his forehead. "Now, make your sister hear me!"

He smiled. "Maeren?"

Talaera pointed toward the center of the camp. "I left her not long ago, arguing with Ra'ael and Takiyah." She sighed and shook her head. "Our Saimahkae must walk a thin line. I'm unsure there is a correct decision for her to make. I only know which way I wish her to decide, but then, my family is at stake."

Taunos nodded again. Talaera smiled, though her chin trembled, and she reached up to pat his cheek, sending him away. He hurried, thoughts spinning through his head like a whirlwind. What had possessed his sister to leave the safety of the camp and go ahead with Eian? Accusations against Galod's students? What had happened while he had been away? And Talaera's mention of a "sudden sleep"—whatever had affected him must have affected his people as well. No wonder they looked so uneasy.

He glimpsed Shana and Taela and dove behind a tent, gritting his teeth. He did not have time to deal with their foolishness today, but sneaking around the back side of the tent only put him face to face with three of the young men of the kaetal.

"Taunos!" one of them exclaimed, clapping him on the arm. "Be aware, Ra'ael is still mad at you for throwing her over that waterfall last time you were home. Watch your back."

The men crowded around him, preventing his forward movement, jostling for position, each trying to wring promises out of him for the Feast.

"After I fix this! I will beat you after. I promise." Taunos raised his hands for patience, forcing a grin, despite his worries. The challenges of the Feast always made him feel... more alive.

"If, you mean," another said, receiving glares from the others.

The first man scoffed. "This is Taunos we're talking about. He will be back with both Kaemada and Eian, and likely before sundown."

Taunos left the three, arguing about his timing, behind him. Barely had he gone five paces before another of his mother's cousins assailed him. After dodging her, he ran into his former betrothed, the healer Uma'arei. A short but excruciatingly awkward conversation later, and he finally managed to get free.

He sigh with relief when at last he heard Maeren's voice and dove into the tent, knocking the top of his head against the frame when he failed to duck low enough. He rubbed his head with a wince. It was just another welcome home for him, being in the land of low doorways. Still, it was good to be out from under the eye of the kaetalyn. His people raised him up to a height where all he could do was fall short of expectations.

Sometimes he felt it would be better to start again from the bottom and work his way up in respect. And yet, he enjoyed the adoration, even if they put more faith in him than any man should have.

"Taunos!" Ra'ael exclaimed.

"You're here!" Takiyah cried at almost the same time.

They stood side-by-side, both wearing belligerent expressions with their long, straight hair—one black, one red—tied back and their packs in hand. Takiyah's bulged at odd angles, and he smiled, wondering how many of her tools she had packed in there.

"Wildling. Tinker." He couldn't help but use the pet names he'd given them long ago. Ra'ael rewarded him with a scowl.

Maeren gave him a tired smile. "Taunos, good."

"My sister went on ahead?" Taunos said, raking a hand through his hair.

Maeren nodded. "Ra'ael and Takiyah want to go find her. They say she caused the sleep."

Taunos suppressed a shudder, remembering his sister's scream as he awoke. He didn't know how she'd done it, forcing so many to sleep unnaturally, but he was certain she had. He'd already been delayed too long.

"She did. Let's go." Taunos turned toward the tent's opening.

"Taunos, wait. Think." Maeren sighed, rubbing her eyes. She looked old, her expression worn and tired, and Taunos's chest tightened. "If you three go after them, it makes this a rescue."

Rescues were never sent because search parties never returned. But someone going ahead alone, aside from scouts, was simply not done, either. Maeren would be weighing the effects of increased scrutiny from other leaders against the chances of success, however strange the circumstances.

Well, worrying about the kaetal could wait. Most pressing was ensuring the safety of his family.

"Right now, only you three and I know the sleep was Kaemada's doing." Maeren shivered. "Who would have thought she had that power?"

"Many think the spirits caused the sleep," Ra'ael said.

"And if you leave and return with a psion?" Maeren asked. "Two psions leaving together? Three of Galod's students?"

"We will figure that out after we find them." Taunos passed a hand over his face, looking up at the tent's cloth ceiling. "But they will know it was her. Even if they do not weave the pieces together, she will give it away at the first confrontation."

Maeren nodded.

He saw it then. The thin line Talaera had mentioned. This was one set of unusual doings after another, and it would certainly attract the ire of the Elders. Maeren was pitting Galod's students against tradition, and relying on their success, even with the accusations Talaera had mentioned.

Taunos would have his status as a hero among his people as a shield from politics. His sister did not.

"As long as we stay on the trail, we should be reasonably safe." He looked at Takiyah and Ra'ael, warning them. "We will have to face the Elders on our return."

Takiyah and Ra'ael's matching glares screamed defiance.

Closing her eyes, Maeren sighed. "Elof, spirits high and low, preserve us from needing heroes. Go, go now. Zeroun and I will see what we can do to limit the damage. But be sure to come back and not to leave the path. The kaetal cannot stand to lose you as well."

Taunos kept his breath to a steady rhythm as he ran along the trail, shadowed by Takiyah and Ra'ael. They'd told him of the attack on the kaetal, and his anger provided fuel to keep his tired muscles going. They had to cover as much ground as possible to find Kaemada and Eian before the sun went down. The last thing he wanted was to leave them out in the wilderness for another night.

Every so often, he caught sight of wolf tracks, confirming they hadn't overshot. An afternoon breeze swept past him, fresh with autumn's chill. Behind him, Ra'ael and Takiyah's breaths came in regular puffs. The woody scent of the scraggly bushes that grew in the area filled the air, and the occasional bird song came from the shelter of the scrub. The trail sloped upward before him, and he increased speed to meet it, ducking under a rocky outcropping.

Tannevar stood in the path, his head lowered, panting heavily. Beyond the wolf, discarded bags and his old cloak lined the trail. Farther on, where the path curved again, his sister lay crumpled in a heap of long, dark honey curls.

Panic crushed him and he staggered to a halt.

The wolf wobbled as he snarled at them, hackles raised. He moved clumsily, stumbling often, his eyes unfocused. Taunos's heart stuttered. Any injury one took, the other mirrored, which meant Kaemada was at least as wounded as Tannevar. And where was Eian?

"Eian!" His voice echoed off the desolate landscape. His sister did not react to her son's name.

He sidled toward the bristling wolf. "Easy, boy. I wouldn't taste good."

"Tannevar! Let us through!" Ra'ael stalked forward.

Tannevar lunged, biting her thigh, and she shouted, kicking Tannevar reflexively. Beyond them, Kaemada jerked inward as if the blow had landed on her. Anger at Ra'ael warred with relief within Taunos. She was still alive. They just needed to find Eian—the boy excelled at hiding—and bring them home.

"Eian!" he shouted again. "Come on out, little man. This isn't a game!"

Ra'ael stood in his way, rubbing her leg and glaring at Tannevar. Taunos shoved her between himself and the wolf so he could pass. If the wolf bit her again, it would serve her right—she knew how deeply Tannevar and Kaemada were connected. As soon as he was past, he sprinted to his sister's side.

Taunos put a hand to her forehead, wincing at how cold her skin was, then gently opened her eyelids. Her summer blue eyes stared out unseeing, her pupils of different sizes, just like Tannevar's. Her fingertips were battered, the nails chipped and broken as if she'd been clawing at something. Taunos tried to relax, reminding himself that her heart was beating and she was breathing.

"Eian!" Ra'ael shouted. "Where are you?"

Takiyah threw him a blanket, and Taunos wrapped Kaemada in it. Moving aside the wooden hunter figurine lying nearby, he gathered her in his arms to warm her. The bruises marring her face—likely from the attack on the kaetal—turned his stomach. "I should have killed Tikatae long ago."

"We... did not know... he was lost... then." Kaemada's voice was weak, the words slurred until they were nearly unrecognizable, and one side of her face remained slack, but still, a rush of hope filled him. The wolf limped over and flopped down beside them, panting heavily.

He squeezed her gently. "How are you feeling, little sister?"

"Too tight."

He laughed in relief, loosening his hold.

Kaemada lurched upward, nearly slamming her head into his, half of her face rigid with terror. "Eian!" Wobbling, she pressed her hands against the stone.

"Where is he?" Taunos asked.

Kaemada shook her head, swaying with the motion. She fumbled, picking up the hunter doll and clutching it close as she mumbled something. Taunos glanced at Ra'ael and Takiyah, but their brows knit, apparently as puzzled as he was.

"Use your mind." Taunos glared at Ra'ael in case the priestess decided to fuss about the law. "No one needs to know."

Gripping his arm, Kaemada stared at him with desperation clear on the one side of her face. The slackness on the other side frightened him, though he'd never let on. He waited a moment, and then prompted, "Cha'atanahn, you're not sending anything."

She trembled and he put a steadying arm around her. Any telepath should be able to send to a willing recipient within touch, and Kaemada was a strong telepath. Tannevar whined, the high-pitched noise unnerving. She looked at him again, her breath hitching, but no thoughts bloomed in his head. Somehow, she'd lost her telepathy.

He squeezed her gently. "Telekinesis?"

Her hand trembled as she lifted it, then she shook her head, shoulders slumping.

Forcing confidence, he said, "I'm sure it will come back to you with rest."

Kaemada took a deep breath and placed a hand on the mountain face, speaking with exaggerated care. "Eian, inside."

"It's a rock, Kaemada," Ra'ael said. "What happened? Is Eian hiding?"

Kaemada bared her teeth. "Inside!"

She wasn't thinking straight. Taunos glanced down the trail for hiding places they may have passed.

"Oh, move!" Takiyah shoved her way forward and began a detailed inspection of the rock face. Taunos smiled at her. If it kept his sister calm, he'd be glad of it.

"No. Eian, inside. Not strong… enough." Kaemada sagged against his arm.

Taunos guided his sister to a rock, seating her there before stepping back, looking along the trail again. The need to move made him jittery.

"I will be back in a moment." He handed her a roll and his water pouch from his pack. "Eat. Drink."

Ra'ael crossed her arms in front of Kaemada. "No one leaves the path. It's against all our most sacred teachings. It's against the law and it's dangerous."

"She's on the path though, technically," Takiyah said, stomping her foot on the trail.

Their voices faded to murmurs behind him as he followed the trail ahead, calling out for Eian. Inspecting the ground, he finally backtracked to the pile of supplies. Kaemada looked exhausted, angry, and lost, while Ra'ael ranted at her as he passed.

There were no hiding places for the boy, but he found a partially obscured print near the supplies. It was about the size of Eian's feet and parallel with the path. He should have looked here more closely, but he'd been so intent on reaching his sister. He crept forward, scanning the ground. Before long, he was back with Ra'ael, Takiyah, and Kaemada, who had buried her head in her hands.

Taunos crouched beside Takiyah, who was still peering at the rockface. A series of scratches marked the stone. He glanced at his sister's battered nails, and then to her wolf who, sure enough, also had broken some nails and worn the others down to bleeding nubs.

Kaemada took a shuddering breath. "I woke. Eian gone. Tracked him... there. I tried... to move stones... Could not."

"And then you screamed in our minds," Ra'ael snapped.

"What?" Kaemada sat back as if she'd been struck, and Taunos reached out to steady her.

"The scouting party and all the psions got it. Some lost consciousness."

"What? No. No..." Horror and guilt twisted her features. Tannevar growled low in his throat.

"I have never heard of such a thing being possible," Takiyah said.

"Neither have I," Taunos said. "I would have said it was impossible, had I not been a recipient."

Kaemada buried her face in her hands, mumbling apologies through her fingers.

Ra'ael continued in a more even tone. "We need to return to talk with the Elders."

"No!" Kaemada clutched the doll closer.

"Go ahead," Taunos said. "I will find Eian."

"You cannot leave the path, Taunos. You know that. It's certain death, even for the hero of Torkae." Ra'ael took a deep breath. "It's bad enough, three psions and the daughter of the Saimahkae colluding in the mountains."

"That's nonsense," Taunos started.

"That's what those against us would say! We need to ask the Elders for direction. There are some who would use this against all of Torkae, which is already in a precarious position."

Taunos frowned. He really needed to find out what had been going on while he was away. Later. "We have to think of Eian."

"I am thinking of him!" Ra'ael shouted. "He has already been missing for a day. We have to salvage what we can."

"Only since this morning!" Kaemada leaned forward, burying her face in Tannevar's fur.

"Where could he be? Not through the rocks—that's a fever dream!" Ra'ael gestured around at the bleak landscape, talking over Kaemada. "We need to bring Kaemada back. At best, we recover Eian's body—" Ra'ael faltered and she looked down, swallowing hard.

"It took us a while to find you," Taunos explained.

"They slept for a full day. That means it's been nearly two." Takiyah turned to face them. "If you're all done arguing, you might be interested to know we can probably break through these rocks. There may be a cave on the other side."

"What?" Hope flickered in Ra'ael's eyes.

"Let's go!" Kaemada scrambled clumsily to her feet, doll still in hand. Of course—the doll must be Eian's.

"Hold on, it's not so easy as that. See here?" Takiyah pointed out a thin crack in the rock face, barely visible, that separated the wall into two parts. She shoved at it, then jammed a rod of metal from her pack into the crack and pulled on it like a lever. It didn't budge.

"Is no one else wondering how a little boy got through here?" Ra'ael asked.

Tannevar growled, bristling.

"Does Eian have telekinesis?" Taunos asked Kaemada. She shook her head. He frowned at the crack in the rocks. Ra'ael was right; if Eian had gone through there, he'd been taken, or at the very least, someone had created a passage for him and then blocked it up again.

A chill ran down his spine. Fae sometimes came this far out, and Eian might have been a fae changeling. He'd been found alone in the forest in Heartwood, and no family had claimed him at the Feasts after. Taunos's hands curled into fists. If the fae had taken him, their fearsome reputation wouldn't save them. Eian was his now. His family. He wasn't giving up on him so easily.

But he needed to be careful not to jump to conclusions. Otherwise, he'd miss things. Taunos extended his fingers, stretching out his fists, then relaxed his hands.

He turned to Kaemada. "Can you make it?"

She glared up at him. "He's... *my* son."

He hefted his water pouch and fixed Kaemada with a stern look, handing it back. "You're dehydrated. Drink."

"Did."

"Drink more. You were unconscious for days. You need water."

She grabbed the pouch, glaring at him again as she fumbled with it and made a show of drinking. He crossed his arms, exasperated. Kaemada was impossible to reprimand, either ignoring him or completely agreeing with him. She never fought him. It was infuriating.

Taunos indicated the rocks with a nod of his head as he took the water pouch back and offered his sister a hand up. "It could be dangerous. You need your strength. Did you eat that roll or feed the birds?"

His sister shook her head, holding on to his arm as she swayed. "*My son.*"

Fondness for her warmed his heart, sharpening his concern. Stubborn, foolish sister, but he loved her. He could have lost her, and he never would have known until it was too late. The thought awakened panic, and he forced a deep breath. He had to be calm to keep them calm. "Come on, cha'atanahn. Let's find your son."

He placed his hands on the rock wall, then looked at Ra'ael. "I could use some help."

"For Eian." Ra'ael nodded, walking over to stand beside him. She placed one hand on the other side of the crack in the rocks and the other on top of his.

Kaemada leaned against him, Eian's doll cradled to her chest, her wolf wavering beside her. Taunos shut his eyes, gritted his teeth, and *pushed*, straining to separate the two halves of the rock. Ra'ael smashed his hand beneath hers as she did the same. The rock was solid beneath his hands, and his arms shook as he demanded more strength. Small rocks tumbled down around them.

And then the rock moved.

His eyes flew open in shock. Grinning, he pushed harder as Takiyah shoved makeshift levers into the widening crack, pulling against them. Slowly, slowly, the crack widened, revealing some sort of cave. As soon as the opening was wide enough, Kaemada and Tannevar stumbled forward, and Takiyah flashed fire into the tunnel-like space. Taunos turned to get a better angle to shove at the rocks, and Takiyah moved around his feet, wedging open the crack.

He waited, muscles trembling, as Takiyah tapped in blocks of metal to keep the crack widened. The rocks pushed against him unnaturally, and he was grateful for her foresight. She grabbed their packs and flashed fire again, illuminating Kaemada and Tannevar frozen and panting a few paces into the cave. Ra'ael squeezed past him, and then Takiyah, before Taunos eased away from the opening, braced for the rocks to crash down on them. The metal Takiyah had placed groaned but held.

Two steps in and Taunos took his sister gently by the shoulders. Ra'ael hadn't gotten much farther before she'd halted, panting in fear. "We're off the trail. We're going backward," Ra'ael muttered. "We should not be underground!"

"Oh, it's not so tight." Takiyah sauntered past them.

His mind rebelled against her calm. Taunos forced himself to take deep breaths. They would not be buried alive. The walls were not closing in. There was enough air. No Rinaryn liked closed spaces, and his sister hated them more than most. Her face was a mask of terror, and Tannevar's eerie high-pitched whining filled the space, unnerving him. Takiyah slipped around them easily, flashing fire to light their way, and a bit of jealousy rose in him.

The rocks behind them slammed shut with a crash, and Kaemada cried out, her broken nails digging into his arm. His own heart thudded in his ears as he tightened his grip on her, thankful for Takiyah's flames sporadically lighting the tunnel.

"I think it's clear Eian isn't here." Ra'ael's voice quavered.

A line of lights at about knee height appeared on the walls beside them, slowly brightening. They were in a small, rectangular, stone chamber of smooth, clean lines.

"The floor's wrong," Takiyah observed as she went back to collect her tools, which lay scattered in front of two flat metal pieces that came together in the middle. Doors.

She was right. It was clean—no dust, no sand, almost as if it had been swept and scrubbed. It was far more a floor than the ground.

Takiyah started back toward them, pausing to stretch her hand over the strips of light. "What is this?"

Taunos shook his head. Seeing the closed space was no better than not seeing it. He struggled to force his floundering brain to think. Takiyah strolled past them, while he stooped to meet his sister's shorter stature and pulled her along. One step, then another. Another set of doors stood before them, two flat surfaces with a thin groove between them. It would make sense for Eian to have gone through there if he'd come this way. He wished the floor was dusty, to show footprints.

"What is this place?" Ra'ael's voice was sharp with awe and fear.

Another step and another. Don't think, just do. "Let's find out."

At a touch, the doors slid apart. No need for telekinetic force. Ra'ael crowded behind, stepping on his heels as they left the tunnel.

They emerged onto a ledge inside a massive cavern, marked by a deep chasm cutting through the middle. Rows and rows of buildings stood cut and shaped from stone, forming a grid of open-topped square and rectangular buildings. Huge pillars stretched to the ceiling of the enormous space, some with arched doorways and windows, within which fluttered curtains of light and airy cloth, and others carved and decorated with intricate designs. More buildings were cut from the sides of the cavern. Everything stood in straight lines, while around the city, the rock of the mountain curved naturally. Wonder banished all other thoughts.

"All these marvels, all this time, hidden right under our feet," Taunos murmured. Another time, he would gladly lose moons and moons to explore down here.

"There must be more than a thousand people living here," Ra'ael said, but her reproachful tone was subdued. He'd almost forgotten—it would be hard for the others to fathom so many people living together. They had no experience with cities.

In the middle of the grids on either side of the chasm, gaped an empty space around irregularly shaped metal buildings, shorter and broader than the stone buildings, linked by something like a heavy rope. The rope glowed with yellow light, though Taunos could see no fire to light it. The ground was paved with stone and lit with lanterns, which Taunos had to give the other three a word for. Ra'ael stared in astonishment, and Kaemada closed her eyes wearily. Takiyah only nodded, leaning over the edge to gaze in wonder until Taunos wanted to snatch her back from the drop.

Eian was nowhere in sight.

"You moved… a mountain," Kaemada slurred.

Taunos laughed. "I will bring this up another time to save myself from my shortcomings."

Takiyah grinned at him, her eyes bright with excitement. His heart understood, leaping with the familiar thrill of the new. Curiosity had sunk its teeth into him, bringing him fully to life with the challenge, eager to learn all he could. If only this was a simple adventure, rather than a search. This was not the fae. Finding Eian in a city like this was an impossible task, but then, Taunos had always taken great joy in achieving the impossible. Surely they could find him.

To the side, stone steps led far, far below them—the only way down.

From an alcove in the rock above the stairs, a person with a hairless, knobby head stared down at them, their mouth tight. They wore a circlet with a red jewel in the center that caught the light as they turned and disappeared behind more rock. There was no clear path from there to here, nor from there to the ground of the cavern. Were there more tunnels inside the rock?

The doors slammed shut. His skin prickled with warning. He and Ra'ael went to the entrance, but no amount of pushing or pulling would open them. They were locked in, locked onto this path, wherever it may lead. A shout sounded from the city below. Pale figures in flowing clothes began to rush around like insects when the hive is knocked over. Some sprinted toward them, and others scattered into buildings. Clearly, there was a peacekeeping force.

The organization screamed civilization, so surely they'd have rules, someone to talk to, to help in their search. Like the guards running toward the bottom of the stairs, if he could calm them down and convince them they weren't an invasion.

Ra'ael's frame was set with tension, but Takiyah seemed unaffected, staring around in open wonder. His sister stumbled toward the broad stairs, and he heaved a sigh.

Kaemada was making things difficult, of course, and if he tried to keep her from her task, there'd only be more chaos. Who knew how the guards would react? Keeping his arm around her, Taunos guided her to the inner edge of the broad stairs, where the wall was worked with metal engravings and gleaming jewels. The wolf tottered at their heels.

"We should stop here," Ra'ael said.

Taunos tossed her a look over his shoulder, continuing on. She knew Kaemada just as well as he did, and they might as well meet the guards halfway. It was certainly better than the guards meeting them while they were locked in a battle of wills with his sister. She'd never fought him before, but her son had never been missing before, either. The others had no idea how to deal with a situation like this. How much trouble would Ra'ael's antagonism cause them? They had to trust him. If they would just follow his lead, they could bring Eian home safely.

"Need... ask... about Eian," Kaemada slurred, not hesitating in her descent.

"There's less maneuverability here," Ra'ael said.

Taunos shook his head. Assuming they were a civilized people, they could ask about Eian, possibly pay a fine for trespassing, and be on their way. A friendly demeanor and smile could open doors that otherwise remained shut—like the doors sealed behind them—while acting defensive could be construed as guilt. Still, tension tightened his shoulders. He refused to glance back at the doors that had locked them in.

"We can fight in close quarters." Ra'ael raised her voice. "We have Taunos."

"Taunos is going to ask them about Eian," he called back.

She muttered something under her breath, and he couldn't help but grin. She was far too fun to needle, and it lessened the tension a bit.

"No need... to fight. We... do not... threaten them," Kaemada breathed.

"You cannot know that, Kaemada," Ra'ael said. "They could be like anything. They're not necessarily civilized."

His sister met his gaze, then faltered.

Taunos forced a grin. "Little sister, you would go willingly into a dragon's claw if it told you it meant you no harm."

She scowled at him. "What little trust! Life... would be brighter... if everyone... gave others a chance..." She trailed off, out of breath and unfocused. He tightened his arm around her. Could he dare hope they had medical facilities they could use, such as the great halls of healing he'd seen among the Dahuti?

"Maybe so, but a little caution helps a long life," Ra'ael said.

Kaemada shook her head and would have fallen if Taunos hadn't been holding on to her. "May find they're... not strange."

"Caution is prudent, but let's not jump to a fight either, shall we?" Taunos gestured to make peace. He needed his attention on the guards, not on bickering.

The oncoming people quickly closed the distance between them. They were tall by Rinaryn standards—about as tall as he was—and so pale that in some places their skin was translucent. Their features were strange, with very little in the way of noses, thin, pale lips, large eyes, and two knobs at the tops of their heads, which were bare of any hair.

The guard force wore a uniform of boots, pants, and a shirt with an upturned collar under an embroidered jacket. Buttons adorned the cuffs and the many embroidered pockets, and ruffles decorated the necks and wrists. The two women among them wore skirts over their pants and broad, fabric belts. The men had metallic belts with rectangular cases attached, and strips of fabric tied in knots around their necks. It looked stifling. Some wore thick-rimmed glass circles on their foreheads and tall hats with wide brims. Each wore a stern expression.

Kaemada's voice wavered as she called out, "We mean no harm!"

"We're only looking for a small boy, lost yesterday morning," Taunos added. He halted, keeping his free hand open and away from his side, and turned his most charming smile on them.

The strangers drew cudgels from loops at their belts. Tannevar growled. Ra'ael muttered, "Twelve to five, my sword and dagger, Takiyah's staff, Tannevar's teeth, Taunos... Do you still keep blades in your boots?"

"We cannot... fight them. Our chances of finding Eian... be less. Show them... not empty words."

His sister was planning something stupid. Taunos narrowed his eyes at her. "Stay behind me."

As he looked back at the strangers, Kaemada shoved away from him, stumbling down the stairs. "We come in peace! We will not harm you. We came to find Eian. He's lost. Please help us!" Her breath failed toward the end of her rushed speech, and her legs buckled, so she crashed against the wall.

Tannevar snarled and Taunos snatched his scruff just before he could leap. He wrestled the beast close to avoid snapping teeth, fuming. Why couldn't his sister follow simple directions? Whenever she couldn't win an argument, she simply did what she wanted, regardless of the consequences. It was Taunos's task to protect her, whether she wanted it or not.

Two of the strangers grabbed Kaemada's arms, batons pointed at her. The doll dropped from her weakened fingers to the stairs, bouncing several steps farther down. She looked at it, her expression pained, but the guards kept a firm hold of her.

"We cannot fight them," she said to Taunos. Then she turned to the guards. "We come in peace! Came for Eian, little boy, lost. Please!"

"You trespass on Kamalti territory. You will be taken to the Council Chambers to await your fate," said a tall man with a red jewel tied at his throat.

Taunos exchanged an astonished look with Ra'ael. The Kamalti were legends; could these really be the people from the fireside tales? Even more, they spoke the Traveller's Tongue. At least they didn't have to worry about translation.

He was drawing breath to reply when another man, this one with an extra layer of lace at his cuffs, broke in irritably. "Well? Move!"

Red-jewel and Lacey steered Kaemada down the stairs past the other guards ascending toward them. Ra'ael shifted next to Taunos. "Kaemada..."

"I'm all right! Do not fight!" Kaemada stumbled again, and the guards caught her roughly. She slurred an apology, the words coming so swiftly and imprecisely that even Taunos had trouble understanding.

Tannevar thrashed in Taunos's arms and wiggled loose. He shot down the steps.

"Kae—Tannevar!" Taunos shouted.

Kaemada turned, slow and clumsy, but still managed to wrench herself sideways in time to put herself between her guards and the leaping wolf.

Tannevar slammed into her, and he, Kaemada, and the guards behind her all tumbled down the stairs. A few of the guards leapt out of the way and turned toward Ra'ael, Taunos, and Takiyah with malevolent looks and ready stances, while others ran to help those who had fallen. Taunos raised his hands. These city guards were among the prickliest he'd ever seen, but at least they hadn't used their weapons yet.

The guards near Kaemada shouted at her while the others regained their feet. Tannevar snarled and snapped, but he was so unsteady he was no danger to anyone. Kaemada put her arms around his neck, shielding their captors with her body once again. Taunos took a deep breath and kept his hands obviously clear of weapons, stepping down another step.

Harsh voices roared at them as the guards shouted in their native language, gesturing forward with their batons. Taunos pushed down his concern and anger. He had to do what he could to steer them toward a path where he could win, and they'd all come out unscathed.

"She will not hurt you!" Taunos called out in the Traveller's Tongue, for they'd spoken in it before.

Red-jewel gestured sharply at them, and Taunos motioned to the others to come peacefully. Kaemada had been right in one thing—a fight would only worsen their chances to find Eian. He picked up Eian's doll, displaying for the guards that it was not a weapon, and allowed them to shove him down the stairs. Two guards hauled Kaemada up by her arms, provoking Tannevar once more.

"Shareil, Tannevar, shareil!" Kaemada pled.

"Tie up the furred one," ordered one of the women guards.

Two men advanced cautiously and bound Tannevar's muzzle shut with fine metal cords, looping chains around his neck as well. All the while, Kaemada turned breathlessly from one to the other, pleading for mercy, pleading for calm, and trying to explain.

"Kaemada, they're not listening," Taunos said in a low voice, watching the guards.

"I have to try! They might listen. But only if we try!" she gasped, looking frantically from their captors to Tannevar and back.

Once Tannevar was bound, the guards stripped them of their weapons. Taunos stood over Kaemada and the wolf while her friends clustered at his back. Kaemada looked miserable, so Taunos pulled her close. "Shh, I have gotten out of worse situations, little sister."

But could he do it again? Without sacrificing anyone close to him, people he couldn't bear to see hurt?

The guards dragged them apart and shoved the end of a truncheon into Kaemada's back. She stumbled forward with a cry, and Tannevar snarled, fighting his bonds. Both fell in a heap.

Taunos snapped. "Leave her alone! Do you not see we're not trying to hurt you?"

Takiyah murmured, "For first impressions, this could be going better."

Red-jewel shouted at the guards beside Kaemada in their unintelligible language. They shouted in return while Kaemada struggled to regain her feet. Taunos clenched his fists, watching their body language for clues. The guards likely did not want their movements hampered by a prisoner who may or may not be faking an injury. He could understand such a concern. He could use that concern.

"Let me carry her," he said.

They looked at him and then each other, muttering. Red-jewel glared at him for long moments before nodding curtly, gesturing from Taunos to Kaemada with his baton. Smiling pleasantly, Taunos gave his sister back the figurine and lifted her in his arms.

She protested, cradling the doll, and he gave her a stern look. "Rest, little sister. You can hardly stand."

The guards shoved Takiyah ahead with a cudgel. She hissed, glaring at the offending guard. "Careful!"

Ra'ael bore the jab in silence. Taunos stepped forward, though Lacey sneered at him and poked him with his baton anyway. Determined not to show his anger, Taunos gritted his teeth. Tannevar brought up the end of the line, led by two wary guards.

They were marched through the streets in stern silence. Taunos kept his gaze moving. Anything they could learn about these people might be an advantage. Everything so far had been posturing and intimidation, not true danger. The civilized air of the underground city increased the chances of some sort of system for justice. The enticing call of a challenge pulled at him. If he could figure out the system quickly enough, it would give him an edge.

The massive buildings were constructed from white stone, sometimes veined with blue, pink, or purple lines. Everything was polished, engraved, and heavily worked. Metal filaments and precious jewels decorated stairways, entrances, and the front of buildings, and the decorations grew more and more ornate as they walked along. Statues carved from smooth stone marked squares and crossroads. Some seemed like tall, bald Rinaryn, while other statues, more worn in appearance, had lizard-like features.

"Look at the lanterns!" Takiyah's voice was thrilled. "The metalwork is beautiful."

Taunos had to smile at her undaunted love of adventure, even as Ra'ael hissed, "Takiyah, stop admiring our captors!"

The air down at city level was much warmer than at the entrance, and the people they saw around them were dressed in a very different manner than their guards. Instead of the ruffles and layers, the regular citizens wore clothes of very fine, flowing fabric in white and muted colors. Jewelry abounded: gold chain belts, metal filament anklets, bracelets, necklaces laden with precious jewels and charms, and circlets made of braided or corded metal filament and hung with gems. The women wore long dresses and wrapped themselves in sheer shawls of white or pastel colors, shimmering like rainbows. The men were clothed in light, short tunics, sometimes open in the front, and simple kilts that went to the knee, held up by heavily decorated belts.

The sea of people around them grew thicker as they made their way deeper into the city. Held back by the guards, the throng grew impossibly large as hundreds of people gawked at them. In the distance, others swarmed about their business, calling greetings, crying wares, arguing over goods. It seemed likely that there were more people here than all the Rinaryn gathered together at the Seeker Tree.

"I have always wished to meet Kamalti," Kaemada breathed with a faint smile. "Your city is beautiful."

The guards scowled more deeply at her until her smile faded away. Tannevar snarled, bucking against his chains.

Ra'ael shared their scowl, though hers was directed toward their captors. "The Kamalti are a myth."

"How can you doubt the evidence of your eyes?" Takiyah asked, looking around in open wonder. She looked up and gasped, her steps halting, and Taunos followed her gaze. A massive glowing ball of lights took the place of the sun, illuminating the cavern. "Look!"

"How do you make it float?" Takiyah asked, but the guards ignored her.

They passed several more buildings, all shaped like boxes and set in grids. The guards in the lead pushed and shouted to clear a path through the throngs of people. One of the irregular-shaped buildings loomed like two arrowheads sitting one atop the other, and Taunos frowned. It seemed clear that the strange, metallic buildings were not made by the same people who laid out the grid. But what did that mean for them? He clenched his jaw. It was too late now. He'd brought them in here, and now he had to deal with the ramifications, whatever they were.

Ra'ael grumbled, glaring around her. "The Kamalti are not real. They're only legends!"

Kaemada shook her head against his shoulder, and he glanced down at her face, slack on one side, but full of a mixture of worry and excitement on the other. "It fits. And even if they're not Kamalti, if they control the mountain, surely they know what happened to Eian!"

Ra'ael narrowed her eyes, but her tone lost conviction. "They could have killed the Kamalti, moved in, and taken over."

Takiyah shook her head. "If someone killed the Kamalti, there would be stories. The simplest explanation is that they're Kamalti."

Taunos nodded. "We keep alert but offer them no excuse to resort to violence. We wait and see if they're as civilized as they appear. No threats of any kind."

Chapter Six

The Rinaryns are prolific breeders—they have to be to survive such high mortality rates. Many families have anywhere from six to ten offspring, and more are not uncommon. However, accidents occur regularly, infant mortality is very high, and childbirth is dangerous for both mother and child.

An example of mortality rates: a family in the nearby village by the surname Tsrian had only three children. The mother died during childbirth along with the fourth child, and the father never remarried. A year after the battle they call the Great Attack, the two younger Tsrians lost their lives during a raid. Before that, the father fell in a hunting accident, leaving only one surviving member.

Another family in the village by the name of Sierso is an additional example of the risks of Rinaryn life. There were once ten children, but two died in a hunting accident. The elder two, along with their families, were killed in the Great Attack. The mother left to parlay with their attackers and died a few months later. The raiders killed the father when he pled for his wife's body, along with the younger son and twin toddlers in the following raid. Of a family of twelve, there are now only three left, and one, being dragonbonded, is effectively dead to the village.

—journal excerpt

The metal building sat like a sharp rock in a stream, ready to gash open the foot of an unwary wader. Kaemada stared with growing trepidation as her brother carried her toward it, his strides immune to the shoves of the guards. He shifted his grip on her, and Kaemada wished yet again that her limbs didn't feel like liquid. The anxiety and humiliation ate at her, her weakness made apparent. How was she to find Eian if she couldn't even walk? Ra'ael was carrying her pack; all Kaemada carried was the hunter figurine that Takiyah had made for Eian. She cradled it, feeling foolish, but it was as close to Eian as she could get.

The metal doors of the building gaped open at them as they approached, and Taunos paused, looking as astonished as she felt. Who moved the doors? One of the strangers behind them struck Taunos's shoulder, rocking him forward, and he stepped past the threshold into the corridor.

"Where are the people who operate the doors?" Takiyah asked. Kaemada watched her from over Taunos's shoulder as her friend peered at the sides of the doors. The guards did not answer.

The hallway stretched far ahead, the ceiling pressing down on them and the walls too close. It was like going down a throat lined with odd lights—smooth, square panels glowing from the walls. Kaemada wrestled with her growing sense of dread.

"Are there lanterns behind those squares?" Takiyah hunched down for a better look at the lights before her guards forced her upright again.

Ra'ael scowled at their guards. "How dare they tear so much metal from the ground! Everyone knows it should be given freely. No wonder they're locked down here, away from the sky and the spirits."

The amount of metal was overwhelming. The floor, ceiling, and walls were all metallic, with occasional panels of a smooth, black substance on the walls. Doors were set into heavily engraved metal frames and themselves bore strange designs. The only hues were black, white, and shades of grey, and Kaemada soon missed the array of vivid colors and natural materials that her people favored. They hadn't seen any wood or straw or bright cloth here. She couldn't wait to be away, to find Eian, to be back under the open sky with the fresh breeze on her face. Taunos carried her through hallway after hallway, and Kaemada's heart raced as if she were carrying Taunos rather than the other way around. She cringed away from the metal surrounding her.

Kaemada tried to reach out to Tannevar, but their link was crippled and she could only dimly sense him. Walking beside them, Ra'ael kept her gaze fixed ahead, her mouth set in a straight line, no doubt wrestling with her own claustrophobia. Taunos's hold on her tightened, and his jaw clenched. The walls converged on them. The ceiling was too low. There was no air. Kaemada couldn't breathe, couldn't move, couldn't think under the weight of the fear that possessed her. She squeezed her eyes shut, struggling to draw each panicked breath.

"Shareil." Taunos's voice was steady, as if nothing was wrong.

His calm was a salve for her fear, keeping the waves of panic from closing over her head and drowning her completely. Every so often, she could gasp a breath through the mind-numbing terror, and she marveled that Taunos and Ra'ael could continue at all.

"Close your eyes, little sister. Envision the forest outside Torkae. We're walking to Galod's clearing. Ready?"

Covering her closed eyes with her hands, she brought to mind the forest. The sound of birds calling to each other. The smell of leaves crushed underfoot. The purpleberry bush that grew under the tatterbark tree which was home to a family of scoundrel tailosaen. Eian laughing and leaping into piles of fallen leaves. Would she ever see him again? Hot tears pricked her eyes, and a sob burst from her lips.

"We're here." Taunos's voice was low. Kaemada opened her eyes.

Another set of doors yawned open for them, and they entered a room ringed with glowing, curved tables. Lights from the ceiling illuminated geometric patterns imprinted on the light grey floor. Large panels of the smooth, black metal they had seen periodically in the hallways prevailed among the walls.

The guards forced them to cluster inside a large, circular design in the middle of the room.

"Do not move from the ring," ordered one, brandishing his baton. The others tossed their weapons and packs into a box outside the door before taking up positions at the edge of the room.

Taunos set her down, and she sank to the floor beside Tannevar, barely avoiding collapse. She loathed touching the cold, hard, metal floor, but she had no strength to stand or even crouch. Kaemada buried her face in Tannevar's thick fur, mumbling apologies while he whined and grumbled. Her eyes burned with the threat of tears, and she gulped around the lump in her throat. Eian was not there. She cast a despairing look around the room, her gaze lingering on each guard, searching for some hope of sympathy for her son.

"This is incredible," Takiyah breathed, her tone a mixture of appreciation and concern as she turned in a slow circle, surveying the room.

"Where is Eian?" Kaemada called to the guards lining the room. They didn't respond, and she tried again, her voice faltering and breathless. "Have you seen a little boy with dark hair in the last two days?"

Still, they ignored her, and she scowled at them, fumbling at the chains binding Tannevar. Her brother crouched beside her, fishing a strange, twisted, red stem out of the herb pouch under his belt. He pressed it into her hand as if to hide it from the guards.

"Here, Kaemada. They might keep us waiting just because they can, so this is as good a time as any."

She took it gingerly. "What is it?"

"It's a medicine from a people I found in my travels. It will make you very dizzy, so you might want to lay down, but it will give you some strength once the dizziness wears off. Crush it between your back teeth."

She hesitated, looking up at him. "Ameyitum. I never meant for all this trouble."

"Hush, cha'atanahn. We will find him, I promise you." He wrapped an arm around her and kissed the top of her head.

She nodded, taking the stem and doing as he said. It tasted terrible and her tongue burned like fire. As he had warned her, the room began to spin, but he caught her and laid her next to Tannevar, who nuzzled his cold nose into her neck. She buried one hand in Tannevar's fur and gripped her brother's hand with the other. The world swayed and rolled, so she had no concept of which way was up and feared to fall off the floor itself. The ground was unforgiving, as uncaring as the guards were to her plight. Closing her eyes, she clung to her anchors. Tannevar was there, even if she could barely feel him. Taunos was there. He'd make everything right again. She just had to be strong enough not to hold him back.

"We should never have left the path. There's no way back." Ra'ael's voice was haunted. They had ignored the sacred law, and now they were here. This was all Kaemada's fault.

Takiyah dismissed her fears. "Stop over-reacting. We're Galod's students. This is only another challenge. How bad could it be?"

"We may yet appeal to their sense of justice," Taunos said. "If we keep our heads—"

"So, what are we doing about it?" Ra'ael asked.

Takiyah's voice overflowed with confidence. "We have Taunos; we will come through this. Your fears are based on nothing more than stories designed to make children behave and listen."

"You're the daughter of the Storyteller!"

"Let's find out how much danger we're in before doing anything rash," Taunos finished.

"What about realmwalking?" Ra'ael asked, switching to Rinaryn.

Taunos shifted, and Kaemada squeezed his hand. "No," he said in Rinaryn. "I cannot bring anyone with me, and walking the realms is inexact. I can rarely jump back to a specific spot."

Ra'ael snapped. "I'm not going to my doom without a fight. You act like you know what to do, you make decision after decision without worry for the consequences, and now look where we are!"

Except it wasn't her brother's fault. It was hers. She opened her mouth to defend her brother, but her voice was choked by the tears she held back. She tried to open her eyes but immediately closed them again as the floor threatened to toss her off. Up and down exchanged places in a dizzying dance. Kaemada squeezed her brother's hand again, hoping he would know she was with him. Silence smothered her until Taunos broke it.

"What do you see?" he murmured.

Ra'ael matched his volume. "That one had a slight limp. I think something's wrong with his left heel, by his gait. That one walks stiffly, probably an old back injury. That one seems strong, but is constantly twitching his fingers. He's nervous. And that one is near-sighted."

"Or he simply prefers to glare at you," Takiyah snorted.

"That's good, but did you see how the one with the limp stays away from the twitchy one?" Taunos asked. "They never even look at each other. And the scowling one? His fingers are red and blistered. They may need bandaging. Finally, see how they're not between us and the door? I suspect the door's locked and these guards are only here for show. Same with the walk through the city—a ceremonial parade. The real fighters are out there."

"When the door opens, we can get our weapons, then fight our way out." Ra'ael's voice was so low it was barely audible.

Taunos scoffed. "You know I would gladly give my life to save yours, but I only have one life to give, so let's be reasonable, shall we?"

Takiyah laughed. "You being reasonable? That would be a sight."

Taunos's tone was light. "All right. If need be, we fight. We have two advantages—unpredictability and strange terrain."

"So… You're making things up as you go along, and we're surrounded," Takiyah said.

"Exactly."

"How are those advantages? You should attempt to make sense if you want to lead."

Ra'ael's questions gave away the source of her irritation. She had always been the leader of their fighting group. It would gall her to give that up, even to Taunos. Maybe especially to Taunos. Kaemada recognized his tone, though. It was the same voice he used when he was needling an opponent into a mistake. The brash overconfidence usually held a strategy, and he'd never let her down before.

Her brother grinned. "They know they have the advantage. When they let their guard down, that's our best chance. If, that is, we're in true danger."

Kaemada glanced at the guards. Was her brother right? Were they simply for show? The world rolled again, and she shut her eyes once more.

Calloused fingers brushed her hair back from her face. "Feeling better yet, little sister?"

She peeked out to see him grinning at her. "I'm going to throw up on you."

He laughed. "It will pass soon. I promise."

"I might still throw up on you. Stop laughing at me." Still, she smiled.

She'd said two whole sentences without pausing for breath. It was all too easy to relax in her brother's care, but impossible to do for long. Not with her son missing. She raised her head slowly to glare at the guards. "Why will they not answer me? Eian needs us."

"Keep gathering your strength, little sister, while you can."

She laid her head back down, weariness forcing her to follow his instructions. Tannevar scrabbled at his chains with his forepaws, and she turned on her side, trying to help him escape the confinement he so hated. The metal refused to yield to her, and the medicine Taunos had given her hadn't completely banished the weariness. She settled for stroking Tannevar's head, hoping to calm him.

"Ameyitum," she whispered again.

Taunos squeezed her shoulder. "Stop apologizing, cha'atanahn."

She reached for the song of the spirits. It seemed muted and distant, and she wasn't sure she could feel it, but she strove to attune herself to that sacred music, anyway.

Looking up at her brother's face, she was struck to find pain in his eyes. He always tried to hide it, thinking she wouldn't notice when he edited the stories of his adventures for her. If anyone could find Eian, it was him. And here he was, trying so hard to keep their spirits up, and she wasn't helping.

She put on a tremulous smile, straightening. "This is just what you expected, coming home, isn't it?"

"It's not a game!" Ra'ael scolded.

He grinned. "But it's so much easier to pretend it is."

Ra'ael glowered at him. "You're a perpetual adolescent, playing games and leaving the adults to clean up after you!"

"Sounds about right." Taunos winked at Takiyah, who choked with suppressed laughter. Kaemada found herself smiling again as Ra'ael sputtered.

"Should I come home, then, Wildling? Live all my days in Torkae?" Taunos asked.

Ra'ael muttered something to herself about the penalty for murder, and Taunos winked at Kaemada this time before turning back. "Oh, so I should continue my 'perpetual adolescent' wandering ways?" He tilted his head, looking so innocent in his entreaty that Kaemada had to laugh, though it earned her a glare from Ra'ael.

"You're impossible." Ra'ael punched him in the shoulder, prompting him to rub it in mock injury.

Taunos threw up his hands. "See? Unwinnable game." He leaned forward and spoke in a softer voice. "Unwinnable games are no fun, you see?"

"What if they insist on being played?" Ra'ael asked, nodding toward the guards.

He reached forward to muss up her hair with one of his roguish grins, speaking softly. "They think we're weaponless because we lack conventional weapons. So let's use what we have, shall we? Such as their emotions?"

Ra'ael slapped his hand away, but a small smile curved her lips. Kaemada smiled at both of them. The Kamalti could never have known what they were getting into when they captured Taunos.

Her brother was laughing when the doors slid open to admit a group of five Kamalti dressed in elegant clothing and gleaming adornments. The Kamalti stopped, staring at them.

"I have never seen prisoners in such good humor before," grumbled an elderly man, casting a disapproving glare at them and their guards. The guards looked down at their feet and shifted uneasily.

The man glanced at the box that held their weapons. "They brought these with them? Lock them away. They will not be needing them again."

He swept his arm in a grand gesture, sending several guards scurrying, then strode into the room with a sniff. The other four followed, doing their best, it seemed, to imitate their leader. Kaemada watched them apprehensively, though anger built inside her like a wave.

Ra'ael leaned over, whispering, "There goes any chance of us grabbing our weapons."

Taunos motioned with his hands, pleading for patience, and Kaemada took a deep breath, hoping to imitate her brother's easy confidence.

"Justice Hedrik, Justice Mezguf, Justice Fandrell, Justice Tydrik, and Lord Reason bring this court to session," one guard said.

The elderly man who had spoken before slammed the butt of his staff on the floor five times, sending vibrations rippling beneath their feet. Kaemada winced. Everything was wrong—the hard, unyielding metal that matched the hard, unyielding expressions of the Kamalti; the echoes of the closed space, rather than justice delivered under the open, in the presence of Eloí.

"If I may have your attention," he said with narrowed eyes and a haughty tone. "You are called here for judgement, having been found guilty of trespassing on Kamalti lands. Do you deny this?"

Called for judgement, not for justice? There was barely any time to respond before the impatient Kamalti shouted at them, "Answer the

Justice!"

"No, but we wer—" Kaemada started, but the Justice cut her off.

"Let the record show the trespassers admit their crime. Further, you forcibly entered our lands, rather than falling upon them by accident and foolishness," he intoned.

Kaemada shifted, feeling off-balance. It seemed the man wanted the conversation to progress at a rapid pace, leaving her reeling at the rhythm. How were they to weave together justice between everyone involved when the Kamalti were so impatient, so demanding? She had been called to stand before the Heartwood Council of Elders once, an experience that had left her trembling and sweaty-palmed, but even that was nowhere near as intense as this.

The Justice frowned hard at them, tapping his fingers on his staff. "You will answer when posed a question!"

Taunos frowned. "How were we to know you were here?"

"The defendants claim ignorance and fall upon their stupidity," intoned the older man, and he turned to the other Elders. "They will be judged for this!"

He spun back around to eye them critically. "What of the plague these days past that caused many of ours to fall into sudden sleep, and others to go mad hearing voices and seeing nonsense? Is this your doing, too? I find the timing suspicious."

Kaemada's jaw dropped open. She avoided the gazes of the others as they gaped at her. Her mind-burst had affected even those who were not Rinaryn?

The Kamalti Elder peered at Kaemada. "This was your doing?"

"It must be," she whispered just as he was opening his mouth once again. Too late, her inner voice screamed at her that these Elders were not trying to draw out the true story so that amends could be made, but were searching for blame. It was not a safe place for true answers, though the thought of deceiving Elders was disrespectful and went against everything she believed in. "I do not know how. Please—"

"There is no tolerance for magic." He tapped a finger on one of the glowing tables of lights. "The Justices for the Scouting Guild send the matter to the Council for judgement. May the accused pray to the gods for mercy, as they will surely need it."

"So, this isn't their Council?" Takiyah whispered.

"We have to endure more of this?" Ra'ael groaned.

It was too much. Kaemada's hands clenched into fists at her sides. "We came to find Eian. My son. We did not mean trouble. Please, help us find him." Her body trembled, but she willed herself to remain upright.

"It matters not. You—"

"It *does* matter," Kaemada spat. "How can you say my son's life does not matter? We only want to find him, then we will gladly leave you to your seclusion. But you will *not* turn us away without telling us if you have seen him."

The leader waved his hands impatiently as if to shoo them away, talking over her. "Lady Answer, take them to the Council. I will stand no longer in the presence of these who will soon be condemned."

One of the women guards who'd brought them to this strange room stepped forward with a crisp, "Yes, Justice." She turned to another guard, waving a dismissive hand. "Chain them up."

Kaemada drew a deep breath and stood her ground, refusing the easy temptation of shrinking behind her brother. One guard spoke in a questioning tone, but Kaemada could not understand the words.

Lady Answer scowled at him. "This is my task. I can handle a few Outsiders."

She spun on her heel and stalked out. The guards forced them to follow. Desperation, rage, and fatigue combined to make walking a difficult task, even with the strength borrowed from the medicine Taunos had given her.

Overwhelmed, she focused on Answer. "Please, ameyitum. I will atone. Please, I must be sure Eian is safe. Then you can do whatever you want to me."

Answer only walked faster.

How could they be so heartless? "Please, please, only tell me if you have seen my little boy!"

~

Takiyah flexed her wrists, straining against the chains. This talk of condemnation and no longer needing their packs or weapons sat uneasily with her. They were bound with metal, walking single file after the guard Answer. Two guards marched on either side of them, and three brought up the rear.

Ahead of her, Kaemada stumbled. She had limped since leaving the Scout's Council, and it was only getting worse. It had better not come to fighting; Galod had taught them to use their strengths as a unit to mask their weaknesses, but Takiyah lacked faith that it would be enough this time, regardless of her boasts.

They walked over cobbled streets and through the throng of people who made way for Answer. The people of the city, garbed in their strange, flowing clothes, crowded the edges of the streets to gawk at them. Parents held their children close, whispering and pointing at them. Takiyah breathed deeply, refusing to let them see her humiliation. Just ahead of her, Taunos walked easily, head high as if all was well.

Let's use what we have, shall we? Such as their emotions? Taunos's words echoed in her memory, and she smiled. Ra'ael may grouse, but she followed his example just as the rest of them did. Maybe it resulted from so many summers growing up in his shadow.

Takiyah kept her eyes moving, partly to be ready for action and partly because, despite their circumstances, she couldn't help but feel drawn to the enormous buildings. Being forced deeper into the underground city, away from the stairs to outside, didn't bother her as much as she would have guessed. Impatience itched at her to find Eian, but what about after they found him and made sure he was uninjured? She raised her gaze to the pillars holding up the cavern's roof. She would find a way to come back here and learn more.

It was as if something in her mind had unlocked, as if a chest full of hidden treasure had appeared, and she couldn't wait to open it and explore. Already, she could see there were differences among the types of stone around her, and she knew, somehow, that each had a name. Rinaryn had nine words for mist and only one for rock—it was ridiculous. Here, all around her, lay secrets waiting to be uncovered.

Takiyah took another deep breath and relaxed her shoulders. Yes, there was danger around them, and she hated being captive, but Galod's training often threw them into dangerous situations. She leaned into the curiosity warring with her wariness, urging her to see, touch, and discover everything around her. Their guards clearly hated that they weren't panicking, and that was something they could use. What kind of people would ignore a mother's pleas for her child?

The row of huge metal buildings on their right ended, leaving an empty space before the ground gave way to a deep crevasse, its vast depths devoid of light. On their left, buildings were carved directly into the rock, and the glow of lanterns illuminated the street. The crevasse crept nearer and nearer to them until it ran parallel to the road.

Takiyah leaned over to look. "I wonder how deep it is."

"Careful, Takiyah."

Takiyah threw Ra'ael a look. Did she really think she'd be stupid enough to fall in?

Taunos spoke to their guards, as casual as if they were on an afternoon hike. "The architecture here is amazing. It's interesting that you Kamalti have not done something with this ravine."

"Have you seen much like this place on your travels?" Takiyah asked, playing along. Beside them, she could sense the guards bristling with annoyance.

Taunos answered with a broad grin. "Like this, yes, but never under a mountain. I spent five moons with a very interesting people who lived in the desert and built their buildings into the side of the red cliffs. They used ladders to get around and could go days without seeing the sun, such as during sandstorms. I spent another two moons with a people who paved their streets with bricks made of dried mud and lit them with lanterns like these, though not of this workmanship."

"No wonder you never make it home," Kaemada said.

Taunos laughed. "If I were home more, Galod wouldn't have time to train you!"

Ra'ael raised an eyebrow. "We could take you."

Taunos scoffed. "Maybe all together. If I was sleeping."

"Silence," Answer snapped, marching onward without looking back. "You must be among the least intelligent of your primitive people, not realizing your peril."

"So enlighten us," suggested Taunos.

Answer spun around to glare at them, and Taunos gave her his most arrogant grin, the one that always made Takiyah want to punch him. The Kamalti woman fumed, then clenched her jaw and spun around to lead them on. Takiyah smirked. Their guard certainly was prickly.

"Answer. That's a pretty name. And in the Traveller's Tongue, too, is it not?" Taunos smiled.

Their leader stalked on, silent.

"Why not use names from their language and not the Traveller's Tongue?" Ra'ael asked.

"Some Rinaryn are named in Traveller's or with non-traditional spellings," Kaemada said, always drawing parallels. "Like Taunos and I."

"But that's your middle name, not your proper name, and Taunos still *sounds* Rinaryn, at least," argued Ra'ael. "Besides, your mother was rather non-traditional—though greatly loved and missed," she hastily added.

"Thank you for that," Taunos said dryly.

"Others might embrace Traveller's as a source for names," Takiyah said. "But not all of them have names in Traveller's. What were they? Hadrik? Very strange. Lots of -ik's."

"Maybe we should ask—" Kaemada began.

"Have you no manners at all? Stop discussing me!" Answer turned to confront them, fury alight in her eyes.

Taunos bumped into Answer, who hopped backward, off-balance. A guard turned on him, staring as if he'd just shot a bird or committed some other taboo.

"How do you dare!" The guard shoved Taunos backward.

"Go!" Taunos urged.

He was right. If they were looking for a chance to escape, now was the time.

The two flanking guards sprang toward Takiyah and Kaemada, but Takiyah twisted and ducked out of the way, her chains flailing around her. Kaemada nearly collapsed, and the guard overshot, while Ra'ael charged the guard next to Taunos. Taunos leapt, getting his hands in front of him, and punched the guard who had pushed him. In the mayhem, Takiyah scrambled to Kaemada, who was evading the guard with grim determination, stumbling over her chains and moving as conservatively as possible. Ra'ael soon joined them, and they fell into the familiar rhythm of a trained fighting team.

The guards advanced in a straight line, in pairs. Ra'ael and Kaemada flanked Takiyah as she extended her wrists, streaming fire toward the oncoming guards. When they dodged, Kaemada and Ra'ael were there, darting forward to take advantage of their opponents' momentary disorientation to deliver a strike to the knee or hip.

That was how it should work, but Takiyah found they had to keep circling to defend Kaemada's slower speed and weakened blows, and their chains hindered them. Tannevar, tied up tightly, was no help at all.

Nearby, Taunos feinted and evaded his opponents, forcing the four guards he was fighting to stumble over each other instead of subduing him. He, like Ra'ael, used his telekinesis to move impossibly fast and deliver extra strength behind his blows. The sound of him laughing and taunting his opponents—even correcting their form!—made Takiyah smile. Taunos always mocked his challengers, and he always won.

Takiyah blasted fire toward Answer as the guard fighting Ra'ael tripped over a foot. They had to get Kaemada relief—her leg looked ready to give out. Ra'ael saw it too, for with the next blast of Takiyah's fire, she ran to engage Kaemada's opponent. Takiyah turned to make sure Ra'ael's opponent stayed down and narrowly avoided burning Taunos. Where had he come from? She scowled at him as he ducked under her attack, but the damage was done. The guard engaged Taunos, and the other two flanked them.

"Get out," he shouted.

"No," Ra'ael replied.

Takiyah turned to face the flanking guards and moved forward, leaving Ra'ael, Kaemada, and Taunos at her back. Kaemada was using Ra'ael's cover to try to free Tannevar. At least she'd been able to get her hands in front of her, just as the rest of them had. Good. They needed every advantage. Galod had drilled them relentlessly over the summers, so it was instinct to know where Ra'ael and Kaemada were and to use each other's strengths.

It was impossible to predict where Taunos would be. No wonder he usually fought alone.

There were six guards against the four of them, and they had already targeted Kaemada as the weak link. The Kamalti slowly pressed them toward the crevasse. Takiyah blocked a blow and shoved the guard toward Taunos, who sidestepped a punch, grabbed the man Takiyah had driven toward him, and threw him toward the guard who'd struck at him.

A weight landed on her back, and she curled, flipping the guard who'd tried to tackle her over her head. Right on cue, Kaemada extended her lame leg, tripping him and then striking his neck once he hit the ground. Takiyah blocked another advancing guard with a stream of fire, taking a side-swipe from a club on her arm as she did so. Pain flared up her arm, but that wasn't the worst part. They were surrounded, and the crevasse was getting too close for comfort.

A lanky guard dove in from the side, grabbing Kaemada. Tannevar foamed at the mouth as he fought the chains around his muzzle, and Lanky Guard kicked him toward the crevasse.

Kaemada shouted and bit the man. He threw her away from him as Taunos surged toward them. Takiyah turned to cover Taunos's advance with a wall of flame. Kaemada flew several feet before hitting the ground, rolling toward the crevasse as she sprawled, desperately trying to stop her momentum, but hampered by her bound hands. She collided with Tannevar, and they both tumbled over the edge.

"Kaemada!" Taunos shouted.

Takiyah kicked out, trying to keep the guards' attention on her so Ra'ael could run to help Taunos. She couldn't help but glance back, her heart in her throat. Kaemada had caught the edge of the drop-off, but she was struggling to grip the stone and Tannevar's chains at the same time. There was no chance she'd let Tannevar go. Taunos dove for the edge. Takiyah threw up higher flames, briefly fencing them in with a wall of fire that she swept back and forth to renew. She peeked over her shoulder.

Kaemada gripped Taunos's upper arm until her fingers were white, and Taunos held her forearm. Ra'ael lay beside him, clutching Tannevar's chains. One of the guards darted in. Takiyah shot flames toward him with blazing heat.

"Get them!" Answer ordered.

"Get back!" Takiyah pulled on her reserves for more fire. She glanced back, hoping they'd hurry. She couldn't hold off the guards by herself for long.

Taunos's fingers spasmed as he held Kaemada, and she dropped a hands-width before he caught her again with a grunt.

"Something's... pushing us," Ra'ael said through clenched teeth. "Ow! Cannot... push it back!"

Ra'ael twisted suddenly to grab Kaemada, who jerked and screamed. She must have lost hold of Tannevar's chains. Lanky Guard slipped around Takiyah's defenses and clubbed Taunos sharply on the shoulders.

"No, wait!" Taunos shouted.

"Stop!" Furious, Takiyah spun and punched Lanky Guard, gaining a dark pleasure at the sound of his nose breaking. But another guard slipped past and smashed Ra'ael over the head with his club.

"Magic!" Club Guard cried. "There will be no magic here!"

Ra'ael crumpled to the ground. Kaemada fell.

"Kaemada! No!" Taunos roared, reaching down into the ravine.

Club Guard slammed his club into Taunos's head, and he fell, face-down in the rocks. The dark swallowed Kaemada's falling body.

Takiyah stood frozen in horror, staring at the empty edge and the darkness beyond.

Blood spattering his clothes, Lanky Guard wrenched her arm. "You will pay for that. Magic is not tolerated." He shoved her away from the chasm.

Her stomach knotted. Nausea rose in her. They couldn't be gone.

Answer confronted Lanky Guard with a glare. "You will stand before the Council for your loss of control!"

"A small sacrifice if they will now treat their situation with the gravity it deserves," Lanky Guard retorted.

Takiyah stared at the ravine. This wasn't real, couldn't be real, but the scene played itself over and over in her mind's eye. Kaemada's eyes widening, her hands flailing for something to hold on to. But there was nothing there.

Kaemada was gone. Tannevar was gone. Taunos and Ra'ael lay bloody and motionless.

Dazed, she didn't object as rough hands rebound her, the chains digging at her skin. How had this happened? They were supposed to just find Eian and be on their way home. The four of them were Galod's greatest students. This was supposed to be an adventure, not...

Takiyah had begun planning her arguments to stay, to learn the secrets of this place. But now, with Kaemada...

Her guards shoved her forward, so she walked, one numb step at a time. Ra'ael and Taunos were dragged ahead of her like animal carcasses along the road. Blood matted their hair and stained their skin. Morbidly, she stared at them. They had to be alive. If she lost them, too, she'd be alone. So very, very alone.

Answer turned to glare at her. "Give me any more trouble, and that is what you have to look forward to."

CHA'A
Chapter Seven

No one could deny the futility of seeking peace with the Darks when they raided the village again, not one year after the Great Attack. Heaping insults around them, they burned and slaughtered animals as well as people. That attack killed the remainder of the families of the telekinetic psion, the telekinetic realmwalker, and the fully functional psion students. The Darks called it a lesson for daring to ask for capitulation of any kind.

The telekinetic psion succumbed to the "blood rage" for the first time during this attack. She did a great deal of damage before the villagers—kaetalyn, in the native tongue—were able to focus her attacks on the Darks. I'm pleasantly surprised to have the chance to tutor and study a person possessing both talents. I expect the possibilities to be quite intriguing.

—journal excerpt

Ra'ael's head pounded. She squinted out from behind the pain. Thick, metal bars loomed in front of her face. She was in a cage, hanging from thick chains looped through hooks in a stone slab above her and then anchored to large hoops in the ground. The ground swayed several paces below. Beside her, Taunos and Takiyah were jammed in metal boxes of their own, empty cages swinging between each of theirs. Taunos lay unconscious, and Takiyah slumped in the too-small space looking miserable.

Kaemada was gone.

The memory hit her like a blow to the stomach. Once again, she was without a family, the only survivor. The last time, Kaemada had quietly gathered Ra'ael's things and arranged them in her hut, and then took Ra'ael by the hand and brought her to her new home. She and Eian had become her family—even Taunos, truly. But now Eian was gone and so was Kaemada. They'd left the trail, pushing aside wisdom for foolish hope, and they were now reaping the consequences of disregarding the sacred laws. Teros, head priest of Torkae, always maintained that those whose story and song aligned with the spirits' would find their paths smoothed and bright. How disappointed he would be in them now. In her, specifically.

She needed the other priests, needed them to surround her, to remind her song of that of the spirits and the greater one of Eloí. She looked up at the cavern's ceiling, the rocky barrier that separated them from the sky. Could the spirits see or hear them, even down here? Could Kaemada's song find her way out? Would she ever cross the rim of the sky?

Taunos awoke with a shout, and Ra'ael jumped, the cage rattling around her. Her heart pounded in her ears as Taunos seized the bars of his cage and shook them violently, screaming his sister's name till froth bubbled at the corners of his mouth.

Below them, Kamalti people turned to watch with overly large eyes, laughing behind upraised hands. Rage bubbled up in Ra'ael like a fountain, and she shouted through the bars, "You killed her! You killed Kaemada, his sister, my friend! Have you no heart?"

They didn't. It was clear from their tittering mirth and the way they eyed their swaying cages as if they were some sort of entertainment while they went about their business. Her stomach twisted. She put a hand to her aching head while Taunos roared wordlessly, throwing himself against the bars. The cage lurched and groaned but held firm. At last, he crumpled silently, eyes open but unfocused.

She needed to check on them. Takiyah and Taunos were her responsibility, even if she only wanted to curl up and weep.

"What happened?" Ra'ael winced at the cracking of her voice, rubbing her forehead.

"They threw us in here for the night." Takiyah's voice was flat, her head resting against the bars. "That one, Answer. She walked away with a stone, talked to the stone a bit, and then came back and said the Council was retired for the day."

Ra'ael scoffed. Stones talking? The absurdity was almost enough to take her mind off the closed space.

The space was too tight. Ra'ael shoved at the door, knowing it was useless but still unable to resist the impulse. Scowling, she pushed at it telekinetically, but it held firm. She focused her efforts on the little box connecting the door to the rest of the cage, prodding, looking for weakness. It sat there, hard and immobile, mocking her just like the people below. Gritting her teeth, she shoved, physically and telekinetically, but nothing changed.

She shouldn't have focused so hard, turning her telekinesis on whatever was pushing at their hands, forcing them away from Kaemada. She should have embraced the blood rage and trampled the Kamalti.

Ra'ael shifted her weight, unable to stay still in the cramped space. The cage rocked and her stomach twisted, sending bile up her throat. What were they going to do now? Even if they escaped, would the Elders allow them back? They'd left the trail and broken into the mountain. They'd met Kamalti, and they were nothing like Kaemada had always dreamed.

At the end of the row, Takiyah stood up, hunching against the roof of her cage, and Ra'ael watched her inspect the cage closely. Grimacing, Ra'ael refocused her attention on her own cage, pushing telekinetically at the door, the hinges, the latching mechanism. Nothing. Seized by a sudden rage, she slammed her hand against it. Pain flashed up her wrist. Ra'ael held her hand to her chest, wrinkling her nose in disgust and frustration.

Takiyah glanced at her, a question in her eyes, and Ra'ael shook her head. Telekinesis would not help them escape.

Taunos remained slumped against his bars. Ra'ael chewed on her lip, the only outlet for her worry. His dismissal of their situation indicated the depth of his grief. He'd never handled the deaths of family members well. She suppressed a shiver, looking into those dead eyes, and surprised herself by wishing he'd make a stupid joke. Much as his casual, playful ways irritated her, they did make it easy to assume everything would work out.

Until he left. It was hard to lean on someone who was never there.

Retreating from the betrayal she'd felt when Taunos had left to wander the realms, Ra'ael came face to face, once again, with the fact that she was trapped. She was going to go mind-sick, stuck in a cage like this. There was no air. She shoved at the bars, claustrophobia clawing up her throat, but she refused to scream. She wouldn't give the Kamalti further entertainment. At least Kaemada wasn't here to endure this. Pressing her head to the bars, she closed her eyes as the tears flowed, helpless to stop them. As helpless as she'd been when the Darks killed her parents.

Kaemada needed a funeral. How were they going to manage that with her body gone? She had to figure out a way. It was her responsibility to make sure they observed proper rites, to see her friend safely to the rim of the sky.

And Eian. Sweet little Eian. Her heart broke for him, the boy who was almost a son to her. How could she even hope he survived? No, no. It had to be faced. Such hope was foolish. Eian was surely dead.

Below her, the Kamalti went about their days. How could they fail to see that everything was different now? They'd been unveiled for the monsters they were.

Focusing on drawing regular breaths, Ra'ael began to rock, shoving down her hatred, her fear, her grief. She had duties to attend to, Taunos and Takiyah to think of. Her voice rose and fell in the funeral dirge, her rocking timed to the beat she'd typically tap with her feet. After a moment, Takiyah joined in softly, brokenly. She glanced again at Taunos, surprised to see his cheeks wet, tears streaming from his dull eyes and trickling down the bars of his cage. There should be a multitude of voices raised in unison, the Rinaryn grieving as they lived—together. Instead, they were alone, cut off from home and their former lives by rock and a people who had proven to be an enemy.

When the song ended, only emptiness remained.

The lights brightened above them. A pang struck Ra'ael; they were missing the beauty of sunrise. There was no dawn to greet here, and she would not get the chance to walk barefoot into the east and give thanks for the new day before cleansing herself. She centered her mind and gave her small thanks anyway, approximating her rituals as much as she was able. Whether or not the spirits could hear them trapped underground like this, she had to try, just in case. It was all she had left.

Ra'ael took a deep breath, her resolve hardening. They would find a way out of this and give Kaemada and Eian the funeral rites. She would not allow her best friend to be condemned to wander forever, cut off from the rim of the sky, cut off from their ancestors. And then... Then, she would teach the Kamalti how far they had erred.

She never should have let Kaemada and Eian go ahead, and she had known it. But the chance to bring an offering had been so tempting, such a salve to the stress of facing the journey empty-handed. Knowing the kaetal's honor was on shaky ground, knowing that Kaemada and Eian had gone out on many journeys together, she had taken the risk. She had let Kaemada have her way, and she had followed Taunos, believing they could make it out, and they'd lost first Eian, and then Kaemada. She refused to lose anyone else.

Activity in the square increased as the Kamalti people began to rise and go about their day. Taunos didn't move, but after a while, Takiyah groaned and stretched, her elbows sticking out between the bars of her cage. When the guards—six of them again—finally came, they lowered them to the ground, snickering as they bumped against the floor so hard Ra'ael almost bit her tongue. Though her cramped, stiff muscles screamed, she forced herself to stand straight as she exited. But Taunos followed orders listlessly, an empty shell of himself, and her heart sank.

The guards led them into the nearest metal building, where they stopped in a small room to relieve themselves. Their hands were still bound, so loosening the ties on their pants and knotting them again afterward was a struggle. Shame and humiliation gathered inside Ra'ael like a storm, but she didn't resist. Neither did Takiyah, although she stared at their captors with a clear challenge in her eyes.

The building was laid out much like the previous one, and noting the similarities helped keep her mind off the cramped hallways. Another set of doors opened of their own accord—for a people who professed to hate magic, the Kamalti certainly used a lot of it—and they were ushered into a much larger room than where they had waited in the previous building. Tables of lights ringed the room, just as in the previous building, and five Kamalti sat at the largest of the tables. Their clothes shimmered with an unnatural, iridescent glow that made Ra'ael's skin prickle with distrust. Spectators crowded together at smaller tables around the rooms. A woman followed them in wearing a simple, white linen gown with a headdress of corded gold filament, from which hung a drop of amber.

"Unchain the prisoners," one of the Kamalti at the large table ordered.

"They are violent and—" began the woman.

"All must stand free before justice," the man cut her off. "You know the Law. Unbind them so that justice may be dispensed."

The guards released them, dropping the chains at their feet and backing away to glare from a short distance, hands hovering near their cudgels. Ra'ael rubbed her wrists, stepping close to Takiyah and casting a wary glance at Taunos. He stood where the guards left him, gaze distant. Ra'ael lifted her chin, clinging to what shreds of dignity she had left, and noticed with pride that Takiyah stood tall as well. To focus herself, just as before a meeting, she reminded herself of her responsibilities. Retrieve Eian and Kaemada's bodies. Get Takiyah and Taunos out. Teach the Kamalti their errors.

A man standing by the doorway spoke in a loud, clear voice. "This session of the Justices of the Council has commenced. Present are Justice Havmis, presiding, Justice Kedim, Justice Fedos, Justice Thafn, and Justice Ket."

"Lady Answer." One of the seated men addressed the woman, and Ra'ael's eyes widened with sudden recognition. "Please present the defendants."

"Great Justices of the Codr Council, these are the trespassers sent to you from the Scouting Guild. There are three here, as one perished in a fall into the Great Divide." In Answer's voice, Ra'ael recognized the formal tones of someone hoping for approval from a superior. "These have admitted to the crimes of trespassing, vandalism, forcibly entering our lands, and assault on our people three days ago. They are responsible for the Sleep imposed on some of our people and the madness of others."

Ra'ael scowled at Answer but kept a tight hold of her emotions. These people seemed to love their rituals, and rituals were something Ra'ael understood. Timing would be essential. Some of the seated Justices whispered to each other until the one sitting in the center rang a crystal before him with a small metal hammer. The crystal sang out with a single clear tone, which seemed to hover and grow in the air before dissipating. "Silence. Answer, explain the events preceding."

"These Outsiders willfully and knowingly left the trail prescribed them, thereby forfeiting their right to safe passage through the mountains as laid down in the ancient agreement between our two peoples, and trespassed on our lands. They assaulted our people with magic, causing the trouble now before us in which some of our people have gone mad, and others slept for an entire day cycle. Furthermore, they intentionally assaulted the entrance to our lands under the mountains. They continued their barbaric ways as they physically attacked the Scouts sent to contain them, and we saw the need to use some force to maintain order and prevent injury. In the presence of the Scouting Guild, they showed an entire lack of respect, laughing while awaiting judgement. We had to bind them to prevent further injury. As we escorted them here, they assaulted my own person in a show of savagery, and then the guards. One of them fell into the Great Divide—"

Taunos broke in, his voice raw and cracking with grief. "She was thrown. She did nothing to you, only admired you, and you killed her."

The leader frowned and rang the crystal. "The defendant will be silent."

"No, no, no, no!" Once more alive, Taunos quivered with fury. Ra'ael edged away, relieved to see Takiyah doing the same. "An accident, I could forgive, but not this. Not this! No civilized person would throw a captive off a cliff."

"Silence!" the Justice ordered.

Guards advanced on Taunos, menace in their expressions, their very strides. He shut his mouth but glared daggers at them.

Relief warred with outrage in her, and Ra'ael frowned at the Kamalti. Taunos's depth of emotion called to her grief, tugged on her heart in a way she could not give in to right now. And yet, was there no true justice here? No chance for the accused to speak their part? On the occasions she'd witnessed the Elders' judgements, the Elders drew the narrative out with both parties together. Standing here, listening to the lies without a chance to defend herself, woke that rage in her that was never very far away. It was bad enough to hide underground as if to hide from Eloí's sight. Where were the questions, the drawing out of the story together, as was done among her own wise Elders?

Answer held her head high, her voice calm. "We had to force them into the cages of Crystal Square. There, they sought to break free, no doubt to continue their wanton destruction. This is the account of I, Answer of the Scouting Guild."

The Justice looked at them. "And the account of the—"

Finally. It was beyond time to let them speak. Ra'ael stepped forward, her fists clenched. "These words are false. Kaemada, who you killed, caused your sleep, and only by accident. She did not remember causing it and had no idea until we told her of the sleep we, ourselves, took. Never would she have done something like that voluntarily."

The lead Justice frowned, nearly cutting off the end of her words with his response. "Do you barbarians habitually slander your newly deceased citizens? And speaking so out of turn—your manners are sorely lacking."

"Judge us as you wish, but know this: we came with the best of intentions," Ra'ael continued. "You talk over us, you barely give us any time to respond—"

"You are insolent. Your slowness to respond disrupts proper conversation," Answer declared.

Taunos stepped forward, trembling, and Ra'ael quieted in the face of his wrath, even though it was turned on the Kamalti. He spoke with exaggerated slowness, exposing the truth of his words for all to see, if these blind Kamalti could see such a thing. "You killed my sister, she who loved you best of all our legends. She preferred stories of the great and noble Kamalti over even dragons. Pah! Not so great or noble. Kaemada brought us here to save a small boy. Did you kill him as well? Did you kill my sister's son?"

The leader rang the crystal three times. "There will be order here, or you will forfeit your chance to speak."

Shoulders taut, Taunos opened his mouth, and Ra'ael grabbed his arm. He shook her off with frightening force but did not advance further.

The central Justice took a deep breath, regaining his serenity. "Now, if you have a calm defense to make, you may speak your part." He waited a mere moment before prodding, "Well?"

Takiyah stepped forward, eyes sparkling with unshed tears. "We did not mean to destroy anything, nor to frighten anyone. We did not come to hurt you. We meant only to find Eian, the little boy, as we were concerned for his safety."

Takiyah was right. Mimicking respect for their Saimahkae and Storyteller might be the best way. Ra'ael shoved her distaste away, adopting a humble tone of voice and forcing the reluctant words out of her mouth. "Losing Kaemada has left us sorely grieved. Yet any who have wronged another must atone for the wrong and make recompense. This is what we offer to you. Tell us how we may make amends for our part in the sad deeds of the past days. Then we can get on with our greater business of finding Eian."

They would atone for their actions, and then Ra'ael would make certain the Kamalti atoned for theirs.

Answer shook her head. "It is you savages and your folly that has brought this sorrow on yourselves."

"We do not kill lost little children and bound women," Taunos shouted.

"You force your children to climb the mountains twice a circulation," Answer replied. "And include them in your low, criminal ways."

"It's a sacred ritual, and we help the children along so they make it all right." Ra'ael glared at Answer, struggling to maintain her composure in the face of such unthinkable lack of faith.

"You are no better than beasts. You should stay off our mountain. The only thing we ask is to be left in peace, not subjected to your ignorance, destruction, and use of magic."

Taunos clenched his fists, his knuckles whitening. "And by and large, you are. But it's you who are aggressive in this, the first encounter we have ever had with Kamalti, and you have been combative since the start."

"I do not go to your homes and break them down as you did mine."

"We did not know," Taunos roared, the veins of his neck bulging with his fury.

"Your stupidity should not be our problem." Answer glared at him.

"Silence!" thundered the leader again. "Lady Answer, your composure, if you please."

Ra'ael hid her smile as Answer was chastened. She sighed her anger out, lest they misinterpret her trembling, and turned to the Elder. "Great Elder of this Council of Kamalti, please, have mercy. If Eian's alive, where would he be? And let us retrieve our friend's body so we may put her to rest."

Taunos bowed his head so abruptly Ra'ael feared he'd collapse. She reached up to put her hand on his shoulder, willing him comfort.

"Some barbaric ritual, no doubt," muttered Answer. More clearly, she said, "It is not possible. No one can go down there."

"What in the lands could you be afraid of?" Ra'ael breathed. "We must have her body. We cannot leave her down here, cut off from the sky."

Answer scowled at her.

The leader stood. "It is as Lady Answer has said—impossible."

"Then tell us what you did with Eian, at least," Takiyah urged.

"Impossible, or you do not want to? Or you're too afraid?" Ra'ael challenged, talking over Takiyah.

"Bind her," snapped Answer.

Two of the guards dug strong fingers into her arms. Ra'ael broke their grip with a sharp tug downward. "Get off me!"

The Justice rang the crystal again. "There will be order here!"

"Ra'ael," Takiyah shouted. "Please, everyone, calm down. This is foolish."

"She's my sister! She must be put to rest properly!"

Ra'ael's voice cracked with anguish. "Her soul will wander in suffering if it's not freed. Do you not see? She must be accorded the proper rituals, she must. Not even the vilest of people go without. At the very least, she must be engulfed in flame to release her spirit!"

Answer gasped and stepped back, horror clear in her face and bearing. The other Kamalti showed the same reaction, revulsion in their faces. "In fire? How barbaric!" someone muttered.

The guards again seized Ra'ael's arms, and again she ripped free of their grasp. How dare they stop her? She was ehreideikae, priestess of Torkae, and this was her responsibility, the last thing she could do for her best friend.

The guards tackled her. Her head slammed against the floor.

~

Taunos held his breath, fearing the worst.

Ra'ael rose with fury, shaking off the guards like so many bugs.

"Oh no," Takiyah murmured.

The other four guards ran to help their fellows, and Ra'ael met them as they came, smashing their heads together or throwing them into the wall. They drew knives, and she faced them unarmed but far from defenseless. Ra'ael's form as she fought was beautiful to behold, graceful and efficient.

Screaming, spectators fled the room, trampling each other as they shoved their way through the doors. Two of the guards shielded the leaders from the fight and the stampeding crowd. A bell was ringing—an alarm. For a moment, in the chaos Ra'ael caused, they were unguarded.

The fight only lasted moments before the last person standing in front of Ra'ael was Answer. Ra'ael advanced. Answer retreated. The woman was shaking, her face as white as her dress, as she backed up slowly. Vicious anticipation welled up inside him. Answer would get her due, and he would get to witness it.

Strength isn't causing harm, Taunos. Real strength is defending the defenseless, no matter who they are or even if you like them or agree with them. How many times had his parents uttered those words, sending him to train with Galod when his play became too rough or edged toward bullying?

Shamefully, Taunos hesitated.

Answer's eyes were wide with terror, and her mouth opened wordlessly. Her raised, empty hands shook. His shoulders sagged. She had no weapon, no defense. Hateful as she was, she was not the one who had killed his sister. It would dishonor the memory of his parents—and of his sister—to allow Ra'ael to do such a thing. Kaemada would be so disappointed in him if he did nothing.

He broke, giving in to his long years of training.

Just as Ra'ael reached Answer, Taunos leapt between them. Ra'ael's punch knocked him backward before he could block it, driving the air from his lungs. He barely dodged Ra'ael's next blow, diverting another, though her fist came far too close to him. He tried to force her backward, wariness screaming with an enemy at his back, but Ra'ael was fast and strong. And unlike him, she wasn't worried about who she hurt.

Coming from behind Ra'ael, Takiyah wrapped her arms around her neck. Ra'ael threw her over her head and into Taunos, then pressed forward, beating them with fists and feet. Taunos rolled clear and charged forward while Ra'ael kicked Takiyah. He came up behind her, hooking one arm around her neck in a practiced motion. With a squeeze, he sent her to sleep, though she elbowed him hard in the ribs before she went.

Taunos collapsed on the floor beside her, gasping to catch his breath, one hand to his bruised ribs. Takiyah sat up, rolling her shoulder and panting, and nodded to him. Two of the guards had staggered to their feet, and they immediately chained Ra'ael, though she was no longer a threat.

Justice Havmis drew himself to his full height, surrounded by the other Justices and a cluster of guards, some nursing injuries from Ra'ael's brief rampage. He looked down at them as if on misbehaving children while spectators continued to flee the room. "It is unprecedented for violence to take place here. It is unpardonable! Where is your sense of civility?"

"What?" Taunos exchanged a weary look with Takiyah. Ra'ael had just attacked them, and their first concern was propriety and civility? These people were insane.

Takiyah winced as she stood. "Ra'ael has the blood rage! She loses all sight of friend or foe and fights until knocked senseless."

"So, this is not her fault, just as the Sleep was not the fault of the one who fell." He frowned at them, obviously unimpressed. "You Outsiders are as children, always with an excuse. Where is your decorum?"

"What sort of civilized people discount the motives or circumstances of the people on trial?" Taunos cautiously regained his feet, rubbing the new bruises on his arms.

"Enough! There will be silence in this hall," the leader demanded, ringing the crystal. Havmis paced, his steps agitated. "These trespassers will suffer for their violence according to the Law, with a sentence of ebrid to last for one circulation, dependent on behavior."

He paused, glaring at them. "That means you will remain here, under the guardianship of a noble family, doing as you are told to make up for your crimes."

The man raised his chin, addressing the room once more. "Afterward, we will send them on to the City as protocol dictates. Send out the word and let any who wish to claim an ebr convene here at the luncheon hour."

Takiyah and Taunos exchanged a glance. Taunos clenched his fists, struggling to keep a firm rein on his temper. They needed to find Eian, despite these troublesome Kamalti. He had already lost his sister. He must find her son.

As protocol dictates. It was difficult to think through his rage, and it took several moments to understand the world of meaning in that phrase. Could they really have sent Eian to some other city? His chest hurt, both from Ra'ael's blows and from the struggle to hope. Impatience flowed through him like the rushing of a river swollen by spring floods. He needed to rescue Eian, to defend his people from the danger posed by these Kamalti. He needed to grieve.

"How much time is a circulation?" Takiyah asked.

One of the judges scoffed at their ignorance. "A circulation is the time it takes for the Outside world to complete a full set of seasons."

"A summer." Takiyah gaped.

"But what of Eian? What of my sister's son, the whole reason we came?" The words broke from him, raw and weeping.

The Justice frowned, then lowered his gaze to the table. He was ignoring them, just as all these people had ignored them. Taunos's shoulders slumped.

"A boy was brought through recently, yes," the Justice said. "And since he did not *break any Laws*, he was returned to his people. You can surely rejoin him after you serve your punishment."

Eian was alive. A giddy grin spread across his face, and he trembled with relief. But an entire summer? How could he wait an entire summer? And yet, the voice of experience whispered, reminding him that escaping a city of enemies was folly. Running or fighting to break out rarely worked, while wit and biding time had better chances. Besides, he'd already tried that, tried to give Ra'ael and Takiyah a chance to get Kaemada out. Much good that had done them.

At least if Eian was back among their people, he would be well taken care of. Rinaryn always cared for children, regardless of who the parents were.

"Thank you." The soft, choked words came from Takiyah, whose arms were wrapped tightly around herself as if to hold herself together.

"Justice Havmis, there is another matter," Answer spoke, her composure regained. "The guard who threw the prisoner into the Great Divide."

She nodded to another guard, and he brought in the man who had thrown Kaemada into the ravine, bound in the same way the Rinaryn were. Taunos stared at him, fists clenching and unclenching.

Justice Havmis waved his hands in dismissal. "This madness must end. He shall share in their sentence. Let him think long before acting without thought again."

97

Chapter Eight

The Rinaryns have a primitive penal system. Breaking their laws may bring one a severe scolding by the village elders or perhaps a whipping if the infraction was severe enough. Only the most heinous crimes are punished by banishment — they call it "being Fallen." Fallen may be hunted by any Rinaryn without repercussion, for the people consider them too dangerous to live near society. Many Fallen, it seems, gather at the last remaining Rinaryn city, the City of the Lost. It's said the gate is guarded by great statues that annihilate any large creature moving outward from the city, effectively making it a prison. I have not been able to confirm this, as no Rinaryn will answer me as to the location of the city, and my explorations have thus far been fruitless.

—journal excerpt

Kaemada plummeted, breathless, unable to scream as the stone around her shot upward. Fear choked her, drowning all thought, paralyzing her. After an eternity of falling, a mind found hers. It forced its way past her battered walls and bruised defenses to her innermost thoughts and memories, scrutinizing them one by one with complete disregard for her comfort. With her abilities lost to her, defending herself was like trying to run on broken legs. Panic engulfed her as she struggled to rid her mind of the intruder. More minds came, ripping into her, tearing her apart. She screamed soundlessly, helpless against the onslaught, until the foreign minds were all she knew.

She woke on packed dirt, her limbs at odd angles as if she had been tossed there. Her injured side ached and her head pounded. The world spun around her as she sat up.

The fear came back first, and then the rest of it rushed back like a rockslide. The fall. The minds. The way she'd been overpowered and invaded. She shuddered again, feeling filthy. On reflex, she reached for Tannevar. Emptiness gaped in her mind where Tannevar usually was. He'd fallen into the chasm. Tannevar was dead. Tears stung her eyes and her breath came in ragged gasps. He had been torn from her, and she wanted only to curl up in the muck and sob with heartache.

She pushed it down, denying the pain and the fear, refusing to face it, for it was too much. How was she alive? How had she ended up here? Where was "here"? She looked around tentatively, trembling with grief and exhaustion as she climbed to her feet.

Deep shadow surrounded her. The stone of the mountains rose behind her, and dirt walls closed in on either side, blocking the light from the sun. She stood in a narrow path between two houses, surrounded by waste. Scrambling forward, her movements clumsy as her left arm and leg refused to work properly, she made her way to the street and stopped.

A tall rock wall sliced through the landscape, running on as far as she could see to the north and south. Small huts crouched along it, with more lining haphazardly twisting roads. People hurried past, their gazes suspicious and wary as they stayed well clear of the path she had stumbled out of. Nothing looked familiar.

She trembled again, the grief and terror like a whirlwind deep within her. She pushed it firmly down, turned her back on it. Eian needed her. With a groan, she leaned against a wall. The left side of her body burned with the stabs of thousands of invisible needles inside, and her left leg didn't want to hold her weight.

The narrow path loomed around her while the wall at the other end beckoned. Her stomach twisted painfully at the discord. Was there a door there? She should go and check, to return to her search for Eian. The tremors took over. Her leg gave way, dropping her in the dirt. The abyss of terror yawned open and swallowed her.

By the time she forced herself, stumbling, along the path to the mountain again, the sun had noticeably progressed on its journey across the sky. She clung to her intention: find Eian. He had disappeared into the mountain somehow. Tannevar had told her where to look. Her brother and friends had enabled her to continue her search.

How would she find him without them?

Gasping, she forced herself to breathe, blinking fiercely as the walls pressed in on her. She crawled the last few paces, the light dimming, the panic rising so she could barely think. She ran her hands across the stone again and again before she managed to focus on her task. Was there a crack in the stone, a door she could open?

Terror forced her back, away from the path and into the open, panting for breath. She checked the sun—had it moved, or was that her imagination? Breath rasping, she sank to the ground in front of the path, looking back along its depths. She hadn't found a crack in the stone, but perhaps claustrophobia had blinded her. Her teeth chattered and she bit her tongue. Bitter bile mixed with the salty tang of blood. She couldn't

S. Kaeth

force herself back there again. Not yet. She needed to take stock, as her brother would tell her to do. It didn't take long—all she had were her clothes, boots, and cloak.

Blinking tears out of her eyes, Kaemada stared at the great wall that stretched out to either side and the vast array of dwellings—square instead of round. The mountains rose up around the city, reaching toward the blue sky. A city, surrounded on three sides by mountains. There was only one remaining city in Rinara.

Even as she reached that thought, she shook her head. She couldn't be in the City of the Lost. She didn't belong in the city for criminals. She couldn't be surrounded by the Fallen, trapped in this relic of a lost age! Eian. She grasped onto that thought instead of the horror she could do nothing about. She had to find Eian. How could he survive on his own? He needed to see his fifth summer. She wanted to celebrate with him at his yah, to dance at his wedding. There was so much he hadn't done yet, so many more memories to make with him.

Only last summer, Takiyah had taken Eian with her and raided a beehive. Eian had come back to the kaetal with a honeycomb in his hand, triumphantly shouting, "Sticky, sticky, sticky, sticky!" She smiled, even as her heart lurched. Tears scalded her eyes, burning tracks down her cheeks.

She surrendered to grief and hopelessness for some time, weeping. Tannevar was gone, and she would never again feel the coarse reassurance of his presence by her side, see his intelligent brown eyes, hear the way he sneezed when he was happy, or feel his warmth in her mind. He had fallen into the chasm, just as she had, and their bond had snapped. How had she survived that fall, the fall which surely killed Tannevar? Could it be that since she survived, he might have as well? But surely if he had survived, she would feel it.

People continued to pass by, avoiding her. No one paused or spoke words of consolation or assistance. She could see no warmth, no comfort here. But eventually, she had no more tears to shed, so she stood and wiped her reddened eyes and runny nose, careless of the dirt staining her face. She pulled in a deep breath. First, she needed water and to find her bearings. The stone wall was a good landmark, rising high to touch the oddly shimmering sky. She took another deep breath, shoving her grief and fear away. She would not let this beat her.

Kaemada followed the wall, picking the direction at random since either choice seemed as good as the other. The people here were different from any Rinaryn she had seen before. Their clothes were ragged, stained, and ill-fitted, often patched and patched again where the fabric was worn through. Most of the women wore large scraps of cloth over their heads. When she tried to greet them or even smile a hello, they glared at her with suspicion and scurried away, holding tight to their belongings. Many shooed her away from their dwellings when she got too close. Even the children were distrustful, stopping their play when she came into view and watching, poised to flee until she passed.

The hair at the back of her neck prickled with unease. Many of these people were disfigured in some way, and no one was clean or well-fed. Was it possible they could have done something to deserve such pain and sorrow? If they were Fallen, they had committed crimes so terrible they had been forced from Rinaryn society. She shoved the thought away. It couldn't be the City of the Lost. What were children doing here? Again she shook her head, muttering to herself.

She longed for Tannevar's reassuring presence, always nearby in mind if not in body. Could it be that Eian and Tannevar had ended up here as well, even if she could not feel the wolf? That hope was her only guide. Each time she saw or heard a small child, her heart leapt. Each time, she was disappointed, and several times, hot tears of frustration rolled down her cheeks. Exhaustion slowed her steps, and she kept tripping over the uneven ground, her left side weak and unwilling to obey her. How could she get out of this place? Was Eian also a victim of whatever horrible mistake had placed her here? She couldn't even walk very far without needing to stop and rest. Frustration turned to impotent rage at her crippled body.

A commotion ahead grabbed her attention. A group of boys—none of them were Eian—laughed and tossed a rag doll while a young girl danced from boy to boy crying, "Give her for me!"

Compassion struck her heart as the laughter of the boys echoed out into this uncaring world. It appeared no one else would teach these children proper behavior—or proper grammar. Pushing back her self-pity, Kaemada approached. Every child turned wary eyes on her, and the boy holding the doll hid it behind his back.

"You sound upset, little one." Kaemada kept her voice soft as she spoke to the girl. She tilted her head to the side and feigned ignorance as she asked the boys, "Might any of you know how we can help her feel better?"

"Go off," said one, and even the little girl backed away, her face filled with fear.

"I cannot simply leave someone so upset."

"Go off!" Hugging herself, the girl twisted from side to side.

Kaemada frowned for a moment, the children's thick accent throwing her off-balance. She took a deep breath and tried again, shifting to take some of the weight off her injured leg. "I—"

One boy spun and raced away from her, and the flurry of his action jarred the others loose from their fear. Another boy shoved a third toward her and took off in a different direction. In moments, the children had vanished, leaving the doll lying trampled in the mud.

Kaemada watched them, puzzled by their bizarre behavior. She picked up the doll, brushing the mud off it as much as possible. She'd lost Eian's doll during the fight and her fall.

She had to force herself to breathe and focus on less painful thoughts. These children were filled with distrust and anger. Her heart ached for them. They should be in a kaetal, cared for by all the adults there, instead of… wherever this was.

"Oowih what you think you're doing?" A thin woman with short brown hair peeking out from under the fabric she wore on her head stood in an pathway, frowning at her.

Kaemada scrambled wearily to her feet, blinking at the use of the Rinaryn question word in front of a question in Traveller's. It was wrong, even if she'd spoken in Rinaryn, since "oowih" was only used in front of yes or no questions. Still, this was the first person to openly acknowledge her in this place. "Ameyitum, but I only woke up over there by the wall a short while ago."

The woman looked her up and down. "Hmph, they did get you, too. Should fight to shelter before nightfall."

"Fight?" Kaemada faltered, bewildered by the woman's brusque manner and strange accent. "Please, I do not know how I got here. Where am I?"

The woman glowered at her. "City of the Lost."

That couldn't be right. "Please." Desperation filled her voice. "I'm searching for someone. Perhaps you can help me."

"Find someone else for bothering."

"He's only a little boy!"

"He's no my concern!" The woman plucked the doll out of her hand and stalked away, quickly passing out of sight.

Shoulders slumping, Kaemada watched her go. This was certainly not the City of the Lost. That would make everyone here Fallen, and she was not Fallen. There were children here; there wouldn't be children in a city for the worst criminals. Besides, she hadn't entered the gates. She hadn't been banished. And if this was the City of the Lost, there was no escape. She did not belong in the City of the Lost. No, she would find Eian, and Eian would be all right. Then they would need to rush to make it to the Feast of Starfall in time. Ra'ael would be furious with her if she missed it.

Deal with the here, not with the maybes.

She nodded to her imagination's impression of Tannevar. It was comforting, even though he wasn't actually there. Was she going mind-sick? She wasn't sure it mattered.

Kaemada glanced up to check the sun. The sky would darken soon. With a sigh, she continued walking along the wall. The houses went on forever. Her stomach growled in earnest and her mouth felt sticky. She was beyond thirsty. Clinging to hope that was increasingly fleeting, she forced herself to smile and properly greet every person she met with a "Betah" and asking everyone she could about Eian and Tannevar. Few acknowledged her, and even then, only with a gruff "No."

Her spirits sank along with the sun. Her side ached. Her bandages needed changing, but she had nothing to replace them with. Her thoughts began to dwell on the feeling of her bond with Tannevar snapping, enduring the pain and sudden solitude over and over. Each time, it took longer for her to push the memory away, and it returned after a shorter time of peace. Despair lurked like a predator stalking its prey.

As twilight deepened, the cramped streets became deserted. Silence blanketed the city but for the occasional scuffle as people scurried into houses.

"My house," cried a man a short distance ahead of Kaemada as another man tumbled out the doorway. He glared at Kaemada and slammed the door shut. The man who was thrown out stood up and looked furtively around, then scuttled away. At a loss for what to do, Kaemada followed.

They hurried through crowded trails and across muddy paths until, at last, they came to what looked like a pile of blankets. On closer inspection, she saw it was a pile of people—men and women huddling close together under a blanket that was much too small. The man dove into the pile, which erupted into much kicking, elbowing, and squirming until everyone was as settled as they could be. Filled with uncertainty, Kaemada hovered, gaining herself baleful looks in return. They needed more blankets.

Rinaryn took care of each other. She took off her cloak and held it out to the nearest person, a woman with dirt covering her thin face. The woman considered her with mistrustful brown eyes, then snatched the cloak away and ducked her head under it so she was completely hidden.

The mass of people heaved and surged, squabbling over the new fabric just as they had the old one. Finally, the squirming settled.

"Stupid," observed someone from behind her.

She whirled to face the speaker, an old man, trying to calm her surprise. "Where would we be without compassion?"

"Alive."

Kaemada smiled. "Worry not about me—"

The old man snapped, "No plan of it!"

He slammed the door shut and latched it. She stared at it, lost, as if some current were carrying her away, and she knew not where. What kaetal didn't share resources in the planting, growing, and harvest seasons so all may survive and prepare for the freezing season?

As the last light faded, the song of the Angels drifted from the sky. Angels. Of course. She scanned the street, her heart pounding. The houses were shut up tight, and what cover there was outside the houses had already been taken. Those huddling in the streets watched her with unwelcoming stares. With no cloak to hide under, what chance did she have? She regretted giving it away, though guilt twinged at her for that regret.

Kaemada pressed her back against the wall of a house, squeezing her eyes shut. The haunting song of the Angels grew louder. Though not as loud as it had been that night with Eian, the multitude of Angel voices created an overwhelming demand. Her will eroded like a soft riverbank in the spring floods. Kaemada covered her face with her hands and fell to the ground, curling up tightly, focusing her will on one simple thought: do not look.

The sound enveloped her, pulling at her, calling to the very depths of her being. Steps shuffled nearby, those who were answering the call. She shivered. Desperately, she longed to give in, even though she knew it was death. If she looked, she would have no hope of finding Eian. With that thought, she cried out, just as Eian had, "We mean you no harm! We are not for eating!"

Her voice joined the cacophony of people crying out in senseless terror. The song went on and on. It surrounded her, became her whole existence.

The ground came up and hit her, pain shooting up her wrist when she landed badly. She shook her head, carefully pushed herself into a sitting position, and looked around, confused. She was not where she had been hiding from the Angels. The Angels! She gasped and covered her eyes, but there was no song. She was safe.

Relief flooded her with such strength that nausea rose in her. She sagged against the house beside her, eyes closed, breathing away tears as she tried to sort out what had happened. The last thing she knew, she had been fighting the song of the Angels.

She got to her shaky feet, turning in a slow circle. She was still in the city, but somehow she'd travelled a good distance. The stars still held their place in the blanket of the sky, but the moons had set. Exhaustion dogged her stumbling steps, and she realized she had several new bumps and bruises.

"No surrender for the Angels' song often, or you'll be Angels-food."

She spun around to see a man, looking as bedraggled as she felt, crouching in the middle of a path.

"What happened?" she asked. That was a stupid question. Obviously, she'd looked. "Why am I still alive?"

He rolled his eyes. "Fall too often for the Angels' song and sense will no come back for you. Angels-food. Pale faces, staring eyes, stand like statues or shuffle around like No-mind—you no miss them."

"Stop noising! Trying for sleep," grumbled another man from under the cover of blankets.

She shivered. Angels-food. She couldn't run from the horror, but she moved anyway, wandering in an exhausted daze. Eventually, she collapsed against a house and slept fitfully, lurching upright in terror whenever anyone came near.

When she woke, the sun shone cold and distant. The dirt paths of the city and the walls of the houses gleamed with condensation from dew and morning fog. The stench of filth clogged her nose. The morning glory of the sun's fire burning away the water in the air—the sacred three combined—was absent here. The fog didn't burn away, it just died. She missed the thick dew that would rise on the grasses and wet her feet as she walked in the morning. She missed the way the fog wreathed the great tree trunks of the forest. She pushed away the thoughts of home and her grief, as if she could force her spirit to lift. But she could hardly stand, much less focus her mind.

She stared at the glimmers enshrouding the homes. She was so thirsty. Careful not to think about what she was doing, she licked the walls of one dirt hovel after another, chasing the precious sheen of moisture. With her broken fingernails, she gouged as much mud off her tongue as she could, but it was not enough. It would never be enough. This city, with all its suffering, was inside her now.

As she soothed her thirst, she avoided the people of the city, giving a wide berth to the doorways. The people, in turn, paid as little mind to her as they did to each other, each ignoring the others as much as possible. Only now and then did she see children, and they vanished upon seeing her. On the faces around her, she saw many emotions, but not a hint of hope or joy.

Once she could think of something other than her thirst, she took a deep breath and straightened her back. She took stock again. She was starving, and she needed to find Eian, Taunos, Ra'ael, and Takiyah. She was trapped here in this heartless place where Angels hunted and left their prey behind. Kaemada drew another deep, shuddering breath, shaking off despair. She would not curl into a ball and weep. She wouldn't even think it. No, instead, she would give thanks for living through the night. She had that, at least. Her life.

She forced a smile and clung to what she knew, greeting everyone she passed with a "Betah" or "Betah teimelei"—her own little rebellion against the horrors of this place. She only received distrustful looks in return but wandered on systematically, looking for Eian and hoping against all reason to feel the tug on her soul that would mean Tannevar was alive and nearby.

The city was laid out around a wide road that led from the gates, guarded by enormous statues which knelt like a pair of men with huge eyes, hands folded in their laps, wings swept upward, and stern, scowling faces. Chills ran up her spine as she gazed on them. The Great Statues guarding the City of the Lost. She turned her back on them, wishing she could shut out the truth so easily, and walked the main road running from the gates into the city. After much of the morning, the road split into two. The fork she followed led to a wide, open expanse of dirt around which stood several stalls selling all manner of things from food to needles, thread, leather, cloth, and wood.

In the center of the space, a large statue of a man reached one hand to the heavens, his hooded cloak billowing around his form in some imaginary wind. Around the base, crumbling rock formed a broken ring. Near one foot, a shaft dove deep into the ground, and a rope dangled into the hole from a post mounted above it.

Tired and aching, avoiding any thoughts that might lead to the despair waiting just around the corner in her mind, Kaemada hunkered down at the edge of the space to rest. Questions did not serve her well here, and she was tired of drawing the ire of these people. The weight of the fears and needs and wants and agonies all around her would surely have crushed her mental walls had her psionics been working. Even so, she trembled under the strain of it all, seeing the desperation and longing in faces everywhere she turned.

A dry, hard loaf of bread caught her eye and her stomach grumbled, even with no aroma to entice her. Around her, people bartered for goods or offered small pieces of metal to those behind the stalls. All she had were her clothing and boots, but she needed those.

A man snuck toward the statue, then pulled the rope, bringing up a bucket filled with precious water. She leaned forward to get a better look.

"Thief! Guards! Guards!"

The man at the stall beside her raised the alarm, and everyone else in the square quickly picked up the call. Armed men in leather armor came running, but not before the man took off, diving for the safety of a cluster of houses nearby. The people scrambled, frantic to stay far away from the guards, even those who had raised the call. One old man was too slow getting out of the way and the guards trampled him. Kaemada clamped her hands over her mouth, staring, then scrambled over to the man. Her hands trembled as she felt the damage to his broken body, the unconscious elder struggling for each breath.

"Where is his family? Who takes care of him?" she cried.

"Take money or go off!" a young man nearby scolded.

Kaemada recoiled, staring at him.

"Not help to him. But my family still lives!" He shouldered her aside and she fell to the hard-packed dirt.

The old man drew his last breath while the younger man rifled through his pockets, pulling out a pouch. He presented it to a man standing near the statue, then pulled the rope, drawing up a bucket from the hole near the statue's foot. The well.

Kaemada scrambled away, horrified. The man behind the stall glared at her. "You need adjust for life here. Newcomers always try for make things better. Truth is, sooner you accept, easier it is for us. It no draw the guards on us."

"Life does not seem very easy here to me."

To her surprise, the man laughed long and hard. Kaemada edged cautiously away, but the sounds of his amusement followed her. She quickened her steps, wrapping her arms around herself to hold her last, dying shred of hope inside. The City of the Lost. At last, not even her own stubbornness could block out the truth. She walked among Fallen.

She squeezed her eyes shut. There had to be a way out. She refused to accept that she was trapped in this nightmare forever. If anyone could find a way to her, it was her brother, Torkae's great hero. Taunos would save her. And he'd enjoy it, too, all the attention and acclaim.

Except he didn't know where she was.

She trudged along, forcing out her muttered "Betah"s to those she passed. She had become used to the lack of response and no longer expected one. She stopped questioning others about Eian, for now, she hoped not to find him, that he was not in the city to find. Stumbling along, she no longer had a goal in mind, but couldn't stop moving, so unnerved was she by the events in the market.

Long after midday had passed, she looked up to see a sparkling stream, tall trees laden with fruit, green bushes rich with various berries, vines climbing trellises, and fields of grains and vegetables. She swayed, dizzy with hunger and thirst and heartsickness. Beyond the fields squatted a large building, which she assumed to be some sort of storehouse. Paving stones—what must be the other fork of the main road—led away from it.

People passed by without giving the fields a second glance, though they were wasted with hunger. It was perplexing. Not even children, dirt-stained and skinny, ventured into the fields to help themselves of its bounty. Some distance away, small groups of people labored to bring in the harvest, watched closely by men in armor. No songs were raised to lift spirits through the hard work, no cheery conversations helped to pass the time. It was eerily quiet.

She hesitated. Finally, she reached high to pluck a ripe fruit from a tree at the border. As she strained to reach, people flooded away from her, pushing and shoving each other as they raced toward a grey stone tower at the edge of the field. She wavered. This must be taboo, somehow, or the others wouldn't be fleeing. And yet, it made no sense that eating when hungry would be wrong.

"Best hurry," said a woman's voice behind her. "Hurry!"

She spun around but saw no one, only the flap of a torn blanket at the edge of a house as a wayward breeze lifted its tattered edges. Kaemada ran to the house to peek around its corner and caught a glimpse of the edge of a cloak disappearing from view around yet another corner. She chased after, but by the time she reached the crossroads, the figure was gone. Who was she, and why had she warned her to run?

Filled with dread, Kaemada gulped the fruit, wiped her mouth, and crept back to the field, peeking out from behind the houses. Guards strode through the fields, their weapons at the ready and their faces grim. A crowd of people, the people who had run away from her, followed a short distance behind, their faces nervous but hopeful.

"No reward," snapped one of the guards to the crowd. "No criminal, no reward." He sneered at them, and the crowd hastily went their separate ways, many casting furtive glances over their shoulders at the guards.

Kaemada withdrew, picking a direction at random. Unsure what to think, she trudged along, bewildered and disheartened, her leg aching more and more severely. As she turned a corner, she nearly ran into a woman clutching a scrawny zeriy as she argued with a man in sharp tones.

"You no can! She's mine!" the man pleaded.

"You no keep her where she belong, I eat her."

"Give her for me!"

"No! I'm hungry."

"Excuse me," Kaemada ventured as she deciphered their thick city dialect, and both turned to glare at her.

"Oowih you want?" both demanded.

"I—perhaps I could help you. You seem in need of arbitration."

"We no need fancy words," the woman snapped.

"Oowih in return?" the man asked at the same time.

Kaemada shrugged a little, wary of hope. "I could use some food or drink."

"No." The woman's eyes flashed as she looked at the man. "I'm no sharing my meal."

"I need her. She catches pests. Let her free," pleaded the man, grabbing hold of the zeriy. The woman twisted away and the zeriy yelped. The man let go, rubbing his hands together in distress.

"What would it take for you to let the zeriy go?" Kaemada asked.

"I need for feeding my family," snapped the woman.

"Well, she will no give you much for eating. Look at her, she's skin and bones!" the man replied.

"You should did-think before you did-take my dinner."

"I no did-steal it and you know it, Mara."

"What was your dinner?" Kaemada asked.

The woman narrowed her eyes suspiciously but the man explained, "Mara think I did-take moldy bread from her. I would rather eat dirt than that foul thing she's so keen on!"

"No forget the roots and strip of jerky, you thief!" the woman shouted.

"Where were they when you last saw them?" Kaemada asked.

"In the pot, simmering, just now. I did-go for call my boy in to dinner and did-leave my girl tending the stew. When I did-come back, she had been attack and the stew take."

"That's terrible," Kaemada breathed.

"It was no me!"

"You was here when I did-return!"

"Ooowih would I hide it? I no had time!"

"You will pay, Takas!"

The zeriy whined, its brown eyes plucking at her heart. Zeriyn had longer legs and shorter fur than wolves, and preferred the prairies instead of the forests. Still she ached, the pain deep and primal, for the bond she was missing. She could not stand by and leave this zeriy to suffer, no matter that she did not know any of those involved. Maybe, just maybe, if she could save this one life, things would get better. Kaemada could honor Tannevar's memory, if she could not find him.

"Let me track down your stew."

The man and woman turned to stare at her. The woman scoffed. "Look in his thieving belly."

"What harm would it be to try?" Kaemada asked. "But please, let the zeriy live until I return."

"Until the sun's one hand above the wall," the woman said finally, indicating the distant wall and demonstrating, holding her hand above where the wall ended and the sky began.

Kaemada nodded with a smile. "I will do my best."

They returned to their argument even as she left them. She wandered nearby for a while, working her way in an expanding circle. She saw no stew pot and no Eian, but plenty of suspicious and hungry faces. Her allotted time spun away, and her spirits sank. Her search for the missing stew seemed to be no more fruitful than her search for Eian had ever been. Her leg hurt, her heart hurt, and it seemed nothing she did made a difference.

One grubby young woman, her shawl tugged close around her face, smiled at her questions. "I did-have grand plans, once. Soon, you will trudge along with us."

Kaemada sighed. "I'm also looking for a little boy. His name is Eian and he would also be new. I only hope he isn't here…"

"Be careful Aleis no see him."

"Aleis?"

"The king's little hunter. Heartless, cruel girl! She look to young, pretty things for please the king. These days that mean mostly newcomers. Best of us already did-ugly ourselves pretty good."

She hardly paid attention, stepping forward with a sniff. Her eyes widened. "The stew!"

The woman's eyes flashed with defiance as she blocked the door to her home. Kaemada feinted to the right, then ducked under the woman's left arm and into the hut. The woman turned, seizing her by the back of her tunic.

The interior was dark, and it took a moment for her eyes to adjust, but as her vision cleared, she saw the hut was packed with people crowded around the stolen stew pot. They watched her, young and old, with a mixture of defiance and distrust.

"Surely there must be other ways to feed yourselves than stealing from someone who has nothing as well!" Kaemada said.

"This's about the pot. The food will be good though, too," the woman said, raising her chin.

One of the inhabitants, a young man, spoke up with pride. "The pot's good and hot, Neia. Did-take me and Yetan holding blankets and our hands covered in clay for get it here."

"Why does that..." Kaemada trailed off. Every person in the hut, young and old alike, had burns on their faces. Every single one except three young children held in the fierce protection of their mothers' arms.

"What—" Kaemada squeaked, but couldn't get the words out for the outrage and sorrow and fear rising in her. She didn't dare consciously acknowledge the guess that part of her mind had leapt to.

Neia released her and looked at her with something akin to pity on her face. "I did-think the same when I did-arrive six moons ago. But then that Aleis did-take my Tinos away for the palace, and I no see him since. All because I was proud of how handsome a boy he was. My folly, and I since did-learn."

She lowered her shawl and swept her hair to the side, revealing burn scars down the left side of her face and throat. Kaemada gasped and recoiled while guilt at her reaction rolled over her like a flood. The woman laughed. "Here, we do you too. Maybe you like. Whatever did-happen for your face, that's not enough for save you."

Kaemada shook her head in denial. "No! No. Surely there must be something we can be do. The guards—"

"The guards!" laughed one of the adults, and the laughter spread through the group as if Kaemada had hit upon an excellent joke. Kaemada stared at them mutely.

Her laughter finished, Neia spat at Kaemada's feet. "There's them Fallen, then there's us Wretched. A Fallen no help a Wretched." She snorted. "They call us Lowlies."

"The Fallen," Kaemada repeated softly.

"Yes. All Fallen are welcome into king's guard. Maybe they will make themselves and the king richer. Few refuse, and those who do end up with us."

"What, were you all caught by the Kamalti?" Kaemada asked.

The woman snorted. "Best of us were born here."

The terrible truth struck her like a physical blow. Nothing stopped the banished from having children. Horrified, she pushed down the nausea rising in her. How many generations had grown up in the City of the Lost, forever punished for their parents' crimes? How many had suffered through generations due to no wrong?

"Enough. Let's get this done," someone said.

"Please, I need to bring that pot back to its owner." Kaemada struggled to focus on the small things instead of the horror she'd just uncovered.

"No yet," Neia said. One of the mothers brought her youngster toward the pot.

"Wait!" Kaemada said. "You need heat, and the other woman needs food, and the man wants his zeriy alive. Maybe all of you can get what you want. Especially… Would you be willing to, to, to… help with others as well?" She swallowed back bile. This city was cruel, and maybe that made cruel things necessary.

The adults in the hut exchanged glances, then Neia nodded. "Maybe it make you leave us alone. Hurry—the pot will no be hot long."

Kaemada nodded and ducked out of the hovel, running back to where she thought she remembered the other woman with the man and his zeriy lived. She tried to shut out the terrible truth in the tent behind her while her mind flashed back to the night after her yah when she had returned to find her kaetal in flames. There was nothing in her stomach to throw up, but her muscles spasmed, doubling her over to heave bile. She no longer had any sort of appetite.

She wiped her mouth and shook her head. Shivers wracked her while her weakened leg threatened rebellion. She needed to think clearly. What sort of horrors existed in this city that a mother would injure her child to save them from greater pain? Nothing like this should exist.

Fueled by burning rage, she found the woman and man where she had left them, though their argument had died down to simple name-calling.

"I found your stew."

"What?" The woman gaped at her.

"Let the zeriy go. I found your stew."

"Let me see first. You will no trick me!"

"Do you know of a person called Aleis?"

The woman hissed. "That hateful girl! Oowih about her?"

"Only that she's the reason your pot was stolen. Your stew can be returned to you. You... may want to bring any children you have, just in case. You will have a decision to make." Kaemada gulped, unable to speak of what she had witnessed.

The woman frowned at her but then turned and called sharply into her hut. Hesitantly, two children peeked out. The girl was almost old enough for her yah, and the boy probably had about eight summers. Still scowling at Kaemada, the mother waved her ahead. Trembling, Kaemada struggled to remember the path she had walked with such intense emotion earlier, but she led them with only a few backtracks to the hut. The man followed behind, grumbling about not letting his zeriy get thrown into the pot.

When they arrived, the third child had just undergone the protective procedure, and was sobbing, cuddled in the arms of his family. The hut stank of burned flesh, and the boy sucked on a piece of meat from the stew pot, his right cheek red and blistered. The scene suddenly seemed distant from her and swam in her vision. She held onto the doorframe to steady herself while the woman released her hold on the zeriy. The zeriy limped, whimpering, to its owner, who hurried to carry it away. Kaemada followed him out of the hut. She ran, stumbling through the streets until she tripped and fell in a heap. Figuring that spot was as good as any other, she curled into a ball alone, shuddering as tears streamed down her face.

Chapter Nine

If anyone causes bodily harm to a citizen, recompense must be made covering all medical fees. If the injurer is another citizen, an additional fine of 1,000 viscram shall be applied. If the injurer is a woman, a fine of 500 viscram shall be collected, and the woman must submit to tutelage under a woman of higher social standing for a period of no less than six faces. If the injurer is an ebr, the ebr shall undergo ten lashes. Any Rinaryn causing harm to a citizen shall be subject to ebrid and forgo lashing. Immediately after the term of ebrid is over, the Rinaryn shall be sent to the City of the Lost.

If anyone causes irreparable damage to or destruction of the personal property of a citizen, the cost of the item must be paid to the owner. If the person responsible for the destruction is unable to afford the cost, that person shall submit to ten lashes. If the person responsible for the destruction is of the three noble classes, the lashes shall be applied in a private setting, while the common man shall be lashed in the Crystal Square. A woman may have a male relation take her lashes, but she shall then wear his favor about her wrist for all to see until the lashes are healed. Any Rinaryn causing damage to personal property shall be subject to ebrid and forgo lashing. Immediately after the term of ebrid is over, the Rinaryn shall be sent to the City of the Lost.

-excerpt from the Code of Law for the Kamalti City of Codr

Ra'ael rounded on Taunos. "What are we going to do?"

Taunos sat slumped against a wall, his gaze fixed on his boots instead of Ra'ael's angry eyes. It was difficult enough to go through the motions of living without also confronting Ra'ael's scorn. "Nothing."

"We cannot just accept this!"

They had been confined to a room off the great hall after their judgement, with guards presumably on the other side of the door. Ra'ael had turned on him as soon as the doors closed. Why couldn't she just leave him alone?

Ra'ael paced, seething. "We need to fight our way out. We cannot stay underground."

"We must, to reunite with Eian," Taunos said. An entire summer, though? It all was so futile, and he was so very tired.

"Even if you went into the blood rage, our chances of successfully

114

fighting our way out of here are very small," Takiyah said. "Our last fight did not go well."

Ra'ael stopped to glare at them both.

Takiyah continued, apparently immune to Ra'ael's ire. "And the risk is very high. We would have to leave you behind or be caught, and you could be killed, too. Besides, then we would never have a chance to learn from these people. Have you seen all this architecture?"

"None of them are innocent. We have nothing to learn from them." Ra'ael stomped back and forth across the floor as if punishing the metal panels.

Killing the citizens of the city would do nothing but doom them further, though the Scouts could use a thrashing. The citizens, though... How many times had he escaped trouble due to the friendship of someone the people in power overlooked?

"There's a time to fight and a time to survive. This is the latter," Taunos said.

"What would you say if the judged fought while standing before our own Council?" Takiyah asked.

"What about Kaemada?" Ra'ael shouted. "We should care more for our lives than theirs. This is wrong!"

Taunos said nothing for long moments, struggling for control. He'd misjudged, had let his curiosity sweep him away. He wasn't used to working with others he cared so much about, wasn't used to worrying about them and accounting for them not following directions. And once he'd realized the risk was too great, that these people were unreasonable, he'd tried to get his sister out, and he'd failed. The hero of Torkae, and he couldn't even save his sister.

His voice was husky when he finally said, "We need to survive if we are to get vengeance. We need to survive to get information on what they did with Eian."

Ra'ael frowned sullenly, her boots hitting the floor with a staccato beat.

"We have already gone over this. Going around and around will not change the matter," Takiyah said. "I would rather be captive for a summer and then be free to live my life than have no chance at living. If we die, what happens to Eian?"

"Tinker's right." Taunos watched Ra'ael pace a while longer, then stood and took her by the shoulders. "Wildling, believe me, if it were not for Eian, I would join you, and together we would take these murderers down with us. But now... I have to think of Eian. Going on a rampage through the city would lose us any chance of information on him, and though the chances are small, I will take them. Can he survive a summer on his own? Is he a captive, too? Is he with another family?"

Ra'ael broke free of his grip with teeth bared. "They're murderers. Who's to say they will keep their word?"

"I will not allow harm to come to you."

"Who's to say you will be able to do anything about it?"

Her words struck true. Part of him wished he could join her in her unfocused rage. Weary, Taunos sank back down on the ground near Takiyah and watched Ra'ael resume her pacing.

Unease sat in the pit of his stomach. The Kamalti had left him in a room unwatched, unbound. They knew they had him, that he wouldn't escape. Their confidence was another blow in itself. He was used to quickly gaining the respect of opponents, not this... apathy. And yet, he deserved no respect from these captors.

Everything had gone so wrong. He intended to protect them, but he had watched, helpless, while his sister slipped from his hands into the crevasse. Now... were the priests right? Was his sister doomed to wander apart from the sun for eternity, cut off from the rim of the sky by this cage of rock? He wanted to ask Ra'ael, but she needed him to be strong right now, and he already felt anything but strong, unable to save them as he was. And then there was the matter of finding Eian. Were all his sacrifices over the years, everything he had given up to help his people and his sister, all for naught? Guilt and grief washed over him like a wave, weighing him down, drowning him. He'd sacrificed happiness with the woman he loved to keep his sister safe, and now Kaemada was dead.

"A summer's a long time to wait," Ra'ael grumped.

"It's much shorter than forever," Takiyah murmured.

A great deal of time passed before the door opened, and guards shoved them back into the main chamber, lining them up in the middle of the expansive room. They were still free of chains, for the Kamalti apparently believed justice could only be done in the absence of shackles. Four guards stood at each of the four doorways, their hands empty, but Taunos expected each carried concealed weapons within easy reach. Two more guards stood a pace behind the three of them, armed with menacing scowls. Beyond, people of all ages crowded the chamber, a sea of knobby heads and pale faces whispering and chattering to each other as they gaped at them. Everyone fell silent when the Justices rose.

The leader of the Justices spoke, his voice ringing. "These three are now ebrs, to serve a term of one circulation for their crimes of trespassing, vandalism, and contempt of Kamalti court. At the completion of their punishment, they will be escorted out of Kamalti lands, never to return." He leaned forward with a frown. "Beware, ebrs, for if you should commit violence, whether or not by magic, your lives will be forfeit."

Taunos exchanged glances with Ra'ael and Takiyah. They needed strength, and he quickly embraced them. "May Eloi's light shine on you. We will see each other again."

"Ebrs may not interact without the permission of their betters! Get them away from each other!" the Justice roared.

Guards tore them apart from each other with more force than necessary and shoved Taunos forward. He glared at the man but kept silent. He had no intention of giving their captors any more reason to punish them. Taunos watched the crowd, wielding eye contact like a weapon.

"The male: a ringleader, strong and spirited. Who will take him?" the Justice asked.

"I will."

Taunos stared at Answer, his composure shattered. He never would have predicted that. Gathering his wits, he shut his mouth. At least it was him instead of Ra'ael or Takiyah. Hopefully, they would have better fortunes.

The guard shoved Taunos over to Answer, bound his wrists before him, and handed the chain to Answer. Taunos gritted his teeth, staring at the leash that bound him to Answer. She ignored him, watching with an expressionless face as the guard prodded Ra'ael forward next.

"A dark warrior-ess. A berserker. Beware, for her companions say when the rage takes her, she knows not what she does. But should she go on a rampage, her life will be forfeit." The Justice leaned forward with a stern expression, and Ra'ael lowered her gaze, flushing.

"I claim her," a large man said. Ra'ael's wrists were bound as well, and Taunos's fists clenched uselessly as the guard handed Ra'ael's leash to the man.

Takiyah stepped forward before the guard needed to prod her, but he did so regardless. She shot him a scowl but thankfully held her tongue.

"This one is quite clearly not Rinaryn, though we know not her race. She throws fire from her hands."

A woman stepped forward. "I will take her."

As soon as the rope was placed in her hand, she jerked on it so that Takiyah jolted forward. Such treatment was not only unnecessary, it was intolerable. Taunos surged forward, hitting the end of his leash before he had gone two steps.

117

"Do not forget your place, ebr, or it will be a longer sentence for you," Answer hissed in his ear.

"There's no cause to hurt—" Taunos started, but Answer slapped him hard across the face.

The Judge fixed Taunos with a look that could have turned anyone to stone. "Ebrs do not speak unless their speech is requested. You have temporarily forfeited the rights of a person, so do as you are told. Any attempt to escape will be met with a forfeiture of your right to live." Then he waved his hand dismissively. "Remove them from my sight. Bring in the disgraced, he who used to be a Scout."

Answer tugged him forward by the leash, just as the others led Ra'ael and Takiyah away. They moved swiftly past the doorway where the guard who threw Kaemada into the chasm waited, guarded by two more Kamalti. Taunos clenched his hands, violence welling up inside him as they approached, but then they were past, and there was nothing for it but to follow Answer out of the building. Outside, among the milling people, their captors each led them in a different direction, and Taunos craned his neck to keep Ra'ael and Takiyah in sight as long as possible. Answer gave Taunos's leash a sharp tug, and soon enough, he had lost sight of them. He trudged along.

Please, please, if anything is listening, let Ra'ael keep her temper and avoid more trouble.

Answer led him toward one of the enormous columns overlooking the chasm, its lines elegant and clean, white stone laced with red. White stone pillars on each side rose several stories into the air. The beauty chilled him; his gaze kept sliding toward the chasm rather than taking in further details.

They climbed the stairs attached to the outside of the column to the third level and then stopped before a wooden door engraved with gold in a strange script. The memory of his sister slipping over the side of the chasm stung him. This is where they forced him to live, in sight of that wretched place? His heart filled with hatred and rage.

Answer unchained him, the metal pinching and scraping against his skin as she pulled it away. "Do not bother trying to escape. They will kill you if you do."

Taunos rubbed his wrists, seething at her, but she seemed unaffected.

"You will open the door for me, as is fitting behavior for ebrs and commoners toward their betters."

Taunos clenched his jaw on his thoughts about Answer being his "better" and obeyed. She glided past him, raising her browridge at him and beckoning him to follow, which he did with a suppressed sigh. There was nothing else to do, trapped as he was—at least for now.

"Why did you protect me?" Answer asked.

He hadn't expected that. He took a long time to compose his thoughts, during which, surprisingly, Answer did not interrupt him. "It wasn't for you. It was for Ra'ael. You killed my sister. I cannot very well stand by while you kill someone else who knows not what they're doing." Taunos did not bother to soften the severity of his tone.

Answer frowned. "You do hold a grudge. You might remember your station. You cannot fall much farther."

"You have taken away the one thing that is most precious to me in all the worlds. The loss of my freedom is nothing compared to the loss of my sister."

Her eyes widened. "In all the worlds?"

Taunos clenched his jaw, berating himself for the slip.

Chin high, Answer turned away and beckoned. "This way."

She led him through hallways with floors of beautiful stonework stamped with geometric designs and stone walls covered by intricate tapestries portraying dazzling lights, prisms, and fractals. Alcoves at precise intervals held gleaming lanterns with worked bronze, and shining crystal designs decorated them as well as the ceiling. They descended rounded stairs, and Answer stopped one step above floor level. She clapped her hands sharply. A moment passed, and then a man dressed in a plain linen skirt, bare of any accessories, hurried to stand before them and bowed.

"My lady?" he asked in smooth, low tones.

"This is the new ebr from the Outside. He is called..." Answer trailed off and looked at Taunos, her browridge raised.

Giving Taunos no time to answer, the man frowned. "You will speak when asked a question."

Again, he barely had a moment in which to speak, with Answer almost immediately opening her mouth to scold. "Taunos."

The man's mouth twitched. Answer viewed him impassively. "It will do. Taunos. Ketrik, you will ready Taunos to meet my parents. I will present him in one hour. Please have him washed and dressed appropriately—not in those filthy clothes."

Ketrik bowed. "Yes, my lady." He stepped back and gestured for Taunos to follow him while Answer ascended the stairs.

They walked at a brisk pace through a hall with plain floors and empty walls where the lanterns hung from simple hooks. Ketrik stopped at a door halfway down the hall and opened it to reveal a modest room with a simple bed, a washbasin with a pitcher of water and a towel, and a small chest. "This will be your room. Wash well and change into the clothes in the chest. I will return shortly. You will need a hurried lesson on manners, no doubt." Ketrik stepped out, and the door clicked shut with finality behind him.

Breathe in. Breathe out. Think. He needed to stay aware, to watch for the chances to find a better road. They would come, but if he let himself be ruled by emotion, he knew he would miss them. Taunos poured water as ordered into the washbasin, then stopped, staring at the ripples as they stilled. It was not proper to care for one's physical appearance during the first seven days of mourning. It had only been yesterday. Had it already been a day since she fell?

He looked around him, his heart empty. Rage was the only thing now that made him feel alive. Driven by habit, he catalogued his surroundings. The room was small but not too cramped. The furnishings were in good condition. Taunos didn't mind sparsity; Rinaryn never had much in the way of material goods. In the chest lay clothes of a sort—a simple white cloth which fastened around his waist and hung to his knees. It left his chest and arms bare, and the fabric, though not coarse, was not the soft alanshorn wool of Rinaryn clothes. Without a tunic, he'd be grateful for the warm air of the cavern floor.

Ketrik entered with a sharp knock and gave a harrumph at Taunos's appearance. Seating himself on the chest, Ketrik began to lecture him on how to behave when presented to Answer's parents, but Taunos found it difficult to pay attention. Where was Eian at the moment? Was he well? Was anyone helping him? His sister would have stopped at nothing to see him well.

He had given up so much to protect his sister, and for what? Now she was dead and his sacrifices were in vain. In vain, he left his land to wander ceaselessly. In vain, he gave up a chance at happiness with the beautiful— He shut that line of thought down firmly but was left with the impression of long, black tresses falling in waves as if to accentuate the muscular fair-skinned form beneath them. Stupidly, he had sacrificed her to keep his sister and his land safe. Surely the spirits were laughing at his expense.

Ketrik stood abruptly, snapping him back to reality. He picked up a small, smooth stick—where had that come from? Taunos berated himself, watching the stick. It had been a long time since someone had been able to draw a weapon in his presence without his immediate awareness.

"Follow," Ketrik ordered, leaving the room without a backward glance.

There was nothing else to do, so Taunos did as he was bid. They climbed the stairs and turned down a hallway to stop before a door engraved with flowers. Ketrik knocked twice on the door.

"Come."

Ketrik opened the door, motioning Taunos to enter before him, and followed him across the threshold. Answer sat on a long, cushioned chair next to two middle-aged Kamalti. The woman was adorned in jewels and the same style of dress of white cloth, her mouth pinched and eyes sharp, while the man, his expression mild and thoughtful, wore a gold vest to match the gold of his belt and his heavily embroidered white skirt. Ketrik bowed low, then rapped Taunos on the leg with the small stick in a blindingly fast flick of the wrist.

"My apologies, my lord, my lady," Ketrik said, shooting Taunos a withering look. "His education is just beginning. I beg you to forgive his rough and crude ways."

Taunos scowled. "Far better to be rough and crude than cruel."

"Silence," Ketrik hissed at him.

Answer frowned and crossed her arms, and her mother sniffed, holding her head high. The father spoke, his voice calm. "You are an ebr in this household, and as such, will remember your station. It is fitting for an ebr to bow before the Lords and Ladies of its house."

Anger flashed through him. It was forbidden for any Rinaryn to bow before another. But these were not Rinaryn, and he had in his travels found it necessary to bow in the past. He just had never wanted so little to do something. Stiffly, bringing to bear all his dignity and pride, he bowed, mimicking Ketrik.

Answer's mother looked at him with disdain and sighed. "That will have to do. Now, ebr, what is your name?"

"Taunos."

Ketrik prodded him again, and again Answer frowned. Her mother looked indignant. Irritation simmered in him. He hadn't been listening when Ketrik went on and on about etiquette earlier, but rather than helping, Ketrik merely matched his thunderous expression.

Well, if he was going to fail at something, he might as well do it with style. Looking once more at Answer's mother, Taunos assumed a broad grin and asked, "What's your name?"

Answer's mother gasped and turned away at an angle, fanning herself with a piece of paper presumably constructed for this purpose.

"Take him away!" Answer snapped, clearly offended. "And Ketrik?

Teach him far better manners."

Taunos allowed Ketrik to hurry him away, which he did with much apologizing and bowing to Answer's family. Once the door was shut, Ketrik rapped Taunos twice more on the arm. Taunos clenched his jaw, entertaining thoughts of snatching the stick away from Ketrik and returning the favor. He kept a firm hold of his temper as Ketrik hurried him down the stairs and back into the lower level of the house, but when he turned and struck him a third time, Taunos ripped the stick from his hands.

"Do you enjoy using this, or is this performance special, just for me?" he demanded.

Outrage contorted Ketrik's features. "You insolent creature! You asked the Lady her name! It is improper ever to ask a Lady her name, even were you the same social standing as she. By the Ships!" he exclaimed. "For you, an ebr, to ask the name of the Lady of the house! Even the lower classes know better than to behave in such a way."

Things did not get better from there.

At breakfast on the fifth day, while Taunos cleared away the used dishes from the side table laden with food, Answer's mother set down her utensils and spoke loudly enough for Taunos to hear across the room. "Something simply must be done about that animal. I am sorry, my dear." She smiled at Answer. "But really, it is unacceptable. Look at all that hair!"

The words washed over Taunos the way the spring floods washed over the fields. He hadn't plucked his sparse facial hair since his sister had died, and his hair was long and rather shaggy, but he saw no reason for that to be offensive. He had far greater problems than worrying about his hair, of all things.

In the days since his capture, Answer and her parents had blocked every attempt he'd made to find a way to recover his sister's body. He had clung to the mourning rituals, hoping somehow they would lift Kaemada's soul out of the mountain to the rim of the sky. He'd failed to save her from death; he could not fail to observe the rituals, not if there was even a chance to spare his sister's spirit from endless wandering. He refused to disrespect his sister by cutting his hair as Ketrik daily hinted he should.

He had been moving through his days numb and empty, but alone in his room, during the rituals, he willed himself to care, to feel. It was the least he could offer his sister. Besides, something about a lack of control and strange hostile surroundings made him long for the rituals and traditions of home.

Answer's mother shook her head. "No, it simply will not do. He is unfit for public sight. He is unfit for private sight! Ketrik simply must bathe that animal and shave off that disgusting hair."

"There are two more days." Taunos's voice was thick.

Disapproving frowns turned on him from everyone in the room, from Answer's father to Ketrik, standing in the doorway.

Taunos struggled to collect his fleeting, half-formed thoughts, which scattered from him as he tried to catch hold of them. "Please. You have made it impossible for us to lay my sister to rest. You have forbidden much of our mourning rituals. I only ask two days to complete this one."

"Nonsense!" Answer's father thundered, browridge knitted. "You, ebr, will control yourself. I will not have such disorder in my home."

Two days were not much to ask for. Rage boiled in him suddenly, and Taunos clenched his fists. "I will not disrespect the memory of my sister!"

Answer's eyes narrowed, but it was her mother who spoke. "You are ungrateful. After everything we have given you, you speak so?"

His reasoning, his bargaining, and his outright pleading were ignored as the family finished their breakfast in stony silence. As soon as one of the other ebrs cleared away the last dish, Answer's father stood, motioning to Ketrik. Ketrik gripped Taunos's arm fiercely, shoving him down the stairs to the ebr's level after Answer's father, while the other two ebrs followed with whispers. Although Answer's mother oversaw the day-to-day dealings with the ebrs, she never actually entered the ebr's level, and it was unheard of for Answer's father to do so.

Taunos balked and slid along, forcing the ebrs to drag him. His body had become slow and weak since coming here, but he held himself ready, in tense anticipation for the fight to come. He wouldn't be able to fight long, so he had to make it count.

Ketrik shoved Taunos toward a chair in his small room, but Taunos gripped Ketrik's forearms, putting him off-balance. Part of him wanted to lay the other ebr out. His honor demanded he fight back, but if he fought too hard, the Kamalti would likely punish Ra'ael and Takiyah for his actions. The Kamalti didn't seem to care about such things as innocence and justice, which only made him care all the more.

Scowling, Answer's father thundered, "I recommend against resisting, ebr."

"I will not dishonor my sister's memory," Taunos grunted, straining against Ketrik.

"Have a little dignity, or you will long for the ability to express any of your savage ways, for they will all be lost to you. And how then will you honor the memory of your sister?"

Taunos braced himself. In this, he could not bend. The other male ebr came in to restrain him, and Taunos threw the chair at Ketrik to keep him at bay while grappling with the other. He should have been able to fight off two at once, but his body was slow to respond and his limbs were clumsy.

Answer's father removed his belt and joined the fray, lashing about him, and Taunos found himself hard-pressed to keep track of anything in the chaos. Several bruises and bloody noses later, Taunos lay on his stomach with Ketrik wrenching his arms behind his back while the other ebr lay across his legs. Answer's father pulled his head up from the cold tile floor by his hair while running the razor across his scalp and face. The pain made his eyes water but Taunos refused to surrender, regardless of the slices from the razor.

He fumed, humiliation gathering in him like a storm. Where were his lauded strength and fighting ability? He hadn't been able to save his sister, and now he was forced to dishonor her memory. He thought of her smile, her big heart, her impossible dreams, and hoped with all his soul that she had found her way to the rim of the sky, because he was failing her. Again.

The ebrs twisted his limbs and pinched him while they could, but Taunos kept his gaze locked on Answer's father, eyes blazing with anger. The man remained stoic, stepping back as soon as he finished and ordering the ebrs to release him. Taunos gathered himself to his feet carefully, weighing the consequences of getting immediate retribution for the shame and dishonor done to him and his sister. He could probably drive the wind from the man, but he would almost certainly be broken for it. Which wouldn't matter if it weren't for Eian waiting on the outside and Ra'ael and Takiyah trapped underground with him. He held himself still, walking a taut rope over the temptation to give in anyway.

Answer's father shook his head. "My daughter did you a kindness, ebr, in having Ketrik instruct you in etiquette and ordering him to show you leniency with your hair. That leniency has now ended. I will have order in my house. I will not suffer an ebr to argue with his betters."

He had to force himself to breathe, force his expression to remain still as his eyes locked with his captor's. Every beat of his heart was a struggle for control, and his nails bit into his hands as his fists clenched. His mind played a fantasy of beating the man senseless, of shoving him to the brink to the chasm and listening to him beg for mercy.

The door clicked shut. He was alone. Taunos sank onto the bed and ran a hand over his newly shaven head, staring with a burning gaze at the closed door.

Answer's family kept Taunos busy with an endless assortment of meaningless tasks. As days went by, the only constants were the boredom, the unceasing blows to his pride, the slow clumsiness of his body, and the mental fog he couldn't shake. He made a show of the lack of coordination and speed throughout the day, but each night, alone in his room, he trained to work through it. He hadn't been able to defend himself, and he was determined not to be caught so helpless again. But he had been determined to follow the rituals for his sister, too, and had been unable to follow through on that resolve. Did anything have any worth now?

When at last he fell asleep at night, nightmares tormented him. Kaemada screamed his name as she fell, snatching at his too-slow, too-weak hands. The force of something massive pressed on his hands, pushing him away from her so she clutched empty air instead of salvation over and over in his mind.

He asked each of the ebrs independently about Eian, and they all gave the same grudging answer—that he would be in a haven with his own kind. Rinaryn looked after children—nothing was more precious. If the story was true, Eian was safe. But he couldn't verify it. He was subject to the whims of his captors.

Time slid past untracked. No sunrises heralded the possibilities and no sunsets farewelled the day with splendor. There were no songs, no stories to pass the night. He went through his days in a numb haze, marked by occasional episodes of unspeakable rage and followed by bone-weakening weariness. Infinite, tedious tasks awaited his attention, all in intricate detail, but he struggled to focus even for the smallest amount of time on the minutiae before him.

Among the many tasks assigned to him was the care of the garden. The family had a large room in the home filled with potted plants and blazing lights coming down from the ceiling. Answer had proclaimed the garden a fitting habitat for her "pet" and declared him responsible for it. The Kamalti rarely went above ground, except for the Scouts on routine patrols. They seemed to abhor the bright light and cool air of the outside. But they needed food, and Taunos had to admit their gardens were a clever solution.

A wide variety of strange plants filled the garden. Taunos relied on drawings he made to help him identify one new species from another. One plant was poisonous, but so far, he could only distinguish it from the plant that bore delicious red and gold fruit by the number of spines on its leaves.

The poisonous plant had three, and the edible plant had five. Then there was a carnivorous plant, which was almost identical to a plant with edible roots except for the slightly rounder shape to its leaves. It should have been easy.

Taunos threw down his drawings after the carnivorous plant snapped at him, yet again. He knelt by the table across the aisle, pressing his hands into his forehead. No matter how he willed himself to focus, nothing worked. He hoped Takiyah and Ra'ael were getting along better, but he had no way to see how they fared. Bitterly, he considered himself a failure in that respect as well. Once, he had been hailed a hero, had been looked up to. Now, he was a captive. Once, long ago, it seemed, he had pushed away from the respect of his people and desired to start at the bottom. But now, at the bottom, he had a rather different viewpoint.

He took a deep breath and stood, determined to complete his task. There would be time enough later to punish himself, or better yet, punish those who had caused this suffering. For now, he needed to complete work and do as he was told. The sooner he became a free man again, the sooner he could look in on Ra'ael and Takiyah. He would find the man who had thrown Kaemada over the cliff and teach him how it felt. He forced himself to believe his sister's spirit had risen past the boundaries of the mountain and reached the rim of the sky—otherwise, he would never be able to continue, with that failure on his conscience.

One of the other ebrs walked past him with a sneer. Taunos glared at him in response, and the other man crossed his arms. "What do you want?"

Rage boiled over in him. "What do I want? I want to hear my sister say something like, 'Look at it from their point of view,' so I can yell at her that I do not want to. I want to grieve properly and put her to rest in a respectful manner. I want to hear her laugh and see her smile. I want her to be alive!"

The man—Tegil, that was his name—picked up one of the fruits he'd harvested and smashed it to the ground, then walked away, leaving Taunos with the mess. The sound of conversation farther down the hallway drifted to Taunos's ears.

"That one has lost his wits, you know."

"I bet they all have. Savages! What do we expect?"

"At least their tree-worshipping rituals will soon be over, and they will leave."

Taunos staggered. The Feast of Starfall was almost over. Dazed, he dropped the watering can with a clatter and walked out of the garden, brushing past the two men blindly and dismissing their outrage as he did so. He went into his little room and shut the door, leaning his back against its solid surface. They had missed the Feast.

Grief drowned him, dragging him under. Flashes tormented him: his sister's laughter as she watched Míyalin Asarred of Stonefield, who danced as she played the pipes; how her eyes glowed with joy listening to the Storytellers spin their craft; the way she half-closed her eyes, miming the beats during the chants of the Monks of Annularei.

He preferred the feasting, the contests, and the mingling with Rinaryn from every corner of the island: the Rinaryn of Life Valley who lived their lives entwined with that of the elves deep in the forests, or the people from the wide open spaces of Dragonmoor, or those who lived in Havenshore where the sea was kind and welcoming, where they could play upon boats in the water, or the people from Stonefield with their wit and riddles, or the brave exploits of the people of Mountainhold.

They had missed it, and what's more, it would never hold the same draw again. Kaemada would never again see a Feast of Starfall. Taunos slumped to the floor and buried his head—his shaven head—in his hands.

Chapter Ten

Thus is the partnership between Rinaryns and Kamalti severed, for they are a people of passion and violence, and there is no place among us for them. Better, by far, to separate and remain true to our vows. They shall refrain from treading our Holy Mountains except during preordained times, and then, only along prescribed paths. For our part, we vow that no law-abiding Rinaryn shall come to harm at the hands of a Kamalti, from here until the end of time. To further demonstrate our constancy (even in the face of Rinaryn whims), Kamalti shall assist lost Rinaryns to be reunited with their kind.

-fragment of a scroll safeguarded by the Monks of Annularei

Kaemada brushed the hair out of her eyes, leaning wearily against someone's home as she watched an Angels-food shamble past. A man roasted a bird a little way down the street, and the aroma made her mouth water even as her stomach turned at the thought of eating the sacred. She turned her back, pushing down nausea, and refocused. How to solve the problem of the Angels-food? It was good to have something to distract her from the city.

She'd followed them all morning, observing from a distance. So much was unexpectedly dangerous here that she'd begun to approach everyone with caution. But the Angels-food were not regular people. They stood or walked until they collapsed, and there they either died or gathered the strength to lurch back to their feet for a little while longer. She never saw them eat or drink, even as she licked water from walls and ate insects when she could find them. Terror paralyzed her at the very idea of taking from the gardens again—especially after she saw the remains of someone the guards caught.

The Angels-food in front of her was a young woman about her age. Who had she been? How had she ended up here? Did she have children as well? Hurrying forward, Kaemada caught up to the woman as she bumped into a wall, turned, and blindly navigated the corner.

"Betah teimelei," Kaemada said.

The woman ignored her, hitting her head on a piece of roofing that dangled from the ruins of a home.

Kaemada reached out to take her elbow. "Here, let me help you."

As soon as she touched the woman, the Angels-food transformed into a screeching flurry of nails and teeth, raking long gouges in Kaemada's arm and cheek. She ducked, Galod's training taking over, and snaked one way and then another to avoid the woman's flailing arms. The woman's fingers curled into cruel talons, dirty, broken fingernails seeking flesh. She fought as she walked—blindly.

"I mean no harm," Kaemada gasped. Her side hurt, and her leg buckled as she dodged another swing of the woman's arm. The Angels-food turned toward the sound of her voice, lips pulled back in a grimace—no, a snarl. Horror gripped her as the Angels-food lunged, mouth gaping. Those teeth were bared as weapons.

Kaemada threw herself to the side, evading the Angels-food's clumsy grab. She pushed herself off the wall of the house, propelling herself past the Angels-food and sprinting down the road. Many houses later, hearing no sounds of pursuit, she slowed and turned to look, pressing one hand to her bloody cheek and the other to her wounded arm. The Angels-food was standing where she'd left her, slowly navigating around that same broken section of the roof. Kaemada panted, her heart beating in her ears, while the Angels-food made it around the obstacle and shambled away as if nothing had happened.

Laughter sounded nearby, and Kaemada stumbled back, her heart racing again. A woman with a grimy face doubled over, slapping her knee as she cackled. "The Angels-food are mind-sick, and you a dreamer for think you fix them."

Kaemada avoided the Angels-food after that. It wasn't hard, as most of them stood near the walls, while she spent most of her time by the market. If Eian was in the city, surely he would find his way to the market, eventually. That would be how she would find him, rather than wandering in random patterns. While she hoped he wasn't here to find, she didn't want to leave any chance of stranding him alone in this terrible place. It was difficult to trust even the few people friendly enough to acknowledge her. It wasn't just the hideous surprises of the city. Every time the people here spoke, they betrayed themselves as untrustworthy. The Great Mothers always admonished children not to shorten their words, not to leave holes for lies to hide in. Here, everyone did it.

She was sitting at the edge of the market when the sound of hoofbeats reached her ears. Horses. She hadn't seen horses since arriving here. The residents drew back swiftly to the edges of the streets, and Kaemada followed their example. Just in front of her, a vendor slipped a large man a bag, and he stuffed it under his wide belt with so casual a motion she almost missed it.

Three men wearing well-made clothes and leather armor rode up, jerking their horses to a halt so they reared up only a few paces from her. The people closest to them drew back even farther from the flailing hooves, grimaces of fear on each face. The press of bodies around Kaemada was dizzying. She shoved her way back to where there was air to breathe, watching everything with wary eyes. Following the guards, two placid horses carried two identical figures, each so completely shrouded that it wasn't clear what gender they were.

The guards dismounted and looked around with sly grins. Kaemada shrank from their gaze.

"Tax time!"

Merchants grumbled under their breaths, pulling out their meager coin purses. One guard walked around the circle, snatching bags from the hands of the merchants, shadowed by one of the shrouded figures on horseback. One man clung to his purse, and one of the shrouded figures put out a hand. The merchant reeled backward, stumbling into the people behind him. His purse fell to the ground and people scurried back from it as if it were a venomous creature. The guard scooped up the purse, then kicked the merchant, who huddled where he'd fallen. Kaemada surged forward, but a man behind her caught her by the arm.

"Oowih you soft in the head? You will make us all purged!" he hissed in her ear. "Just keep your head low and the guards will tire."

She glanced back at the man holding her, his brown eyes glowering at the guards, then returned her gaze to the shrouded figures. The one must have telekinesis; was the other a psion as well?

The guards dumped the coins on the ground in a large pile, throwing the empty bags to the side. They scooped up most of the coins in heaping handfuls, pouring them into the pouches at their sides, while on horseback the two shrouded heads surveyed the crowd.

One of the guards raised his eyebrows at a young man who watched in clear outrage. "You there. Something for saying?"

The young man shook his head, fists clenched and teeth grinding.

The guard grinned, his voice dripping honey. "Tell me... Do you think we're unfair?"

"You're very fair," the young man replied, edging backward.

"No, no, I wouldn't want you for thinking us unfair. Let us bring you for the palace and make sure we're just in using your money," another guard joined in.

The young man paled, but the guards caught him before he could run.

A woman wailed as the second shrouded figure pointed her out, and the guards grabbed her, too. In moments, they hauled both of them away, trailed by the shrouded psions. Only when they were out of view did the crowd relax like a sigh of relief.

Kaemada gaped around her. "What happened?"

"They's dead and gone. The guards will bring them for the palace, have some fun, then kill them," the man behind her grumbled.

"But... They took the merchants' money!" Kaemada objected.

"Hush! No let them hear," hissed another.

"That was taxes," spat the man.

People began to go about their business again, many surging forward to fight with the merchants over what was left of their money. The burly man from before took the pouch out of his belt and returned it to the merchant, who smiled and bobbed his head.

Kaemada stared down the road where the guards and psions had gone. She hadn't felt the presence of the psions, only seen the evidence. A shiver crawled over her skin. Was her ability still broken? Would it ever return? For the first time, she truly understood why psions might be regarded with distrust or even fear.

"The psions," she whispered.

"Psions are the king's, loyal for him."

"What if a psion isn't?"

"Then they's dead." The man walked away, vanishing among the others leaving the market.

Kaemada frowned, glancing around the marketplace. The sound of hoofbeats came again as she crept her way toward the burly man. The psions were in the lead this time, flanked by the guards.

"Someone," a guard growled, "didn't pay their taxes."

The merchants stared at each other, murmuring and shifting as the shrouded figures turned this way and that. In unnerving silence, one raised an arm, pointing toward the burly man. The guards tore through the crowd, thrusting people aside as they chased the fleeing man. It was unfair, unjust. She couldn't stand by while they tormented people. Kaemada shoved a load of empty barrels over, blocking the way the man had gone.

The guards scowled, turning toward her. She ran, twisting and ducking through the crowd. Glancing back, she saw the guards had turned back for their horses, and the crowd made way for them lest they be trampled. Kaemada made the most of her few, precious moments, slipping into an alley and pressing herself against the side of the house, desperate to make herself as small as possible. The horses galloped down the street and passed her. She peeked out, her heart pounding as they wheeled back toward her.

A ball rolled into the street, and a small child ran after it. Gritting her teeth, Kaemada gave up her tenuous hiding spot and sprinted across the road, scooping up the boy and tumbling out of the way of the hooves. The guards yanked their horses to a halt, and she released the child, scrambling to her feet. As she ran on, a woman snatched the boy into a house, scolding him.

The guards leapt from their mounts to chase her on foot as she bolted into a narrow alley. Gasping for breath, Kaemada pushed away the fatigue claiming her. She had regained some of her strength in her days of walking, but couldn't keep up the pace for long. She scrambled up alleys and down side passages, trying to stick to areas she'd grown somewhat familiar with. Rounding a sharp corner and seeing her chance, she dove into a refuse heap, covering herself hastily. The stench of rotted wood, feces, and decomposition filled her nose, but she resisted the urge to gag, trying not to breathe. Her muscles drawn taut as a bowstring, she waited, listening as the guards searched for her.

Finally, their steps faded away. She waited for as long as she could force herself to and then emerged, shaking herself off as best she could. A thankful sigh escaped her. She had gotten away, though she stank so badly anyone could find her if they knew to smell for her. She wiped off the worst of the garbage, especially from her hands and face, even though she'd never be clean again.

No longer caring where her feet carried her, she stumbled away. Her legs trembled and her knee shot hot pain through her every time she put weight on it, the old injury acting up again. How was she going to survive here when almost every day she managed to re-injure herself? How could Eian survive? She shook her head. He had to be alive. She had to keep hope it was so.

Her legs were shaking so hard she could barely walk when someone stepped out from an alleyway. Her feet stumbled to a stop, her weary muscles protesting the sudden change. She stared. The woman she had met her first day scowled at her.

Warily, Kaemada mumbled. "Betah."

To her surprise, the woman responded, her voice curt. "Betah."

Kaemada shifted her weight. It had been so long since she'd had anything approaching a normal conversation—about three days since she had arrived in the city, although it seemed much longer.

"Come," the woman beckoned, glancing around.

"Where?" Was this some new horror?

"Oowih you want for live long enough for find your boy?"

After a moment's hesitation, Kaemada fell in step behind her. The woman wound her way through a series of streets and alleys. At one point, she stopped with a "shush" and waited in the shadows while a group of guards walked down the street before continuing. It was a long walk, and Kaemada bit her lip against the flaring pain that lanced through her with every step.

Finally they reached a small house far from the wall and the woman ducked inside. Again Kaemada hesitated, then she pushed aside the curtain in front of the doorway and entered. A giant of a man rose to his feet, snapped the curtain out of her hand and back into place, and sat back down on a rickety chair that groaned under the strain.

Kaemada looked around the house's only room. The woman tended the fire to bring some warmth to the cold room, while the man bent over a pair of shoes he was mending by the dim light, utterly ignoring her.

"Betah." Unease muted Kaemada's voice. She could feel the walls pressing in on her, the low ceiling threatening to entrap her. She watched the couple, trying to distract herself from her claustrophobia. Recognition hit her like a slap in the face. This was the man from the marketplace earlier. He should have stood out by his size alone, being taller even than Taunos, but many of the guards were built like her brother as well. "You! You made it away!"

"Keep your voice down," the woman snapped.

Kaemada blinked. The woman had spoken without an accent. She softened her tone. "I'm relieved."

The man glanced at her, then returned his attention to his work, his expression inscrutable.

"Ameyitum," Kaemada whispered. Shivering with exhaustion, she sank the the floor, uneasy and unwelcomed.

The woman blew on the flames and poked the sparse wood with a long, sharpened stick. "Did they catch you together?" she asked.

Kaemada sat up straighter, blinking at the question. "Eian and myself? The Kamalti? No. He disappeared a little over a day before me. I was looking for him."

"Then he has likely been here several days already." The woman fixed Kaemada with a frank look. "The Kamalti bring all who trespass on their mountains here."

"All?" Kaemada frowned. "Why?"

The woman shrugged. "Maybe they enjoy watching us scrape out a living. Your boy, he could be anywhere."

"Who might take him in?"

The woman scoffed. "We all have enough mouths to feed as is."

Kaemada frowned in silence. In normal Rinaryn life, those who had plenty aided those who needed help, the way she shared her home with Ra'ael. But the woman's words confirmed what she'd seen here. No one would help Eian.

"Tell me what your boy looks like."

The back of her neck prickled with suspicion. "Why are you ready to help now when you refused me before?"

"Lucky for you that you got away with that fruit. Ignorance will not save you from the king's wrath."

She shivered. "There are no kings in Rinara."

"Pah, but you're in the City of the Lost, and here, we have a king. No one steals from the king."

Kaemada scowled. "That makes no sense. Who could own the trees? Wait… You! Were you the one who told me to run?"

The man snorted.

The woman frowned at him as she answered Kaemada. "I wanted to see what you were made of. You may have your head in the clouds, but you have decent instincts. You made it out of that scrape. Barely, but you did it."

Kaemada's frown deepened as she seethed against all the cruelties she had witnessed in the last few days. "There's so much hunger and suffering here. There should not be when others nearby have so much plenty!"

"Welcome for the City of the Lost," the man rumbled.

"Now. If I'm going to help you find your boy, I need to know what he looks like."

Kaemada sighed, tempering her hope. "He has four summers and dark brown curls with brown eyes. He's a quiet boy, thoughtful. We're from Heartwood, from the kaetal of Torkae."

The woman and man exchanged a glance, and the man shook his head. The woman thinned her lips. "He may already have been brought to the palace."

"Then to the palace I will go," Kaemada said, climbing to her weary feet.

In a flash, she found her way blocked by the woman. "And what good do you think will come from you being killed? Or captured by the Fallen?"

"It's my risk to take."

"That's what comes from helping a newcomer."

The woman glared at the man and then turned her anger on Kaemada. "Stop your foolishness. You asked me for help. I'm going to help you. My way will find this little boy you profess to care so much about faster than you aimlessly searching!"

"Why are you willing to help me now?"

The man put down the shoe and leveled his gaze at her. "Why did you help me? You could have got killed, and I'm a stranger."

"It was the right thing to do," she said. "Just as you trying to help that merchant was right."

"You have been stirring up quite the ruckus meddling in things," the woman said.

"I have only tried to help where I could."

"Most people here are simply trying to get through the day. Worrying about what's right and what's wrong's risky business."

Kaemada raised her chin. "How can anyone make the world better if they let fear stop them?"

"And what will happen to your boy when your head's so stuck in the clouds it's easily lopped from your shoulders?"

All the atrocities she'd seen piled on her. The mothers scarring their children to save them from the guards. The guards bullying people. The Angels-food. The hunger, the want, the fear. She sank to the floor again, her voice breaking. "With all this suffering..." She scowled. "If I do nothing, nothing changes. But maybe, just maybe, a person standing up for what's right can make a difference. There are no safe paths in life."

The man and woman exchanged a look. "She'll get herself killed, and us with her," the man said.

"Yes, but she fights. She has not given up." She looked thoughtful, rubbing her chin with one hand.

"What are you talking about?" Kaemada interrupted.

The man and woman exchanged a glance, but neither answered.

Kaemada sighed and tried to start over. "I'm Kaemada. Orianne Hope Tailae Kaemada Sierso, from the kaetal Torkae in Heartwood."

"You said." The woman pursed her lips. Her rough demeanor cracked after a moment. "I'm Elisabei Waliko. This is my husband, Reinan. Here, we only use our last two names, forsaking the first three as we forsook our freedom."

"Someone told me... the guards, they are all Fallen?"

Elisabei snorted. "Henchmen for *him*. The Fallen, once they come here, become guards like those you saw in the market." She glanced at Reinan.

"Or, some guards grow up in the palace, raised and trained by the guards there. Their leader's the self-proclaimed king. They bully the rest of us, especially we who were sent here by the Kamalti, those false, arrogant..." She trailed off, grumbling.

"We did need be sure you're no working with the guards," the man said.

"Why would I?"

The woman snorted. "With your overzealous idealism? You come off as a bit hard to believe."

"Is it so bad to dream?" Reading the skepticism on their faces, she faltered. "It seems a bit of dreams and goodness could be well used around here."

"Better to have food and water and not be beaten by the guards," Elisabei said.

"Sounds like you're a dreamer as well." Kaemada folded her arms in defiance. Elisabei grimaced.

Kaemada deflated, looking down. "It's not right."

"None of this is right. But out there, pampered, it's easy to forget the hard things. The ones who suffer."

"How long have you been here?"

"I came six winters ago—summers, you would say. My husband was born here."

"Born here!" she exclaimed.

Elisabei gave her a frank look, but Reinan didn't react.

"Saiameyitum. I wish I could make it right." Kaemada looked down at her hands in her lap.

"Wishing will not get you two steps. Here it's all hard work. Get your head out of the clouds, and you and your boy might survive."

"What about the psions?"

Reinan and Elisabei exchanged a look again, their faces worried. Elisabei answered, "The psions patrol with the guards to sniff out trouble and other psions. Psions are brought to the king, and if they are to keep their lives, they become loyal to him. Why?"

Kaemada watched them. It wasn't fair for them not to know the danger of taking her in. But if she confessed to being a psion, they might not help her. Visions of Eian beaten or dying filled her mind, choking out her confession even as guilt filled her for hiding the truth.

The man seemed to reach a decision. He stood and passed out a small handful of jerky and a small cup of water to each of them. "Eat. Drink. Then sleep."

Kaemada's thanks for the food, water, and shelter went unacknowledged. Reinan peeked out from behind the cloth covering the doorway, then hefted the table, jamming it into the doorway and sealing them in.

Kaemada nibbled on the tough jerky to make it last, then took her cue from her hosts and curled up on the floor. Surprise hit her as she realized her claustrophobia had lessened just a little, maybe because the city only offered cramped quarters. Before, she would never have been able to stay in a place so small, but now, she could handle it as long as she didn't think too much about it. She fought to focus on the few good things until she drifted off to sleep.

The sound of singing woke her. She leapt to her feet, heart racing in her throat.

"Lay back down," said Reinan. "It's the Angels."

"Go back to sleep," ordered Elisabei.

Arms wrapped around her shivering body, Kaemada lay in the dark and hummed the counter-tune to the haunting song of the Angels. She concentrated on giving thanks, though her heart was tinged by sorrow for those without shelter this night. Inevitably, her mind turned to Eian, spinning her pictures of him cold, alone, and afraid. Or worse.

ÌTAL-AETHA
Chapter Eleven

Thus spake Naran to Torkaema, "Let one city remain, as a monument to our history." And thus did Torkaema reply, "It shall remain, as a testament to our folly." And so were all the cities destroyed but one, and after generations, that city became known as the City of the Lost, and the banished inhabited it for their own.
—excerpt from a scroll safeguarded by the Monks of Annularei

Kaemada woke as dawn brightened the sky, light streaming through the cracks between table and doorway. She stretched and crept to the hearth, cleaning out the ashes and building a morning fire from the meager fuel. As the flames lit, she turned to see Elisabei and Reinan watching her.

"If you have a rag, I can clean your table."

Elisabei snorted. "Rags we have in plenty."

She buffeted Kaemada aside and poked at the fire, then handed her a small, worn cloth while Reinan pried the table out of the doorframe and set it back in the middle of the room. Kaemada forced a smile, unsure how to respond to her gruff hosts, and focused on wiping down the table.

Reinan picked up the shoes he had mended last night, inspecting them while Elisabei brewed some weak tea. There were very few tea leaves left to them, Kaemada saw, and no food, but even so, Elisabei handed her a cup. She accepted with quiet thanks, to which Elisabei and Reinan only grunted a reply.

"Eian may go to the market." The words came out of their own accord.

Elisabei nodded. "I will join you. We can watch the road to the palace."

Kaemada glanced at Reinan, but the burly man ignored her, picking up his chair and setting it outside the door, where he sat drinking his tea. Once they finished, Elisabei wiped out the cups, then tossed Kaemada a large scrap of fabric.

"Hide that hair." Elisabei fussed with the cloth, tying it around her head. "There, that will do for now. You will fit in even more maybe you learn dialect. Keep distance from me."

As she spoke, Elisabei slipped into the speech of the city, leaving Kaemada gaping. The woman left the house without a word, and Kaemada hastened after her toward the market.

Elisabei flowed through the crowd, blending in so effortlessly

Kaemada lost sight of her multiple times. She tried to stay several paces away—covering more area increased the chances of finding Eian. Still, there was no sign of him on the way to the market, nor once they were there. All through the morning, Kaemada searched the crowd for any sign of Eian. Time spun on, and she alternated between sitting on her heels, then standing, then pacing, then sitting again, until finally a merchant drove her away from his stall with a knife.

Passing near Kaemada, Elisabei paused, making a show of inspecting some spoons a woman was selling. Kaemada twisted her fingers together, keeping her eyes on the crowd, and Elisabei murmured, "You draw too much attention. Frighten people. I did hear a rumor—the guards maybe bring prisoners. Go watch the road for palace. But keep out of sight of guards."

Wrapping her arms around herself to hold in hope, Kaemada trudged down the road. The furtive language of the city, with all its hidden words and wrongness, ebbed and flowed around her. She clenched her hands, wiping her dirty palms on her filthy pants. What if Elisabei was lying? She and Reinan were the most helpful people she'd met, but nothing here was as it seemed. Kaemada's heart ached for the easy trust of home.

Movement caught her eyes—people fleeing the road. A group of guards approached on foot. The rumor was true, then? Muscles taut, she dashed to a side alley, keeping her back to the wall as she peeked out. At the edge of the market behind her, Elisabei stood watching, her posture tense. So far, Elisabei had been helpful. How could Kaemada mistrust the only kindness she'd seen while here?

She focused instead on the guards, and her stomach turned. Several dirt-smudged children trudged along with their heads down, their hands behind their backs. A heavily muscled man led them, flanking a young woman with a smile, while two more guards brought up the rear. As they drew nearer, the man in front paused, stiffened, and headed straight for Elisabei. Kaemada held her breath, her gaze darting between Elisabei and the children. One boy tripped, and a guard snatched him up by his shirt.

The child cried out, "Mahkae! I want my mahkae!"

Kaemada's heart skipped a beat. Eian?

She sprinted onto the road. One of the rear guards shouted, and the burly one turned, his eyes narrowed on her as she sped toward the group. Several of the children leapt on the distraction, plowing into the guard who held Eian while the other rear guard struggled to get them back under control. Their sheer numbers overwhelmed their captors as they scattered.

Eian's voice filled her ears, becoming a battle cry. "Mahkae! Mahkae!

139

Mahkae!"

Kaemada kicked the massive guard in front of her, her foot landing high on his hip and driving him back a step. She whirled, striking the back of his knee, and then punched him in the neck once he'd dropped.

"Mahkae! Mahkae!"

The woman faced her, brandishing a knife and a too-broad smile. Surprise halted her motions, for she was just a girl, only a few summers past her yah. But she had Eian. As she stepped forward to kick the knife away, the guard she'd hit drove his fist into her stomach, knocking her to the street.

"Eian!" Clambering back to her feet, Kaemada dodged another blow, but her weak leg put her off-balance and she stumbled. In moments, the guard pinned her arms together behind her back.

"Keep her confined," the girl ordered, wrinkling her nose as she looked at Kaemada.

Kaemada twisted and squirmed. "Eian!"

"Mahkae!" Tears made tracks through the dirt on his face.

The other children disappeared into the alleys, ushered on by Elisabei. The woman glanced at her, regret shimmering in her eyes, before she, too, dove out of sight. But Eian, the one she'd come for, was still captive. The girl stared around them with a petulant expression, then waved the guards back to her. "Forget about them."

Kaemada stomped hard on the guard's foot, wrenched her arms out of his grasp, and flung herself at her son. She clung to him as he sobbed into her neck, even as a guard hauled him backward. Eian. She held back the tears that choked her, relief warring with dread. Her son was alive, and for the moment at least, in her arms. But they were in terrible danger, if the people of the City were to be believed.

"Well, isn't this lovely?" The girl smiled, eyes twinkling with cheer. Kaemada shuddered.

"A mother and son pair's easy for controlling, Aleis. A good catch." The guard she'd kicked seized Kaemada's arm. Kaemada tightened her hold on Eian. This girl with sparkling brown eyes and hair light as summer grain was Aleis, the hated and feared minion of the king? Eian's tears soaked her shirt.

"Let him go!" Kaemada said. "Take me instead, but let him go!"

Aleis laughed, tossing back her head. "Oh, this's sweet! How marvelous! I do like this pair much better."

"Let him go!" Kaemada repeated.

"Oh, let go of him or he'll choke." Aleis waved her hand at the guard.

She pointed her knife at Kaemada. "But he's not going free."

The guards didn't tie them up, but they didn't need to. Outnumbered and weaponless, her knee throbbing, Kaemada wrapped her arms around Eian. She managed to untie his hands, but the guards shoved her forward, and so she carried her son, too terrified to let him go. Eian clung to her neck so fiercely it was difficult to breathe.

They walked up the lonely road toward the large building in the middle of the fields, and soon her muscles burned with weariness. The prick of knives at her back was enough to keep her in line, even if the guard she'd kicked wasn't walking next to her, occasionally grinning at her. Her skin crawled. Eian wouldn't stand a chance if they tried to run. They'd cut him down before he went two steps.

The white walls of the palace loomed above them. Two wooden doors yawned open, ready to consume them.

Kaemada shivered.

Aleis laughed. "Welcome home!"

Pretend calm. Scared is prey.

Clinging to the advice she knew Tannevar would have given, Kaemada strove to emulate Taunos. "Oh, no. There must be others more worthy than I for such a home."

Again the merry laugh rang out, and the hair on the back of her neck rose. "It's not an invitation. This honor's given only on merit that the king sees. This's your home—I suggest you do what you can for keeping it that way. It's much better for living here than out among the Lowlies."

How could she have so much joy in this place? Or were the people of the City wrong in their fear? Aleis's accent, and that of the guard next to her, was much lighter, and part of her reached for a sense of belonging with these people who hid fewer of their words. They couldn't be so bad, could they? Surely the stories were exaggerated. And yet, her skin prickled with danger, something within her screaming not to go inside.

Eian trembled, his arms tightening further. Kaemada squeezed him back, but the reassurance was hollow.

They wound through a maze of corridors, up and down staircases and through so many twists and turns that Kaemada wondered if Aleis was deliberately trying to confuse her sense of direction such that she wouldn't be able to find her way out. It wasn't necessary—all the hallways looked the same to her. It was all so far from the pulsing life of the forest or the buzzing of the prairie. It was all a trap.

Finally, Aleis stopped before two enormous doors and pushed them inward to reveal a large room. Polished stone, scrubbed until it glistened, made up the floor. Paintings and woven tapestries hung on the walls, mostly depicting hunting scenes and men with yellow rings around their heads. Chairs of polished wood with colorful embroidered cushions on the seats furnished the room. Kaemada had never seen such workmanship before, not even in her brief time under the mountain.

Aleis laughed and flashed her dimpled smile again. "These are your rooms to now."

"For now?" Kaemada corrected in a whisper.

"Yes, until the king meets with you for seeing if you're desirable."

"Desirable?"

Aleis laughed again. "Yes, for becoming part of the family! Now. There's a washroom on the left, and the right's a sleeping chamber."

Thinking of Elisabei, Reinan, and the others was easier than focusing on the danger she and Eian were in. The overwhelming, muscle-freezing tension turned to rage. "All these things could go a long way toward making life more bearable for the people out there."

"You don't give fine things for rodents." Aleis turned to leave.

"They have nothing!"

With another merry laugh, Aleis left, closing the doors behind her. Kaemada turned a slow circle in the room, her heart sinking. Multiple rooms in the same house? Multiple houses in the same building? It was too much. In the sleeping chamber, a wooden platform raised the bed above the ground, and the feather-filled mattress was covered with linens while over top, a thick, embroidered blanket spread. Seeing it only made Kaemada long for her familiar sleeping mats and simple hut. There were windows, but whatever filled them was so strong it did not break even when she threw a chair at it.

Everything here was a trap.

She looked gravely at Eian as he tested the cushions on the seats. "We take only what we need."

Wide-eyed, he nodded. She gathered him close, holding him until shadows stretched long through the room, and kissed his forehead. "I was so worried about you."

"I love you, too."

"You were on your own for several days. How did you…?"

"I wasn't alone."

She frowned at him, but his expression was so solemn. He looked toward the mountains. "People underground fed me, but I missed the sky. And then I was here, and I hid. But then I heard you calling for me. I'm sorry I did not come right away. I was scared. But then I looked for you, but the guards found me first. They said they would bring me to you."

She didn't understand, but she didn't need to. Finally, something had gone right, and Eian was in her arms. That's all that mattered.

Except for the looming sense of doom.

"We're in danger here, Eian." She made her tone as gentle as possible. It was no use to deny it—denying hunger to avoid hunting never brought meat. Her denial of the horrors of this place had gained her nothing. Instead, she needed to protect them, and that meant safeguarding certain truths. A passing thought from Eian could alert their captors to her gifts.

She drew in a deep breath and looked at him seriously. "We need to build our mental walls. These people cannot find out I'm a psion."

Everyone could form mental walls, psion or not, but all psions were taught the process as children. Normally, she projected a telepathic image into their mind so they could learn to block it out. But she didn't know if her abilities had returned—she would only find out if she tried to use them—and the use of her telepathy would alert any psion nearby to her talent.

She forced a smile. They'd have to do this the hard way. "Acha'iyih, think of yourself, but think in a whisper. Just a whisper of yourself. Pull it back into the very core of you. Keep pulling."

As she spoke, she retreated into herself, too, building up her walls. The higher and deeper the walls, the safer she would be. If Eian could build his walls sufficiently, the psions wouldn't be able to scan him in passing, unless he thought in a shout.

"Why do you not just take us out of here?" Eian asked.

Her concentration shattered. "My abilities were broken, and it's too dangerous to test them here. Even if they have returned, I cannot simply whisk us away. Please, acha'iyih, concentrate."

Eian scowled. "I want to go home."

"I know. I know, acha'iyih."

"Please?" He turned those big, brown eyes on her, and her heart broke.

She reached to embrace him. "Soon, Eian. Soon." She hoped.

He clenched his fists and curled up tight into himself and then flung himself at her, burrowing his face into her stomach as he clung to her. "I'm scared."

Lights flashed as fresh pain stabbed through her from her wounded side. She nearly fell over, catching herself with one hand, the other wrapped around Eian. "I know, acha'iyih. I know. That's why we have to build your mental walls." She rubbed his back. "I will hold you—you tell me when you're ready."

Finally, he pulled away and nodded, and she forced another smile.

"Pull back into the core of you. Imagine a wall. Build it branch by branch, stone by stone. Build it high. Build it deep."

"Can you fight the psions?"

Kaemada's eyes snapped open. "Eian, this is important. You must concentrate."

"I cannot do it!" Eian scowled, his little hands curling into fists.

"You must concentrate."

"No! Use telekinesis."

Kaemada's smile faltered. "Acha'iyih, even if I could, I do not see how that would help."

"Break down the wall and let us out!"

"I wouldn't be strong enough—no single psion would be. Telekinesis does not add that much to my natural strength, and it only allows a push."

"Be right next to the wall. To add strength."

"It's not unlimited. To push down a wall, many psions would need to link to each other, but we have no way to know who would be safe to ask for help."

"If you fought the psions, we could leave."

Her heart ached with longing for that to be an option. She was failing her son, and yet, she couldn't see a way out. Perhaps one would appear with a little time or help would arrive. She held her ragged composure together with breath and prayers, for if she came undone, her son would be lost.

"I know it's scary, Eian. I would love to take you away from here. But there are too many psions—all the psions in the city are here, they said. And with the guards, too... Better to hide and wait for a chance to escape."

Eian sulked at her. "Taunos wouldn't wait. He would fight his way out."

A sigh gusted out of her, and she gathered Eian in her arms again. It hurt that he was right. The odds never seemed to affect Taunos—he could talk or fight his way out of anything. But what could she do? How long would she be able to keep them both alive? How long could she hold him next to her heart? She didn't have Ra'ael's confidence to lean on, nor Takiyah's resourcefulness. She didn't have her brother. All she had was herself, and she felt woefully inadequate.

Over the next two days, Kaemada huddled against the window, as far from the door as she could get, and worked with Eian to build his mental walls. It was frustrating, nail-biting work, for Eian's mind continually wandered, and he either couldn't or wouldn't maintain the focus needed to build his protection. It became clear there was only one last option.

Hunched beside the window, Kaemada held Eian close, resting her head on his, to build his mental walls for him. She couldn't tell if it was working, and she fully expected to be found out. Every time she used her abilities, she would be like a flare of light for any psion close enough and looking. Distance decreased telepathic strength, but she couldn't count on the distance being enough to hide her.

She tried to choose times when, she hoped, they'd be least likely to be discovered, but every time the door opened, she froze, certain the guards waiting outside would seize her and drag her away. But each time it was only the servants delivering food and wood for the fire, taking away dishes, or emptying the chamber pot. The servants and guards were silent, and terrified she might somehow betray her secret, Kaemada avoided them.

On the third night, the stars began to fall. Kaemada knelt by the window with Eian, pointing out the streaks of light in the black. Quietly, she sang the starsong, though tears clogged her throat. There were none of the festivities that should go along with the display. No music, dance, or games lifted spirits here, neither inside the palace nor outside its walls so far as they could see through the window. Kaemada sent her prayers flowing upward, for the spirits were closer when the stars fell, and she strained to hear their tune and harmonize her song with them. But caged inside the stone walls of the palace, she couldn't hear or feel that song.

They were alone, cut off even from the spirits. Cut off from Eloí. She forced herself to breathe through the terror making knots in her stomach. She couldn't give in to it. It couldn't be true.

On the morning of the fourth day, the door opened to admit Aleis. Her eyes flashed with a strange, unfriendly light as she smiled that dangerous smile. "Hurry, darlings. The king's waiting, and that's something he intensely dislikes."

"The king?"

"Yes, and you're planning for going looking like that?" Aleis raised her eyebrows.

They had no other clothes. Kaemada drew in a breath slowly, clinging to calm. "Yes."

Aleis's teeth flashed at them, and Kaemada turned her back to shut out the sight, crouching in front of Eian.

"Eian, listen to me. I love you. I will always come for you, and I will always find you. I promise."

Eian launched himself into her arms. "I'm scared, too."

Aleis laughed. "Come, come. You want for making a good impression, yes?"

Giving Eian one last squeeze, she stood and took his hand. Aleis flounced out of the room, and Kaemada followed with Eian, glaring at the girl's back and trying to ignore the guards behind them. Once again, she led them by a roundabout path. Though Kaemada tried to remember the ways they had gone, the complexity of their route and the strangeness of the surroundings quickly overwhelmed her. Her palms were slick with sweat, but chills filled her core, and her heart seemed weighted to her stomach.

Finally, they came to two tall, intricately carved doors which together made an arch. Beyond them stretched a grandly decorated hall with intricate stonework and wood carvings. Flowering plants filled the room with their fragrance. A long, narrow woven rug on the floor led to a wide chair covered in cushions, upon which lounged a middle-aged man with light brown hair and brown eyes, facial hair—though it was neatly trimmed—and an enormous, multicolored cloak wrapped around his form. He regarded them intently and Kaemada quailed under the scrutiny, avoiding his gaze. Two figures stood like statues halfway down the hall, dressed in robes head to toe. Psions. Kaemada's heart pounded in her ears. She couldn't breathe, couldn't move. They would discover her.

Aleis dragged them about a third of the way down the hall, then knelt, yanking Kaemada down until her forehead nearly brushed the floor. Kaemada stumbled, then recovered her balance, gripping Eian's hand tightly.

"Bow!" Aleis hissed, her gaze fierce.

Eian looked up at Kaemada with wide, terrified eyes and dropped into a low bow, whispering, "Or die!"

A shudder gripped her at her son's words. This place endangered her son. There would be no placating them.

How would her brother get out of this situation? He once told her that he always found his way home by remembering who he was. Kaemada shifted to a ready stance.

Who was she? She was a Rinaryn, and Rinaryn do not kneel.

She was of Torkae, they who struggle to maintain the original vision.

She was a student of Galod's, trained to be a fighter and a psion.

She was a friend of Takiyah and Ra'ael. She was Taunos's sister. What would they do? Taunos taunted the guards when they were captured. A show of confidence, then—but not too much, lest they take it out on Eian. Just enough to find a way for harmony.

146

The man rose to his full height, staring down at them. "Bow before your king!"

Show no weakness to a bully of a leader. A lump formed in her throat as she thought of dear Tannevar. She would never see him again.

She straightened and returned the man's gaze, striving to mimic Ra'ael's confidence. "Rinaryn are forbidden to kneel to any other Rinaryn."

"Or to demand the bent knee of another," Eian finished in a whisper.

The king laughed, and Kaemada fought to suppress shivers, holding tight to Eian's hand as if by maintaining a hold on him she could keep them safe. Except they weren't safe.

"I do like spirit." The king smiled, seating himself again with a whirl of his cloak. "You're in my City, where my reign is indisputable, and you will bow."

"I'm only a traveller. My duty is to the laws of Rinara, and so I'm forbidden to do this." Kaemada struggled for Taunos's easy charisma.

"Why do you care to Rinaryn laws? You're here, never for going home. The sooner you cease fighting, the easier it'll be. I'm the king, and you would do well for simply accepting that fact." The king spread his arms as if to indicate his domain.

"I must first test for truth." Her voice did not sound nearly as confident as Takiyah's would have.

The king scoffed. "We'll see how long you test. That your boy, then?"

Her face heated. Kaemada drew Eian close and raised her chin.

"Funny, he looks nothing like you. Except maybe the hair."

Wrath broke through, easier to accept than the terror beneath the surface. "Who decided that you should sit comfortably in here, toying with people, while others are denied even clean water and food?"

"You know, I have decided. I'm keeping you. Both of you," he said lightly.

"You cannot own someone."

"You'll do as I please, and believe me, you will please me."

Kaemada's heart raced, and she shifted Eian behind her, prying his fingers from her clothes. Would she be able to fight if it came to it? The weakness was no longer apparent, but she could still feel it inside of her. No, there must be a way to reconcile with these people. If only she could find it!

The king stood again and strode down the carpet toward her. Kaemada concentrated on breathing evenly. Her heart felt like it would burst, her head light, somehow distant.

"Aleis, my bird, take the boy."

Aleis leapt forward, seizing Eian with a knife to his throat. Kaemada held tight to his arm as he cried out.

"Let him go or his blood coats the floor!" Aleis hissed. Eian's brown eyes were huge and Kaemada hesitated.

"Shareil, Eian, shareil. It will all be well." She couldn't keep the quaver from her voice, and her fingers trembled as she let him go. Swallowing hard, she watched as Aleis dragged him to the side of the room, one arm wrapped around him, the other holding the cruel blade close to the tender flesh of his neck.

The king had stopped about halfway down the hall, between the two shrouded psions. "Tell me your name."

"Please, let him go! I'm Kaemada." She couldn't tear her eyes away from Eian, from the blade against his skin.

"Look at me."

The words took a long time to process. She hesitated. Would Aleis hurt him when she wasn't looking? Her thoughts raced too quickly to be held onto.

"If you don't obey, the boy doesn't live." His tone was light, almost pleasant.

Her gaze darted to his face. "No! Please, let him go!"

With a smile, the king held out his hand. "Kiss my ring."

She glanced at Eian, still as death, and at Aleis's bright eyes. She moved forward as if wading against a strong current. This was a nightmare. She had to be sleeping. She would wake up and find none of this had happened, and Talaera would scold her for something, and Galod would berate her for not being better, and everything would go back to normal.

Except she didn't wake up. Tears stung her eyes, and her nose began to run. She blinked back the threatening tears as she stepped toward the king, searching his face for any glimmer of compassion. He was like stone, with no life in him. As if someone else was moving her body, she bent, touching her lips to the large green stone on his ring. Trembling, she retreated, glancing behind her at Eian. Still alive.

"Please, let him go!" she whispered, hope dying within her.

"Tell me what you did do in your kaetal." The king sounded bored.

Kaemada stared at Eian. She couldn't answer that question. Yet, she was no good at deception, either. All she could hear was her heart trying to escape her chest.

"Look at me!" the king snapped.

She jumped, obeying.

"Better. Now, answer."

She licked her lips. Her voice had dried up and withered away inside her. "Mostly get scolded," she whispered.

The king waved his hand. "It matters not." He crossed his arms over his chest and stared at her. She felt very small under that gaze. How could she hope to escape? How could she think to save Eian?

"Now. Kneel before your king."

In spite of herself, tears filled her eyes once more.

Do not cry! her memory of Tannevar admonished her.

She bent her knee, feeling as if everything she'd known about herself was slipping away. She would break any law for Eian. How could she say she respected the law, then? How could she have pride in being Rinaryn, in being of Torkae? She couldn't get out of this mess. How could Ra'ael, Takiyah, even Taunos condescend to be seen with her, to associate with her? Her abilities were weak and broken—how could she say she was a psion? And without that, Galod would have nothing to do with her. All just as well, for there was no way out of the palace, and no escape from the City. She would never see any of them again.

She bent her head as she knelt, knowing, even so, that she couldn't hide the tears streaming down her cheeks. They fell, marking the stone below her with drops of darkness. She turned her head and looked at Eian once again. She had shown the king defiance, and moments later, Eian had watched her surrender. He'd watched as she bowed, a thing she said she'd never do. But impossibly, there was still trust in those brown eyes.

She spoke, pleading into the uncaring silence. "Please, let him go. He's innocent."

The king seated himself again and waved his hand. Aleis lowered the blade and Eian ran to Kaemada. Resolved not to let such a thing happen again, Kaemada backed up a few steps, keeping Eian behind her so Aleis would have to go through her to get to her son.

The king laughed again. "Ah, Aleis, take this one away and show her their new quarters, my lovely. Then return and give your report."

Aleis beckoned them with twinkling eyes, and Kaemada followed, holding tight to Eian's hand, torn between the desire to hurry out of the king's sight and the desire to keep distance between herself and Aleis. She would have to find a way to get her bearings. She had to find a way out. To do that, she needed patience and a plan. An attempt to fight their way out would only end in death, and she could never, never, let Eian be in such danger again. She held herself stiffly against the shudders threatening to overtake her, knowing somehow that publicly breaking down would doom them both.

Aleis led them down a corridor lined with many doors on each side. She stopped at one and opened it onto yet another extravagant room. "This's yours. Enjoy!"

Guards turned the corner, patrolling with stern faces, their boots ominous against the stone floor. Aleis shut the door, which latched with cold finality, ringing the truth deep into her song. There would be no mercy here.

Interlude

Maeren buried her face in her hands. "What will we do, Zeroun?"

Zeroun, Storyteller of Torkae, stared at his daughter's sleeping mat, folded up in his hands. She had no more need of it, but somehow, he wasn't ready to lay it on the fire. Not yet. His daughter's things still littered the hut—a comb, neatly folded clothes, a pile of colored stones, scattered strips of leather, and a sack full of various things from shards of metal to bark scraps. Takiyah had loved to collect things and insisted on being ready for anything, including events that only her imagination could come up with. It did not seem possible he'd never chide her again to leave a project for time with the kaetal.

Maeren mumbled into her palms. "Everything is falling apart. Did you meet with Galod?"

"No. He's taking the loss of his students poorly. He has the anger of Thassen in him and will not speak to me." Zeroun set down the woven bedmat and held his wife, gazing over the top of her head at the dried grass walls of their home. Here, he didn't have to be the Storyteller, to balance everything and have the answers. But it didn't help that he felt... lost.

His wife shook her head, leaning against him. He tightened his hold on her as she spoke. "It's bad enough we lost them. Now, with Teros and Talaera dissuading the rest from learning from him..."

"Teros and Talaera may become a problem. Only ten of his students continue their lessons. Every day the grumbling against Galod grows."

"Those two may well push the Councils to depose us, and the Councils are already..." Maeren choked off. "We failed them, Zeroun. We failed them all."

"We did what we must, as we continue to do."

Even he scoffed at the words that came from his mouth. They were empty, just like the hole in his heart where his daughter should be. Instead of being able to grieve properly for her, he was forced to spend his time and energy keeping the peace. Teros and Talaera had come back from the Feast of Starfall pressuring him to force Galod to leave. The Feast had allowed them to stoke the flames of their dislike of the hermit, fueled by others who distrusted him.

He didn't want to deal with such childish grudges. Not now. He would never see his daughter again. No one came back after leaving the paths of the mountains, and even his foolish optimism hadn't survived the journey back home without a sign of Takiyah. Even so, he would spin endlessly through the ages before he'd allow her to be gone in truth. He refused to avoid speaking of Takiyah or thinking of her, though his wife was as yet unable to say her name, instead focusing on the other four that were lost.

"If anyone could have beaten the odds, it would have been them," Zeroun whispered.

"I should never have let them leave. In my folly to save Kaemada and Eian, I lost our kaetal Taunos, Ra'ael, and, and—!" Maeren's voice broke and Zeroun tightened his embrace

"They would have gone anyway. It's what they trained for."

"I never should have let her take Eian in the first place! But I was swayed by fear for our kaetal and look where that got us. We have lost much honor. I do not know if we will survive this."

"We will."

"Oh, my love! I regret so much. Never marrying them off. Never seeing them truly find their places. They were close. Ra'ael was blooming, and her song was so strong… But I wished to give Taunos something to stay for. A wife, perhaps."

Zeroun tried to avoid stiffening, but Maeren pulled back before he had time to collect the right words and looked at him suspiciously. "What is it, husband?"

"Taunos wouldn't have stayed for a wife."

"For the right one, he would have. I just hadn't found her. Uma'arei haunts him still."

"He never did give his heart easily." Zeroun winced and sighed. The secrets no longer mattered. "Taunos's travels were not wholly his. The Heartwood Council listened to his tales and sent him out with goals to search for, questions to answer. It grieves me that you're more correct than you know. If Lína knew what we put him through, her wrath would know no bounds."

Maeren set her hands on her hips. "You kept this from me?"

"It was a Heartwood Council affair, not a Great Mother affair." It was a weak excuse, but it was all he had. Maeren was right, of course. If he'd talked with her about these things before, he'd have seen how flimsy the reasoning was. He wouldn't have been so alone, striking out on the wrong path like Naran.

"It is a Great Mother's affair when that young man comes to me again and again to seek forgiveness for taking the lives of mother's sons that he had no right to take!"

"He told you this?"

Maeren crossed her arms, glaring at him. "He never said more than that, only asked absolution after absolution, which I gave him freely. Did you know, when he went to Teros at first, as was right, Teros named him a murderer? As if there wasn't enough bad blood between them!"

He should have known of that. He hadn't realized things were so bad, hadn't realized Taunos suffered so much. Or perhaps he hadn't wanted to notice these things, so that he'd be able to continue making the hard decisions to put the man in the path of danger, time and time again. The weight of his guilt lay like a boulder on his shoulders. "I'm glad he had you. I did what I could to protect him, spirit and body, from the more dangerous tasks. But the Elders—"

"The Elders had no right to keep secrets from the Great Mothers! And clearly, the priests did not consent, either!"

"Teros was eager to send him away. And the Elders no longer work as closely with the Great Mothers as they once did. I fear we are to become Torkaema and Naran, our paths ever split."

"You, husband, should have told me!"

Zeroun nodded, crushed beneath the weight of their cares. "I should have."

Maeren sighed, tears glinting in her eyes, and he knew she was thinking of Takiyah. Her gaze was distant for several moments before sharpening on him again. "I fear the future, Zeroun, as I never have. Eraeos, the messenger from Storyteller Utalen, came before the Feast looking for a fight, and Takiyah said he threatened us. And you know Utalen was behind much of the dishonor on us this Feast. It wasn't so hard for him, since we had no sacrifice and had lost four of Galod's students along with a child of the kaetal. Some wish for our dishonor, willing to disgrace all of Torkae to get it."

"Perhaps the path they walk must be out and away from the story of the kaetal, as with Daevin," Zeroun said, taking comfort from the ancient tale. Could it be they were still alive somewhere, unable to return? Or was he being a foolish old man? "Wherever they are, the spirits know."

"I'm worried, Zeroun. What was that display at the Feast? The Council of Elders is disrupting the balance of our people."

"They should not have rebuked you so." Anger at the other Elders set him dangerously apart, but they had picked out his wife to shame in front of all their people. How could he feel otherwise?

"No, I deserved that, even publicly. The mistakes were mine, and Talaera told me at every turn not to make the choices I made. But the Great Mothers submitted a rebuke to the Council, as apparently, they agree with you, and the Council refused to hear it."

"The other Elders believed the Great Mothers overstepped themselves. I could not get them to see reason, but fortunately Storyteller Sarik persuaded those calling for stripping you of your power to choose mercy."

His wife's eyes blazed with fire, and her voice grew sharp. "The Council of the Great Mothers balances the Council of the Elders and makes certain the Elders give fair judgements! It's as important as the balance between Storyteller, priests, and Great Mother. If the Council will not listen when they go too far, what will happen?"

"The Elders are on edge because of these dreams. I pray it passes soon. I do not intend to change my position, Maeren. I am a rock battered by the seas, and no man may move me."

She deflated, rubbing her forehead. "I will stand against the seas with you, as I have promised. I only wish I could have spared our kaetal from these trials. But I failed, even against those I saw coming."

"Fānitos failed to save himself, but his failure saved many others." The ancient tale of Fānitos was eerily applicable to present times. He hoped their story didn't end as disastrously as that one had.

"We must keep Torkae out of trouble until we can show the others we are not tainted, and we are not to be disrespected."

"I know, my love. I know." Their path was as precarious as those in the mountains. Any further false steps could throw them into dishonor so great they'd be hard-pressed to rise back up from. And how, then, could he protect... No, the greatest heroes of Torkae needed no protection now. They were gone, lost to the mountains.

"And you cannot shut me out anymore! I do not care what the other Elders are doing, I'm the Great Mother, and I'm also your wife and you will no longer keep things from me."

How had he gone so far astray? He'd seen the sense in Maeren all those summers ago when they'd first courted, love blossoming in all its tender newness. When had he begun to turn away from her, to hide away with secrets like a Kamalti from legend? "You're right, of course. But Maeren, these dreams. Most of the Elders are having them, and they are nothing you want to experience. I do not even want to tell you their stories, they are so horrifying."

"You're the Storyteller; tell me the lessons."

Zeroun shuddered. Maeren's arms tightened around him, and he anchored his song in her steadfastness, letting his gaze go distant as his voice came out in a dry croak. "Danger in places that should be safe. A flock of birds, split again and again, until only a small group remains. A rot spreading, multiplying until the whole fruit is bad. Removing oneself from disease or injury, or wrongness… like a harsh winter. The whole separating so that the people might live, but there is only gladness and joy, no grieving for those who did not return to the kaetal. It's profoundly wrong."

The trembling became uncontrollable as he continued. "And the fear coming with these dreams, the sense of impending doom. It's like seeing a boulder coming down a slope, and there you are, stuck in the mud, unable to move out of the way."

Silence blanketed the hut. Maeren appeared thoughtful, and Zeroun waited. He'd done too much without her. It was past time to be patient and sort through his worries with the Great Mother.

When she looked back at him, her mouth was creased with worry. "These dreams, they would drive anyone to search for conspiracies and secrets. And we have not only Galod, which other kaetaln have already snubbed us for, but now we have lost four of Galod's best students. It does not take much to understand that the Elders will likely shiver in fear of our 'nefarious' plans should we stay our course, and then the Councils will remove both of us. They will want to get rid of Galod, and they will not stop there. Under the influence of such fear, no one will make wise decisions, as you failed to when you left me out of this."

Zeroun nodded. "And Teros's pride could bring down ruin, as could Talaera's vengeful dissatisfaction. Teros is wroth at losing one of his priestesses, and he blames me. Talaera is upset—rightfully so—at losing family members and wont to take it out on you. Both mistrust Galod, even more now. And with Ra'ael no longer here to give her harmony to balance Teros's…"

"Zeroun, you must have an apprentice. We must convince the other kaetaln we are no threat. We must no longer stand out. Right now, differences are dangerous."

He waved her suggestion away. "There are no suitable candidates."

"There haven't been for many summers, so you say. Lower your standards and choose the best fit."

After a long moment, he bowed his head. "I will follow the wisdom of the Great Mother."

"Good! It will do you well," Maeren said. "But it still will not be enough."

"Bow to the fears of the other Elders? What about standing with me against the battering seas? Torkae should lead by example. We should honor our daughter. Takiyah's very spirit was that of Torkae's—strong in the face of adversity, unyielding."

Maeren's face crumpled in grief, and she sagged against him. After a long, shaky breath, she shook her head. "Can one lead if no one thinks your example is worthy of following, or if the social price is too high? That is what we are faced with now, Zeroun, whether or not it makes sense. What is the cost of dishonor?"

Zeroun closed his eyes, leaning his forehead against his wife's. "Loss of influence with the other Elders and with the other kaetaln, no aid when needed... Some of the other Elders may actively argue for the opposite of what I want just to oppose us. We would make enemies of them, Maeren. And yet... is that worth compromising all our values and history? Must we cave to this disastrous pressure?"

"Torkae cannot stand against the opposition of the Council of Elders." Maeren sighed. "We must bow our heads to the fears of the others. Our daughter would be so ashamed."

Chapter Twelve

None may profit from the sale of ebrs. After a period of one circulation, the ebr shall be returned to society, his or her debt paid. Ebrs shall be treated honorably and only struck when punishment is necessary to alter behavior. An excess of blows reflects poorly on the honor of the owner, while a well-kept ebr who works hard and returns to society a productive citizen gains his owner great honor and respect. Thus, the great majority of ebrs end up serving the noble houses.
—Justice Trekl's notes on the Kamalti City of Codr's Code of Laws

Iron. Her chains were made of iron with just a little sulfur. The urge to use her flames on them grew like an itch she couldn't scratch. She thinned her lips to keep from smiling—she felt truly alive for the first time in her life, despite her circumstances. The metal was cool on her skin, and she knew she should despise it—part of her *did* despise it for what it represented—but it also brought her knowledge.

Quandary hated it when Takiyah smiled in chains. That was part of the reason she continued to do so, even though Quandary would lock her in a closet for the night as punishment again. It would have killed one of the others, but Takiyah had begun looking forward to those nights, even hiding a dull knife in the closet to use, not for escape, but as a pick.

Each morning, she emerged from the cramped space exhausted but triumphant. Somehow, touching and handling bits of rock and metal unlocked bits of knowledge in her mind. Actually working with the materials unlocked even more, of course. She'd learned so much from working her little forge back home. But this was different than learning through practice. Instead, she felt like she'd already known these things and was remembering long-forgotten memories.

The sheer breadth of information in this place, just waiting to be known, was staggering. It was intoxicating. It was distracting.

Beside her, Quandary's servant scowled. "Do not fool yourself. You will not have it any better where you are going. There is a reason I am always careful to stay in Lady Quandary's good graces."

Takiyah scoffed. She'd been a model worker. "Quandary should decide how hot she wants her bathwater if she's going to throw such a tantrum about it. It's a wonder she's given any responsibility at all in the Scouts, the way she handles setbacks."

The servant spun, finger pointing at her, mouth open to scold, but nothing came out.

She bit her lip to keep from smiling at the fear and anger in his eyes. They never harmed her. Galod's training had been far more physically grueling than the work they set her to, and their mindset was easy to manipulate. Of course, she'd seen the gloating in Quandary's eyes when she would emerge from the closet in the morning, stiff and exhausted and rumpled, but she'd also gained so much, not the least of which was the satisfaction of Quandary's expression when she saw the damage done to her walls. The knowledge gained was more than worth the petty insults and degradations.

The servant closed his mouth and turned, jerking on her chains. With a swagger, she lengthened her stride, trodding on his heel as she did so. He yelped, skittering ahead, and she smirked, though she soon smoothed the expression from her face. What was she doing? Her mother would shake her head to see her tormenting the man like that. Even if he deserved it. They all did, regardless of how the man who had thrown Kaemada into the chasm was being punished.

Their boots echoed on the quiet streets of Codr. The massive orb above was dimmed to indicate "night time" and lanterns chased shadows from the corners. She still hadn't gotten enough of the city in the scarce opportunities she'd had to see more of it, and she craned her neck to take in as much as possible, her hair swinging behind her. She'd taken to braiding it as a concession to the warmer air down here, though she'd contemplated cutting or shaving it off. It was the solution that made the most sense, but her parents would collapse of shock should she return with short hair.

Because they *were* going home. They only stayed thus far to accommodate Kamalti "justice" so they could find Eian. She didn't mind as much as she'd have thought—it gave her time to snatch at all the knowledge she could from these people. Much of it could help her people if she could convince them to use metal.

The servant skittered ahead of her, keeping his body turned as if afraid to have her directly behind him. "Lady Quandary's cousin will sort you out. And good riddance to you! I have never seen such disrespect nor such incompetence!"

Takiyah scowled. "I worked hard and followed directions. What more am I supposed to do?"

He sniffed, glancing at her with his head back so he could look down his nose even though she was taller. It was a ridiculous position. "A good servant predicts his master's needs at all times, with never more than one request necessary!"

She wrinkled her brow. "So… a good servant uses telepathy?"

He jumped. His feet actually left the cobbled streets, and he turned with an expression of such surprise it was comic. "There is no magic allowed here! Savage!"

Takiyah let that go. There was no arguing with these people on that subject. Besides, if one defined "savage" purely in terms of lack of knowledge, the Kamalti did have a lot of knowledge she had previously lacked. Too bad they had no sense of civility. A pair of patrolling Scouts passed by them. Before turning the corner, the Scouts waited, watching her pointedly.

She sighed at their suspicion. What she wouldn't give to see Ra'ael and Taunos again. She hadn't seen them since her captivity began. And Kaemada… The darkness she'd been holding back rolled over her like a wave. Her life would never be the same, even after they got out of here. Without Kaemada, Ra'ael would isolate herself and lash out at everyone else. Taunos would just leave again, losing himself in other worlds. And her parents would keep an even closer eye on her as if she were a child.

No amount of knowledge managed to fill the ache in her. She missed her freedom. She missed home, the way things used to be.

And would the Kamalti keep their word and let them go, or would they have to fight?

Their shadows stretched long, thrown by street lanterns, while above, the strange orbs cast their faint gleam. Quandary's servant turned sharply and bounded up metal stairs that zigzagged up a massive tower of stone. She smiled, brushing her fingers against it. Granite. Kamalti houses were built into the columns which reached up to the cavern's ceiling. The rich lived near the bottom, while the poor lived toward the top, sometimes ten-and-five levels high.

Chains rattling, Takiyah raced after the servant, up several flights of switchback stairs until he finally stopped, panting, with a wary eye on her. She turned to gaze out over the city with pointed calm as she got her breath back. They were so high that the pair of Scouts they'd seen earlier looked like tiny insects. She grinned until the servant yanked on her chains, causing the metal to bite into her wrists. He led her along a rickety balcony, then rapped on a door. Takiyah scowled at him while he fidgeted, and when the door opened, he jumped again, shoving Takiyah inside. She caught her balance and turned on him, but he was bowing to a woman, gripping Takiyah's chains with white-knuckled fingers.

Takiyah took her chance to find her bearings. The woman who greeted them wore clean, well-cut clothing, adorned only by a thin gold circlet and a matching chain woven between her fingers and around her wrist. She lacked the jewels and finery Quandary favored. The room around them had simple furnishings and bare stone walls. Almost nothing in their small dwelling seemed devoid of function. Takiyah rather liked it.

"What is this?" the woman asked, her tone heavy with suspicion.

"A gift from your cousin, Lady Quandary," the servant said.

She spat. "I want no gift from her. She can keep her charity."

"This is an ebr from the Outside. It is said she can summon fire." His wheedling tone made Takiyah wince.

"Come to burn my things, is it? I will have none of that!" She waved them away.

He fidgeted, rattling Takiyah's chains incidentally. "Mettle, I am certain you can find a use for her. And if you cannot, then trade her."

Takiyah set her jaw and clenched her fists. She would endure. She had to.

The woman, Mettle, looked her over roughly, turning her face this way and that. "Fire, pah! Lying stories to cheat me. You tell Quandary I am wise to her! You want to see me embarrassed when I try to trade her, claiming what I cannot?" She waved Quandary's servant away. "Be gone with you! Get out of my house!"

The man unlocked Takiyah's chains and retreated promptly, relief lighting his expression. Takiyah ignored him, studying the woman in front of her.

Mettle scowled at her. "Get to work! The fire is dying!"

Takiyah suppressed a sigh. More rudeness, more simple, mindless work. What she would give for a chance to really test herself! She couldn't remember the last time she'd been so bored. Moving with a show of care, she set more wood on the fire, arranging the pieces to allow air to flow. The flames licked upward, and she turned to find Mettle hovering over her shoulder. She held herself still. Had the woman been testing her, expecting she would waste her fire on so simple a task?

The woman stepped back, frowning at the fire. "You, ebr, will prepare dinner and take care not to burn it, hm?"

Biting her cheek, Takiyah looked around the barely furnished room. "Where do you keep your food? And is it just you?"

Mettle glared at her. "Keep a civil tongue in your head. You will cook

160

for three adults and three children."

Takiyah scowled. Why were all the Kamalti so prickly?

Her expression stern, Mettle pointed to a small silver handle in a wall, and when Takiyah pulled it, the wall opened up to reveal a well-stocked pantry. There were so many interesting new foods down here, and Takiyah quickly chose some protein and roots, placing them on the table. Mettle had disappeared, so with more clattering than necessary, Takiyah searched for pans. Annoyance rose in her at the pointless difficulty of the mundane task, even after finally finding the pans behind another moveable piece of wall. There was no stove like Quandary had, either, and she looked along the walls, pushing and pulling at them with no success before settling for using the fire. Mettle checked on her twice while the food cooked but never spoke, her mouth set in a firm line, leaving the room quickly when Takiyah saw her. However, as Takiyah set out the plates and utensils, the family straggled in to claim spots at the table.

"Serve the food, ebr," a sour-faced man ordered. The children wrinkled their noses. "Such detestable service."

Biting her tongue, Takiyah served them, trying not to let her frustration show. She'd done the best she could in a new kitchen, with little help in finding anything, and no direction!

Guessing at her place, using the knowledge gleaned from living at Quandary's house, Takiyah retreated to a corner of the small room. The children complained and pushed their food around, and Mettle and her husband, Hardy, berated her for the "disgusting taste." Those comments stung—Takiyah had always been a good cook. She'd tasted the food as it cooked, and the dishes were seasoned well, all things considered. Her only reprieve was the elderly man, who shoveled it down silently, eyes fixed on his plate.

Finally, everyone left the kitchen, though Hardy stabbed his finger at her as he exited. "Lazy ebr, clean off this table! I will not have you slacking off."

Takiyah took her frustration out on the pots and pans, determined that at least they wouldn't be able to find fault in cleanliness after she was through. Her stomach growled, but when she started to finish the children's supper for them, Hardy was there again, knocking the plate to the floor and splattering food everywhere.

"Do not try to take advantage of our goodwill, ebr. You were not excused to eat!"

Surprise filled her when the woman intervened. "She might be hungry, Hardy."

"It does not matter, Mettle! Your cousin's gifts are always curses in disguise. I deal with enough disrespect from the other nobles, thinking they are better than us. I will not tolerate such an attitude from an ebr!"

Takiyah made a show of dumping the excess food from the plates into the washing water, though it was a terrible waste and made more of a mess. She'd known men such as Hardy, their ambitions squashed by those with more power, and she'd seen how they took that frustration out on others. Only here, she had no way to escape his power. She would have to endure.

Hardy left the house, slamming the door behind him. Takiyah wiped down the wall where he'd splattered the food with exaggerated motions. Behind her, Mettle clattered the dishes left on the table, scraping silverware against the plates. When Mettle called for her attention, Takiyah took a deep, calming breath before turning around.

Mettle pointed at the plate where she'd scraped the last of the leftovers into a pile. "Eat. Then put this kitchen back in order."

There was no visual appeal left to the slop, but Takiyah ate, barely stopping to chew. She was still hungry when the leftovers were gone, but she was accustomed to times of hunger. She hurried to finish cleaning to avoid yet more unfair scolding. Finally, aching with exhaustion, she was allowed to fall asleep in a small pile of blankets in the corner.

In the morning, Hardy roused her early to start the fire, which had gone out overnight. Still weary and grumpy from yesterday's demands, she piled the kindling and looked for the tinder. Every cabinet proved fruitless, and she barely kept from slamming them in her growing frustration. Takiyah peeked over her shoulder. No one else was there. Extending her wrist, she spurted a small stream of flame. The kindling lit readily and in no time, she had built a crackling fire. She stood and turned. Hardy leaned against the wall, staring at her with a gleam in his eyes. Her heart sank. This would not go well for her.

"Make breakfast," he ordered, and he left the room.

By the time she served breakfast, the family was ready for their day, and Mettle gave her a strange little smile. "You will clean yourself up now, and then you may eat. Be quick, for we are going to the market."

Takiyah bit back her questions and quickly obeyed. She was eager to wash, anyway. After a hasty scrub in a small tub in a tiny room, only a single biscuit remained for her breakfast. She bit her tongue till she drew blood as Mettle and Hardy chided her for her laziness. Hardy hefted a bag, and he and Mettle hurried her out the door. Her skin prickled with danger.

The market was bustling already, and Hardy shoved her over to one of the few unclaimed stalls. Mettle opened the bag and draped a cloth over the wooden front of the booth, while behind, Hardy chained Takiyah's ankle to a stake secured in the stone ground. Takiyah eyed the iron links, dread rising in her.

"Come and see! Delight your eyes, awe your children! Only 1 viscram per person!" Hardy bellowed.

Mettle interrupted, frowning. "This is debasing."

Humiliation heated her face. Takiyah glanced at her tether, then around at the market. Few of the other stall owners were calling out, so Hardy's shouts were drawing a lot of attention, including glares and looks of disgust from the other sellers. Shouting must be considered impolite among the Kamalti, just like eating and breathing.

Hardy turned to his wife, and Takiyah barely caught his harsh whisper. "What is debasing is having to choose between paying the rent and eating. This will only be for a little while. When our debts are paid, we will regain our proper place in society. Trust me." Hardy smiled briefly at his wife, though it turned to a scowl when he met Takiyah's gaze.

Mettle reached out and tugged Takiyah forward to the limit of her tether. Smiling at the crowd, she hissed in Takiyah's ear, "You perform well, you eat well. You make trouble, and my husband will beat you bloody."

Hardy waved a small board in the air, rapping the wood with his knuckles. He dropped it in front of Takiyah. "Light it."

Takiyah scanned the area for other options. Apprehension tightened like a knot in the core of her, stronger each moment.

Still smiling, Mettle dug her fingernails into her arm. "Be good to the crowd, dear—they love a show." Her voice dropped to a hiss. "Do not test me."

No options. They couldn't actually beat her, but still, something screamed danger. Gritting her teeth, Takiyah blasted the piece of wood into charcoal. The crowd whispered and some tossed coins at her, which Mettle quickly scooped up.

It felt good to release some of her frustration, but that satisfaction died as Hardy set a length of ragged cloth in front of her. "Light it."

All day, they forced her to light all variety of things—big, small, cloth, wood, fire-resistant materials, and more. They tested her accuracy, range, and control, then added obstacles. She rebelled about midday, exhausted, and Hardy circled behind her. Something hard hit her calf, and she jerked in surprise. Her tether checked her momentum, and she crashed to the ground. Recovering, she found him smiling at the crowd, assuring them that the show would continue after a brief break. Behind his back, hidden from their spectators by the stall, he held a thin cudgel.

She glared at him, only to receive another sharp strike. Smiling, Hardy spoke encouraging words to her, his tone coaxing, yet the blows kept coming, always where the crowd would not be able to see. Takiyah hunkered down, but with her body out of view, Hardy had more targets for his cudgel. She tried to avoid him, but her tether was too short.

She didn't mean to do it. Frustrated, humiliated, exhausted, and in pain, she snapped, falling back on Galod's lessons. As Hardy's arm swung back for another strike, her hand shot forward, hitting him square in the sternum. He staggered back a step and then surged toward her. Mettle shouted wordlessly. Hardy tackled her. Her tether wrenched on her ankle. She raised her hands to defend herself...

And two Scouts were there. Her relief was only momentary, however, as they piled on top of her with Hardy, fists and cudgel bashing into her such that she could hardly think. She curled up, trying to protect herself as blows rained down on her fingers, sides, neck, and back.

"Hold on now," a voice said, and the Scouts reeled back, hauling her upright, though the world swam before her. It took her a moment to see that a man in fine clothing with a thick, gold circlet on his head—definitely a Kamalti "noble," then—was standing before the stall, frowning. "It is not acceptable to beat an ebr so! Compose yourselves, gentlemen!"

"She struck me!" Hardy said. "Out of control, this ebr is. Had to be taught manners!"

The man drew himself up, staring down at them. "Scouts?"

The Scouts exchanged a glance before nodding. "The ebr was on a rampage. We restored order."

The man narrowed his eyes at them. "Did you see any improper behavior before this... rampage?"

"No, Justice. We would have intervened if we had," one of the Scouts said, stepping forward. Takiyah glared, straightening. She'd be next, then, to tell her story.

The Justice sniffed. "Well, then. Ebr, remember the penalty for attacking a Kamalti. You and your companions are in a precarious position. Another show like this could see you and the other two put to death."

Takiyah gaped as the Justice walked away. Where was her chance to speak?

"Get her out of here," one of the Scouts said. "She is not fit to be seen."

"Of course," Hardy said smoothly, giving the Scouts a deep nod. His fingers dug into Takiyah's arm. Mettle was there in a moment, having apparently packed up while Takiyah had been busy defending herself. Busy getting a beating.

"How much did we get?" Hardy asked, yanking on Takiyah's arm. She barely kept from biting her tongue.

"We can pay the rent."

Hardy smiled at Mettle. "We will be free of our debts in only a short time, my dear! And you, ebr, will remember your place next time, yes?"

Takiyah's stomach turned. "You do not have to hit me."

Hardy turned so he was suddenly nose to minimal nose with her. "Ah, but you cannot hit me. Do we understand each other?"

Takiyah clenched her teeth and nodded slowly. The ride was over, she realized. With Quandary, it was a challenge, a test of how far each could go without crossing that invisible line. But Hardy had crossed that line straight away, going for blood. This could not be forgiven.

"You obey orders from now on, understand?"

"I ran out of flame."

"Liar!"

"If she had flame, would she not have used it when attacking you?" asked Mettle, the voice of apparent reason.

Hardy shifted, his features twisting, and he spun, tugging Takiyah along. "You will do more tricks tomorrow."

"People will get bored, eventually," she said.

Hardy grinned at her. "No they will not. Visitors will come from other Cities. Do not worry, your performances will be in demand long after your sentence is up—even if you behave yourself perfectly."

The knot of apprehension went cold with fear. The rules she'd depended on—the rules the Kamalti seemed to prize so highly—had evaporated like mist. She was in deep trouble.

ÌTAL-BAE
Chapter Thirteen

There are many uses for an ebr. Violent or dangerous ebrs must be worked physically to rid them of the excess energy. Intelligent ebrs can help their household even as they pay their debt to society with bookwork and organization. And some ebrs, the very few, may be raised to bodyguard status—once they have proven their loyalty, of course.

-excerpt from Etiquette for the Modern Noble Family

Ra'ael hummed her song to the spirits as the warm soapy water splashed over her skin. She lifted the dish, inspected it, and set it aside, reaching back into the basin to scrub the peculiar utensil Dode called a "fork." As she worked, her gaze rose to the unholy barrier of the cavern's ceiling. She could imagine her song bouncing off it, just as captive as she was. Rinaryn were not supposed to be underground. How could the spirits see her under the stone? How could her song join theirs?

Lifting the fork, she gave it a shake to clear the water from the metal and dropped it to the side. She started work on Dode's favorite cup next, scrubbing the metal clean. So much metal here! It was disgraceful, yet Dode seemed to think it was something of an honor to tear the metal ore from the ground. She scowled.

Her first captor had traded her like an object to an elderly woman named Dode. For all that Dode seemed rational—at least for a Kamalti—and even friendly, she was still her captor. In the beginning, when Ra'ael had flatly refused to prepare a bird for dinner—instead, committing the body to the flames with proper reverence—Dode had merely watched her with a faint smile. She hadn't brought home a bird carcass since. Rather, she stocked the kitchen with vegetables, breads, and strange gelatinous cubes that apparently passed for food among the Kamalti.

She'd been captive for a moon—the Kamalti called them "faces"—and hadn't seen Taunos or Takiyah even once in that time. The worry weighed on her like a stone. They were her responsibility. She'd already failed in her duties, giving in to their ridiculous schemes that landed them all here. All she could do now was focus daily on her goals: find Eian and get him to safety. She'd even asked Dode, who suggested the boy might have been taken somewhere safe, out of the mountain. Ra'ael's own future was ruined—she no longer had any chance of ever being made Great Mother, no matter how long she atoned for. It would be a miracle to regain a place in the kaetal. But Eian was only a child. She had to hope for him. He was the reason to continue her song—that and the nagging fear that if she should fall here, she'd never make it out of the underground and across the rim of the sky.

Ra'ael dumped the dirty water out the window into a chute that would take it down a system of pipes until it reached the ravine. After rinsing the dishes in a few ladles of clean water, she poured out that water as well, watching it flow away, the sacred held captive by that which had been ripped from the ground. Shaking her head, she dried the dishes with a clean cloth and pulled water from the bucket beside her to fill the kettle.

Dode would return soon and want her tea. Then would come the questions. Yesterday, Dode had asked what Rinaryn did if a storm blew down their huts, and before that, she'd asked how they got enough metal to make things if they didn't mine into the ground. The woman didn't understand. How could she? Dode thought it amusing that Ra'ael preferred sleeping in the kitchen, unable to fathom the truth. The house of stone, divided with walls inside, was distressingly tangled and hopelessly removed from the flow of life. At least the kitchen was more proper, for it held the fire. Close to the hearth, Ra'ael could make sure the fire never went out—another thing her captor couldn't seem to understand.

The door opened and Dode entered, thin and slightly hunched, her sandals scuffing lightly on the stone floor. She smiled at Ra'ael and gently closed the door. "Come, Ra'ael. I need your assistance carrying supplies."

Ra'ael paused in the middle of lifting the steaming kettle. There was a consistent rhythm to Dode's routine. After she came home, she had tea, asked questions, and then retired to her office until supper time. Foodstuffs had been delivered to her door three days ago, and it was another two days before Dode would go to the market for the morning.

Dode smiled. "Do not worry, we can converse on the way."

"On the way where?" Ra'ael set down the kettle, following Dode out the door. Unease fluttered at her heart. The change in routine highlighted her lack of control these days.

"I find myself in need of a few books and some writing supplies."

"Now? It cannot wait two days?"

Dode chuckled. "Am I so predictable?"

"Yes."

The old woman gave her another smile, the corners of her eyes crinkling, and then her expression became serious. "Now, you have not come with me to the market before. There are things you must know, social customs you must follow. As an ebr, you must never pass me but always remain at least one step behind. However, you must be seen to be busy and move quickly."

"How, then, will I not pass you?" Ra'ael challenged her.

"I expect you will have to shorten your stride." The woman's light tone and gentle expression only heightened the humiliation of the whole scenario.

Ra'ael glowered.

Dode turned, walking along the exterior corridor with one hand trailing on the lattice banister. "Come, Ra'ael, I think you will enjoy this. The Codr marketplace is a fascinating experience even to Kamalti of other cities."

Glaring at her back, Ra'ael followed, belatedly remembering to shorten her stride so she scurried like some rodent. The Kamalti were not better than Rinaryn. No marketplace could hold a drop of water against the rushing river of Rinaryn celebrations.

She was speaking before she knew it. "Why do you Kamalti not come out of hiding and help us if you're so superior? My people never know when the Darks will attack. You could give much needed aid."

Ra'ael could *sense* Dode smiling ahead of her. She never should have asked a question! The old Kamalti had been waiting for this, hadn't she.

"Our place is not that of the Outsiders. Our place is not for war." Dode pressed a button on the wall. Chains rattled along the outside of the column, and a vertical platform lowered itself toward them.

The Kamalti pride, yet again. Ra'ael's fingers twitched. "Our place is not for war, either. All these machines and inventions you have—they could save lives."

"Not all Kamalti see the deaths of your people as a waste," Dode murmured, lowering her gaze briefly.

Unclenching her fists and taking a deep breath to settle herself, Ra'ael ground out the question that had been grating on her. "Why do you ask so many questions if you believe we're so much lesser than you?"

Dode laughed. "I chose the Philosophers upon gaining my majority because I love the search for wisdom and truth. You cannot truly know a thing until you have looked at it from all of its sides," she said. "Likewise, how can we claim to understand life until we know how others see it? Now hush a moment on the lift—it would not do for others to overhear such talk."

Such foolishness! Ra'ael shook her head but pressed her lips together.

The platform bumped to a stop, the button springing outward again, and Dode stepped on. Ra'ael hesitated, eyeing the five other Kamalti standing on the lift, but Dode's hand snaked out, grabbing her wrist and pulling her onto the lift just as it began to descend again. They bumped to the ground and Ra'ael stumbled, the only one not holding on to a handrail. As the others stepped off, Dode ushered Ra'ael along the city streets.

Heart pounding from the experience, Ra'ael twisted as she walked, looking for landmarks. She nearly missed Dode's nod of permission as the streets thinned. Again, the foolish Kamalti ideas of what was proper!

Her tone sharpened more than she planned. "You cannot simply stand by, ask a few prying questions, and then claim to understand a people. You must live among them. This is important no matter your position—Great Mother, priestess, hunter, or Kamalti."

Dode's smile looked suspiciously triumphant. "Yes, I suppose one would have to live with one of you," she mused with twinkling eyes. Then her browridge raised. "Priestess, you say?"

She hadn't meant to let that slip. Still, why shouldn't she be proud? "My role among my people."

Surprise and delight glowed on Dode's face. "Oh! So you guide your people in their beliefs?"

Ra'ael's brow knitted. "I make sure the traditions and ceremonies are conducted as is proper. How can any guide another's beliefs?"

Dode had the gall to look disappointed. "I see. Here, a priest has a vital task. He guides the sacred rituals, but he also guides the people to the sacred truth, away from the lies seeded by selfish thought, cowardice, and laziness. This is the job of a proper priest."

"In the end, the spirit must make its journey alone. How can we expect that it's proper for another to guide that spirit? We celebrate and live life as a community except in one thing—each practices his or her faith in solitude. Only alone can we see Eloí unencumbered by the expectations of others." Ra'ael found herself warming to the debate. She hadn't realized how much she'd missed arguing with Takiyah, the way they kept each other's mind strong through opposition. Conversation with Dode would have to do as a substitute for now.

"And the journey up the mountain?"

"We worship separately except for twice a summer."

Dode laughed. "I will introduce you to your Kamalti counterparts one day. Among my people, we have no priestesses, only priests. They are very important, though not everyone listens to them."

"Who do your Storytellers and Great Mothers confer with? Who settles disputes of philosophy and morality? Who helps your Storytellers guide your people into the future?"

Dode's browridge crinkled in confusion, and she gestured toward a man standing on the next corner, waving his arms in the air as he told tales to the crowd around him. "Storytellers? No one listens to them, not seriously. They have nothing of wisdom to say, merely frivolity to amuse the poor. As for guiding my people, that is for the nobles, not the priests."

Ra'ael gazed at the man on the corner. Such a man was not a Storyteller, not a leader. Once again, Dode didn't understand. She didn't know what she didn't know. A group of Kamalti "nobles" glided past in a bubble of serenity, all draped in their finery, while ebrs scurried about, invisible to those better off. Even those who entertained others, like the man playing music, were only visible as novelties.

The commotion increased as they entered the market, and Ra'ael's skin prickled as she strove to watch for danger. Machines were displayed and demonstrated, but for the most part, sellers stood quietly except to speak with customers. Bits of metal flashed as people exchanged coins for goods, and Dode explained everything as they walked, though Ra'ael tried to maintain an uninterested expression. There was an order to it all, and Ra'ael hated that she appreciated it. Those who called out for attention tended to wear coarser garments and less jewelry. The crowds they attracted also appeared to be of humble means. It baffled her, such distinctions between those with wealth and those without.

A commotion to her left drew her eye. A child bolted from a stand, apple in hand. Shouting, the vendor caught the boy by the collar, cuffing him on the shoulder with his free hand. Rage bubbled up in her like the steam the machines belched. Didn't these savages know how to treat children? Any child should be able to eat freely, offered food and comfort by any nearby adult. This situation showed, once and for all, that the Kamalti system was broken.

She took off toward the man and boy. Dode, moving faster than she'd ever believed the elderly woman could, blocked her path.

"Stop, Ra'ael, stop now!" she demanded.

"No adult should strike a child! Are you a race of bullies and cowards, only able to—"

Dode's hand cracked over her mouth, and Ra'ael stopped, stunned.

"Home. Now." Dode ordered.

Inwardly seething, Ra'ael followed, holding one hand over her reddened cheek. Dode had… she had *hit* her? The walk passed in a daze, for while the pain was minor, she could not fathom the reason for this.

Dode had seemed so meek, so gentle, even frail. Right until she struck. Dode remained silent all the way back, not once looking at her as the rattling contraption lifted them up the column to the level of Dode's home.

Once the door was shut and latched behind them, Dode sighed, sagging a bit. "I apologize for striking you. I needed to stop you before you caused greater harm."

Ra'ael clenched her teeth and glowered at her. Dode's secret was out—all Kamalti were awful people with no sense of justice or morality. Dode was not the sweet elderly lady she appeared.

"As for the child, how else is he to learn what is acceptable behavior?" Dode asked.

"Through instruction! Children should always be treated gently—they're precious," she seethed. "If one adult cannot handle a child's antics any longer, another should take over so the child is always treated with patience. Every Rinaryn knows this."

"Regardless of your views, I cannot have you acting so foolishly in public. It reflects poorly on me, and that can be dangerous for you."

A knock interrupted, and Dode frowned at Ra'ael. "You did not see the Scout in the marketplace."

It was not a question. The hair on the back of Ra'ael's neck stood up as Dode answered the door, revealing a Scout in all his regalia. The Scout stepped inside, scowling at Ra'ael.

Dode, however, smiled smoothly. "Ah, my lord, may I make you a refreshment?"

"Of course, Lady Dode," he returned easily. Dode gestured to Ra'ael, who narrowed her eyes but turned, setting the kettle on its hook and swiveling it over the fire.

"Send the ebr away, please."

Dode laughed. "What, my lord Scout, am I to make you tea with my own hands? That would be a breach of etiquette, given our positions. My ebr must do it."

"Your ebr was seen rampaging through the marketplace."

"I would hardly call that minor slip a rampage."

"I will not accept food or drink from her hands."

"Then I am afraid I will not be able to offer you a refreshment, and as it would be unseemly for you to visit without a refreshment, you must go. What awful manners!"

The Scout stiffened, hesitating long moments before he finally turned to the door. "Keep a sharp eye on this ebr of yours. Should she... slip... again, she will find her life forfeit."

Dode nodded, still smiling, as she shut the door behind him. Once the door was latched again, she turned to fix Ra'ael with a frank look.

Ra'ael folded her arms.

"The Scouts have something against you. You must tread lightly, or I will not be able to save you." Dode took a slow, deep breath and gave her a gentle smile at odds with her stern words of before. "No Kamalti interferes with another's children unless they break the Law. In such a case, one could rebuke the child and administer a little slap to help the lesson sink in."

Ra'ael stared her, a storm raging within, but held her tongue. She turned to dump the water from the teapot, but Dode stopped her. "Put the kettle on. I think some tea would do us both some good after that misadventure."

"Misadventure" was a mild word for it. Even so, Ra'ael brought out two mugs and dropped the tea leaves into the kettle.

Dode sat in silence for a while before asking, "How do your people handle children?"

Ah, a chance to prove her people's superiority. Ra'ael straightened, brushing her hair back behind her shoulders. "In Rinara, all adults in the kaetal parent all the children except inside the family home. Lessons are taught by explaining the consequences of actions and what to watch for or by telling ancient stories to illustrate the hazards of certain actions and highlighting virtues. If needed, the kaetal elders are called in to talk to the child, and if nothing else works, the older child may be briefly submerged in water to wash away willful disobedience." She was quite put off when, after finishing her explanation, Dode smiled.

"Oh, child. You are so blinded. Do not look so cross—so am I! But Kamalti would interpret what you have said by saying, 'You are so lenient with your children that when their willfulness takes hold, you must threaten them with drowning to persuade them to behave!'"

"That isn't it at all!" Ra'ael protested.

Dode nodded, still smiling. "I know, child, I know."

Ra'ael glared at the teapot, pouring a bit of tea to test the color. It was almost ready, just a little light. The elderly woman reached for her favorite mug, one of silver with an intriguing pattern engraved on it. She paused, frowning at it, then handed it to Ra'ael.

"This needs to be washed."

"I just washed it. That discoloration will not come off the metal, but the cup is clean."

"Oh, see, now it is marred. It will never be as perfect." Dode pursed her lips in annoyance.

"It was once a blank canvas. Now, it has written on it a story. That makes it even more beautiful," Ra'ael replied. Surely, Dode would recognize Rinaryn wisdom in this.

Dode looked at her quizzically, then handed the cup back, murmuring about "strange notions."

"If nothing can be less than perfect, how did your people create all this?" Ra'ael gestured around her, challenge in her voice. "Surely buildings and statues, even roads, must deteriorate with time. What, then, do you do?"

Dode stood. "Come with me."

Ra'ael followed her to her rock garden in a back room where Dode liked to meditate. Dode scooped up a handful of pebbles and pressed her other hand over top, squeezing the pebbles between her hands. A repulsive metallic twang filled her mind, setting her on edge, and Ra'ael winced and stepped back. Dode seemed not to notice it, and when she opened her hands, the pile of pebbles was now a single, smooth rock, and the metallic twang had gone.

Ra'ael gasped in amazement, and Dode chuckled. Reaching out to touch the stone, Ra'ael stopped short. An instinctive dread and something akin to hatred welled up deep within her, and her hand shook.

Again, Dode didn't seem to notice, offering her the stone. "You may take it."

Ra'ael clasped her hands behind her back instead. "Why not do that with your cup?"

Dode sighed. "It is not so easy with refined metals. There will always be some imperfection."

"I thought you Kamalti hated magic."

Dode smiled at her. "That was not magic. That was the Gift from the gods."

~

That very next morning, Ra'ael accompanied Dode to a nearby chapel, for Dode said it was high time she introduced Ra'ael to the gods and to Kamalti priests. Arches high above their heads attached the heavily engraved building to the buildings on either side. Dode glided up to the door and reluctantly, Ra'ael followed.

A man wearing purple robes and a satisfied smile opened the door for them. Lanterns hung high above their heads from chains attached to the arched ceiling, which was made of more panels of colored glass set in beams of stone. Light streamed in from the cavern outside through the glass roof and through windows of various shapes and sizes filled with glass of all different colors. Everywhere, the metal was worked in beautiful, twisting designs. Kamalti filled the bench seats, with ebrs standing against the outer walls. At the front of the chapel sat a stone table worked in gold and silver and inlaid with brilliant gems of various colors and sizes, slender candles burning on it. Another man, also wearing purple robes along with a large crystal that hung from a gold chain around his neck, stood beside the table.

Ra'ael couldn't help but stare. It was stunning, even if very different from the decorations of wood, antler, horn, and bone from home. Nothing with life in it was used for Kamalti decorations, it seemed. Still, the beauty lifted her heart, although she wondered how and who the Kamalti worshiped. Did they worship Eloí? If so, they worshiped in a much more ostentatious manner. And if they did not, they were heathens, abandoning Eloí for falsehoods.

"Let not your heart be filled with darkness, child," Dode said.

Ra'ael thinned her lips. Dode only smiled patiently and directed Ra'ael to stand along the side and keep silent. The service began as the priest turned his back to the people and spoke in Kamalti. The people followed his movements, kneeling when he knelt and rising when he rose, and Ra'ael doggedly watched the strange rituals while keeping an eye on the other ebrs around her.

Through the service, she gathered from the smattering talk in Traveller's that they worshipped a god called Kellendine who held all the creative power and had made everything. This was similar to Eloí, but Eloí was properly worshipped in the presence of all the life they brought forth. They were worshipped under the openness of the sky, not in a building of stone buried underground. She caught mention of several other names repeated during the service—other gods worshipped by these heathens, no doubt.

After the service, Ra'ael peppered Dode with questions, and smiling as usual, Dode brought her to one of the metal buildings in the City.

"You who judge others would not yourself appreciate being judged so hastily." Dode entered the metal building before Ra'ael could reply.

Simmering with questions, she followed, winding through the hallways until they came to a great room. A shimmering image born of light was displayed on a wall, and Ra'ael gasped as the image changed. Who was doing such magic?

"This shows the faces of the demigods to the Chosen. By Chosen, of course, we mean us." A rueful smile twisted Dode's lips.

Ra'ael peered at the image as it changed again. The images were fuzzy, but they looked far more Rinaryn than Kamalti. Both men and women appeared bald and wore strange clothing somewhat similar to the costumes of the Scouts. There were several of them, and Dode told her about each one, devotion filling her voice: Reri, the goddess of mothers, Tilo, the god of artists, Noru, the goddess of love, Voric, the god of alcoholic drinks, and more.

"All these serve under the great Kellendine who holds all power. My people have long honored those who assist Kellendine. Long ago, Kellendine was helped in his creative works by a group called the Prusotak. They built the world as we know it, but they were not long for the world and soon diminished. As they did so, these Takanis came to take their place as the helpers of Kellendine."

"So, when you changed the pebbles into a single rock, you said it wasn't magic but a gift from the gods. Which gods?"

"The Takanis, of course."

"How does one receive such a gift?"

"It is a sacred ritual, available only to some. Never to ebrs."

Ah, yes, the secret of Kamalti society. Money. "Only to the rich, you mean."

Dode raised her browridge. "Only to nobility, yes, but not all nobles have the Gift. Your priessshood is restricted, is it not? Does, perhaps, your own parentage influence your status?"

Ra'ael scowled at her, irritation twisting her heart. Her mother had been highly honored, and Ra'ael longed to make her proud. Had her mother's deeds been taken into account when she'd been made priestess? The truth sang uncomfortably in her head.

Her feet dragged as she followed Dode to another room farther down the hall, a shrine to the Prusotak. A massive statue stood in the middle of the room, carved to resemble a being raising up mountains with his hands. He looked much more like the Kamalti than the images of the Takanis, but somehow even stranger, almost lizard-like.

Ra'ael shook her head. "How can you worship those who do not look like you?"

"And what does your Eloí look like?"

Again, the priestess shook her head. "Eloí has no shape, no form. They're a force like the wind which whips around the mountains and carves their shape."

Dode smiled. "I could ask you as well how you could worship that which does not look like you."

Caught in truth, Ra'ael couldn't help but smile a little.

Ra'ael awoke from her cot. Her exhausted body protested, still weary from all the errands she and Dode had run that day. They'd ended with another trip to the shrine, another discussion. She'd even begun to enjoy herself, and had fallen asleep with a feeling that approached… happiness.

But something had awakened her. She crouched beside her cot and held her breath, ears straining, peering through the dim light of Kamalti nighttime. Some perception that had not yet drifted to her conscious mind filled her with wariness.

Movement caught her eye—a shadow. Someone was in the house.

The shadow moved down the hallway, and she crept after it, racing forward as the intruder opened the door to Dode's room. He approached Dode's bed, pulling a knife. Ra'ael leapt, tackling him. They hit the floor hard, and Ra'ael quickly had him pinned.

With a gasp, Dode sat up in bed. She lit the lamp next to her and Ra'ael blinked in the light.

"His knife is there," Ra'ael said with a nod of her head. The intruder lunged to break her hold, but she held tight. He was no match for her.

Dode, however, shook visibly as she wrapped herself in a robe. "We must convene the Justices." She paused, then hurried out of the house, her frame filled with tension.

Once the outer door had shut, Ra'ael grabbed the man, forcing him into the kitchen. He was of average height and build for a Kamalti, and if she'd passed him on the street, she wouldn't have given him a second thought. But he'd tried to kill Dode. The fury that filled her was surprising.

She snatched a length of rope and tied the man to a chair, ignoring his protests that the ropes were too tight. Anger stole her words, so Ra'ael yanked harder on the ropes until he quit complaining. She was checking her knots when Dode came back in, but the woman walked past her without speaking, hardly seeming to see her. Filled with concern, Ra'ael checked the knots one more time and gagged the man even though he sat quietly. She slipped down the hallway to check on Dode.

Dode sat in front of a mirror, wearing fresh clothes and painting her face. Her hands were still shaking, however calm her face appeared. "The Justices will deal with this intruder, this attempt on my life," she said.

Dode must be terrified to speak such obvious truths. "You seem to have many enemies."

"I have not risen to my station without upsetting some people," Dode said. She smiled, and Ra'ael returned the smile.

Admiration welled up within her at how Dode strove to hide her terror. "You do not seem to be the enemy-making kind," Ra'ael confessed. "You seem so mild."

Dode put her paints away. "The Scouts will soon take in this... visitor. I will go with them to see the Justices. You will stay behind."

"When we were brought before the Justices, we had to wait until morning," Ra'ael said.

"An attempt on the life of a noblewoman, a Philosopher, carries greater weight."

Ra'ael snorted her disdain. Why should one life be worth more based solely on birth?

Dode's hands continued to tremble. The elderly woman was in no shape right now for debate. She reached out a hand and set it on Dode's.

It wasn't long before the Scouts rapped on the door. Once they'd all left, including the prisoner, Ra'ael grabbed the soap and washbucket and scrubbed the floor. She couldn't go to sleep now—not when Dode had nearly been murdered in the next room.

The entire floor of the large house was sparkling by the time Dode returned, looking haggard. She latched the door and leaned against it, trembling. Shock froze Ra'ael, seeing the old woman's composure so damaged.

"Did everything go all right?" she asked.

"Yes, yes," Dode said, taking a deep breath and straightening her shoulders. She sat down at the table, outwardly calm but for quivering fingers.

Almost by reflex, Ra'ael prepared a pot of Dode's favorite tea. When the tea was ready, Ra'ael placed a cup in the woman's hands. Dode's browridge rose as she emerged from whatever thoughts she had been pondering.

"Be careful, child, or I may start thinking you do not completely despise me."

Ra'ael sat next to her. "I never despised you. I only despised my role."

"I, for one, am glad you are here." Her expression darkened. "The Justices thought you might be part of the plot. No, do not worry. I told them in no uncertain terms that you are innocent. Their prejudice and suspicion will be their undoing!"

There were no words to say that would not hurt Dode, so Ra'ael said nothing.

Dode mused silently to herself while she sipped the tea, her lips moving occasionally. After draining the last drops from her mug, Dode took a deep breath and fixed a sharp gaze on her. "Ra'ael, I cannot release you from ebrid. However, ebrs have many functions. How would you like to be my bodyguard?"

Ra'ael's mouth dropped open. Bodyguards were an honored occupation among the Kamalti.

Her hand trembling only a little, Dode reached out and gripped Ra'ael's hand. "It seems obvious there are some who are not happy about the influence the Philosophers have been gaining. Some may raise a fuss over you as my bodyguard, but I have no care for their thoughts. You have kept me safe without my asking. It seems only fitting I now formally ask you."

Ra'ael smiled. "Of course, Dode."

Dode nodded and sat back with a deep sigh as if a weight had lifted off her shoulders. "This is good. You will now accompany me almost everywhere I go. In public, you will still need to be deferential and invisible, as an ebr should be, but Ra'ael?" She smiled, weariness lining her face. "I am honored to be in your company."

ÌTAL-DEITAE
Chapter Fourteen

The gracious hostess is certain her household staff is in order, not just the rooms themselves! She trains her servants and ebrs in proper etiquette and insists on protocol. Since many servants and ebrs come from the lower classes, their knowledge of etiquette may be insufficient for a noble house, so they must be taught proper form: to speak only when spoken to, to answer promptly and succinctly, and to keep their gaze down when talking to their betters. While it is polite for those of her station or better to look her in the eye, this is unacceptable for the lower classes. Nothing is so evident of poor breeding as the staff whose gaze wanders while his betters instruct him!

Of course the well-bred young lady must be attended by female staff, while male staff is required for young gentlemen...

-excerpt from The Young Ladies' Guide to Etiquette

Answer hurried through the streets, her boots clicking on the cobblestones. She longed to break into a run, but that would not be seemly, and she'd surely hear about it from her mother later. So she kept her pace as swift as the rules of decorum allowed and greeted those she passed with distracted nods, recalculating her schedule instead of paying attention to the streets. At least her home was not too far from the Scout's Council, and she'd finished her rounds on the Upper Fifth on the stair-ward side of the City right on time. Once home, there should be just enough time to change out of her uniform, bathe, and dress in civilian clothing. She'd have to hope her mother hadn't busied all the ebrs with frivolous tasks so she'd have someone to carry goods for her while she shopped. The merchants were just opening their stores, and she could hear the sounds of arguing as those less well-off set up their temporary stalls in the marketplace.

Two rings sounded from Timepiece Tower, the massive mechanism the artificers had made last circulation to prove that Codr's artificers were the best of the best. The pride of Codr, it drew the envy of the other Kamalti Cities. The City of Detr had even had the gall to threaten to subjugate Codr once more, but of course, the Scouts all knew that with Hadr's support, they could stand against Detr. She sneered for a moment at the tunnel on the Detr-ward side of the cavern before smoothing her features once more. They'd thrown off Detr and its taxes a generation ago and had only grown stronger.

Answer stared at the lift as it crawled its way up her column. She should wait for it, for decorum's sake, but time was already short! She needed to get to the market while the stalls were still fresh, before all the best goods were gone. If she bought the Justice Zhedr an impressive gift, she could turn his eye to her. Courting him would significantly increase her rank, and it didn't hurt that he was young and handsome.

The lift was too slow. Decorum would cost far too much if it meant she missed out on the market. She bounded up the stairs, climbing the switchback flights as quickly as she could. The day of the ball was fast approaching. With Scouting and training Taunos and dealing with the pressure from other noble houses, which were worried about the savage ebrs, she'd nearly lost track of time and only had two days left to find the perfect gift. If she missed this chance, it would be several faces before the next social occasion where Scouts, Philosophers, and Justices mingled freely with one another.

Throwing open the door, she poked her head into the library to find Ketrik polishing the wooden shelves. She paced across the thick rugs as he bowed to the precise angle he should.

"My lady Answer?"

"Ketrik, draw me a bath. Afterward, you will come with me to the market. I have some business to attend to."

"My deepest apologies, my lady, but I cannot. Your mother has decreed that after I finish here, I must shine her best circlet and be certain her crystal earrings are spotless. It would not do to disappoint her."

Answer twisted her gloves in frustration. "Then who can attend me? Where is Kajat?"

"Kajat is at the tailor's, collecting the gowns for the ball, my lady."

She frowned. "Send me Tegil, then."

Ketrik sighed. "My apologies, my lady, my deepest apologies. Your father has taken Tegil with him to a meeting. I can take Taunos from cleaning the dishes if you wish. Or, if you could wait two hours, Kajat should have returned by then."

"Two hours is too long! All the best merchandise will be gone from the market by then, and I must have the best."

"Then Taunos is your only option, my lady," Ketrik said, blinking his apologies.

Answer took a deep breath. It wasn't fair of her to take out her frustration on Ketrik. It was her mother who was ruining her plans. "Fine, Ketrik. Please have Taunos dress properly for the market and send him up to me. I will draw my own bath."

"Very good, my lady," Ketrik said.

She turned and ran from the room as he bowed.

Her hurried bath in the large copper tub was far from relaxing, for the water wasn't heated as thoroughly as she liked. That's what she got for not having the ebrs do it. The water encouraged her not to linger—she didn't have time for a soak, anyway.

There was a knot in her stomach, and it only tightened as she dressed, picking through her jewelry for just the right pieces. Her ebr was dangerous, there was no doubt about that. It was one of the reasons she'd chosen him. After all, if she could subdue a violent savage, surely the other nobles would respect her further. It should increase her reputation and therefore rank, which meant more power, more freedom. That was how it was supposed to work, anyway. Instead, her superiors pressured her to trade Taunos for a more suitable ebr. And then, when she was home, the ebr rarely missed an opportunity to remind her that he held her responsible for his sister's death, no matter how they disciplined him.

She slid her feet into a pair of sandals that complemented her outfit and gazed critically at her reflection. Satisfied that her appearance was free of defects, she turned and hurried back to the library. Taunos would not cause trouble, surely. After all, they'd be in public, so it wasn't like he'd get away with harming her.

But he knew how to damage the family's reputation.

About a face ago, the Outsider had accompanied her family while they bought crystals to comfort Answer's ill aunt. When Taunos reached for the bag, her mother realized he was not wearing the proper gloves—he'd failed to change his white gloves for black ones—at the same time as the shopkeeper noticed. While the shopkeeper didn't take offense, he did let his tongue run freely. The other noble houses had lectured them for days, and they had only recently regained some of the status they'd lost due to the fiasco.

"After all," Necessity, Answer's superior in the Scouting Guild, had told her firmly, "if you cannot keep a single ebr in line, how can we depend on you to study the Gifts? Details are important, and precision is key!"

But she had to chance it. She raised her chin. These days, he no longer committed such breaches of etiquette as trying to walk on the inside of the walking ways or speaking when not spoken to. He remained so slow and clumsy that he was more a danger to himself than anyone else. She considered having Ketrik alter the dosage of the herbs he used in Taunos's food and drink. Then again, it was prudent to err toward caution and be certain the Outsider could make no trouble with his magic.

She couldn't wait to show the ebr off as a symbol of her status. The savage from the Outside, civilized at last. But her work was not entirely done. Taunos was still infuriatingly slow to speak and spoke in barbaric phrases, and she still hadn't broken him of the habit of roaming his gaze over the entirety of any and every room he entered. It seemed almost a compulsion for him! Once she could trust him to act respectfully without being constantly watched, she would claim victory, but not until then.

Still, that meant she had to test him now and again to look for improvement.

By the time she strode into the entryway, Taunos stood waiting for her, and she suppressed a smile at the annoyance plain on his face. She wasn't sure why she enjoyed needling the Outsider, only that it was a satisfying hobby. Her head high, she walked past him with all the dignity a Scout should possess and gestured to him to follow.

The main marketplace sprawled near the center of Codr, between the great stairs to the Outside and the Great Divide, close to the Scout's Council. Shops surrounded the square, with hanging signs indicating what they sold along with pictures for those unfortunates who could not read. Temporary stands sprang up daily on grids in the square, offering a new variety of goods each day. At the center of the market, still more storefronts sold sacred items inside the middle one of the metal buildings.

There were no signs there. If a person didn't know what those stores sold, they had no business being there.

Answer walked along the main path with Taunos shuffling the appropriate distance behind her. She discounted the stalls that sold necessities—they would have nothing worthy of Zhedr. She breezed past the fruits, vegetables, meat-birds, and fish, delivered to the market daily from the large-scale growing facilities on the City's edge. The merchants selling cloth, twine, and thread were likewise ignored, though she had to give a nod to her tailor when he noticed her. His shop, of course, was not one of those selling dresses and suits in the open—these stalls sold to those too poor to have their clothes made to order.

Once through the central stalls, she lingered at the edge, browsing the shops that sold or repaired the machines that worked by an intricate system of gears and ran on steam power. Nothing was quite right, though she did order a sweeping machine to be delivered to the house. The aromas from the nearby eateries and taverns enticed her and her stomach grumbled, but she didn't have time to lounge. She sidestepped a boy sweeping the street clean of debris and dodged a grubby-faced family with patched clothes.

"Care to buy some flowers, my lady?"

Answer cultivated a neutral expression. Most of the stalls knew better, but the wandering sellers were a problem. How rude it was to call out to passers-by. At least the ruckus made it easy to avoid the corner where someone was shouting about a fire display. What was the market coming to?

Another grubby girl accosted her about some handmade crafts—as if that would be an appropriate gift! No matter how "unique" it was, it would never be worth anything. Taunos fell behind a few steps, and she turned to find him folded in a crouch, speaking to the girl. How mortifying! If anyone saw—but anger and haste were not the correct responses.

"Taunos, attend me," she snapped, walking onward. She listened, tense, ready for his disobedience, but his sandals flapped along behind her in his characteristic scuffing step. She pressed her lips together. So uncoordinated. He was always moving, never still, and yet it seemed a miracle he stayed upright sometimes. When she had first seen him, there had been a swagger, but now…

An urchin careened into her, and she snatched him by the arm before he could tear her purse free and flee. "A poor choice, boy. You will not enjoy being locked up with the Scouts."

Whimpering, the boy struggled, pushing at her with unseemly desperation. She grimaced as he kicked out, spreading filth all over her dress. A steamwagon trundled past, loaded down with merchandise and snorting steam. Its driver hollered for people to make way.

"Answer," Taunos began, but she cut him off.

"You do not speak to me! Remember your training, ebr."

He seemed about to speak anyway when the boy twisted free, bolting. He careened off the side of the wagon and picked himself up from the road, quickly losing himself in the chaos of the markets.

Rage shattered the composure she worked so hard for, and she whirled on Taunos. "Do you see what you nearly caused? That boy could have been killed!"

"It did not—"

"Silence!"

He obeyed, thankfully, though his eyes spoke of violence.

Answer turned back to her shopping. A Scout passed by, too late to offer assistance. They were always easy to pick out in their formal uniform of hats, ties, coats, goggles, and boots. Just knowing several Scouts patrolled the market always made her feel better about the chaos, the people of all stations talking, shopping, and occasionally squabbling.

A noble greeted her, and she stopped, forced to exchanged pleasantries. Taunos shifted his weight from foot to foot, looking around with an expression of increasing exasperation, and she smiled, taking slightly more time in conversation than needed.

She led Taunos to another shop, purchasing a trinket even though there was nothing appropriate for Zhedr, and handing the purchase to Taunos to carry. After all, she needed to make up for taking up the merchant's time. As they left, a lower-class man greeted her, and she nodded, sweeping past. She would not have it said she was rude to any free citizen of Codr, but a lower-class person didn't require the time spent chatting that a noble did.

A pack of wayward children raced past, nearly tripping her, and she pursed her lips, checking her pockets reflexively. Taunos juggled the packages he was carrying to tap a little boy on the head as he passed, a hint of a smile at the corners of his mouth. It was odd, almost… gentle.

But her ebr was a creature of violence.

Another steamwagon trundled past, raising a cloud of dust and smoke in its wake. With a huff, Answer pulled Taunos between herself and the vehicle to avoid getting too much dirt on her dress. She gave him a look. Clearly, she would have to have Ketrik remind Taunos of his etiquette lessons.

He walked next to her with a grim expression, carrying the ever-growing pile of packages as she visited shop after shop. Her frustration grew as time passed and she still hadn't found the perfect gift. The shopkeepers did a poor job hiding their irritation with her when she asked them if they had anything else not on display, and to make it worse, Taunos's smile grew with their annoyance.

Finally she found it. They were in an expensive wood shop, and it called to her from the shelves—a beautiful polished wood box, the lid engraved with an image of Temris, goddess of wisdom, and inlaid with gold filament. As with all wood, it was quite expensive, but it was worth it. She carried it to the front delicately, relief bringing a smile to her face. She couldn't take her eyes off it as she handed over the coin. The shopkeeper wrapped it well in paper before putting it in a cheaper metal box and setting it on top of the pile Taunos carried in his arms. With a roll of his eyes, the ebr held it in place with his chin.

Answer beamed. The gift was perfect. She was ready for the ball.

Thanking the shopkeeper, she turned for the door.

Three men burst into the shop, nearly running her over. "Hand over your money!" one shouted, brandishing a knife.

Cold suffused her fingers and she stared at the weapon. By the Ships, all three men had knives! Her muscles locked up and made a statue of her, though she inwardly screamed at herself to move. She braved the Outside, and yet here she was, frozen in place. How dare they rob the store she was in? She'd never been in a fight before, being too well-bred for patrolling. That was reserved for the lowest-born nobles, those who hardly deserved the name Scouts.

And where were the Scouts on patrol? They should be here now! Trembling seized her, chattering her teeth, but she managed to back away. The sharp knives glinted in the light. How much would it hurt if they stabbed her?

Two of the thieves stepped past her, grinning as they did. How dare they? Didn't they know who she was? They shouldered their way past Taunos, making him stumble. One went to the shopkeeper for the cashbox while another strutted to another customer—a woman frozen in the middle of the store looking as terrified as Answer felt.

The third smiled at Answer, boldly taking her jewelry off her piece by piece with his filthy fingers. She shivered, the rage and terror roiling in her, but couldn't move, even when he tugged her purse free from her frozen fingers. Her breath came in little gasps, her eyes fixed on the blades.

A gust of relief went through her when he turned to Taunos. The Outsider shrugged with a foolish little half-smile, his arms filled with her purchases. Of all the ebrs to have attending her during such an emergency, it had to be the one she trusted least, the one holding a grudge against her!

The thief ripped the packages out of Taunos's graceless hands, and Answer cried out. Turning toward her again, the man brandished the knife, and she backed away, covering her mouth with both hands.

He kept pace with her. "Pretty little noble lady. You think you are better than me?"

Her back hit the counter. She was trapped, held at knifepoint by a thief with no respect for his betters. "The Scouts will catch you," she squeaked, willing herself not to come completely undone.

The thief smiled at her. "Maybe, maybe not. What you should ask yourself is, 'Will the Scouts come in time to save me?'"

Answer shook her head, warding off the knife with her bare hands. Her fingers shook visibly. If she made it out of this alive, her mother would have words with her about keeping her composure. The thought was so incongruous, it made her laugh, though it came out more like a choking sound.

Ever since she'd brought in the troublesome Outsiders, she had encountered more violence than she was accustomed to. Why wasn't Ketrik here to protect her? Anyone but Taunos, who would likely laugh if she died at the hands of these impudent thieves. She couldn't die now, not just days after finally receiving the Gift of the Takanis.

The Gift of the Takanis.

Her skin itched where the needle had pierced her during the ritual, almost as if the supernatural knew she didn't believe. She'd only gone through with it for the status it conferred, even though the skin piercing was barbaric. But they said the Gift gave a person sacred abilities. Maybe it could save her.

Fire would be excellent. She conjured up an image of the thieves running from flames. Nothing happened. A gust of wind? Still nothing. Simple, inelegant death? The thief smiled. Frustration and despair fought within her. She hadn't been to Orientation yet—that wasn't for nine days. She could really, really use a miracle right now.

"Please," she whispered.

The thief chuckled. "Do you know where 'please' has gotten me?"

She shook her head. Her voice creaked, her mouth gone dry. "Take everything. I will not tell the Scouts."

The thief stepped closer. His blade rested on her arm. She stared at it, unable to look away, her breath ragged. Tears ran down her cheeks. He traced the edge gently on her arm, and she shuddered. A sob broke from her lips. The thief pressed down, and Answer held her breath, mesmerized by horror. Her skin, miraculously, did not break.

And then Taunos moved.

The ebr grabbed the thief's knife hand and swung him around. The thief almost got away—what did the Outsider think he was doing?—but then, all at once, the ebr ripped the blade from the thief's hand. He threw it, burying it deep in the chest of another thief. Answer gasped. Taunos's expression chilled her to her bones. He looked as calm as if he was at a meeting, except he could very likely get them all killed!

Taunos's fists pounded into the man he had disarmed, landing again and again on his face.

Answer whimpered, covering her face. She didn't want to see, didn't want to hear. There was so much blood! Would he kill them all? What kind of monster was she standing next to? Or was he saving her life?

She forced her eyes open as the sounds faded and Taunos stepped back. Disgust, fear, and gratitude all fought for dominance. Such a close call, but the thief couldn't hurt her, not anymore. The third thief fled, and the shopkeeper approached.

"Thank you, my lady! Thank you."

She struggled to gather her wits. Two thieves lay bleeding on the shop floor, and the ebr stood there, looking surprised. He stooped, retrieving what he could of her things, then held out his hand to her.

She hesitated, still trembling. Her mother would say his victory was her victory. Act like a lady. The ebr had finally done something right. Her family could now claim guardianship of a hero ebr. Which meant *she* had done something right. All the risk of bringing in an Outsider was paying off.

But Answer searched Taunos's eyes. Would he turn on her? Surely not in public, not after... this.

Her voice quavered as she straightened, ignoring his hand with every scrap of pride she had left. "Are you making a habit of rescuing me?"

"I will always defend the defenseless." He clenched his jaw. "But you kill the defenseless, tossing prisoners off cliffs."

Of course he had to bring that up again. She took a deep breath and lifted her chin. She was above him. She would not stoop to his level. "Do I get a lecture, again, on my evils?"

"Do you want one?"

She turned away, staring in silence at the door until the Scouts finally came to restore order. She controlled her breathing, wrapping nobility around her like armor, stilling her trembling. She would not show her fear. She pushed all feelings aside as if nothing had happened. Her mother would be proud of her composure.

Answer gave her statement, berated the Scouts for not being on hand, then left, her ebr trailing her in silence. She gripped her gloves tightly, wishing she could keep her calm so easily. All she wanted was to go home and weep. People were too close to her. There were too many eyes. A gentleman accidentally bumped into her, and she yelped before she could stop herself.

Turning a corner into a less-used side street, she paused and stared at the cavern's ceiling. She had to calm herself. The panic waiting for her could not beat her. Again, she focused on her breath, clinging to her control, blocking out the bustle of the marketplace she had just left. Regaining a small amount of composure, she turned back to the street and stopped, struck by surprise. Taunos stood with his back to her, still holding all her packages. She'd have guessed he'd take his chance to run while she had been distracted.

"I am sorry. About your sister." Her mother would have been furious to hear those words, but they needed to be said.

Taunos grunted. "That will not bring her back."

Answer stifled a sigh. She should have expected as much.

But then he held out the box with her gift for Zhedr. "You may want to check if your present is intact."

She took the package, regarding him with curiosity. "Are we melting down our swords?"

"I thought I would try a new way."

"Well, I rather like it." She checked the present carefully, happy for the distraction. "Good, it is not damaged." She sighed, replacing it in its box. "Still, I should get something else. This has been through a near-tragedy."

"It has a story with it. Nothing else will have that story. And you seemed excited about it," Taunos said. "My sister—no, no reminders of guilt this time—my sister always carried with her an old cloak of mine. The edges were worn and frayed when I left it behind, and now it's even more tattered. But she loves it because it reminds her of all the good times. Reminded her."

Answer gave him a stern look. "I thought you said this was not for placing guilt."

Taunos spread his hands. "Anyway, I never bothered to give her a new cloak because it wouldn't have been the same. She would still have favored the old one."

She hesitated, looking at the box. "I have never heard of any Kamalti treasuring something old and broken over something new and pristine."

"Your obsession with the new—is that why you keep pestering your father to buy those steam-belching machines with gears?"

Answer frowned. "It is not an obsession. It is progress."

She started to hand the package back to him but recoiled. Blood spattered his hands and far up his arms, even sprinkling over his chest. She'd been too worried about herself to notice it before. "Were you injured?"

He chuckled. "No, this blood isn't mine."

Her hands flew to her mouth. Taunos had nearly killed someone right in front of her, and now he was acting as if nothing had happened. How was he so calm? What kind of animal had she brought into her home? Except he wasn't an animal. He knew exactly what he was doing.

That was even more dangerous.

She shuddered. Composure. She must keep her composure. Her

mother would be very disappointed in her if she made a public scene. She turned, walking carefully toward home, with Taunos following her just as his position dictated. She'd been saved by an ebr. Taunos had saved her when she was vulnerable.

And yet, his life was in her hands. His frightening, violent life. What was she to make of that? How could she repay such a debt? Indebted to an ebr, indeed—her mother would be appalled at such a thought!

She kept a firm hold of herself, even ignoring the vagrants she had begun to see more and more often near her home, until she shut her front door behind them. She paused there a moment, eyes closed, leaning against the door.

"Shall I send up a cup of tea?" Taunos asked.

Answer blinked at him. Bile rose in her, and before she could dash to the washroom, she vomited all over Taunos.

~

Answer smiled at her guests to cover the stiffening of her shoulders as Taunos entered the dining room. Around the table sat her fellow Scouts, all dressed in their finery as befitted a dinner party. Everything was going smoothly. So far, Taunos had maintained his manners, leaving her waiting for the inevitable disrespect. Ever since the incident in the market, she hadn't decided what to make of him. He frightened her, and yet...

Oracle was ranting. "Did you truly hear the Justices this morning? I believe they think they are better than us simply because they interpret the Law. But who upholds the Law?"

"The Justices have their function, just as we have ours," said mild-mannered Rubric.

Taunos ladled the soup into bowls and served them, the saucers clattering as he set them down.

Answer winced, but no one took any mind, so she let it go for now. What a shame that the same herbs that blocked him from accessing his magic made him so very bumbling as well. She needed him to impress her guests—there was no way they could top the distinction of having civilized an ebr from the Outside.

"They should give us more credit, that is all," Oracle said.

"How much more credit do you want, Oracle? Truly, I think you wish the Scouts to lead the Kamalti people!" Epiphany waved Taunos away as he paused to fill her goblet with wine.

Taunos shuffled to the staging table on the far wall, where Tegil was arranging bread on a tray. He picked up a teapot, and Answer stifled a wince as Tegil rebuked Taunos loudly enough to hear across the room.

"Not that one, the red tea. The black tea comes after the meal, you imbecile. And don't forget the bread," Tegil scolded. "You do not have much for brains, have you?"

Answer plastered her smile in place, though she wished she could hide in her humiliation. Taunos hadn't forgotten. This was another of his small rebellions. She would have to talk with Ketrik afterward. Her guests didn't seem to mind, but both Tegil and Taunos needed further lessons in etiquette.

"And why not? It is we, after all, who protect the entire Kamalti civilization," Oracle replied.

Answer spoke up, hoping to distract her guests from the mess her ebrs were making. "There is a balance to maintain. Yes, in some things we should be consulted first, I agree on that count, Oracle. But the Justices are better suited to some tasks than we, and the Philosophers in others."

Tea kettle and bread in hand, Taunos returned to the table just as Victor spoke, eyeing her ebr sidelong. "Are you not afraid, having it here?"

"And does the smell not bother you?" Rubric asked.

"He only smells of the Outside. I have made him wash many times, but it does not come off. It must be their natural smell." Answer waved her hand.

"Well, I could not stand it. I do not know how you do." Rubric eyed Taunos as he placed the bread before her and filled her cup with tea.

Their criticisms irritated her like an ill-fitting shoe. They were meant to be impressed, even jealous. If she were to be honest, she would confide that Taunos was an assault on her senses. He smelled of the Outside, and his movements were too big and too fast. They lacked the careful, focused precision she was used to, although every once in a while, she caught him attempting to attain those attributes. His voice was too loud and without nuance. She occasionally heard him singing dreary mourning songs full of melancholy, and his voice had none of the refinements of the fine Kamalti opera singers she was accustomed to. Still, she did not forbid him his singing. Indeed, she'd been surprised to learn the savages *had* music.

"You know their history. It could snap at any time," Victor said.

"I do not think so," Answer said, watching Taunos critically as he placed the other plate of bread on the center of the table, filling the rest of the teacups as he went.

Ever the perfectionist, Epiphany gawked at him. "Look at all the scars. What savages, to deal out such punishment!"

Numerous scars were scattered across his torso, arms, and legs. His old, crude clothing had hidden most of them. Kamalti clothes were more proper, but they revealed all those imperfections. Taunos had told her most warriors Outside, including the two who had come with him, had many scars from battle, mostly on the left side of the body. Her fellow Scouts—those who were trained for patrolling, anyway—were better than the savages, weren't they? Or did they have scars as well?

"You know, they are not proper people. They will not rejoin Kamalti society after their ebr term is up," Victor said.

Answer nodded as Taunos left the room. "I only hope to civilize him a little before he leaves, even though he fights me every chance he gets."

"Why are you so soft on it?"

"He saved my life twice. No civilized person has ever done that. I think that earns him some favor."

Her friends scoffed.

"Anyway, he has some fantastic stories and strange ideas. He is quite entertaining," Answer said, finding herself compelled to stand up for him. "Just the other day—"

"Oh, Answer," interrupted Bluff. "Are you a Scout or a Philosopher? You are talking like your father. Your mother would know better than to say such things!"

"Be careful that your fun does not keep you from Opportunities," agreed Specter, who had been fairly quiet. "Were you to cease to be a Scout, you would also cease to be Answer."

Bluff raised a finger, assuming the same pose he took when lecturing on the Guild floor. "You have your Future to think about, remember? What a shame if some savage should be the cause for you to miss out on Advancement—or a good marriage!"

"What was your name before you joined the Scouts? Do you want to give up all you have earned, including your Scouting name?"

Answer scowled, fury rising in her. Her guests were the closest thing she had to friends, but they were not friends the way she'd learned Taunos thought of the term. His life sounded so simple, without civilization's constant pressures to outperform one's peers. None of her guests would worry about her beyond jostling for position and reputation, nor did she concern herself with them. "Let me worry about keeping my name."

"Anyway," whispered Victor, his tone eager, "Is it true he has magic?"

"Victor! This is not polite conversation for a dinner table," said Bluff.

"Yes. I witnessed it myself. It was horrible," Answer replied, relieved at the change of topic. Maybe now they would be duly impressed.

"Tell us about it!" urged Oracle, waving away the protests of Bluff, who was now glaring his disapproval.

Answer leaned forward. Here, she could demonstrate her greater knowledge. "They can move faster than any being should. They can move things without touching them."

"How terrifying!" breathed Epiphany.

"How do you keep it from killing you in your sleep?" Victor asked, only to be sternly rebuked by Bluff.

"Victor!"

Victor gave an apologetic shrug.

Answer waved him off. "No, it is all right. It is something I thought of. After all, they are barbarians. I could think they might be fine with something like that. So, I have been putting a little of that sleep medicine in his food and drink."

"How do you manage it?" Victor wondered.

"Well, I had to bring my head ebr into the arrangement. He thinks Taunos knows."

"Excuse me, I am sorry, Answer, forgive me for interrupting you," broke in the man who had been cautioning them all about etiquette. "But... Taunos?"

"That is his name."

"You use its name?" exclaimed Oracle incredulously.

"This is exactly what I mean, Answer," said Bluff. "I think you are too close to this ebr. It is an Outsider, after all. Be watchful lest your fondness for it be misconstrued."

"Honestly, Bluff, perhaps you care overmuch about my image," Answer snapped.

The man shut his mouth, set his jaw, and sat back, drawing proper manners and etiquette around himself like a robe of dignity.

Answer sniffed and lifted her chin. "Anyway, Ketrik forces him to drink and eat every day, to make sure he has enough of the medicine."

"It is a boon to have a faithful ebr like Ketrik," Bluff said stiffly. "We must hope he can save you from your folly."

ÌTAL-EHREI
Chapter Fifteen

Courtship is a boring thing, but I will include notes on Rinaryn courtship only because you plague me so, Lenatis! The one initiating courtship will carve a wooden bowl, sometimes offering it to their partner at the beginning of formal courtship, sometimes not until the end. This seems to depend on the solidity of the relationship and on how complex the engraving is, for some get quite intricate with scenery carved into the outside of the bowl. The courtship proceeds with the initiator giving gifts and doing tasks for their partner which they're very much capable of doing on their own, and the parents of the couple consult with the heads of their villages on the match.

—journal excerpt

Kaemada stared out the window. Everything was wrong here. Dread sat in her stomach like a stone from the moment she awoke until she finally drifted off to a restless sleep, cradling her son close as if she could spare him from the terrors that entrapped them.

But there was no way to save him from the cruelty of the palace. She strove against the horrors, even knowing she would lose, because she couldn't bear to surrender. Grateful tears sprang to her eyes every time the servants brought their meals to their rooms; her heart struggled to beat for fear each time they came with dresses for her and suits for Eian. The dinners were the hub of the palace's torture, the life spring of Eian's nightmares.

The past ten meals had featured the king: decreeing a section of homes to be burned, leaving their inhabitants to choose between fire or Angels; accusing one of his guards as a traitor and forcing each of the others to take a turn flaying him during the meal; and beheading his head chef for overcooking the meat, serving his head the following morning at breakfast on a platter.

The worst part was having to remain expressionless. Those women who ruined the king's mirth by sobbing or vomiting were singled out for additional cruelty. There was a vast difference among the women. Captive women and children all lived in the same wing. Others like Aleis, those who joined in with the king's carefree laughter, apparently had rooms elsewhere in the palace and tended to be seated closer to the king, a fact that suited Kaemada just fine. The farther she was from those awful eyes, the better.

Kaemada sighed, brushing a lock of Eian's unruly hair back from his face. He had finally fallen asleep after being up all night with nightmares. She needed to find a way out of here, but every plan she'd thought of was too risky. If they caught her, they'd hurt Eian—or kill him. Where were Ra'ael and Takiyah and Taunos? They should be here by now if the Kamalti took everyone they captured to the city. But how could she contact them? She had tried to think like them, to see the solutions they would see, but such heroics evaded her. As always, she needed them. She leaned her head against the invisible barrier that covered the window, wincing at its cold hardness.

Homesickness gripped her like a plague. She longed to walk through the forest and feel the ground beneath her feet, to let the bird song and fresh air renew her. She missed the ancient stories and songs that steadied her spirit and the easy medicine the forest provided so generously. Worst of all was the lack of wind. Without it, she couldn't breathe. She'd never realized before how much she depended on even the brief presence of a breeze, but here, locked away from the wind, the spirits seemed dead.

The sun shone on the barrier as she watched, and her prayers flowed like futile tears. *Eloí, please help us.* They had to get out of here. Somehow, everything would be all right. It had to be. The alternative was too terrible to bear thinking about.

The door loomed at her across the room. Somehow, the palace psions hadn't discovered her yet. Nightmares of her time in the throne room, of what the king might do to Eian, stole her sleep. She shivered. The comforts around them mocked them, also mocking the suffering of those outside the palace. She avoided them, instead curling up at night in the center of the room in a tight ball with Eian, as if they could shrink together and disappear.

She shivered again, the window's cold biting at her. She was always shivering, growing thin from sleeplessness, fear, and the fact that supper was bird more often than not. Kaemada still couldn't choke down such sacrilege, though her stomach grumbled. Her son shifted in her arms and she brushed his smooth cheek with the back of her fingers. Her fingernails were ragged and bloody. She didn't remember chewing them.

Desperately, Kaemada wracked her mind for any way to escape. She'd tried the window but couldn't break through the barrier, even after she'd smashed furniture on it and filled her hands with splinters while trying to poke holes in it or pry it away. She'd tried the fireplace, but Eian had slipped before they'd gotten halfway up the chimney, and her left arm and leg had nearly given out at the same time. She'd tried eluding her guards, but when they caught her, they ripped Eian from her arms and pinned him to the wall by his throat. Meanwhile, two others beat her, then crushed her into the stone blocks until she passed out from lack of air.

She hadn't made another attempt after that. No matter how hard she fought to protect her son, the guards were stronger. Her left side was still weak and tended to droop when she tired. How could she risk Eian in another escape? Or was it riskier to wait and try to find another way, braving the king all the while? Closing her eyes, Kaemada forced herself to take a breath, shuddering with the panic clawing its way up her throat.

To distract herself, she turned her thoughts to the peril of the other captives. She hated the sight of the women's carefully expressionless faces, and the children were more like statues than children, their eyes always filled with dread of the next coming horror. She couldn't bear to consider the possible reasons there were no boys old enough to go on their yah, while girls ranged in all ages. It was worse to know that she and Eian were well on their way to looking the same way. How could she help them when she couldn't even save herself and her son?

A sharp knock sounded at the door. Eian jerked awake, clawing at her in panic, and she clung to him in return, her heart racing. She kissed his cheek, eyes fixed on the door. Another rap echoed and she trembled. The servants always just came in. Why would someone be knocking?

Gently untangling Eian's arms from around her neck, she motioned for him to stay put. As if approaching a wild animal, Kaemada crept to the door. Her hand shook as she hauled it open.

A guard stood in the doorway. Her eyes flickered over his face, some small relief whispering through her. He was not one of the guards who mimicked the king. Instead, she had marked him as one who at least did not go out of his way to cause misery. It seemed he caused harm only to keep up appearances, to save his own skin. But why was he at her door?

The guard raised his eyebrows at her scrutiny and walked past her, breaking her grip on the handle with casual ease. He stopped in the center of the room as she quickly shut the door and watched him, frozen with fear at the unwelcome change. His eyes flickered over everything, but when he stared too long at Eian, crouching by the wall, Kaemada placed herself between them.

"Why are you here?" Fire laced her voice. Guards had never entered her rooms, not since the first day.

He stared down at her, and she frantically donned her mask of expressionlessness, her only flimsy armor against the nightmares of the palace. He tucked his hands behind his back. "Are you comfortable?"

Kaemada stared, frozen into that blank mask.

His mouth twisted. "I know you heard me."

"I'm a prisoner here." Her tone was flat. "My life and the life of my son are in danger."

He smiled. "My name's Theron. If there's anything I can do for making you more comfortable, let me know."

She shook her head slowly. "You... want to make us more comfortable... while we're prisoners."

"There's no reason you can't live in comfort. Why think of yourselves as prisoners?"

"I would think we weren't prisoners if we could leave." The words were out before she realized, and she shut her mouth so hard she bit her tongue.

"I won't help you escape."

"Then there's nothing we need from you," she said, gathering Eian in her arms again. Her son trembled, his eyes never leaving the guard's face.

"Are you certain? What have you been doing with your time?"

"Not much." She narrowed her eyes at him, not sure she enjoyed talking with him. He was a danger. And yet, wouldn't Ra'ael or Taunos use this opportunity to their advantage somehow?

"That seems very boring," the guard said, smiling again. He had a kind smile, one that reached his eyes, which was unusual here. "Do you do needlework?"

"I'm not very good."

"Well, then. What did you do in your free time?"

She tightened her arms around Eian, her mind whirling. Could she do what her brother would in her place? Swallowing hard, she answered carefully, "Mostly walking through the forests or helping wherever needed. I had no special skills." Or at least none safe to share with him.

The door opened and the dressers entered, carrying a gown and a suit. Her stomach knotted and a bitter taste filled her mouth.

The guard nodded at her. "Tomorrow, I'll bring you a new painting."

She shivered as he shut the door behind him.

~

"Why do we tell the stories and the songs here?" Eian asked. "They do not change this place."

It was the next day, and they sat on the stone floor in the relative haven of their rooms, sharing a midday meal.

"No, but the songs and stories are not meant to change the outer world. They're meant to change you, the inner world."

Eian frowned at his stewed vegetables, pushing them around with his spoon.

Kaemada brushed his hair back from his face. "We tell the stories because they're part of us. Our stories are entwined in the greater stories of our people, our songs in their songs."

"Ra'ael said participation is most important, even when you do not know the words."

Kaemada nodded. "She's right. Participation first, then rhythm, then tune, then words. All are important, but the doing is most essential—the singing of the songs, the dancing of the dances, the telling of the stories. Pieces of the song Eloí sang when they created the worlds are found in the songs of all, so singing your song is important. Just as your story adds to the story of the whole, so your song adds to the greater song of all Rinaryn."

"But we're not home."

Her gaze went distant, a realization striking her. "It's the same for life, isn't it? Participation first, the trying. Then the rhythm, to help all around you to continue the energy, the āti. Then the tune, joining your song to the greater one. Finally, but still important, are the words. Finding the right words is hard, but if you can do it, great good can come about."

"Do the other mothers here tell their children the tales?"

She shook her head. "I do not know, acha'iyih. I do know the stories are important. We, at least, will not forget where we came from. This place takes much away from us, but we will not let it take our past."

She would not let it take their lives, either.

A knock sounded and the guard from yesterday opened the door. With a broad grin, he entered, carrying a covered canvas.

"Here!" he said, sweeping the cover from it. The canvas was painted with greens and browns under a swath of blue. Among the tall trees danced a woman with hints of yellow in her dark hair.

Kaemada stood there gaping until Theron's voice prodded her out of her surprise.

"Don't you like it?" He frowned.

"No, um..." She twisted her fingers together, her thoughts racing. Would he get angry with her if she didn't like it? What would he do if he was angry? "Um, no, it's lovely. It's only... unexpected."

He laughed. "You didn't expect for finding such beauty here?"

She hesitated, then let herself smile a little. "No, not really. But I'm glad to find it."

"You're not alone. If you look only to darkness and monsters, that's all you'll find. Life may be hard here, but there's also beauty."

She was still gaping as he turned and left the room, the door closing with a soft click. Kaemada stared at the painting throughout the day. What did it mean? Did she dare hope for some safety, some reprieve from the endless fear? Or was it another trick? It loomed over her, smug in its own mystery. Even when the dressers and the stern guards came to escort them to dinner, she thought about the painting. She tried to watch Theron as he ate and laughed higher up the table toward the king, but he never looked her way and she was left with her own uncertainty.

Soon enough, the king caught her eye and gave her a too-broad grin. She fixed her gaze on her mostly empty plate. She'd avoided the meat entirely, for she wasn't sure what it was and had a suspicion it was something horrible. The king laughed, his voice ringing off the stone walls around them, at a joke he had made about cannibalism. Catching the terror in Eian's eyes, Kaemada squeezed his hand under the table. She placed her fork to the side of her plate, wincing as Eian's fork clanged against the plate when he moved to do the same. Head down, scalp prickling, she waited, but no retribution came from the head of the table, so she sat gripping Eian's hand and praying.

As soon as the king left the room, Kaemada rose, cautious to avoid seeming too eager, yet goaded by the pressing need to be anywhere but the hall. Women and children with empty eyes formed an orderly line, and she and Eian joined it. Following their guard escorts, they filed out of the doors. The carefree women swished down the hallway past them, sometimes jostling the line. Others ran past giggling, hand in hand with guards, and disappeared around a corner into a wing of the palace she'd never seen.

Kaemada forced her gaze back down to the floor, checking quickly on Eian. The line of captives turned down another hallway, silent and tense. The line thinned as each reached their rooms, and Kaemada couldn't help but fix her gaze on her own door at the end of the hallway. It was so close —not safety, but the nearest thing in this place.

A hand grabbed her, slamming her against the wall so hard it drove the breath from her lungs.

"No, please, no," she mouthed, unable to speak, unable to breathe. Pushing with her feet, she flung herself from the wall, tackling Eian.

They'd worked out a system: he crouched in a ball as she hit him, curling around him, every part of him shielded by her body. They couldn't get at him this way, and all she needed to do was outlast the guards. Not until help came—help never came in this place—but until the guards got bored.

One of them grabbed her by the hair, yanking her head back. The pain sparked tears to her eyes, but she tightened her hold around Eian. The line of women continued to move, every head down. No one could risk helping. She couldn't blame them, knowing what would happen.

The guard pulled harder, and she gritted her teeth, squeezing her eyes shut against the pain. Her arms tightened further around Eian even as hair ripped free from her scalp. He huddled up as small as he could get, and she locked her arms around him.

The pressure on her head ended with a sharp tug. She landed back on the floor, the stone bruising her knees, and she ducked her head, concealing Eian again. The sounds of a scuffle reached her ears, and cautiously, she peeked up.

A guard had slammed another against the wall in much the same manner as Kaemada had been. Snatching up Eian, Kaemada sprinted for her door on trembling legs. Guards rarely fought in view of the captive women, though she suspected they often fought amongst themselves. What else could explain the bruises, scrapes, and black eyes so many of them wore?

"I claimed her," one guard was saying as she scuttled past, his voice incongruously calm. "Spread the word. No one touches her unless they want for dealing with me."

There was a murmur.

"The boy too. I'll view it as a challenge if anyone touches the two of them, and you know how I deal with challengers. Have your fun elsewhere."

Her neck prickled and she shuddered, glancing backward as she fumbled with the doorknob. Theron shoved away from the guard who had attacked her, his expression thunderous. Fear closed up her throat. Her door finally gave and she burst inside, slamming the door closed behind her and racing to the farthest corner of the sleeping room to huddle with Eian.

The door to the main chamber opened and shut. Shaking, Kaemada pried Eian's hands from her neck and shoved him under the bed. Her muscles quaked as she crept forward. She wasn't sure what she would do, but no one was going to harm Eian.

Nothing happened.

She peeked out of the room. There, sitting on one of the chairs she and Eian refused to use and staring at the painting, lounged Theron. Kaemada paused, terrified of what would happen next, and very, very tired of being so constantly afraid. She took a deep breath and approached.

"They won't bother you anymore," he said with a smile.

She stood there, uncomfortable in her rumpled gown, desperately wanting to believe him and terrified to do so. Danger continuously came here when she least expected it, but it was exhausting to be constantly on edge and ready for it.

"Are you all right?" he asked, surprising her further.

She nodded slowly.

He smiled again. "Go on back and sleep. The left half of your face droops when you're tired, did you know that? I'll sit here and watch, so you know no one will disturb you."

Kaemada stared at him. But at last, exhaustion overcame terror. She turned without a word, closing the door of the sleeping room and lying down in front of it. Face wet with tears, Eian crawled across the floor and cuddled up against her. She wanted to sing him a lullaby, but the music wouldn't come. She'd had no time to herself since being captured, and Eian was increasingly needy. She had nothing left to give. She was empty, her soothing words made meaningless by their surroundings. So she just held him and lay with her back to the door, waiting for the next terrible thing to happen.

~

It had been a long time since she'd heard laughter, so when Eian laughed many days later, it startled a laugh out of her, even while tears sprang to her eyes. She watched Eian chatter away at Theron and smiled through tears. The rooms were full of Theron's gifts, from paintings to poems to carvings, and he'd come early that day, before supper, bearing flowers and a basket full of sweets from the kitchen. Eian grinned around a mouth so full his cheeks bulged while Theron shoved two rolls in his mouth and made a face.

Kaemada looked down at the necklace in her hand, the latest gift from Theron.

"Beauty for enhancing your beauty," he had said. Except she wasn't beautiful, and she knew it. Still, it was nice to have the comfort Theron offered, comfort she sorely needed. He always smiled and waved to Eian during these visits and sometimes came with gifts especially for him.

Fingers trembling, she fastened the necklace around her neck. Her eyes roamed the shelves full of his other gifts. Was Theron courting her? She shivered, her mind flashing back to the gifts Tikatae had rained on her and how badly that had ended. She had no interest in courtship, and even if she did, this was not the time or place for romance. And yet, how could she say no? If she did, their danger would increase. Not that they were safe now. He was the kindest person she'd met in the palace, but that didn't exactly say much. She and Eian were still trapped. Still in danger.

Having Theron on her side was an enormous benefit. Already, the guards were keeping clear of them. Her brother had told her countless stories of getting out of tight spots due to the friendship of a guard. She could do that too, couldn't she? Was this the way out she'd been looking for? And the flowers. The blue blossoms were spirits' tears, good for calming nightmares, and the yellow ones were dasavu, which took down swelling. The small purple petals were from bitterroot and could be crushed and made into a salve to help heal cuts, while the roots soothed pain.

"Do you like them?" Theron asked.

Tension radiated from her shoulders down her back, but she nodded. This was something, at least. Something they could use to make life better until they could get out of here. "Are there more?"

He nodded. "As many as you like."

She forced a smile, taking a jam-filled roll for herself. They wouldn't have to eat at supper if they filled up now, and she had to admit the food was delicious. Theron turned and grinned at her.

Searching for something to say, she voiced a question she'd been wondering about since her arrival. "Why is it that when it snows it does not fall all over, but only in certain places? The snow hangs in the sky in a way I have never seen before."

"That's the dome."

"The dome?"

"You don't know that word?"

She shook her head.

He smiled and illustrated with his hands. "Here's the city, under. And above is like an overturned bowl, only with holes in places. So, when the rain and snow hit the bowl—the dome—and they slide away except where there are holes. That's why crops are only planted under the holes."

"Can you escape using the holes somehow?" The question was out before she knew it.

Theron's tone hardened like the stone surrounding them. "There's no way out, Kaemada. Turn your thoughts for surviving the here and now. Life will be much better that way."

She lowered her head, shrinking in on herself. Eian froze, holding another roll halfway to his mouth.

The door opened and her heart sank. The dressers had arrived. Without a word, Theron rose and left, and her stomach churned while the dressers stuffed her and Eian into fancy clothes as if they were dolls. Once their silent work was done, the dressers left, and Theron came back in. She twisted her fingers apprehensively, trying to stammer an apology.

He looked down at her, and she felt very small. "Don't apologize, Kaemada. Just put thoughts of escape out of your head. Is it so bad here?"

Yes, she wanted to reply, but she bit her tongue before the word could escape. They couldn't lose the dubious safety of his presence. "I… I'm glad to have met you," she managed.

He smiled at her and swept his arm toward the door. "Time to supper. Ready?"

She nodded, taking a deep breath as she assumed her mask of impassivity. Squeezing Eian's hand and glancing down at him to be sure he was ready too, she followed Theron into the hallway.

They were nearing the dining hall when one of the carefree women of the palace approached, blocking their path. Kaemada drew Eian back toward the wall with her, lowering her gaze. Before, she'd actively avoided the carefree women, but now, there seemed no need. After all, Theron was with her.

"Theron, instead of duty in the dining hall, you're for riding into the City. There's a potential plot against the king you need for learning the truth of," the woman commanded.

Theron bowed. "As my king demands," he replied, presenting her with the deference the women normally assumed for the guards.

Dread coiled at the core of her. Theron would not be at supper to protect them. And this plot—she had seen the suffering of the people with her own eyes. They needed justice, not punishment. The woman sauntered off and when Theron began to walk away as well, Kaemada clutched his arm.

"Theron, do not go. Does not everyone deserve a little mercy?"

He backhanded her. The floor slapped her as she fell. Kaemada pushed herself up, dazed and shaking, pain roaring in her face. Had she been completely wrong about him? Eian crouched behind her, trembling, and she held her hand to her cheek, pushing Eian behind her with the other. Fear, confusion, and outrage filled her, and she resisted the urge to shake off Eian's grasp on her arm.

Fighting would do no good. Theron was stronger, and if she fought, she would only be condemning Eian to death. She clenched her jaw briefly before wincing and gingerly touching her cheek and jaw again. She tasted blood. Theron gazed down at her as she scrambled backward with Eian, awkward in the fancy dress.

"I go where my king demands." He turned and strode down the corridor, the sound of his boots on the floor fading as he left.

Later that night, a knock sounded at her door. She opened it and promptly blocked the doorway with her own slight body when she saw it was Theron, struggling to shut it on him. He sighed and picked her up by the arms with ease, moving her out of the way so he could enter. Fear's cold fingers clutched at her heart as she cast a glance to the other room where Eian slept.

Theron set her down and gently touched her bruised cheek and jaw, where she'd rubbed in the crushed dasavu petals.

Kaemada froze, her heart pounding against her ribs.

"I wish you hadn't made me do this," he said.

She stared at him blankly.

He took her hands in his. "I regret having to hit you. I didn't wish you pain."

Kaemada pressed her lips together, unable to trust herself to respond. She hadn't made him do anything.

Theron let her go, turning away. "I must serve my king. And if any doubted my allegiance, well... you know what would happen. You have seen it with your own eyes. Tell me you don't wish that fate on me."

Despite herself, sympathy rose in her to join the other roiling emotions. Perhaps she hadn't been wrong about him. Perhaps he was still a good person at heart. His poetry reminded her of her father's, and how could such an artist be evil? All he needed was a chance, wasn't it?

Theron's voice lowered. "There are things we all must do in life. Things we may or may not want for doing. But they don't need for defining us."

She shivered, lowering her gaze and trying to think of how to respond.

Then he was there, kneeling in front of her, holding her hands in his once more. "Listen. Here, with no one around but me, you are safe, always. I would never wish you harm."

"The king is a cruel man." Kaemada frowned, drawing away from him, every muscle tensing.

"He does what needs for doing. Order must be maintained."

"Have you seen all the suffering, both inside and outside the palace? No one with the power to stop it should allow it to go on!"

"The king doesn't need for letting anyone live here in the palace, you know. But he does, and now there're servants who're well paid and beautiful accommodations for his guests," Theron said, gesturing to the room around them as proof.

"That does not mean the way things are is good."

"We're all trapped here, Kaemada. All of us, trapped in this ancient, ancient city. The king's king, and doing the best he can."

Kaemada shifted, staring down into his earnest eyes. She wished she knew what to do next, what path would lead to safety. She was drowning, out of her depth. It was too hard to keep looking at him, so she looked around the room instead, but that was no better. There was nowhere she could look that she didn't see him in the gifts he had given her. And she had begun to enjoy the time he spent with them, despite her misgivings. She'd enjoyed trading tales with him and talking more freely. And the medicine. She could use that to help the other battered captives, at least a little.

She drew a deep breath. Theron was in danger, just as she was. At any time, the king could turn on him, and for no reason at all. He was right. She had brought his strike upon herself with her foolishness. Some part of her railed against the notion, but she pushed it far, far away. It was better to accept things as they were, to accept her own fault. It was the only way to have any peace to this place.

"I should not have asked that of you," she whispered. "I should not have asked you to disobey the king."

"I'm a loyal man, Kaemada. That doesn't mean I don't care to you."

For a moment, Tikatae's face flashed before her eyes, his voice in her ears. Her stomach clenched, but she breathed, pushing the fear and nagging unease away. She would work instead to avoid causing any commotion, and surely she could convince Theron to help them escape.

After all, he was only doing what he needed to survive. Just like her.

Chapter Sixteen

To be sure, it falls to the noble classes to lead the common people into the Future. We have the advantages of Birth, Prestige, and University. Of course, these can be said to be disadvantages as well, but no matter. We must ensure the continuation of the Right of Elect, regardless of what others may say! It is crucial to continued success in our efforts at balance to allow our children, upon reaching the age of majority, the choice of joining the Scouts, Philosophers, or Justices. Boys of noble Birth must, of course, finish University first, but the young ladies should continue to have their chance...

-scrap of a letter between two noble houses in Codr

Ra'ael centered the dress on its hanger, slipping it into Dode's wardrobe. Worry nibbled at the edges of her mind like a pest, regardless of how she tried to focus on the details of the mundane chore. Dode was at a meeting with the other nobles, and she wasn't there to protect her if another assassin came. The Scouts forbade Ra'ael's presence, and most of the Justices backed them, even though she'd been on her best behavior for nearly four moons. When had she begun to care so much about Dode's wellbeing? Every meeting, Ra'ael found herself pacing the floors, cleaning obsessively, and straightening what was already tidy, even though a pair of Scouts escorted Dode to and from meetings. Having a Rinaryn bodyguard had not made Dode more popular, and Ra'ael loved her for that.

The door in the entryway slammed. The hanger nearly leapt from her hands, but she caught it, setting it down with the clothes she was holding. Who could it be? Dode always shut the door firmly but quietly. Never slamming. But why would any intruder slam the door? Ra'ael cautiously crept to the threshold of Dode's bedroom, reaching it just as Dode burst inside. She would have knocked right into her if it weren't for Ra'ael's quick hop backward.

The old woman rubbed her hands together, a manic light in her eyes. "I have wonderful news!"

Ra'ael pressed her lips together, taking deep breaths to slow her racing heart.

With a quick step past her, Dode tore through her wardrobe, holding up gowns and then tossing them away. Ra'ael stared at Dode. She'd never seen her so excited.

Throwing aside another dress, Dode continued, "I have convinced the Opera House to allow a little entertainment in seven days. We have little time to prepare. You and your friends will be brought together, and you will sing your folk songs and dance your folk dances. It will be a wonderful evening!"

Ra'ael bristled. She'd just put all those clothes away. Dode hadn't even acknowledged startling her, so wrapped up was she in this fantasy of hers. Folk songs and folk dances, indeed. Ra'ael had no intention of putting her culture on display to be sliced into pieces and dissected by the monster of Kamalti high society.

"We're to be your entertainment?"

Dode dropped the clothes she held in a heap, finally looking at her. Disappointment lined the edges of her frown. "I could order you to do this, you know. It would be fully within my rights. But I hoped you would enjoy this, that you might think of this as an opportunity to help Kamalti get to know Rinaryn ways."

"You assume that's a goal of mine." Ra'ael eyed the pile of clothes heaped on the floor. She'd have to put everything away. Again.

"I thought we had gotten past this." Pain formed an undercurrent of Dode's voice. "You have served me well these four faces, and I hope you think I have been kind to you. Why should we let the nonsense continue to spread that your people are animals?"

"Why should I care what they think? My people do not—the Kamalti might as well not exist from their perspective."

"Well, do not let that stop you from having a nice evening." Dode's tone gentled further. "I thought you might be getting homesick and want to see your friends."

Ra'ael hesitated. She yearned to see Takiyah and Taunos again. Dode had checked on Taunos twice for her, reporting that he seemed well-treated, all things considered, but there was no word about Takiyah. Still, Takiyah was smart and strong. Taunos was the one who needed watching, to make sure he didn't do something stupid. There was no longer Kaemada to worry about. She had to make sure the others didn't die as well, murdered by sneering Kamalti. In that moment, seven days seemed too long. She wanted to check on them right away, to talk to them, to see for herself that they were well.

Dode pressed on. "You take solace in your familiar habits. I know you do. This is a chance to let them spread like seeds sprouting in the gardens."

"Will it be honorable? We're not to be mocked." Ra'ael drew herself to her full height, despite the fact that she was much shorter than Dode.

A smile lightened her expression. "Do you think the great singers and performers of Kamalti society think themselves mocked? No! Well, not when done correctly. When done right, it is uplifting and exalting. And it will be done correctly for you—authentically. I have reserved the Opera House, did I not mention? All Kamalti performers strive to one day earn the privilege of performing at the Opera House."

Ra'ael tapped her finger against her lips. Kaemada had longed to bring Kamalti and Rinaryn together. Perhaps this spectacle would honor her memory. At least it might open dialogue and sow curiosity. Maybe they could find a way to make the Kamalti more lenient toward those who left the paths. And even if none of Kaemada's dreams came true, this would be a chance to check on Takiyah and Taunos.

"Fine."

A broad, giddy smile split Dode's face.

The next few days were a whirlwind of activity, filled with meetings with the Opera House, tailors, and other vendors as Dode rushed to plan the event with Taunos's and Takiyah's captors. In the evenings, Ra'ael and Dode argued about content with raised voices, a bent plate, and a cup with a crumpled handle bearing witness. After three vicious nights, they agreed on some children's songs and a few group dances. Ra'ael banned all religious dances and songs and refused to budge regardless of how hard Dode pressed her. Eventually, Dode relented.

The evening of the performance, Dode grabbed Ra'ael by the hand and pulled her into the small guest chamber set aside for her that Ra'ael never used. With a flourish, Dode opened a bag. Inside lay Ra'ael's own proper Rinaryn clothing, clean and folded. Ra'ael gasped. Tears sprang to her eyes, and her hand trembled as she touched the soft alanshorn wool. It felt like home.

"I had these professionally cleaned so you could wear them tonight. And look. Look farther in the bag."

Ra'ael dug her hands in, pulling out her clothes. The thin blue shroud of priestesshood lay beneath them, also clean and folded. She threw it over her shoulders immediately, though it sat wrong on the too-smooth Kamalti dress. Something else weighed down the bag, and she reached back in, drawing out her small hand drum and the rattles for her wrists and ankles. She stared at them. They had been in her pack.

Dode smiled. "I managed to get your pack from storage. I thought you would like to wear your own things tonight."

"Thank you." The words came out in a whisper. It was strange, the depth of gratitude she was floundering in. They were only things. And yet they reminded her of home, and she had missed home so very much.

Dode nodded and pulled the door shut behind her as she left. Ra'ael wasted no time discarding the Kamalti garb. As she pulled on the familiar clothes, serenity filled her. She tugged on her boots and then finally the priceless blue cloth, which draped perfectly. A glimmer of optimism rose in her like a fresh spring breeze. Dressed like this, comfort and authority filled her once more. Dressed like this, she was a woman in control of her destiny. She was loath to ever take these clothes off again.

It was difficult to remember the Kamalti protocol regarding ebrs as she left the house with Dode. She'd gotten used to the silly rules, but now, with everything about her screaming Rinara and home, she found her head rising, her steps quickening, and her lips curving upward. Her loose hair flowed about her like a sleek, black waterfall, and every movement sang of grace and strength. Kamalti heads turned as she passed, and she smiled fully, enjoying that power again. Let them look. Let them see her and remember.

The Opera House's columns of carved rock towered several stories above them. The building formed a perfect circle, open at the top. Of course, that was not unusual for Kamalti public buildings—there was no weather here to ward off with roofs—but somehow, the Opera House made the design feel artful instead of unnecessary. Ra'ael followed Dode to the side and paused. A sign hung above the door, and while she couldn't read the blocky Kamalti letters, she had no trouble reading her name in flowing Rinaryn script.

So that was why Dode had asked her to write their names. She grinned at Dode, who beamed in return.

"I hope you feel honored," Dode said.

Honored, valued, maybe even loved. Maybe this wouldn't be so bad, after all. "I do. Thank you, Dode."

Stepping into the lavish interior after Dode, all words were stolen away. She still cared little for stone, but here, the polished stonework gleamed in the light of hundreds of lanterns. Wooden decorations, polished and stained, accented the hallway with luxury. And this was only an entryway! If the entrance for performers was so grand, what did the main entrance look like? Of course, it was nothing compared to a grassy meadow under the open sky, but it was the best these Kamalti could do since they insisted on hiding underground.

The hallway opened to a thickly carpeted chamber with curtains hanging along the walls. Dode pointed out the dressing rooms, which Ra'ael had refused to use, and then the simple door that led onto the stage. Two Kamalti approached, a shuffling older man and a younger man with a powerful stride. The older man bowed and made empty platitudes toward Dode, which Ra'ael ignored. The younger man grabbed her bag. She tightened her grip, narrowing her eyes at him. Itching for a fight, was he? There was no way she was letting go of her drum and rattles again, and certainly not to an ill-mannered Kamalti.

"He has to check that you brought no weapons, Ra'ael," Dode said. "Honestly, Kerim, I assure you there is no need for worry."

Staring the man down, Ra'ael let go of one of the bag's handles, keeping a firm grip on the other.

He scowled, grumbling under his breath as he searched the bag far more thoroughly than was warranted. Finally, the Kamalti threw the other handle of the bag back at her, which she caught easily. He grimaced, and she smiled at his back while the two walked away.

Dode raised her browridge. "You need not provoke security so."

"He provoked me. Where were his manners?"

The entry door opened again and Taunos stomped in. His shoulders slumped and his entire head was shaved bald. There was not a hair on his head, no stubble on his face, even his eyebrows were gone. Tension lined his face, but a fire burned in his eyes. She didn't see any signs of injury or mistreatment, even with the Kamalti clothing baring his torso and arms, but his gait was so... wrong. Fear crawled up her spine as she stared at him.

Taunos glowered at the floor, barely glancing up at all as he crossed to the dressing room and slammed the door. Behind him, an older man walked with an inscrutable expression, his gaze flickering over Ra'ael before he focused his attention on Dode, giving her a very proper bow.

Dode returned the formality. "It is good to see you, Lord Mekl."

"And you, Lady Dode."

"I missed seeing you in Council last meeting."

"Yes. I had an urgent matter to attend to. Did you hear about my daughter?"

Dode's expression turned sardonic. "Your daughter, Answer, who chose the Scouts over the Philosophers?"

"She was with the ebr there when the market was held up."

Ra'ael's gaze flicked to the dressing room, and she bridled some in Taunos's defense, though she held her tongue. He was far more than "the ebr there."

Dode raised a hand to her mouth. "By the—! How terrible! Is she all right?"

"Yes. The ebr is slow, but he managed to take down the culprits. Even so, it was quite the ordeal for any lady to go through, even a Scout."

"A daughter needs a father. And you are a good father, Lord Mekl."

Ra'ael watched Taunos carefully as he emerged from the dressing room in his Rinaryn clothes, which suited him much better. His anger made sense. She'd be angry too if she'd had to save the life of that terrible Scout, Answer.

Taunos stumbled toward her as if he'd drunk too much firewater, but she could smell none of the drink on him. He had none of the loss of inhibition, either—if anything, he was more inhibited, less casual than his typical self. The sense of wrong screamed louder, and the hairs on the back of her neck rose.

"What's wrong with you?" she hissed.

Taunos stared at her for a while before speaking, and she found it difficult to read his expression. "How are you, Ra'ael? Are you being treated all right?"

Ra'ael frowned at him. She looked good—she'd made certain of it. It should be obvious she was being treated well. Taunos, however... His face was worn, his eyes weary, with none of the twinkling that had always irritated her, as if he was laughing at some joke of the spirits. There was no laughter there now, just an angry fire. She resisted the urge to shudder.

"Yes... Are you?" She threw the question back at him pointedly.

"Fine."

"What in the realms is wrong with you?"

"You're not looking forward to this, are you?"

"We have a chance to partake in our own culture and maybe honor Kaemada's memory by inspiring some curiosity among these people."

"I'm not a dancing tailosae to gibber and jump around on command," he snapped.

"I had the same initial thought. But we have to do this, so we might as well enjoy ourselves." Ra'ael winced inwardly as she echoed Dode, but she kept her gaze steady.

Taunos shook his head, his eyes smoldering. "You feel free to enjoy yourself. Being scheduled entertainment like this... It's debasing."

"What good will come of this anger, Taunos?"

"Who says I'm angry for some good to come about from it?"

Ra'ael's mouth twisted. "Well, do not take it out on me. This wasn't my idea."

"I had thought you would be dead set against it."

She shrugged. "I changed my mind. Taunos, I do think some good can come of this. We could use some good in our lives. I wanted the chance to see you and Takiyah again. I thought you would be fighting to honor your sister's memory, not sulking."

His expression darkened with such violence she drew back. "This isn't sulking. This is anger."

"As you say." Worry gnawed at her. Something was seriously wrong with him—his heavy movements, the dead look behind the anger in his eyes. How bad was it? Were his reflexes affected? She threw a punch at him, an easy thing to block.

Her fist collided with his jaw. He staggered back and crashed to the floor. Ra'ael stared, speechless, as Taunos took his time recovering. Her punch never should have landed, even unexpected as it was. Even if he hadn't dodged, he should have been able to catch his balance easily. This was Taunos, the hero of Torkae. And she'd laid him flat out.

"Ra'ael, what are you doing?" Dode snapped.

"What in the Clouded Crystals is going on here?" Mekl swore at the same time, apparently forgetting his manners.

Opera House guards descended on her, clutching her hard by each arm. The Kamalti were entirely too touchy about her blood rage, but there were bigger troubles here than them. Her focus remained on Taunos. What were his captors doing to him? And why would he put up with it?

"Taunos, what's wrong with you?" Ra'ael shouted.

He rubbed his jaw, shaking his head.

"If she is unstable, perhaps we should call off the event. We do not want a stampede if she erupts," Mekl said.

Dode stepped toward Ra'ael, but Mekl held out a hand, stopping her. "Take care."

"Pah! I will be fine, Lord Mekl."

"Are such barbarous shows of violence common among your people?" Mekl looked at Taunos, his gaze critical and aloof, with no sign of concern for his wellbeing. Ra'ael resisted the urge to snarl at him.

"I'm fine." Taunos dusted himself off and gestured at Ra'ael. "She's fine, too. You can let her go. She's not going to hurt anyone."

The guards looked at Lord Mekl for confirmation. His gaze darted between Dode and Taunos, and he gave a reluctant nod. "Let her go."

"Whatever got into you?" Dode asked Ra'ael, at once angry and concerned.

S. Kaeth

Ra'ael shook her head, trying to contain the rising panic. She wanted to run over to Taunos and shake him until he told her everything. She wanted to whisk him away from his captors, but she couldn't leave Takiyah alone. If Taunos was affected so, what was Takiyah enduring? "He should have blocked it, and easily. I never should have been able to land that punch."

"Is that how your people greet each other?" Dode's voice held judgement.

Ra'ael clenched her fists. How could Dode not understand? "Something is wrong with him!"

Dode shook her head, and Ra'ael knew this conversation wasn't over. Dode would expect an explanation at her home, and Ra'ael fully intended to give her one. There were protocols to observe here, just as there were at home. She would find out what was going on, but she would go about it in such a way that she could use Dode's resources to aid in her investigation.

"Are we to continue?" The older Kamalti from before was back, wringing his hands and looking askance at Ra'ael. She refrained from glowering at him or provoking him—barely. Mekl, Dode, and the administrator—what was his name... Kerim?—stepped to the side to discuss the potential dangers of proceeding in hushed whispers. Taunos began to pace, though it was more of a trudge, his grace and balance and energy stolen from him somehow.

Ra'ael stood in his path, but he barreled through her like she wasn't even there.

"Taunos, what happened to you?" she asked again, walking beside him. He gave her a black look and stopped, leaning against the wall.

"Taunos, please."

"I do not believe you, Ra'ael. Going along with this?"

"I'm sorry I hit you. Why did you not block it?"

He scowled. "You know I'm not mad about that."

Ra'ael crossed her arms, her temper rising. "Why did you not dodge?"

"It does not matter," he said and stared up at the ceiling.

Ra'ael narrowed her eyes at him. He was impossible. Clearly, he'd already decided something, and that something didn't include telling her. Nothing would change his mind—he was as bad as Kaemada in that. As bad as Kaemada had been.

Hastily, she turned her thoughts elsewhere. She stared at the entry door, waiting for it to open and admit Takiyah. Behind her, Dode was insisting that the risk was low, and the administrator worried about recuperating their costs if they cancelled. Ra'ael waited, letting Taunos

212

sulk while hushed voices made plans for their future without consulting them. Did she want to continue with the event? She didn't know. She did want to see Takiyah, she knew that much. Was Takiyah being treated like Taunos?

The administrator nodded, bowed, and hustled away. Dode came over to her with Mekl walking at her side, and Ra'ael straightened. Beside her, Taunos continued to lean against the wall, staring at the ceiling, and Ra'ael shifted to stand between him and Mekl, a strange flicker of protectiveness washing over her.

"We will proceed," Dode said. "Two famous opera singers are scheduled after you, so we may as well. However, Ra'ael, I feel I must warn you again about your precarious situation with the Scouts."

"I know," Ra'ael snapped. Eloi's light, she hadn't meant to hit Taunos at all!

Dode frowned at her but said nothing else. They waited, the four of them, in silence while the murmuring of voices filtered in from the door leading to the stage. The seats must be filling up out there. Attendants ran in every direction, readying final preparations and shouting orders to each other. And yet, the door drew Ra'ael's eye, and Takiyah still did not come through.

Finally, the lights dimmed. "It is time," one of the attendants said breathlessly, pausing by them. His gaze was on Mekl and Dode, instead of Ra'ael or Taunos. "Are they ready?"

"Takiyah's not here!" Ra'ael protested.

"We must stay on schedule." the attendant said.

"We are expecting another Rinaryn. The tall one," Dode said. "You will be sure to have someone watch for her and send her right out when she arrives."

"Yes, my lady," the attendant said. "Come, the usher is here to show you to your viewing boxes."

Dode turned and smiled at Ra'ael before leaving, but Ra'ael found it hard to smile back. She glanced at the door again. Where was Takiyah? Taunos began pacing again, and she noticed him looking toward the door, too. The attendant beckoned to them, but Ra'ael ignored him. What did time matter when Takiyah wasn't there yet?

The attendant stabbed his finger toward the curtain. "Get over here, you animals, or I will have the guards force you. And if I do, mark my words, your Kamalti betters will not let you see the daylight orbs for many cycles!"

Well, that wouldn't help her make anything better for Taunos or

Takiyah, wherever she was. Ra'ael walked over, touching Taunos's shoulder lightly as she passed to draw him with her. She glanced at the door again before the stage swallowed them. The spirits had to hear them, didn't they? She'd been careful not to include any religious songs, but that didn't mean she couldn't pray as she danced. The music always made the prayers flow more freely.

Lights blinded her. Dimly, she was aware of a sea of Kamalti hidden somewhere in the darkness, watching. It felt more like a dream than reality. Taunos began the beat on the drum, and the sound reverberated off the walls, filling the air. His timing was off and the sound did not float freely in the open sky as it should have. Suppressing a wince, Ra'ael turned in a slow circle to begin the Preparation Dance. Taunos's clumsiness made it difficult to follow the rhythm, and sometimes she found herself leading him, though the dancer leading the drummer was wrong, wrong, wrong! Still, she did her best to embrace the dance, performing the sweeping circles that would allow small prey animals to flee, clear the land of small rocks, and lay the grass down flat.

Taunos's expression, caught in glimpses as she turned, was creased with concentration. Dismay clenched a fist in her gut. The beat was something a child of five summers could keep. Taunos should have been able to do it with ease, yet he failed at the rhythm. The side door continued to call her, where Takiyah still did not appear.

The Preparation Dance ended, and Ra'ael took the drum from Taunos, standing next to him. She met his gaze, trying to give him some reassurance or comfort, but her heart was low, and her head was full of worries. She tapped the beat, then nodded the cue to begin the next song, a child's lullaby such as she'd sung to Eian. Taunos's baritone was strong and clear, but he sang as if he was sleeping, and they were sorely missing Takiyah to lend the complexity of a second harmony. Frustration and worry roiled like a storm inside her as they ended, and she was left with intense dissatisfaction. Songs were important. It would have been bad enough, ruining the music at home. It was even more humiliating to do so on display in front of people who despised them when they thought of them at all. This had been a huge mistake.

But the Honoring Song was next, and Ra'ael threw her heart into it. Taunos remained behind the beat more often than not, scowling to himself as he tried to match time with her. She imagined the lines of Rinaryn that should stretch beyond them as they circled and twirled, honoring those who were no longer with them: Kaemada, her own family, and all those whose voices no longer joined their song. Their song, which was so much smaller than it should have been.

The Seeker Song's strong beat and indomitable air seemed to re-energize Taunos somewhat, and the sound of the rhythmic stamping as they clapped their hands against each other's hands, chests, arms, or legs in the complex rhythm filled the space. At one point, Taunos's palm hit her hard, rocking her backward. She came right back at him on reflex, resuming the rhythm, part of her eager for a spar. They were both Galod's students, after all. And for just a moment, he grinned, and there was a glimmer of the real Taunos in his eyes, ready to meet her challenge. Pride filled Ra'ael in the wild rush of music, a balm to her soul as they followed up with two children's songs.

Taunos ended their selection of songs playing on a borrowed pipe as Ra'ael lent her powerful contralto to the ancient lay of Emarfah the Fair. The instrument was slightly different than a Rinaryn pipe, and the sound a little off, but it was better than nothing.

Then it was over. Takiyah had not come, and as Taunos returned the pipe and stomped off the stage, his shoulders drooped once more. Ra'ael sighed as Mekl collected Taunos and brought him up the stairs to the balconies of the Opera House. He left without a word to her. She'd failed him. This event had helped nothing. Something was wrong with both Taunos and Takiyah, and it was her responsibility to fix it. Yet as a captive, what could she do?

"That was beautiful." Dode swept over with a smile.

Ra'ael looked at her and then the stairs Taunos had trudged up, unable to force a smile in return. Applause rang out as she followed Dode out of the Opera House, and then a single, undulating tune wavered and hung in the air, without the intricacies of harmonies or complex rhythms. The Kamalti opera had begun.

"Where was Takiyah? And what is wrong with Taunos?" she asked as she and Dode began the walk back.

The older woman nodded. "Yes, I saw it during the concert. Though I still do not understand why you felt the need to punch the poor man in the face."

"I told you, I never should have been able to land a punch."

"I will inquire of Lord Mekl when next I see him."

"Do you think he will answer truthfully?"

Dode shot her a warning look. "Do not forget your place."

Ra'ael glowered at her, but held her tongue and dropped back a pace to follow Dode through the throng of people coming and going in the market square. She'd speak her mind at Dode's home, where there were no

Scouts to worry about.

~

Now was her chance, and there may not be another one. No chain bound her any longer—her captors imagined her spirit was sufficiently broken. Takiyah's body ached, riddled with bruises. Someone threw twine in the air for her, and like a well-trained animal, she incinerated it. She glared at the Kamalti who thought they could own her as they haggled over the price for viewing her "magic." The price didn't matter. It had no effect on her treatment.

Several entertainments dotted the market, but one draw her eye like the metal drew her heart: a great, round piece of fabric attached to a little basket. They called it a "balloon" and used it to clean the massive collection of light orbs overhead that marked the day and night cycles. Afterward, it gave rides to children. Just now, the balloon's driver was helping some children out of the basket, while others jumped about, clamoring to get on.

As soon as the last child left, she could make her move. If she could drive the balloon, she could escape. She wouldn't be able to bring Taunos and Ra'ael along, but she might be able to bring them some help. Taunos had looked well enough, though very strange with his head shaved, when she glimpsed him just before the incident in the market. A few days before that, she'd seen Ra'ael, just as striking as ever and apparently almost friendly with her captor. Hopefully, she was right and they could wait for rescue. Otherwise guilt and regret would crush her. But she couldn't take another beating.

The last child finally stepped out of the basket, and Takiyah surged forward, leaping over her booth. Kamalti shouted, scattering before her, their voices filled with fear. That's right—she was a savage on a rampage. She shot little bursts of flames before her, encouraging the people to be quicker about getting out of the way.

"Stop!"

"Get back here, you maggot!"

She ignored the demands of her captors, just as she ignored the cries of the people she nearly ran over. This was her only chance. She would not let it pass her by.

Takiyah's feet pounded the stone, gripping it and throwing her forward as her hair streamed wildly behind her. A sense of dreaminess, of having done this before, tickled the edges of her mind. The thrill of racing toward danger, of testing herself against the unknown. The rightness of it. She narrowed her eyes, dismissing the fancies. She darted around the line of children and leapt over the side of the basket, shooting small bursts of flame up into the hollow of the balloon. The children and the balloon's owner spilled out and away with screams and cries. She turned one hand outward, shooting fire at any who got too close, keeping the crowd well back. She bared her teeth in a feral grin at her captors' horrified faces, turning her flames on them when they neared.

But now was no time to gloat, for her escape had only begun.

"Cut the ropes!" she ordered the balloon's owner.

"That is my balloon!"

She leveled her hands at him. "Cut the ropes."

"Get the other one!" Someone in the crowd pointed at Ra'ael, bright in her priestess shroud. What was she doing there, and how had she regained her old clothes?

Another Kamalti threw themself at Ra'ael, and the two fell to the ground, while more circled around Ra'ael's captor, who was scolding them all in outrage. Futile. These people were monsters. And none more so than the man who rose to his feet, a knife to Ra'ael's throat. Her captor, Hardy.

"If you leave, she dies!" he yelled.

"You will not do it," Takiyah shouted.

"Watch me."

Ra'ael met her eyes as Takiyah weighed her options. Then the priestess warrior smiled. The message was clear: go and leave her behind. Leave her in this nest of monsters.

But if anyone could get out of that bind, it was Ra'ael.

Takiyah nodded. She shot fire upward so the balloon strained against its ropes, then burned the ropes until they snapped. With a jolt that nearly threw her off her feet, she was free.

A breath of prayer left her lips as the crowd churned below, and Ra'ael fought for her life. Please, please, let Ra'ael make it out of this. Let them all make it out all right.

Takiyah turned her attention to the balloon's controls. The spark of her curiosity had dimmed till it guttered, nearly extinguished by her captivity. Now, it flared to fill her with the need to know everything. The familiarity of it soothed her aching spirit, and tears sprang to her eyes. A contraption hung from the left side, and she turned the handle. After a few moments, the balloon drifted to the side. She swung the handle to the other side, smiling when the balloon followed after a delay. Turning to the central flames, she twisted a knob. The fire went out. The balloon dropped, and

Takiyah shot fire upward with one hand, quickly spinning the knob in the opposite direction with the other. The fire didn't reignite, though her flames kept the descent slow. She didn't want to go down, though! She shot a small stream toward the fire-maker, and a swoosh sounded as the air caught fire. A cackle of laughter escaped her, though the fireball had singed her hair. The balloon was rising again, fire spouting upward from the fire-maker in the middle.

This was how she was meant to live—on the edge, with a chance of survival, of adventure. Not that captivity she'd run from, but this wild freedom, where only her choices, her wits and her strength, determined whether she lived or died. Whether she crashed or flew.

Takiyah checked below her. The fighting seemed to be dying down, and she searched for Ra'ael. She had to be all right. But she couldn't see any sign of her, though the light blue of her shroud or the sleek black of her hair should be easy to spot. She couldn't decide if that was a good thing or a bad thing, and it didn't matter. She'd made her decision, and there was no going back now.

The rock wall of the cavern loomed, and Takiyah turned the rudder to the side. The word had just popped into her head. A rudder. Only, somehow, not quite. She didn't know what was wrong with it, but now was not the time to examine her randomly appearing new knowledge. The sharp rocks were getting closer. Was it just the delay of inertia, or had she swung the rudder the wrong way? She was running out of time. She slammed the rudder to the other side.

Too late. A sickening rip sounded as a rock tore through the fabric of the balloon. The whole thing plummeted. Takiyah raised her hands, her stance wide for some small hope of balance, and erupted flames upward to slow the balloon. Still, the ground rushed toward her.

She leapt at the last second, trying to roll to distribute the impact, but the basket, ropes, and the balloon itself tangled her, and her world reduced to darkness and pain. Someone grabbed her arm, dragging her out of the mess. She struggled, but her limbs wouldn't work right. Her head swam with agony, the world dimming and going out of focus as she moved. Her dreams of escape were as ruined as the balloon.

Angry, shouting masses surrounded her. Takiyah clutched at consciousness, refusing to let it go, forcing herself to look around. More information meant more chances of... something. Hardy glanced back at her, his face twisted with scorn as he and Mettle dragged her away to "correct" her in the privacy of their home.

Chapter Seventeen

I encourage you, my son, to continue as I have begun. Do not let any psion know who the others are. Their shame is our power, their need for secrecy, our strength. Always keep at least two, preferably three, close by, and treat your psions well. In the event of a mutiny, they will not know if they can trust each other. Never allow weapons in the presence of your psions on pain of death, for an overly ambitious guard will strive to take them out first before coming for you. Guard them as you guard yourself.

-letter fragment found in the palace of the City of the Lost

Kaemada gave Eian an extra squeeze as she finished the story of Āssipos's faith and then loosened her hold, checking to see if he was ready to be let go. He snuggled closer and pressed his cheek against hers, his unruly curls getting in her eyes. She wrapped her arms around him tightly once again, trying not to stiffen at the pain of his weight on her bruises. She ached everywhere. Sitting on the cold, hard floor telling stories didn't help.

Eian straightened, pushing away from her. His too-serious brown eyes searched hers. "Mahkae, you saved me." He hugged her again. "I was so scared."

"I will always save you, acha'iyih. I would do anything for you."

But would she? She still hadn't found an escape, and it was becoming clear that befriending a guard wasn't the way out. Theron hadn't helped at all, though at least he'd been honest about that moons ago. She couldn't expect him to help when it was her against the king.

She shivered, the events of that night's dinner flashing before her eyes again. How quickly she'd nearly lost her son. The king had become bored, he'd said, and with a flick of his hand had ordered a guard to stab Eian. The words hadn't made sense to Kaemada's horrified ears, not until the guard was nearly on them. She'd flung Eian out of the way and the knife struck her just below the shoulder. Theron had simply watched.

The king had been furious with her for bleeding on her gown. Once they were back in their rooms, Theron had come to visit. She had decided to forgive him, but he'd been furious with her for embarrassing him. Fortunately, Eian had been hiding, so he hadn't seen Theron beat her. She hadn't been able to fend off the blows. He was so much bigger than her. So much stronger.

She drew in a deep, slow breath. Where were Taunos, Takiyah, and Ra'ael? She was tired of being confused, tired of being frightened. She wasn't strong enough. She hadn't even been able to save Tannevar, and her heart still hurt for missing him. Her back ached, especially between her shoulder blades, from all the tension she'd held over the moons. Her bruises hurt all the way to her bones. No, deeper than that. The pain went to her very song.

She should have been more careful, shouldn't have frustrated Theron so much. Would he continue to protect them from the other guards? He was a good man, deep down inside. The stacks of teas, salves, and balms in her rooms were made from the plants he gave her as gifts, and they, in turn, did much good when she gave them out to servants and the other captive women. Deep inside, Theron wasn't bad.

She repeated that like a mantra, desperately needing it to be true. And yet, she'd never left Eian alone with him. Part of her always rebelled against fully opening up to him. She squeezed her eyes shut. Perhaps if she had trusted him, things would be different. Was it too late? She could keep Eian safer if only she didn't frustrate Theron so much that he left them. Everything would be better if only she was better, more open toward the only safety in this place. More loving even. Surely that would not be too great a sacrifice, convincing him she loved him back? So why couldn't she respond to his affections?

Theron had begun kissing her before leaving—except tonight—but she always froze, remembering Tikatae. Perhaps that was driving him away, inhibiting the good man inside of him. Such a poet as he was, such an artist, could not truly be evil, could he? No, not Theron. He was only misguided.

He only hurt her when she provoked him. She should be wiser than that. The pain came from her mistakes.

She deserved it.

"Mahkae, is it my fault?" Eian's small voice brought her back to the present. "Did I do wrong? Is that why we're here?"

Anger smashed through her confusion, guilt, grief, and pain, rolling over them like a thunderstorm in the sky. "No, my Eian. No. That isn't how life is written."

She busied herself helping him out of his dirty shirt, her motions careful to avoid opening her wound and bleeding through her bandages, then handed him a clean one.

"Teros said the path is easy for those who do no wrong. This place is horrible. I hate it here. It's hard, not easy, and I want to go home!" The new shirt muffled Eian's voice as he struggled into it.

"Ra'ael says Teros is full of idle chatter like a tailosae," she reminded him.

"But Teros is the head priest!"

"That does not mean he cannot be wrong."

Eian frowned, and Kaemada sighed, tousling his hair. "Would you say Āssipos deserved his trials? All that long time waiting, hoping his sons would return? No life is ever perfect, but it's important to choose the best we can."

"But how?"

Kaemada shrugged. She wished she had that answer. "The bad spirits are tricky and will disguise their way as good and right, especially if you let fear, pride, and anger sway your thinking. Sometimes a bad choice will at first seem like a good one..." Kaemada trailed off, her words turning to dirt in her mouth. So many of her own mistakes had landed them here. Decisions fueled by fear, anger, pride. Choices she had thought were good but had landed her son in this place of torment.

They needed a way out. And she was weary to her bones of not being able to see a way. Weary of every escape plan she thought of being too risky. Weary of the palace's casual cruelty. Weary of trying to hold on to hope in a place where hope was murdered on a daily basis.

The words poured out of her before she could think better of them, raw and passionate. "This is wrong. You were never meant to be here, Eian. This part of your story is wrong."

Eian clung to her, panic contorting his face, and she clutched him, kissing the top of his head as tears fell from her eyes. It was wrong here. All of it was wrong.

A soft knock sounded on the door. Kaemada's breath caught and her muscles tensed. Theron was on patrol duty. Was it the psions, finally coming to take her away? It could be one of the women asking for medicine, or it could be danger. Life in the palace had taught her that her imagination was not nearly broad enough to contain all the cruelty people could think of, and now she might have driven away their only protection. The door was left unlocked these days, but she'd learned all too well that was not a chance for freedom—it was a trap.

Leaving Eian in the sleeping room, Kaemada crept to the door. Her hand trembled as she slowly opened it.

As soon as the door cracked open, a figure swept in, spinning around and shoving the door shut behind her. Kaemada stepped back in a half-crouch. Her visitor was one of the captive women she often saw at dinner, someone she'd given tea to a few days ago to soothe a cough. Olorah.

"Forgive me," Olorah said. "When you took so long for answering..."

"Do you need more tea?" Kaemada ventured, willing herself not to cast a glance back at the sleeping room.

"He took him away! He said the cough was bothering him, and he took him away. Oh, will I ever see him again?" The woman dropped into a chair and buried her face in her hands. The muffled sounds of weeping escaped.

Sympathy won over fear, and Kaemada knelt beside Olorah, her hand on one shoulder. "Who?"

"My son! My little Ilos! The king took him, and I fear I'll never see him again!" she sobbed. Ilos had about twelve summers and was one of the oldest captive boys she had seen in the palace. Kaemada embraced her from the side. Olorah clung to her and Kaemada rubbed her shoulder, hiding a wince as her bruises protested. She knew all too well how quickly a mother could lose a child here.

"I sorrow with you," Kaemada whispered, knowing the words were not enough. She looked over toward the sleeping room. Eian stood wide-eyed at the threshold. Her heart lurched. Finally, Olorah released her, and Kaemada gave her a small cloth to wipe her eyes and nose.

"We must get out. You and the others as well," Kaemada murmured. Somehow.

"I have a plan. But... I can't do it alone." Olorah clamped her mouth shut. Tremors wracked her and the knuckles of her clenched hands went white.

Her fear of risking Eian had not kept them safe. The king could kill them at any moment and Theron would not stop it. In the past moons, Theron had received many black eyes, bruises, and cuts. She wasn't sure it was entirely selfish for her to think they were wounds taken on her behalf. At any moment, the psions could find her out. Surely her powers had returned, hadn't they? Or was she doomed to never get them back?

Rinaryn did not leave others to suffer. Even in the hard winter three summers ago, she and Ra'ael and Eian had clung together until the thaw, drawing on each other's strengths.

Spirits above, let her not bring doom upon them in taking this chance.

Kaemada nodded. "Tell me how I can help. I would do anything to keep Eian safe. And your other children need you now more than ever."

Relief flashed across Olorah's face. In whispers, they cobbled together a plan, and Olorah named several other captives to help escape, people who wanted out and would not betray their plans. "Not like Aleis," Olorah explained. "That girl'll turn any situation for her advantage if she can see a way."

The next few days held an odd sort of relief. It was good to have a purpose again rather than the moons of idle terror. She kept her thoughts firmly on their goals: get out with the other captives, and find her brother and friends. It made it easier to deal with the numerous tortures the dinners served up for them and to deal with her confusion over Theron. It seemed like he was still mad at her, and that anger didn't make sense. Surely, he would never expect her to stand by and allow harm to come to Eian.

She ripped the bedsheets she had never used into strips and wove them into long ropes. Other women occasionally visited her room, strips of bedsheets hidden under their gowns. Olorah was doing the same work, separately so as not to draw attention. Some sheets she made into slings for the babies and small children, using Eian to size them.

It was difficult to go about her days as if nothing had changed. The worst was two days after Olorah had come to see her, when Ilos's body was found outside the palace. Her heart ached as she passed Olorah in the corridor. Any show of compassion would only doom them both and risk their children, but Olorah's stern, cold face masked such pain. She wept that night, feeling awful for Olorah and even worse for withholding her sympathies.

The risk of being discovered increased with each day that passed. It was a relief when Olorah popped into her room one morning and said "Tonight," disappearing as quickly as she'd come.

Kaemada continued washing the floor as if nothing had happened, cautioning herself to remain as calm as possible. Eian cheered, making her smile even as she hushed him. A knock sounded on the door a heartbeat later, and Kaemada dropped her cloth. Had someone heard Olorah? Heart pounding in her ears, she started to climb to her feet, bruises and stiff limbs protesting, when Theron entered. She froze, watching out of the corner of her eye as Eian dropped to the floor and crept away. He'd become terrified of Theron again ever since she'd taken the knife for him.

Theron scowled. "The servants wash the floor."

"So do I." She raised her chin. Had she said the wrong thing? Was it all over now? Her head felt light as she kept her expression still. She couldn't let him see her panic.

Theron shook his head with a sigh. His boots were loud on the stone floor as he approached her. He raised a hand, and she flinched, gritting her teeth.

Pain pinched his mouth and shone in his eyes as he stroked her cheek with the backs of his fingers. "You know I don't like hurting you. We'll talk tonight, after I return."

"Return?"

"I'm out for getting taxes. Please, stay in your room and don't make trouble while I'm gone."

She nodded. This might be the last time she saw him. "Theron, I'm sorry."

He turned back with a smile. "I know."

A confusion of riotous fear, sorrow, anger, joy spun through her mind, chasing each other over her heart. She wanted to invite him to escape with them. It would be good for him—he would be a good man if only he was free from the influence of the king. And yet, her tongue seemed glued to her mouth, revolting against the idea.

She followed him to the door, struggling to breathe, struggling to make sense of everything. He'd protected her and Eian. He'd hit her. He made art and wrote poems like her father had. He was loyal to a monster. He was only trying to survive. Eian was afraid of him.

So, as he left, she said only, "Goodbye, Theron."

"Goodbye," he said with a little smile. His footsteps receded down the hallway as she shut the door.

Kaemada leaned her back against it, struggling for calm. If Theron was out for taxes, that meant many of the guards would be out of the palace with him. No wonder Olorah wanted to escape tonight. They'd agreed sundown would be the best time, as they could use the darkness of night and the presence of Angels to cover them. And tonight, the loyal women would be entertaining the king.

It was hard to wait. Jittery and unsettled, Kaemada poured herself into washing the floor and checking her ropes and dressing Eian in clean, warm clothes. They couldn't take anything with them—that would be far too suspicious. When everything was done, she told Eian stories and tried not to worry.

Finally, the sun descended beyond the wall. There would be no dressers tonight, no dinner without the majority of the guards. Women had been coming to her for basic medicines any Rinaryn should know for some time now, so it made sense to use her room. But the waiting stretched out, thin as her nerves.

A knock sounded on her door. She opened it, and Olorah whirled inside, her toddler in her arms and an older boy quick on her heels.

"Finally!" Kaemada whispered. "Did you have any trouble?"

Olorah shook her head, unwinding handmade ropes from under her dress. "Can you pull the others up on the roof?"

Kaemada winced and shook her head. Between the weakness that remained in the left half of her body, the lingering stiffness from her bruises, and the still-healing wound in her shoulder, she'd never be able to climb up alone.

Olorah turned to the oldest of her two remaining children. "Taban, up you go. Rope around your waist, remember? I'll come after you. Kaemada, can you fit my little one with a sling? I'll pull her up next."

Kaemada nodded. "And then, I will watch the door."

While she tied the sling snug around the toddler's chest, Eian scrambled into the chimney, feeding the ropes upward and making sure they didn't get caught on anything. Within moments, Olorah was up top with her son, and two ropes hung down the brick opening. Kaemada led her daughter into the chimney and attached the ropes to the sling, fighting the strangling claustrophobia that threatened to overwhelm her. She breathed a sigh of relief as she stepped out, and the little girl was pulled up the chimney.

While Eian watched the ascent, Kaemada went to the door. She'd hardly gotten there before there was a soft knock, and Kaemada cautiously opened it, hardly daring to breathe. Another of the captive women darted inside as soon as the door opened, along with two small children.

"Hurry, to the fireplace." Kaemada shut the door behind them.

She fitted the children with the slings while showing the woman how to use the ropes to help with the climb. As more of them got to the roof, there would be more help available for the climbers, and as long as they stayed low, they should be fairly safe from discovery. Just so long as no guards or servants came. After gaining the roof, the next bit of danger would be coming down and evading recapture and the Angels.

But they had to succeed. They had to. Kaemada darted back and forth from the door to the fireplace, letting in captives and then helping with slings and ropes. Before long, Eian was helping them on his own, and while pride filled Kaemada's heart, worry also simmered there.

"Eian, climb up. I will join you once everyone has come," Kaemada said.

He paled and shook his head. "I want to stay with you."

"Please, Eian. I want you safe."

"No! I'm staying with you!"

Kaemada winced at his shout and sighed, leaving the argument for now. If someone heard, it would doom them all. Another knock sounded at the door, then another. The captives streamed in, all white-faced and worried, and Kaemada's heart leapt with fear of discovery every time.

A loud rap on the door startled Kaemada, so much different from the timid taps of the captives. Terror seized her and Kaemada ran to the fireplace, where Eian stood covered in soot and a woman holding her infant waited for the ropes to be lowered once again.

"Masa, hide!" Kaemada hissed. Her gaze went to Eian. Maybe, just maybe, she could boost him up, and Olorah could pull him out. It had to work.

"Eian, grab the ropes!" She lifted him with a groan, her body protesting, and Eian clutched at her neck in sudden fear. "Shareil, Eian. Can you reach them?"

She struggled to balance him as they teetered against the walls of the chimney, but the ropes were too high.

Someone grabbed her arm, yanking her out into the room, and Eian fell with a scream. She barely managed to grab his arm and steady his fall, but her head slammed against the edge of the fireplace. She blinked hard, trying to focus her eyes as she held one hand to her forehead and clutched Eian in her other arm.

Theron scowled at her.

"Theron, please!" she begged. "If you could lift Eian, maybe he could reach the ropes. Surely you can see this is no place for a child."

"You two're in a lot of trouble," Theron said, tucking Eian under one arm. But he did not step into the chimney. He gripped Kaemada's elbow and dragged her out of the room—a room that seemed empty. Had Masa been able to hide? What was Theron doing?

Eian shouted, kicking and squirming.

"Theron, please. You could say no one was here when you got here. Please, please, help me protect Eian!"

"I'm the king's guard. I'll always be the king's guard."

"You could be so much more." What was he doing here? Why wasn't he in the city? "How did you know?"

Theron shook his head. "You, foolish woman, are terrible at keeping secrets. You said goodbye. It felt like a real goodbye."

Tears of fear and pain blurred her vision. Why was she always so blind to the way things truly were? "Are you really going to turn us in?"

"I told you, I'm the king's guard. I'm a loyal man, Kaemada." The sound of his boots on the floor echoed, as useless to argue against as the vice grip he had on her arm.

"Theron, I thought you were my friend! You said I would always be safe with you!"

He shook her. Pain shot through her arm and she bit her tongue. Her head hurt, and the room spun around her as she was snapped back and forth like a rag. Fury twisted his expression.

Why would he be furious at her? Of all things... the discrepancy sliced through the fear and pain.

"Are you mad at me?" she asked when he stopped shaking her.

"Of course, I'm angry with you! You think I want this?" he roared at her, resuming his stride. "I don't want this!"

"I'm not making you do anything."

"You can't truly be that stupid. You think you can try for running away and not pay the price?"

Kaemada glared at him, planting her feet, but she barely slowed Theron at all. Eian was screaming, struggling uselessly in Theron's other arm. Blood dripped from her forehead, and her knife wound tore as she fought, coating her with blood.

"I thought you were smarter than this. After all I did to you. I saved you! And this is how you repay me?"

She barely bit back a retort, and he snarled at her. "You realize, don't you, that the other guards would have visited you had I not staked my claim? Not all of them are as pleasant as I am."

"That does not make it right!"

Theron took the corners quickly, bouncing her off the walls, as unaffected by her struggles as a rock to water. Battered and bloody, she tried to claw his grip off her arm like a rodent beating at an alanshorn. Through the whole nightmare, he remained impeccably groomed. Theron's hands would remain clean, even while he took her and her son to their deaths. It was unbearable.

He wrenched her into the throne room and shoved Eian into Aleis's grasp. The girl held tightly to him, offering Kaemada a too-sweet smile.

Doubled over from the pain shooting through her arm, she growled at Aleis. "You do not want to hurt him."

The psions stood at their posts, like shrouded statues. She would have to fight them. Eian would die if she didn't at least try, so keeping her abilities secret didn't matter anymore. And her psionics had to have returned by now, didn't they? It had been five moons.

The king scowled at her, sitting on his chair.

"My king, I caught this one trying for escaping up the fireplace." Theron bowed, his fingers digging into her arm.

The king leaned forward, placing his chin on one hand. "So, then. Were you alone in this folly?"

"Let Eian go!"

"How many others joined your escape attempt?"

"Let Eian go!"

"Tell me!"

She stared back with all the defiance she could muster, though she trembled so hard she could barely stand. Her eyes flickered to the psions. Could she do it? Could she beat them? Bile rose in her throat. Psions fighting psions? Those days were supposed to be long done.

The king waved his hand in dismissal. "I tire of this. Let the psions glean what they will from her mind." He smiled at her. "I'll know what you know, no matter how you fight me. Take the boy away, Aleis. You can play with him however you like. I care not."

Tears streamed down Eian's face as he squirmed in Aleis's grasp.

"Let. Him. Go!" Kaemada screamed.

Theron shook her again. Agony burned from her elbow to her fingers, and her teeth clacked together. As soon as the world stopped swimming, she lashed out at Theron telepathically. There was no finesse, no skill, only brute force and desperation. His grip on her arm broke as he turned toward her, a look of horror on his face.

"Psion! Psion!" unfamiliar voices screamed.

The gleam of metal flashed in her eyes, and then Theron plunged his knife into her stomach once, twice, again. Pain consumed her, and black dotted her vision as she grabbed his arm, her blood coating his once pristine hands.

See, decide, act, and face the consequences.

His hands grabbed her throat, and she beat at him, desperate for air as the pressure on her neck tightened. Eian's screams filled her ears, her every muscle tight with desperation. She wasn't strong enough to do this. Not this way. Because she wasn't like Taunos. She wasn't like Takiyah or Ra'ael, to beat him with strength or wits. She was Kaemada, and she could only ever be Kaemada. But she was strong in other ways.

She let go.

Forgetting her body, Kaemada scrambled into his mind, past his barriers. His horror surrounded her, and she rode that wave of emotions to his greatest fears. She paused, struck by the truth in front of her. Theron's loyalty was his pride, but it was a mask. She pulled it away, and beneath it, the relief of not having to make decisions, of not holding the final say, shone through. He was afraid to lead. No wonder he was happy to do whatever was asked of him, so long as he didn't have to take responsibility for the consequences.

She wove a hasty dream around those fears and solidified it in his mind to haunt him. Coming back to herself, her teeth clacked together. Theron was convulsing, and another guard whipped her back and forth, grappling to get at her. She dealt him the same treatment, so his nights would be filled with the agony of being burned alive, and his days filled with the horror of remembering it.

Her head pounded and her stomach twisted. Her ears rang. She was doing too much, but there was more to do. These horrors wouldn't end until the king was dead, and the pressures of the psions weighed on her mind. She was cracking, squashing like an egg. Light lanced painfully through her head.

Aleis shouted.

Kaemada hurled her mental attack at the king. There was a swirling around her as the psions rebounded, caught by surprise. She struggled against the mental walls they'd built for the king. The mental imprints of many, many psions were stamped on those walls, and her own walls were crumbling as the psions lashed out at her. They beat against her like a drum, ever louder and more violent.

Eian was screaming, but she couldn't pay attention long enough to understand. A glimpse of Aleis fleeing the room.

Awareness of physical surroundings only divided her attention. The king was too far away—she needed to be closer to deal more damage, to break through his walls. She needed every ounce of power to beat them, to give Eian a chance to run, a chance to hide. If only she had Tannevar to help her! A battle cry ripped from her small frame, and she dreamwalked, lending power to her telepathy while her broken body slumped to the bloodied floor.

Everything became clear. There was only one important thing: the king. The psions would be dealt with afterward. She shot toward his cruel song through the swirling dreamscape like a dagger, plunging into his mental walls. Gathering herself, she crashed against them again, her mental power stronger in the dreamwalking state. The psions' songs were touched with indecision, and that gave her the time she needed.

Kaemada burst through all at once, sliding through a crack in the king's mental walls. *You should have let us go. I will not let you hurt Eian.*

She boxed herself up tight, affording herself some flimsy protection from his prying as he scrabbled at her mind. There in his head, his inner thoughts and plans, the tragedy of his memories, it was all clear to her. He displayed pride in all the wrong places, and though there was regret, it was covered by entitlement. He'd made so many sacrifices, traded so many lives for comfort, and he thought it was worth it. And he would continue to do even more. Revulsion shook her.

And the king laughed at her.

She and Eian and the other captives were just tools to be used, rewards to hand out to the loyal. They were nothing to him, though she herself was becoming more annoying than she was worth. Eian, though, the king could let live. For a while, at least. Sometimes toys got broken, but there were always replacements.

Kaemada flung her mental daggers at him. The life spark of the king extinguished. Shock froze her for a moment, both her own and echoes of the king's surprise as he died. It left a heavy sense of responsibility, of guilt. Of grief for what could not be.

The king's psions besieged her, only moments too late. Kaemada fought them with what remained of her strength. They smothered her, drowned her.

Eian, be safe.

White light burst, with a feeling as if something had broken or been loosed, and then everything went black.

ÌTAL-HAETH
Chapter Eighteen

An ill-treated ebr may choose to seek asylum. At such time, the ebr will be put up for auction and awarded to the highest bidder; the proceeds shall benefit the Scouts. Few will mistreat a thing they have paid a great deal of money for.
—excerpt from the Kamalti City of Codr Code of Law

"But what place would the Outsiders have if we admitted them into society? Already, Detr imagines a Future in which we are once more subjugated under their rule."

"And you and I have both heard the rumors that the City of Rhedr is warring against its neighbors. How long before such unrest reaches our own cave system? No, we have enough to think about without throwing the savages into the mix."

"Savages, Lord Tetl?"

With her back turned to the Philosophers' meeting, Ra'ael poured a glass of water from the pitcher at the side table. She smiled to hear that tone in Dode's voice. It spoke of danger for the unlucky person she directed it on. The last time Dode had used that whipcrack was nearly a moon ago when the mob set upon them during Takiyah's escape attempt. If only Takiyah had succeeded. If only Ra'ael could check on her.

The meeting wore on Ra'ael's nerves, but at least their verbal sparring would bring some entertainment. Of course, not even the Philosophers would ask "Outsiders" what should be done about them. They considered themselves enlightened, and yet they ignored her.

With smooth movements, she slipped between the chairs to set the drink in front of Dode, who grasped her hand in thanks, taking a moment to smile at her. Ra'ael smiled back, knowing the proud nobility around the table would take offense at this breach of manners—but how were simple gratitude and decency a breach of manners? It was all a scene played out with intention by Dode, and thrilling amusement filled Ra'ael whenever she partook in the game.

She took a step back, ready to head back to the wall where the nobles would say she belonged. The world went fuzzy and dark at the edges. At the table, Dode stiffened, then slumped forward. Ra'ael reached for her, but the world tilted, slid, and went black.

~

Takiyah gritted her teeth and blasted a scrap of fabric into ash. She staggered, but when they tossed the next item in front of her, she blasted it as well. Sweat poured off her, her breath came in ragged gasps, and exhaustion numbed her. She longed to sleep for days, but that wasn't an option.

Don't think. Only see to the next flame. Then the next.

How much longer could she keep this up? No, she shouldn't think, just keep going. She had to put off the next punishment as long as she could. Her leg still throbbed where her captors had broken it, and the brand on her cheek, gifted to her three days ago, was raw and blistered.

Chaos erupted in the market. Some of the Kamalti just... stopped. Some fell to the ground, and others shouted and ran about as if they were seeing or hearing things. More stared at nothing and rocked themselves back and forth. A steamwagon careened off the road, its driver incapacitated, and plowed through several stalls, and onto another road.

More importantly, her captors lay crumpled by the table. No one was paying attention to her.

She paused, breathless, leaning against the table in front of her. Did she dare believe it? Yes. She had to.

Takiyah ran.

~

Taunos followed Answer through the streets, barely paying attention to his surroundings. Galod would have scolded him, but it was so much effort just to put one foot in front of the other without stumbling or appearing as exhausted as he truly was. Answer's Scouting meeting had been so mind-numbingly boring he was looking forward to polishing the silverware. He suffered through the meeting, since Answer had begun using him as her bodyguard, mimicking Dode's use of Ra'ael. It was just another chance for her to show him off. He tolerated it. The only blow was to his pride, and that was in tatters, anyway.

A familiar force nearly knocked him off his feet. He could almost hear his sister's battle cry ringing in his mind. He staggered against one of the massive pillars before regaining his balance.

It couldn't be so. It had to be his imagination.

A steamwagon rocketed down the road, weaving erratically in their direction, its driver slumped over the controls. Answer stumbled at the side of the road, falling in its path. Taunos yanked her out of the way, a force of will more than anything else.

Darkness crashed over him.

Figures hovered above him. He was lying on the ground. Adrenaline surged through him as he fought his way back to consciousness. Snapping open his eyes, Taunos grabbed one of the figures, rolling them onto the floor and switching places with them. As he did so, he grabbed the other's leg, tossing them to the ground. The world rolled around him, up and down flip-flopping. He gripped the figure beneath him by the shoulder, more for stability than anything else, solidifying that direction in his mind as down while his stomach turned.

It was Answer, he realized, wide-eyed with fear and anger. He was in the entryway of Answer's home straddling her, and the other figure was a strange woman, just now getting to her feet. Answer grabbed his hand in both of hers, breaking his grip on her shoulder. Up and down switched places again and continued tilting dangerously. Taunos's back hit the floor, and he found relief in at least knowing where down was again. He held his open hands by his head, yielding, as he closed his eyes to shut out the spinning world.

"My apologies. I wasn't aware it was you, Answer." He clenched his jaw, nauseous from the effort of speaking.

"It is fast. I will give it that," murmured the strange woman.

Taunos risked opening his eyes. Thankfully, the room's spinning began to slow.

"And strong." Answer rose, looking down at him. "If you bleed on my rugs, you will have to wash them."

She turned to the strange woman. "See that his injury is closed. And should he give you any trouble, let me know, and he will answer dearly for it. When he is cleaned up, send him into the parlor to arrange the lanterns for my dinner party tonight. He should be well enough for that, yes, Doctor?"

"Yes, I think it will be well enough to serve. It may have a nasty headache."

Answer hesitated, then sniffed and lifted her head. "Yes. Well, then. I leave you to your work, Doctor."

The room rocked, threatening to spin again, and Taunos closed his eyes once more. The woman's hands were firm as she stitched him up with apparently no more care than she'd give a piece of cloth, even though it was his head she was stabbing with the needle. He felt nothing, oddly, and spent the time trying to decide how much pain he should be in, trying not to think of the other capable hands he'd rather have stitching him up instead. The Doctor murmured to herself about how soft his head was and how he should take better care of it, but Taunos tuned her out.

He had gone black again. The only other time that had happened, Kaemada had been the cause. What did that mean? How could she have survived that fall? It was impossible. What, then, caused the black that had enveloped him? The Sleep? And Answer... she'd been affected. He'd never seen her trip and fall like that.

The Doctor stood, packed her bag, and left without a word to him. Slowly, Taunos picked himself off the floor, holding on to the wall as a wave of dizziness threatened to overwhelm him. He brushed his fingers over his forehead, grazing over the stitches. Step by step, he made it to the parlor, leaning against the doorway for a moment to fend off vertigo.

Answer sat on the couch with her mouth pursed in thought and her gaze distant. He almost shook his head but thought better of it. Apparently he had lanterns to clean.

As he walked toward the first side table, one hand trailing on the wall for balance, Answer stood and blocked his path. He clenched his jaw. Why did she have to make everything more difficult?

"Why did you save me?" Answer asked. "You have made it clear what you think about being my bodyguard. It would have been a good way to rid yourself of me."

The room swayed around him. He felt even woozier than what had passed for normal the last five moons. Stifling a groan, he leaned against the wall to stay upright.

Answer continued. "There were none of your countrymen there, nor any innocent bystanders to save. If you did it to gain favor, you should know I have no power in your term, nor will I treat you as more than just an ebr."

"You, at least, do not refer to me as 'it.' You're dangerously close to treating me like a person."

"You are infuriating." Answer scowled.

"I'm told it's one of my many talents," Taunos grimaced.

"Tell me, is that why you did it?"

"No."

"Then why?"

Taunos shook his head and immediately regretted it as his vision swam. Why had he done it? He hadn't even thought about it.

"You needed saving," he said at last.

Answer stared at him as if he had two heads. "I have been awful to you, and you respond like this? Your people are mad."

Taunos chuckled. "You may not be entirely wrong on that count. But we're a lovable sort of mad if you let yourself."

"How is your head?" Answer asked. "You cracked it open on a wall when you blacked out. You would not have if you had let fate run its course."

"I believe we make our fate. And my head's fine. I have had knocks on the head before." He paused for a moment, and then added, "You might be glad I have been training to overcome the effects of your drug and was able to drink some untainted water this morning."

Answer considered him silently for long moments. "I cannot risk my position and Prestige by treating you as a person in public. And you are still my ebr. But... I am not ungrateful." Answer fidgeted, frowning at her hands.

"So... You lied about the dinner party?"

"No, I am having a dinner party. But I do not truly need your help to prepare for it."

"I'm not entirely sure what you're trying to say, then."

"You are still my ebr. I cannot change that. But... When not in public, you may have some more leniency and my respect, person to person."

Taunos raised his eyebrows. "You have my gratitude for that." He might as well pounce while Answer's prickly guard was lowered. "Is there any way my sister could have survived that fall? The last time I lost consciousness like that, it was she who caused it."

The imperious air returned. "That is impossible. The ravine goes down to the roots of the mountain and is controlled by monsters."

Taunos frowned. "What other explanation is there? Your people knew nothing of this, and my sister was the cause previously."

A small, sad smile touched her lips. "You must have loved her very much to keep holding her death over me and to risk your neck doing so. You were so very angry, like a parent losing a child to a horrible accident."

"We were very close, the last of our family. Except for our sister the dragonbonded."

Awed amusement replaced the smile, and Answer shook her head. "You are a family of surprises. Yourself, a sister who makes others lose consciousness, and another sister who lives with the dragons."

A bell rang from the front hall, summoning Scouts to an emergency. Had there been another breach into the mountain? Taunos's fists clenched.

"You cannot come," Answer said, apparently sensing his tension. "It would not be seemly with your wound."

Ah yes, the ever-present obsession with what others thought. He wouldn't be much help anyway, unsteady as he was. Besides, it was probably just more Scout drama. Despite his sister being on his mind, it was unlikely to be a Rinaryn—the next Feast of Starfall was a moon away.

Taunos forced himself to let out his breath and picked up a lantern. "I have these to tend to."

As Answer left, Taunos drifted about the room, cleaning and lighting the lanterns. It was quiet as he arranged them in the parlor for a cozy ambiance. Answer's parents were away at a meeting in another city, and they had brought Kajat with them. Ketrik had been sent out in the morning to inquire about a custom-made bookcase, and Tegil's term of service had ended a few days ago. Now that Answer was gone, he was alone in the house, an event increasingly common as Answer's family grew to trust him.

It was nice to have a little solitude. It gave him time for his own pursuits.

He collected spare food from the kitchen in a metal pail. As he put it outside next to the back door, he winked at the little boy who scampered up to it. He'd been sneaking food whenever he could for that little boy and his father, both living on the streets of Codr, and had grown unexpectedly fond of them. There was beauty here among the Kamalti, hidden amongst the decay of corruption and selfishness.

Kaemada had seen it, had believed in it. Could she be alive? Why had he and so many others lost consciousness again?

A tap sounded at the door. He made his careful way over and opened it, nearly falling backward when Takiyah burst inside. She flew around him to slam the door shut, wild-eyed and wild-haired.

"Takiyah!" Taunos reached for her shoulders, in part to keep the dizziness at bay, and found her stiff and trembling, her breath coming in ragged gasps.

"Takiyah, come here. Let's get you away from the door." He spoke gently and guided her to the parlor, keeping his movements slow and sure, as if dealing with a wild creature. Nausea and vertigo kept creeping up on him, so slow movements were doubly good. "Sit down. No one else is here."

Takiyah limped badly, leaning on him even as he leaned on her. She settled on the couch, but after only a moment, she jolted up, looking around in a panic.

Taunos gentled her back down, then poured the warm water leftover in the parlor's teapot into a cup along with some tea leaves. "Shareil, Tinker. What happened since last I saw you? You disappeared! Answer said she sent word to ask about you, but I hadn't heard back."

Takiyah dug her fingers into Taunos's arm. "Do not let them send me back!"

This was a powerful warrior who had proven herself again and again in battle. He'd never seen her so shaken. Anger burned in him, struggling to burst free as he held the taller woman, trying to soothe her. "I will not, Tinker. You're here, and if I have to hide you, I will. I will not let them take you. Now, tell me what happened."

Taunos kept his arms secure around her, letting her cling to him as she slowly told her tale, shaking and crying and often needing reassurance. Fury built inside him, and he kept himself very still as he listened to the circumstances Takiyah had been forced to bear. Grimly, he examined the soot marks on her red and swollen hands and wrists, the fresh lacerations, the bruises on her face, and the red, angry burn where they had branded her. Her broken leg had been badly set and had twisted as it healed. She'd never regain full mobility. Horror chilled him.

He took her chin in his hand to look into her green eyes. "Mark my words, Takiyah, these things will never happen again."

Takiyah buried her face in her hands as her shoulders shook. "We cannot fight back, not if we intend to survive and find Eian. You, yourself, said we simply needed to endure."

"The humiliation, yes. But not this. Never this!" Taunos left her to pace, his anger subdued slightly by the nausea that flared when he spun too quickly.

Violent shivers overtook her, and she curled up in a ball, her eyes tracking his movements. "How's Ra'ael faring?"

"I saw her a couple days ago," Taunos said. "Some Kamalti were after her about something, but that old woman she's with is crafty."

"That's good, that's good," Takiyah said, nodding excessively with her eyes unfocused as she repeated herself.

A noise outside made her leap up and join Taunos's pacing. He stopped and brought her to a halt.

"Tinker," he murmured. When she didn't respond, her gaze far away, he spoke slightly louder, careful not to startle her. "Tinker."

Her gaze darted to him, and he guided her back to the couch. "Be at peace. I will do anything, pay any price, to save you from further abuse. I will not let this happen again."

She sniffed and nodded, burrowing her face in his chest. He wrapped his arms around her again. Her shoulders shook as she sobbed while Taunos stroked her hair and held her and let her cry.

After a while, she sat up, wiping her eyes. "Thank you."

"Anytime, Tinker."

"Now my eyes and nose are probably all red." She sniffed.

He grinned. "It's all right. They match your hair."

Her eyes lit with mock anger, but she smiled as she shoved him away. "Get me a cloth to wash my face."

"Ugh," he groaned, standing. "Am I to be forever ordered about?"

"Get used to it." A hint of her former sass lit her voice. She would be all right. He started away, but Takiyah broke in.

"Taunos?" Her voice quavered. She'd always been so bold, so confident. A deep hatred filled him for the insecurity in her

"Yes, Tinker?"

"Be quick, please?"

He smiled gently. "I'm not leaving."

He took a clean cloth from the pile for polishing and used the last of the warm water from the teapot. Not only did he not want to leave her alone, but he was also wary of his dizziness. Takiyah washed her face and the soot marks off her arms, and Taunos cleaned and bandaged her wounds. He stood to put the items away, returning quickly to drape one arm around her shoulders as she leaned against him. They sat quietly for the most part, occasionally speaking of events long past. Talk of the present or future was too difficult, and they avoided it.

Eventually, the front door of the house slammed. Answer bellowed for Taunos. With a squeeze of Takiyah's shoulder, he left, closing the parlor doors behind him.

"Taunos!" Answer shouted as she stomped down the hall. "Taunos!"

"Answer." He made sure his voice was quiet and calm.

"Do you forget your life is in my hands? Do you forget your place? I will never again be so easily swayed by your wiles," she stormed.

"What do you mean?" His brow wrinkled.

"What do I mean?" Disgust, anger, and betrayal distorted her features. "One of your countrymen has escaped her captivity. The red-haired, tall one. Do not dare to look innocent. Now I see your plan. You set all this up to sway me, and it nearly worked. But it will not work. It will never work. Tell me where she is! I am handing both of you back to the Justices."

Shock turned to confusion and then anger, which Taunos channeled into defiance. "This wasn't some grand plan. If you will list—"

She slapped him, stopping him mid-word. Trembling with the wrath which reddened her face, she shook a finger at him. "They will never let me forget this. I will never forgive you. Tell me where she is. Did you coordinate her escape?"

"What? How could I?"

"We will not stand for your continual disrespect for our Laws and customs. And I will not tolerate traitorous, conniving, lying, two-faced manipulators in my home."

Taunos took a deep breath. His voice rumbled low with warning. "Do you know what they were doing to her?"

"Where is she?"

"Did you know?" he shouted.

"Yes, I knew! Now tell me where she is!"

Taunos stepped back from her. "You... You're animals. Worse than animals!"

Answer stepped forward, face to face with him again. "No, you are the animals. You have forfeited your right to personhood again and again. You continually attack my people and our way of life. If we come down from the mountains and your lands burn, the blame is on your heads."

She spun around and raced to the crystal mounted by the door, ringing it. The Scouts would be here to enforce order at any moment. Taunos stared at her, stunned by her threat of war. But Answer did not have that authority. And yet... she knew people who did, people who likely harbored ill-will toward his people. Her words carried weight, as one who "owned an Outsider ebr."

"You do not want a war," Taunos said. Suddenly, this had grown much bigger than them. All he'd worked so hard for, all he'd sacrificed to protect his people—all of it was in danger of being brought down by this spoiled Kamalti brat who desperately wanted to be treated like an adult. "Your people would die as well, and you do not want that. You would have to show yourselves, and it's clear you fear us, even as we're in awe of you. We have lived in peace for generations. Do not let it end with you."

"I will not lie down while you attack my people and tromp all over our traditions. This war starts with you."

"The fault will lie with both of us. Do you not see? Neither side would benefit."

"Tell me where the rogue ebr is."

"I cannot allow any more atrocities to be done to her, come what may."

"Then we are at an impasse."

"Answer, do not do this. I wish you no harm, but I cannot allow this.

239

We both have made mistakes. We both have said hurtful things. For my part, I'm sorry, but I plead with you to stop this madness. You can end this."

"I can. I choose not to. You will pay dearly."

"We both will," Taunos agreed, his voice soft.

He leapt at Answer. She did not go down easily, and the moments slipped away while his head protested the quick movements the struggle demanded. Takiyah arrived with the cord from the curtains, and together, they bound and gagged Answer.

"You did not kill her," Takiyah observed as Taunos finished tying the bindings on her hands and feet.

"Whenever it's not necessary to kill, it's preferable not to," Taunos replied evenly, adjusting the gag. He wasn't sure how much force would knock out a Kamalti without killing her, so he laid the struggling woman down on the floor of the parlor. It was an interior room and would muffle her cries for help, especially with the gag in her mouth. But Answer was resourceful, and Taunos had no doubt she would be free after a short time. There had to be other Kamalti who would balk at the threat of war, though he felt a chill, recalling how so many considered them mere animals. If nothing else, they were out of options. They needed to escape. He only hoped he had gained them enough time.

"She will come after us," Takiyah said.

"I know," Taunos took her arm gently, looking into her eyes. "So we move fast. No going back."

He guided her out the door and locked it behind them. They hurried through the streets, trying to look as if they were simply on errands, clumsily leaning on each other or the walls far more often than Taunos would have liked. It would be a miracle if they got out of this alive. The guards would be looking, and Takiyah was rather conspicuous, but perhaps the citizens would take no notice of them.

"Where can we go?" Takiyah asked.

"We need to get to Ra'ael."

"That's the first place they will look for us." Takiyah's tone was matter-of-fact.

Taunos smiled grimly. "Then we will have to be quick."

No outcry was raised, and soon Taunos tapped on the door of the house where Ra'ael dwelt. Takiyah fidgeted, looking around in all directions. As soon as the door opened, they both rushed inside without waiting for an invitation and pressed the door closed behind them. Ra'ael stood there with a look of surprise on her face, staring at them.

"Takiyah, what happened to you?" Ra'ael reached for her.

Takiyah swept Ra'ael into a tight embrace while Taunos looked down the hallway warily, blinking and keeping one hand on the wall to help make certain up stayed up. Ra'ael released Takiyah and hugged Taunos, who pulled free first.

"Ra'ael, we must go. We're all in grave danger. They were torturing Takiyah, and I must get her to safety. If you do not leave with us, they will take it out on you."

"Trying to escape… As you said yourself, Taunos, it's madness!" Ra'ael replied.

"Madness seems to have fallen on the City," spoke an elderly voice.

Taunos stepped in front of his sister's friends, fearing that the battle had already begun.

Ra'ael's captor, Dode, walked toward them calmly. She raised her hands. "I mean you no harm."

"I cannot let Takiyah go back," Taunos said, a warning in his voice. Ra'ael frowned at him as if affronted by his tone. "Answer threatened war. We must go—this is bigger than us, and your people seem immune to reason."

Dode continued to advance, her attention shifting to Takiyah. "Child, what has been done to you? Is this the cause of all the ruckus?"

"The Scouts came here searching," Ra'ael said. "Searching for you, I suppose, Takiyah."

Takiyah shrank back, and Taunos shifted to shield her more fully.

Ra'ael placed her hand on Taunos's arm. "Taunos, please. I trust her."

Taunos considered her and then Dode, his thoughts racing. Reluctantly, he let her pass. "All right, Wildling. But we need to be quick."

Takiyah stood frozen, her breath coming in shallow pants. Taunos wrapped his arm around her shoulders to lend her strength.

"Oh, Kiy!" Ra'ael breathed, taking Takiyah's hands in her own.

Taunos recounted the abuse Takiyah had suffered while Dode clucked her tongue and murmured ineffectual but necessary sympathies.

"We must get you to asylum, child," she said.

"Asylum?" Takiyah repeated, her gaze darting to Taunos for clarification. The word would be foreign to Takiyah and Ra'ael, of course.

"Are ebrs allowed to seek asylum?" Taunos asked.

Dode nodded. "When they are misused as she has been, yes. Asylum would not negate your ebr state, but it would force your owner to put you up for auction."

"But then she could be bought by someone as bad or worse!" protested

Ra'ael.

Takiyah's legs buckled, and Taunos leaned against the wall as he held her. Ra'ael embraced Takiyah from the other side until she recovered.

"It might be better to take our chances on the run." Except that he was in no shape for a fight. He'd barely managed to take down Answer. But they could be separated, and worse could happen to Takiyah. "I dislike the idea of being separated again. I must make sure nothing else happens."

"You're not responsible for us," Ra'ael told him.

He smiled sadly down at her. "I will always feel responsible for you, Wildling."

Dode was shaking her head. "There is nowhere you would all be together, unless you all were under the same noble, and that is unlikely. I would snatch you all up to know that no more atrocities were committed," she glanced at Takiyah, "but I do not believe I would be able to afford the asking price. I would do what I could, however. And as for Answer, well. She is a foolish child, and any who would support war over a personal vendetta can be easily dealt with."

"Where would the nearest asylum be?" Taunos asked.

"You could seek asylum at the Hall of the Saints," Dode said.

"That's the place we brought decorations to, yes?" Ra'ael asked.

Dode nodded, and Ra'ael turned to them. "I can lead you there."

Wariness filled Takiyah's voice. "Is that the best option?"

"This sector of the City is under the jurisdiction of the Scouts. They have authority in matters concerning the Outside, but they must abide by our Laws. If you were to run and be caught, you would be tried by the Council of Scouts. If you made it to asylum, there would be no trial, only bids to buy you, the money to be given to the Scouts," explained Dode.

"So the Scouts would want to drive up the price as high as possible," Taunos said.

"Could we make it out?" asked Takiyah.

"It would be a hard thing to hide you, child, with your hair and your height. And look at the two of you, both of you having trouble standing upright! No ebr has tried to escape out of the mountain before, to my knowledge, but then, I do not ever remember Outsiders as ebrs," answered Dode. "I wish I could give you a satisfactory answer to your question, but I simply do not know."

"It's difficult to find a way into the mountain," said Takiyah, "But you probably do not try to keep your people in. It would be easier to find a way out, providing we could get there."

"If you could get there." Dode nodded. "We rarely have trouble with

Kamalti wanting to walk the surface, and those who do tend to be the impulsive youth."

"The Scouts are searching for us. We need to decide and quickly. If the Scouts are in charge of this area, we're standing in the middle of the fire," Taunos said.

"Try for asylum. I will lead you to the chapel, and then come back here," Ra'ael urged, suddenly decisive.

"You should stay then, if the Lady Dode can keep you safe," Taunos said, indicating Dode with a deep nod of his head.

"Will you be all right?" Takiyah asked Ra'ael.

"I will do what I can," Dode said.

"Is there a reasonable chance you can keep her safe?" Taunos needed to be sure.

Dode inclined her head. "I believe so."

Taunos nodded as well, a little reluctantly. "You remind me of the Great Mother of my kaetal. We will forever be grateful to you for your help."

Dode chuckled. "I am not a mother, much less a Great Mother."

"The Great Mother is she with the most power in a Rinaryn kaetal. She leads the domestic and everyday tasks and provides the true names for the kaetalyn as they become adults. She's loved and respected by all." Ra'ael smiled. "And you remind me of her as well."

"Well, I am flattered. Now, go, go, and take care! May your path be lined with stone and lit with crystals, and may danger yield from you at every turn."

Dode threw a blanket over Takiyah as they left, and Takiyah hunched under it while Ra'ael hurried them down the stairs. They kept their pace swift, just under a run. Takiyah lurched along with her injured leg, and Taunos willed the threatening dizziness away.

Shouts rang out behind them. They dared not look back.

"How much farther?" Taunos asked Ra'ael.

"Nearly there. It's just ahead." She pointed.

"Stop!" demanded a voice behind them.

"Run!" Taunos slowed to cover them, pushing Takiyah forward. Ra'ael yanked open the doors of the chapel. Takiyah and Taunos rushed inside. Ra'ael hesitated in the doorway.

"You are in violation of the Law! Surrender!" cried the Scouts, running toward them.

Ra'ael slammed the door shut behind her, securing them all in the building.

They were not alone in the chapel. A woman kneeling before lighted candles stared at them. A man sat on a cushion near an elaborate stained-glass window, deep in meditation. Another man in a gold robe trimmed with purple, with a golden ring around his head surrounded by droplets of crystal, glided toward them.

"He's the priest," Ra'ael whispered. She stepped forward. "Mercy, your grace. We seek asylum."

"You are the ebrs from the Outside." His voice was soft, but there was a smooth sort of power there. Could they persuade him to their side? "All may seek asylum here. Do not fear. Fear clouds the crystal of the mind and blocks the thoughts from meditation on the holy."

"We did not wish to make such a fuss," Ra'ael apologized. "We're being hunted."

"All is well now. Come, light a candle." The priest gestured toward the front of the chapel.

Taunos glanced at Ra'ael, who nodded and led them forward. Behind them, the priest swept to the heavy wooden doors through which they had entered, and tension gripped Taunos. He paused while Ra'ael and Takiyah continued on.

"They are granted asylum," the priest called out. Outside, people were clustering in front of the chapel. "None may harm them while they stay within these walls. Let the Scouts arrange judicious redress as necessary."

Taunos nodded to himself—the priest did have the voice of a natural orator. Now, how best to get them safely out and make sure war did not break out? He'd never considered the Kamalti a source of danger to his people. There was still Eian to find, too.

The wooden doors creaked closed, and Taunos let out a breath, pushing back the encroaching dizziness. He despised the clumsy weariness he'd lived with the past many moons, and now it was worsened by his head wound. How was he going to get them out of this mess? But running was no longer an option unless he could manage the impossible.

A smile broke out on Taunos's face. The impossible was what he did, and now that he was with Ra'ael and Takiyah... He caught up to them and took their hands in his.

"What are you doing?" Ra'ael whispered.

"Concentrating."

He closed his eyes, his brow furrowing with the strain. If he just tried hard enough, perhaps he could do it. If he realmwalked with them, they would all be safer—if he could keep their every detail in mind to make the shift. They'd cross together into the Everything between realms, crushed

244

and pummeled by the endless possibilities and chaotic energies there. And then his waypoint, where the sky was void of stars, a silver expanse around a black sun, where the endless grey dust rose into the air and avoided the clothes but clung to the skin. Then it'd be back through the Everything and somewhere else, somewhere safe on Rinara.

Sweat beaded on Taunos's brow, and his hands shook with the effort. He pushed further, gritting his teeth as he dug deep, but it was like pushing against a mountain—one that didn't have doors in its side.

Finally, he released them, stepping back to catch his balance and instead collapsing on a bench. He gasped for breath as the room spun around him in a mocking dance, his muscles like liquid.

"What is it?" Concern filled Takiyah's voice.

"I cannot do it," he gasped. He dragged himself up, slumping forward with his elbows on his knees, head in his hands.

"You tried to realmwalk with both of us?" Ra'ael whispered in awe.

"I'm not strong enough."

Takiyah sat next to him, her shoulder against his. "Thank you for trying."

Taunos didn't acknowledge her. It hadn't worked. Ra'ael's hand rested on his other shoulder, giving him some small comfort. His breathing eased as he recovered, and he sat back.

"Come," Ra'ael said. "We should light some candles. We may still get out of this."

She knelt before the candles and picked up a stem resting nearby. Murmuring to herself, Ra'ael lit the stem from an already burning candle, ignited a new candle, and passed it to Takiyah, who knelt and did likewise. Somewhat bemused, Taunos followed their example, then extinguished the stem and set it back down. The woman kneeling nearby gave them an appraising look before returning to her silent prayers.

They stayed there, Ra'ael murmuring softly and Takiyah's lips moving slightly, though she was silent. The priest passed behind them, shifting the arrangement of some crystals to the side. Taunos stared at the flame of the candle in front of him, wishing he knew the way out. Was the priest the answer? Dode? A wild, reckless chase through the city? No, he wouldn't be able to pull that off for a while, not without rest. Was his sister alive? And what about Eian? Would Answer drum up war against the savage Outsiders her people thought so little of? He'd seen people go to war over less.

Takiyah rose, retreating to one of the benches where she sat leaning forward with her elbows on her knees and her head bowed. Restless,

Taunos joined her, watching the chapel.

Ra'ael finished her prayers and stood, making her way to the priest, her voice low. "As we're within your house of worship, it's only right that I ask the favor of our worship here."

The priest waved his hand toward the candles. "You have already lit candles."

Ra'ael nodded. "And we thank you for that. But our worship isn't always silent, and we do not wish to disturb your other worshippers or you who have been so kind in providing asylum for us."

The priest looked thoughtfully at her. "What exactly does the worship of those who live on the Outside look like?"

A bit of unease crossed her face. That was interesting. Worship had never made Ra'ael uneasy.

She shifted. "It depends on many things. We have no houses of worship like this one. We only worship together during rituals."

"Is that true? That is very odd," the priest said.

"But I thought a chant may provide some comfort to our friend there, Takiyah. She has been through much."

"Let your priest there begin the rituals."

Oh, that wouldn't go well. Taunos stamped down on the laugh before it could break free.

"*I* am priestess." Ra'ael drew herself up.

The priest's mouth worked in astonishment before he found his voice. "You?" The priest shook his head. "You Outsiders have strange, strange ways, but who am I to say? The very thought!"

Rejoining them, Ra'ael began the chant, her voice quiet but strong. Taunos closed his eyes, taking their hands as the rhythm of the chant washed over him, easing his worries somewhat despite himself. This was why Ra'ael had wanted to be priestess, and she was very good at it. She never could have known she would perform her duties so very far from home.

ÌTAL-IHNISH
Chapter Nineteen

In memory of Torkaema and Naran, and in deference to the spirits, all Rinaryn should speak the Traveller's Tongue when congregated together for the holy Feasts of Starfall. Instead of attending to navigating the mixture of dialects, all will then be free to focus on the gathering and aligning all together to the will of Eloí.

-fragment of a scroll safeguarded by the Monks of Annularei

The curtain in Elisabei and Reinan's doorway was flung to the side as someone entered. Reinan had the intruder pinned against the wall before the shoe he'd been mending hit the dirt floor. Elisabei flanked him an instant later, her knife bared. Only then did they get a good look at her.

"Olorah? How...?"

"Shh!" Olorah hissed.

They strained to listen, Reinan's grip on his cousin relaxing. Only the silence answered, and finally, Elisabei released the breath she had been holding.

Reinan caught Olorah in an embrace that was fierce but brief. "Where's Masa?"

"She was meant for joining us. Six of us got out. I don't know what happened for her, Reinan, truly I don't."

Elisabei made Olorah sit down. "Tell us everything. How did you finally escape?"

Her voice trembled as she began with the tragedy of Ilos's death. "When the king took him, I knew something awful would happen. I took a chance—it was mind-sickness, I expect—on a newer captive. The spirit hadn't been beaten out of her yet. She made medicines and gave them for the rest of us. Anyway, when the king took my Ilos, I went for her, and Kaemada said—"

"Kaemada?" Elisabei interrupted.

"That was her name."

"Was that not the name of that foolish woman we helped find her child a few moons back?"

"The one Aleis took?" Reinan shrugged.

Elisabei nodded, scowling. "She should have kept her head down."

247

Olorah's gaze flickered from one to the other. Elisabei shook her head and gestured for her to continue.

"Well, she said she would help. I thought surely we would be found out and executed. But the king killed my boy! For my surprise, I and some of the others got for safety. But the guards came, and we needed for pulling the ropes up. The danger was too near—we needed for saving those of us who had escaped. The last I saw of Masa was the night before. She had planned on coming. Somehow, oh, Reinan, I'm so sorry! I do not know if they caught her, too."

"The king'll pay, I promise you," Reinan rumbled at last, his face as hard as stone. The day the king took Reinan's sister Masa had been almost as bad as the day the Kamalti had found Elisabei and brought her to this terrible city. Reinan had searched tirelessly to discover if someone had betrayed Masa to the king. All his fighting to free his cousins and keep them free, and then his sister was whisked right back to the palace.

When at last Elisabei could speak, she asked, "How shall we repay our king?"

"I'll organize the rest of the Resistance to a strike," Olorah said.

"We cannot do a full-scale strike. It's too dangerous." Elisabei shook her head.

"You're not for letting him get away with this, are you? Masa? Ilos?" Olorah snarled.

"Of course not," Elisabei snapped. "But that's no reason for getting us all killed."

"We go precise. In and out. Test the new batch of Boom," Reinan said.

"The guards would catch us immediately," Elisabei objected. "It's foolishness."

"Not if there's a distraction," Olorah said.

Reinan shook his head. "No."

"I can do it."

"The children," he reminded her.

"How long do you really think I can hide them? Their best chance at life is if the king's dead. Now that they're out of the palace, my sister can look after them."

Elisabei opened her mouth to voice another protest, but Olorah cut her off. "No. You cannot change my mind. This is my payment for the king taking Ilos away from me."

Elisabei sighed. Perhaps it was Olorah's mention of the woman, but her mind flashed back to Kaemada that night in their house, exhausted, overwhelmed, and yet fierce.

Is it so bad to dream? the woman had dared to ask them.

What were they really accomplishing, nipping at the guards here and there? Perhaps it was time to reach for something big, especially if they could give Masa a chance to escape.

"We're probably all mind-sick," Elisabei grumbled. "When do we go?"

"How soon can you be ready?"

"Immediately," Reinan said.

"Give me until the moons rise over the wall. You go in by the orchards. You know the door. I'll confront the main gate."

Elisabei nodded. There was not much time. Reinan stood and embraced his cousin again. "Go softly. Go well."

Olorah smiled at him. "You as well."

She turned and was gone, the curtain rippling behind her. Reinan and Elisabei hurried to ready themselves, digging out all of Reinan's Boom from the assorted hiding spots and loading it into bags they could carry to the palace. No words were needed but for a nod to each other when their tasks were completed.

Just as the second moon peeked over the wall, Elisabei and Reinan crept through the shadows of the night. Shrill, otherworldly screams broke the air, sending shivers up Elisabei's spine. What could cause such a noise? Not a single person was in sight, but when Elisabei chanced to look up, her breath caught in her throat. A massive crowd of Angels pressed against the dome of the City, screeching down at them. Elisabei shuddered, disconcerted and slightly relieved—the glance hadn't frozen her. But the sound filling the night was not the haunting Angels' Song. It was a cry of rage that made every hair on Elisabei's skin stand up. All she wanted was to flee.

Reinan squeezed her hand and she nodded, running with him toward the palace. The screaming of the Angels was an oddity they could take advantage of, and Olorah would expect them to. They dashed across the fields, approaching the large, elegant building.

Aleis sprinted through the shadows toward them, glancing over her shoulder now and then. Surprise struck Elisabei dumb as they ducked behind a purpleberry bush. Rebelliously, Elisabei took a berry and popped it in her mouth just to taste the forbidden fruit while they hid. Then, Aleis was gone and their way was clear.

They entered by the servant's door. The thick wood muted the shrieking of the Angels, and some of the tension oozed away from Elisabei. Creeping along the abandoned hallways, they deposited little bags in strategic locations behind them. Thanks to Olorah's force assaulting the main gates, they only encountered a few guards on their way, and those they interrogated fiercely.

Door by door, they searched for Masa. Elisabei's hopes were dwindling when they heard a scream. Reinan rushed forward and Elisabei flanked him. They rounded a corner, stumbling on Masa, baby in her arms, cowering from a guard.

Elisabei flicked her knife forward just as Reinan lunged. By the time her husband reached him, the guard was on the floor, Elisabei's knife in his eye.

Masa ran to them, shaking. "Olorah made it out?"

Reinan nodded with a broad grin.

Relief relaxed the lines of Masa's shoulders. "A woman helping us was caught. She had me hide, else I would have been caught, as well."

Elisabei collected her knife. "Is it on the way out? Olorah's attacking the main gate, but her distraction cannot hold for long."

Masa nodded.

She led them through the hallways to a long room with an ornate, raised chair. Two psions lay crumpled on either side of the rug, bleeding from stab wounds, and the king sprawled on his throne, his eyes staring sightlessly. Halfway down the room, a woman lay next to two unconscious guards. Blood soaked into the carpet beneath her, and bruises mottled her skin.

"That's her," Masa whispered.

Kaemada. The woman had certainly found the trouble she'd been looking for. She was still breathing, at least. Stomach turning, Elisabei draped her cloak over her to cover her injuries.

Reinen had paused by one of the guards, crouching next to him. With a shake of her head, Masa put a hand on his shoulder. "Theron's no worth it. He would have turned me in."

Elisabei glanced at her husband, her stomach sinking at the pain in his eyes. His past cast long shadows, but they had to move. Shaking himself, Reinan turned and scooped Kaemada into his arms. The wounded woman gave a low groan of protest at the movement.

"Destruction will be limited while carrying her," Elisabei said.

Reinan's eyes were hard, his voice thick. "We Boom what we can while we get out."

Elisabei nodded, casting a glance at his unconscious burden. If they survived this... Well, the first thing was to survive this.

A tiny form sped toward them from behind the throne. A child. He beat on Reinan's leg with his little fists. "Leave my mahkae alone! Leave my mahkae!"

"Oh, poor child!" Masa gasped. "That's her son."

The door loomed, empty for now. They had to leave right away, before guards came in force. They had what they came for and more.

Trapping Eian's fists in her hands, Elisabei knelt to look him in the eye. "Now, look here, little boy. We're getting you and your mahkae out of here, but you must be silent. Do you understand?"

He paused, tears filling his eyes, and then nodded, sniffing and wiping his nose with the back of his hand. Elisabei took his other hand. What atrocities had this boy witnessed? They had to get him out of the palace.

They retreated, trying to avoid jostling Reinan's burden so as not to provoke another moan of pain that might give them away. The little boy was remarkably silent. As they moved down the hallway away from the throne room, Elisabei lit a scrap of fabric with her fire stones, then threw the vial it was attached to. Her aim was sure, and it landed near one of the packets they had placed before. The explosion knocked the boy off his feet, sending up a cloud of dust.

Hauling the boy up, they sped on their way. A few paces farther on, Elisabei threw another lit vial down a side corridor, and Masa threw a third. By the fourth explosion, they could hear the shouts of guards trying to organize themselves. Elisabei smiled grimly. The corridors off their path were all trapped with Boom, and as they ran onward, Masa and Elisabei turned the guards' paths to rubble.

They burst out of the palace, Masa clutching her squalling baby tight in one arm, and the little boy clinging to Elisabei's hand. Elisabei cast a quick look back, smiling grimly at the destruction.

They wove through the chaotic streets. Screaming Angels were pressed to the dome everywhere. Twice they saw the bronze skin and large wings of death itself actively inside the City. Huddled clusters of people trapped in alleys or houses shouted. People hurtled through the streets, searching for safety. Their panic joined the shrieks of the enraged Angels before inevitably turning to howls of agony. Elisabei's heart pounded in her ears. Over all the horrific noise, how many had even heard the explosions from the palace? Even if their attack had been heard, no one would care—not when the Angels were tearing through houses and ripping people apart. Nowhere was safe.

Even so, they turned toward their house. Kaemada and Masa needed to be tended, their wounds bound. They needed to decide their next move, and if Olorah survived her assault, she'd send a messenger to their house. Two streets onward, a flash of bronze skin blocked them. They threw themselves into an alley. Elisabei pressed Eian close to the side of a house with her, giving Masa and Reinan a side-long look. If the Angels were singing their typical hunting song, they would already be Angels-food. Tonight, though, the stakes were even higher. Based on the sounds around them, if the Angels found them, they would kill them.

Masa's breaths came in rapid, shallow gasps. Reinan had his stern thinking face on, Kaemada limp in his arms. Only Eian seemed unaffected. She narrowed her eyes at him. He looked around, a far-off gaze to his eyes, not a hint of fear on his face.

"I wasn't expecting you for coming for me," Masa whispered.

"All you did need was a fighting chance, Masa. That's all you ever did need." Reinan smiled down at his sister.

The boy spoke. "To the door."

Elisabei scowled. Didn't he understand how much trouble they were in? "We can't get there. The Angels are everywhere. Even if they weren't, no one can leave the City."

Eian shook his head. "To the door. It's safe there."

"We will take you home with us, figure out our next move."

"The Angels will leave when we get there. They're just mad now." The boy stared east toward the mountain.

Sympathy quavered in Masa's voice. "He's touched, poor child."

Elisabei sighed. "We can't hide here forever. We must keep moving."

They waited a little longer, every muscle tensed, ears straining. When the Angels' screaming quieted to the west, they edged in that direction, racing across intersections to the precarious cover beyond. They slunk forward past two alleys until the shrieks and cries forced them north and then east again. Elisabei winced. They were moving toward the palace once more. Beyond lay the impenetrable mountains. They turned north to avoid a mob of people and almost immediately heard Angels bearing down on them until they ran east again.

"Elisabei! Reinan!" A hoarse whisper sounded to the north, and they dashed across another alley, at every moment expecting the Angels to catch them. In the shadows waited Olorah and a host of others, some familiar and others, strangers.

"We're being herded," Elisabei groaned, setting Eian on his feet and rubbing her aching arms.

Eian remained facing east. "They will leave when we get to the door. They will not be angry anymore."

"Who are they?" Elisabei narrowed her eyes at the strangers with Olorah. She removed a needle and thread from her bag and hastily began stitching up the woman in her husband's arms. No use failing to multi-task, especially since they were blocked from home. They would strategize in the street, since they had no other options.

"Palace psions. We found them unconscious."

"They're no dead," rumbled Reinan.

Olorah shook her head. "We broke in, saw guards breaking down doors, killing psions, bodies everywhere. We found a wing with psions still alive, just unconscious. Toah's potions brought them around, but as you can see, they're still stumbling. Freed some captives, too. All in all, our biggest success in... ever, that I can remember."

"Why did you no kill them?" Reinan repeated, narrowing his eyes.

"I was defenseless many winters," Olorah said, her voice like ice. "The psions were captives of the king, just like we were. Now we have them, and we know who they are. They think if they link together, the telekinetics might be able for pushing through the wall, especially with the help of your Boom. Think of it, Reinan! Freedom!"

"And if no?" Reinan asked.

Olorah shrugged. "Running away from the death of the king? Mighty suspicious, I think. Dragging them through the streets was hard work—we lost some good people."

Masa tilted her head toward Kaemada. "After they captured her, during the chaos, I heard some guards shouting about a psion in the throne room."

Elisabei's eyes widened, though her hands kept busy bandaging the larger wounds. She? A psion?

Olorah leaned forward, her words quiet but intense. "We're leaving at dawn, as soon as the Angels leave. We'll punch through the north wall by the gate. All we need is a place for hiding until then."

"We keep trying for getting home, but the Angels are always there," Elisabei said.

Masa nodded. "We split up. Perhaps we can break through this herding."

"The Angels are out there—it's a death trap!" Elisabei objected.

Masa smiled. "So will the City be when the guards come to revenge. Meet you at the northern wall near the gates at dawn."

Reinan frowned. "Masa, be careful."

Head high, baby cradled in her arms, Masa's defiance radiated from her like starlight. "Thanks to rescuing me, brother. I see another fighting chance, and I intend for taking it."

Elisabei drew her cloak back over Kaemada's body, veiling her like a corpse. With a tight smile at Olorah, Elisabei nodded, gathering her courage.

A nod from Reinan. "We go."

Olorah's expression was tight. "The wall at dawn."

"The wall at dawn."

Elisabei peeked around the corner, ducking back for a moment and signaling to the others it was clear. The Angels' shrieking rose and fell around them, and the cries of victims sounded not far off. One more deep breath and the group scattered. Elisabei sprinted beside her husband, and it quickly became just the four of them. Eian's hand clutched Elisabei's, and Kaemada lay silent under the shroud.

Two streets down and they had to change directions, then five more streets and they had to turn again, nearly trapping themselves in a dead-end. Once more, they were inexorably driven east to the wall, and every time they attempted to break free, the net of screaming Angels tightened around them. There were no guards, but then, why would there be? The guards would be happy to wait for their revenge until after the Angels were gone. They tried to pass by a group of Angels-food, but the normally mindless creatures reacted, pinning them against the wall of a house. Fingers snatched at her clothes as Elisabei fought and dodged her way free.

Elisabei shuddered as they drew closer and closer to the grey rocks. They needed an escape, but it seemed the only option left was to see if they could find the place where the Kamalti dumped those they caught. At least there, the Angels couldn't catch them. The spooky little boy might have a point.

They turned another corner. A crowd of Angels-food shambled in their direction, only a few houses away. They were pinning them in.

"Here!" shouted Reinan over the swell of Angels' screeching.

Elisabei scrambled toward him, away from the Angels-food, whose shambling picked up pace as the screeching around them swelled. Gritting her teeth and panting hard, they dashed into an alleyway. As they did so, she recognized it—the alley everyone in the City loathed. So many winters ago, the Kamalti had declared her guilty of trespassing, and then she had woken up in that alley, wondering how she'd gotten there.

Reinan pointed to the end of the alley, where the rocks were cracked open like a strange sort of door. If they could get through, it might provide some cover from the encroaching Angels and Angels-food.

Still, a great foreboding came over her.

"We will need to block the door behind us, assuming we can get it open." Elisabei's voice was strained.

The boy released her hand. He strode forward with a wide sweep of his little arms. "Beholuun Osundo!"

The doors shifted, then glided aside. Elisabei stared at Eian as he hopped through, seeming almost eager. "The door is open and someone is home!"

Reinan grimaced as he followed Eian in, carrying Kaemada. Elisabei tripped over something as she crossed the threshold in the dim light. The door crashed shut behind them.

Darkness surrounded them with eerie silence. Elisabei took a lantern from her pack and lit it. As the light flashed, Reinan gave her a look, one of his looks that spoke volumes without him ever saying a word. They'd overcome so much together, and now the king was dead. What was a spooky tunnel next to that? She forced a smile, feeling ever-so-slightly better as Reinan walked beside her, a hulking shelter against the dark. Eian strode forward as if he were home, pulling her onward. The tunnel floor sloped upward. Elisabei's breath came faster as fear pressed on her mind, primal and irrational.

Abruptly, Eian let go of her hand and ran forward. "Hello!"

The shadows swirled as four creatures came toward them. They were grotesque, with impossibly pale faces and skin so translucent Elisabei could see the blood moving through their veins. Their knobby skulls were bare of hair, their eyes were too large, and they had no noses. Reinan stepped back into a defensive stance. Staring, Elisabei's stomach clenched. She'd been so shocked the first time she'd seen Kamalti. This time, she saw details she didn't remember from winters ago. These seemed much paler even than she remembered. Some had lumps on their skin, some shuffled along as if their limbs didn't quite move properly, and some had open sores. All were dressed in rags.

One spoke, his voice merry but rough, as if long unused. "That is all right. You are as ugly to us as we are to you."

Kaemada moaned something, her voice breathy with pain and fatigue. Her eyelids fluttered.

The one who had spoken frowned. "No, no, no, we do not speak to you. Not to you who have the Gift. Only to those wretches lacking the Gift."

The creatures stretched out their hands. The gesture seemed ominous, and Elisabei stepped back. Kaemada bucked in Reinan's arms, cried out in pain, and then fell still once more.

"Stop, stop!" Eian screamed.

S. Kaeth

Elisabei shouted too, the words flowing before her mind caught up. "What are you doing?"

"You are not supposed to be here," sang another, stepping forward.

"You're—AH!" Reinan fell to his knees, dropping Kaemada, who rolled onto the stony floor.

Elisabei started forward, and the creatures turned on her. Pain crashed into her like a landslide. She couldn't move, couldn't think.

"Pain, pain, pain, fear, ahh!" Eian babbled, wringing his hands.

"You would attack a child?" Elisabei's only terrified thought was to shame them.

"We do not hurt him. He is too special to risk damaging," spoke one of the Kamalti.

"A precious vessel," said another.

"He has come again," said a third.

"Do you know in whose presence you travel?" asked a fourth, pointing at her.

Elisabei did not know, and soon she knew nothing at all as she sank into oblivion.

Chapter Twenty

Chapels and holy places are protected under Law, for what is a citizen without the guidance of religion? Priests must diligently attend to their duty in guiding the City and its beliefs so that all may thrive. Any person seeking to destroy, dismantle, damage, or steal from a chapel or holy man merits the highest punishment.

-legal proposal circulated among the Justices of Codr

Taunos peered out the colored glass window at the crowd growing outside. He grimaced. It seemed every time he checked, it had grown. Restless energy demanded he move, and he paced back to Ra'ael and Takiyah, glancing over the others as he went. The woman who had been lighting candles had already left, and now the man who had been meditating rose, exiting the building. Tension filled Taunos's shoulders as the doors opened, and the sounds of the mob grew louder. But the doors swung shut again and the priest latched them, shutting out the noise of the crowd. They'd stayed away from the doors, but no one had tried to enter the chapel. Still, all that kept the Scouts from entering seemed to be their sense of decency. They were trapped.

Taunos perched on the edge of a bench. His stomach growled, but there was nothing to eat. Scrubbing his hand over his bald head, he stood again, going back to the window once more. The ever-changing mass of angry Kamalti outside surrounded the little building. The lights dimmed as the night cycle began, but that didn't seem to bother the mob.

This wasn't the first time he'd been in a tight spot. Galod had put him in seemingly impossible situations all the time.

Climb to the top of that tree and bring me a feather from the raptor's nest without getting scratched up.

How many eggs are in the tserwora den? Nevermind that they're venomous, temperamental, and extremely territorial.

He'd been turning him into a legend. The Elders were the same, constantly expecting miracles. And he had delivered again and again.

But now, his people were in danger, especially if Answer made good on her threat. It was easier to balance the danger when he was far from them—less chance of a mistake finding its way across the worlds to harm them. Now, with the loss of his sister, how could he risk her friends? When they'd first been captured, he'd expected only to be confined for a little while. It would be boring and humiliating, but a safer bet than fighting their way out, and they could probably negotiate for a lesser sentence with time. After all, they'd only been trespassing. He hadn't realized...

They had tortured Takiyah, maimed her, branded her like an animal.

He passed his hands over his face. Ra'ael sat with her arm around Takiyah, their heads bowed close together. Terror crawled up his spine at the thought of losing them as well. If he returned home without them, Galod would be furious. Rightfully so. And the Elders, they would rant about the law and threaten him with banishment, but of course, they'd let him come home. They always did. He was too valuable for them to lose. If he could keep Takiyah and Ra'ael alive and get them home, the Elders would threaten and posture, but still, they'd welcome them.

Answer's threat haunted him. He had to warn his people just in case Answer drummed her Kamalti fellows into war. By the looks of the crowd outside, that wouldn't be too difficult.

He gritted his teeth, clenched one fist in the other hand, and paced along the wall again.

"What happens if the priest leaves?" Takiyah murmured.

"There's nothing stopping them from coming in and forcibly taking us right now," Taunos said, eyes on the priest.

"Fear not, my children. I will stay to light your way through the long night." Ever calm, the priest smiled at them, lighting lanterns along the wall.

"Why?" Taunos narrowed his eyes at the priest, moving aside as the robed Kamalti passed him.

"He's an honorable man," Ra'ael said. "Dode often comes to worship here, and the priest has never shown hostility toward me."

"Fear, hatred, and violence are not the way of Kellendine," the priest said, lighting another lantern. "Order and composure are achieved through control of the self, not through giving way to base emotions."

He turned to walk along the wall again.

"Taunos, stop pacing. My nerves are tighter than the drums I dance on without you adding to it!" Ra'ael snapped.

With a sigh, Taunos brought himself to a halt despite the urge to move.

The priest smiled at him. "Fear clouds the mind, my son."

"I'm not your son." Taunos clenched his fists. He shouldn't be snapping at the poor man. He should be talking to him, getting him on their side. His soul ached, strained like a branch bent to the snapping point.

The priest's smile didn't dim. "We are all children of Kellendine, even Outsiders."

Taunos stared at the flickering flame, fighting for control over his frustration and fear. "Will you remind your people of that if they work themselves into a frenzy? Will you keep them from thinking of war?"

The priest frowned. "War? What, with the Outsiders? The Scouts would need to gain the agreement of the Justices and Philosophers for that."

"The people seem ready enough," Taunos said, tilting his head meaningfully toward the wall.

The priest shook his head. "The people do not mind you. The allies of Scouts make up the majority of that mob."

"Can you help us?"

"I am sorry, my son. I will speak for you, but I cannot take sides. The nobles would not listen, anyway. Kellendine has raised them much higher than I."

Taunos snorted. "Seems you need to talk to Ra'ael. She would happily enlighten you on the respect my people give our priests and priestesses."

The priest smiled. "I have heard. She and Dode come here often to worship."

"Dode said we were in the Scouts' sector. Would it have changed if we were elsewhere?"

The priest shook his head. "Not to any degree that matters to you. Two ebrs of the Scouts claiming asylum, and one of you from a highly respected family—the Scouts take offense to such things. They patrol all districts of the City, but if they caught you in a district controlled by one of the other noble factions, they would report to them. That you also claimed asylum in a Scouting district, this only heightens their anger."

"What happens if we're still here when a crowd comes to worship?"

"I will give you my own room if you wish it, to be sure no one tries to capture you. I promise you, on my faith in Kellendine, I will hold to the Honor of the Law. No one will wrest you from asylum on my watch. But once the Scouts organize, there is nothing I will be able to do. I am sorry. I will pray for you."

Taunos nodded.

"You carry heavy burdens." The priest laid a hand on his shoulder. "Who put these on you? Set them down."

Who had? The Elders, he thought immediately. But that wasn't so, not truly. He'd been protecting his people ever since that night at the end of

Ra'ael, Takiyah, and Kaemada's yahs, when he'd woken to find his kaetal attacked by Darks. The night he'd first been called a hero.

How could he release himself of that burden, of the responsibility for his people? He wasn't sure he wanted to, heavy as it was. It didn't seem quite honorable. And yet, here in the chapel, Ra'ael shone and Takiyah no longer trembled.

"I do not know if I can set them down," he confessed. "But I will see what I can do about sharing them."

The priest smiled, inclining his head.

"Tāt woowanihum bunlaey, dasa woodisāum nlaey, reln wooteirihum nlaey." Ra'ael was chanting as they paused by the bench.

A questioning look on his face, the priest paused.

Taunos translated. "Fire walk with you, water guide you, mists protect you."

The priest bowed, his expression pleased. "May the Gifts of the Takanis light your way, the Gifts of the Prusotak clear your mind, and may the love of Kellendine guide your heart. I will be just around the corner if you need me."

Taunos woke from a restless sleep. The clamor of angry voices filled the air. He leapt to his feet, tensed and ready. A blanket fell to the ground, and he picked it up, turning it over in his hands. The priest must have covered them at some point in the night. Odd, that he hadn't woken. No one else was visible aside from Ra'ael, sitting up warily, and Takiyah, who was stirring.

Taunos went to the window. The crowd had grown larger still, including several Scouts in uniform. The priest had been right—nearly all the people in the crowd wore finely woven garments, and several wore jewels. A line of people struggled to get through the mob, Dode among them, but the crowd blocked their way. Chanting rang out, voices seasoned with hatred and fear. Some called for the priest to stop harboring fugitives. Others cried out for the priest to be dragged out to face the Justices.

His expression worn and anxious, the priest emerged from his room carrying a tea tray. Still, he greeted them warmly and poured cups of steaming tea.

Taunos held up the blanket. "Thank you."

"It is nothing." But the priest rubbed his bald head as he peered out of the windows, pacing from one to another.

Ra'ael invited him to share the tea, and the priest reluctantly joined them. Silence stretched between them as they drank. Taunos forced himself to appear calm, but that task became harder and harder, his nerves fraying as the clamor outside increased.

A sharp, metallic taste assaulted Taunos with a scent like the air after a storm. Ra'ael wrinkled her nose, clearly sensing it as well.

"What is it?" Takiyah asked, gripping their hands.

"It's as if you bit down on the flat of a blade, only in your mind," Ra'ael explained.

"That's the Gift of the Takanis." The priest's tone was thoughtful.

"What?" Taunos asked. It was the same feeling he'd sensed before he'd fought the thieves, but he'd never gotten an explanation.

"I have felt it before, in Dode's rock garden. She made a handful of pebbles become one rock somehow," Ra'ael said.

Taunos raised his shaven eyebrows.

"What are they doing?" Takiyah asked.

The walls shuddered. That did not bode well. Would the mob storm the chapel to seize them? Every exit was blocked, the entire building surrounded. Taunos ground his teeth, looking around. There had to be a way out.

"They would not dare! They would not dare!" The priest ran from one window to another, fear etched in every line of his body. His eyes darted around his precious chapel, his fingers fidgeting at his robes.

Taunos took Ra'ael's hand as the building shuddered again, dropping dust from the ceiling. Takiyah cried out, her face twisted in panic. As she clutched at Taunos's shirt, fresh hatred for the Kamalti filled his heart. He pulled them both to the middle of the chapel, away from the walls.

"The blasphemy!" The priest scowled. The metallic twang rose abruptly—coming from him.

Whole sections of the ceiling cracked and shifted, raining debris and shattered glass. Taunos and Ra'ael, their fingers entwined, pushed at the larger sections with their telekinesis, but the dust rose and choked them. Somehow, the ceiling didn't collapse. The priest stood next to them, his face rigid with strain, hands raised upward much like theirs were. Even united, they were barely holding the ceiling together.

A stained glass window exploded, and the priest cried out in anguish. A section of the ceiling fell on the candles next to the beautiful crystals on the altar.

"No, no, no, not the crystals!" The priest raced to the altar.

"No, come back," yelled Ra'ael.

The weight of the ceiling on his telekinesis increased, and Taunos's knees buckled under the strain. He groaned, the pressure growing further as Ra'ael reached out toward the priest. A pane of glass from the ceiling fell to the side of the priest. A slab of stone shifted, sliding toward them. Taunos shouted, pushing it away, but it was too big, and he was too exhausted. The stones came down, the dust rose up, and they were buried alive.

Claustrophobia pressed against him, snuffing out any thoughts. Taunos struggled blindly. Ra'ael flailed, kicking him in the shin. Sparks flashed, and he glimpsed Takiyah's face. She grabbed his hand, and he held on tight as she pulled. Rubble shifted around them, smothering him. Another flash of fire, another pull. He kicked his way free of a large rock. And then, suddenly, there was light and air. He gasped, dragging himself to the surface as Takiyah pulled Ra'ael, kicking and clawing, to the top as well. Taunos grabbed their hands as they lay on the ruins of the chapel.

They had to move, but he couldn't summon the strength. All he could do was cough and struggle to breathe. His head pounded, his vision dimmed from the strength of the telekinesis he'd used.

"There they are!" someone cried.

"Get them!"

Rough hands seized them, pressing his face into the sharp stones. He twisted and fought, roaring his defiance even as his hands were bound behind his back.

"It's not your fault, Taunos," Takiyah shouted beside him. "It is not your fault."

But it was. He should have seen this coming, shouldn't have allowed the situations that put them here. And Takiyah had suffered the worst of all of them.

The man holding Takiyah down struck her, shouting, "Be quiet."

"Leave her alone. Leave her—" Taunos struggled to no avail.

They dragged him to his feet and backward, away from Ra'ael and Takiyah, wrenching his arms. He gritted his teeth and fought harder. The desperate terror on Takiyah's face as she was yanked farther from Ra'ael seared through him. A cold iron collar snapped around his neck, heavy with captivity and cruelty, and all he could do was watch as collars were fastened around Ra'ael's and Takiyah's necks, too.

"What is going on here?" Dode's voice was cold with fury, coming around the edge of the rubble.

"Go away, Dode." Answer's tone was just as icy.

Hearing her voice, Taunos twisted. The Kamalti holding him struck the side of his head, sending him to his knees.

"What happened to the chapel!?" cried Dode in disbelief and outrage.

"It fell," Answer snapped. She turned away, but not before Taunos saw her struggling to remain composed.

"The priest!" Ra'ael gasped. "He ran to save the crystals. The roof fell. I could not stop it."

Murmurs ran through parts of the crowd, while others remained silent, glaring. Answer glanced back and winced, guilt all over her face.

Dode's voice shook with rage. "It is true they no longer have asylum if there is no longer a chapel. Could you not find another way? Was this worth it?"

"This was done when I got here," Answer protested.

"But did you know about it?" Dode glared at the crowd. "Clear this rubble. Can you not see? We must find out if you have murdered a man!"

Chapter Twenty-one

It is a great sadness when a child is born with a deformity or stain, such as magic blood. However, those who use magic or who are too deformed for society must be cast aside for the greater order to prevail. Those who shield such creatures should be fined to teach them to obey, especially given the reasons…

-letter scrap in the City of Codr

Pressure built inside Kaemada's head like she was an egg being cracked open. It was just like after she fell, during her first encounter with these people. In remembering, she felt the sensation doubly: in the present and in the past, together at once. The strangers forced their way through her defenses while she once again was unable to use her powers. Fear seized her. If they continued to force access to her psionics, could they cripple her permanently? She shivered and pushed back at them, panicked that her abilities might be forever lost to her.

Nonsense! clamored voices in her mind. *We are careful. You will see. We are gentle.*

The voices rose louder, hundreds of them all demanding her attention such that she couldn't focus to hear or see the outside world. She struggled against them, choked on them, drowned in them.

Stop fighting us. You have the Gift. Use the Gift. The Gift makes us one, and you will be one with us. This is the Great Sharing. The Magnificent Cooperative. The Glorious Collective. The Splendid Union.

Kaemada floated. The ocean surged around her, at once as tumultuous and dangerous as Dead Man's Sea, yet also as inviting and comforting as the seas of Havenshore. It was an ocean made of the minds and thoughts, the desires and feelings, the personalities and hopes, dreams, and fears of the Kamalti psions. They were welcoming and reserved, excited and angry, understanding and quick to take offense. They washed over her and around her such that sometimes she floundered and sometimes she soared.

In such a sea of persons and minds, she kept losing hold of who she was and what she wanted and how she felt. Was this how it felt to be an untrained psion who had lost all sense of themselves? It was liberating and terrifying all at the same time. The ripples of her own feelings spread throughout the collection of minds merged around her and with her.

The time she spent in the oblivion and fullness that consumed her—and yet *was* her—seemed at once infinite and minuscule. She was there for moments. She was there for an eternity.

Far away, soft hands patted her face. The touch was familiar, and a great love rose in her. Small hands, frantic. She fought her way free of the lull and the pull of the other minds. She was lying on the cold, hard floor of the tunnel. Eian was patting her face, sobbing. Was he all alone?

The answer came immediately to her mind. *The others are lying near you, sleeping.* Images of Elisabei and Reinan bloomed in her vision. *They threatened the Collective and have been punished. They are bad, dangerous. They should be sent back to the City.*

No! They were her friends! They were good people, and she trusted them. They weren't going to hurt anyone. They only felt attacked.

Attacked. The Kamalti psions are being attacked. You are a psion. Stand with the Collective. Stand against the intruders, except the small one.

No! Her thoughts kept merging with the Collective's, her will melding with theirs. She struggled, focusing on the impossible task of keeping herself separate. *No, they're not a danger.*

She needed to wake up. Could she wake up? Would it hurt?

The pain in her head was gone. The damage had been soothed and the pain had been shared and diluted.

Eian was frightened. She needed to comfort him.

Images, emotions, and thoughts washed over her, spinning her around and disorienting her as thoroughly as the time many summers ago when she had slipped and fallen under a waterfall, pummeled by the waters. Her song was mixing with the larger, louder song of the Collective, becoming only a harmony to theirs. If she'd had Tannevar with her, she could have relied on his steady presence and the strength of their bond to anchor her. Instead, she was besieged by images and spun around and around until there was no edge between herself and others. There was only being.

A babe and a very young woman sheltered beneath the Seeker Tree with its unique white bark and silver leaves. The grass around grew lush and green, then brown and brittle, then frosted and covered with snow, then sparse and light green, finally back to the lush green of before. The babe and the young woman completed a cycle of seasons under the Seeker Tree. The woman disappeared, and the babe was left alone until a cloaked figure came and took the infant.

Kamalti moved about, reading aloud to vast audiences from ancient, well-maintained, and beautifully engraved books. An angry crowd shouted and shook their fists, throwing objects. They pushed the Kamalti forth from them. A door shut firmly, leaving the exiled on one side and the community on the other.

Great scraps of burning metal fell, and strange people emerged who looked much like Rinaryn but taller, with no wings. They looked like Takiyah and Galod. Kamalti greeted them, bowing low with awe.

There was her, walking up on high, then falling toward the edge of the ridge. Many telekinetic pushes reached up and shoved Ra'ael and Taunos's hands away. *Be one with us.* They cradled her, gently bringing her to the bottom of the chasm.

Kamalti psions ventured out into the City of the Lost in the chaos following the king's death, drawn by curiosity about her mind-burst. Pleasure filled them as they spoke to sleeping psions and confusion boiled in them as those minds winked out again and again. Their hatred and fear of the Angels, their worry over the screaming Angels, surrounded her. Light caught them and blinded them, and therefore her, painful and blazing. Their fear of the sunlight she loved so much flowed through her.

Emotions spilled over her with the images—fear, respect, admiration, shame, anger, hatred, honor, love, joy, jealousy, confusion.

Kaemada's head spun. Some of what she saw was symbolism, had to be symbolism, but which parts? The onslaught of incoming thoughts and images and emotions made it impossible to process any one thing. Shock struck her like a splash of cold water in the face. The people down here were all either psions or those considered deformed by the Kamalti. Tossed down here with the refuse.

That was wrong, just as surely as the conditions in the City of the Lost had been wrong.

The ancient stories ran through her mind, how the psions grew powerful in the Great War so long ago. She told them how the people became afraid of the psions and targeted them first in battles, together with those who had wings. Some even targeted and killed psions on their own side. Torkaema brought the people together, ending the wars. He was tolerant of the psions, and now psions were accepted, so long as they used their powers only for the good of the community.

We're not broken. We're not deformed. We are powerful. We are strong. We're not subject to their judgement of our worth!

She rode on the waves of the minds around her, rudderless, out of control. No! She needed an anchor. She missed Tannevar, grief overwhelming her.

The wolf fell, died, and fed us, living on in our bodies. The sacrifice was worthy.

No! Anger and nausea filled her, and confusion at her own rage, echoing from the psions' confusion.

She tore herself apart from them. She was separate. She was not one with the mass of minds. She was her own!

At long last, she was released, and she crawled back to her body, or in what direction she hoped her body was. She needed to regain her senses. Eian. Eian had been crying. She was Kaemada. She was separate from the melded minds around her. She had to check on Eian.

~

Elisabei woke first, to the sound of Eian weeping. Her head pounded as she struggled to sit up. The Kamalti stared at them, looming from the shadows. The old horror of seeing them for the very first time washed over her. Despite herself, Elisabei shuddered.

They should go out the door they'd come in, escape into the city. Olorah would be looking for them. But the Angels might be lying in wait, or if they were gone, the guards would be thirsty for blood. And how to account for the Angels-food? Would they be mostly docile again, or would they remain dangerous? She peered down the tunnel. The strange vanishing door had crashed shut. Could they get out that way now? Even if they could manage to get it open again, even if the Angels-food and Angels were no longer an issue, they'd have to battle their way through the guards and hope the psions had blasted through the wall.

Perhaps there was another way out of the mountain. The Kamalti had captured her when they found her off the trail six winters ago. But they hadn't listened then; there was no reason to believe they'd be more reasonable now.

The little boy crouched by Kaemada's body, where she lay crumpled in the tunnel, shaking her. Reinan sprawled nearby on the floor. With a groan, Elisabei crawled over to her husband to check for breath. Eian watched her, his sobbing quieting.

Once she was sure that Reinan and Kaemada were merely unconscious, she looked at Eian. "How long were we out?"

Eian wiped his nose with the back of his hand and hiccuped. "A long time."

"How long?"

"I'm hungry."

How was she supposed to make a decision with such awful

information? Elisabei gritted her teeth.

Eian's face crumpled, and he curled inward on himself, rocking back and forth.

Well, that hadn't helped at all. Awkwardly, she pulled the boy close for a hug. "She's only sleeping. It may do her some good, help her heal."

Eian nodded, sniffed, and hiccuped again. "I was scared."

Elisabei patted his shoulder. "I know. So was I."

After a little bit, Elisabei pulled over her pack, cast a wary glance at the statue-like Kamalti, and opened it, sharing some food with the boy.

"Not too much. We do not know how long we will be here," she cautioned. Devouring her own meager meal, she then turned her attention to stitching and bandaging Kaemada's wounds as well as she could. The dangers now were blood loss and infection, at least from what she could see in the dim, flickering light. But why wasn't the woman awake?

Not long after she repacked their supplies, Reinan finally stirred and woke. He grumbled, shooting a dark look toward the Kamalti. Then, he indicated Kaemada with raised eyebrows.

Elisabei shook her head, answering his unspoken question. "She's only unconscious."

With a grunt, Reinan sat back against the wall. At least here, they were not in immediate danger. They would wait a bit for things to calm down out there and give Kaemada time to heal. If she was mobile, they would have their hands free, just in case they needed to fight. They waited in silence, keeping track of the time by the amount of oil their lamp was burning. It did waste fuel, but without the light, they might not make it through the waiting sane. The tunnel remained utterly changeless save for the occasional movements of the psions as they shambled in and out of the darkness beyond their tiny pool of light.

The psions kept their distance, but the constant staring made Elisabei shudder. After what she guessed was a day of waiting, both she and Reinan were eager to move. But where to go? Backward was as dangerous as forward.

Reinan bent to pick up Kaemada, but four of the psions advanced, arms outstretched. "We have not finished conversing."

Her husband hesitated.

Elisabei clenched her fists, unnerved by the prospect of feeling that mental pain again. "Are we prisoners here?"

"No. Go, stay, we care not. But this one stays until we finish our conversation."

"We should move on," Elisabei said to Reinan.

"I'm not leaving my mahkae." Stubbornness filled the boy's voice, and his eyebrows were drawn in a line.

Reinan sat in thought for some time, then nodded. Eian scowled at them as they rose. Reinan picked up Kaemada while Elisabei took the boy's hand, but as soon as they took a step, the Kamalti psions were there. They tried to go around, and pain roared in their heads, crumpling them. By the time Elisabei could think again, Eian was crouched over his mother once more, while the Kamalti hovered at the edge of the shadows.

She exchanged a glance with Reinan. The city hadn't hardened her that much, to just abandon the boy. She flicked her gaze to Eian, and Reinan nodded, but when Reinan picked the boy up and stepped away from the mother, he screeched like the screaming Angels, kicking and clawing. The Kamalti advanced on them again, hands outstretched. Reinan quickly put Eian back down.

"Haven't you finished your talk yet?" Elisabei's frustration poured out in her voice as she turned on the psions.

"No."

How long could a conversation last, and what exactly were they talking about that was so fascinating?

But there were no better options. They waited.

Finally, Kaemada groaned and stirred. Relief sighed out of Elisabei. She laid a calming hand on Kaemada's shoulder as the woman jerked and flailed, trying to sit up. Recognition slowly flickered in Kaemada's eyes. She relaxed some, especially when Eian squeezed her, burrowing his head in her shoulder. She groaned, but clung to her son, kissing his hair. Tears leaked past her eyelashes and down her cheeks.

Elisabei grabbed their supplies, throwing them in her pack. They needed to move. "You're finally awake. Good. At least rest helped you heal some."

Kaemada said something, her tone almost wistful.

Elisabei clucked her tongue. It had been several winters since she'd heard Rinaryn. "Why are you speaking Rinaryn?"

Kaemada shook her head. "Aonat mino Waneidei Vair!"

"I'm speaking plain Traveller's." Eian's translation prompted a quizzical look from Kaemada.

Biting back her exasperation, Elisabei leaned forward. "No. You're not."

Kaemada shrank back, clasping shaking hands over her mouth. "Elisabei? Lameis! Lameis onsa nlaey ehreiuw!"

Eyes. Something about eyes. Elisabei rubbed her eyes absently.

Confusion wrinkled Eian's brow as he translated. "You're bleeding! You're bleeding from your eyes!"

Elisabei sighed. "I'm not, Kaemada. You're seeing things."

Reinan shook his head. "She's mind-sick."

"This kind of thing can happen in those who have had a great injury to their heads," Elisabei said.

One arm around the boy, Kaemada rubbed her eyes, then squeezed them shut. She said something in sorrowful tones.

Eian translated, "They said they would fix me."

A snort escaped Elisabei. Clearly the Kamalti psions had lied—they hadn't fixed her at all.

Another murmur. "You helped me. Thank you."

Elisabei shook her head. "And you're not even surprised, are you?" She glanced at Reinan, then back at Kaemada. "Well. The king is dead. Two key captives escaped, among several others, and many guards are dead. Oh, yes, and we no longer have to worry about the king's psions."

Laid out like that, it was a great victory for the Resistance, especially if they'd managed to break through the wall of the city. Gratitude lifted her heart in a reluctant wave.

"I never would have dreamed it possible," Elisabei said. "We will likely have someone worse set themselves up as king, but now, for the first time, I have some hope. Thank you for that."

Kaemada closed her eyes as she rested her head on the wall behind her, looking pained.

"You will recover, Kaemada," Elisabei said.

"At what cost?" Kaemada cried over and around Eian, who continued to translate her words. "I have done nothing well or right or good! I have only brought suffering and death where there has already been too much of both! I keep intruding on the minds of others and sending them from consciousness. I tried to escape and nearly got us killed because I trusted the wrong person! I cannot protect myself. How can I protect Eian? It was my fault Eian went missing, my fault that my friends and I were caught by the Kamalti. And where are they? I do not even know if they're all right. I lost my wolf when I fell—poor Tannevar died because of me! And I miss him so. All I want is to help, but I seem to only bring pain and trouble. It's no use!"

Kaemada shut her mouth abruptly, flushed and shamed. She buried her head in her hands.

"Come on," Elisabei snapped. "You're alive. That's what matters right now. We need to go before those Kamalti decide to have another little talk with you."

It took a moment before Kaemada spoke again, and she did so with her eyes closed while Eian translated. "They wanted to talk. They speak with people before they go to the city, and sometimes they go into the city to find people to converse with. That's how you found the door. I think... Yes, I think the Kamalti send all their psions down here as soon as they're discovered, along with those they consider deformed. They're afraid; the Kamalti think they're dangerous."

"I'm inclined to agree about these particular people," Elisabei grumbled. "Will they let us go?"

Pack shouldered, Reinan watched the silent, still psions.

Kaemada considered the Kamalti quietly, then nodded. Eian translated, "Yes. We wanted to talk. I mean, they wanted to talk. Just to talk."

"Better go before they change their minds," Reinan rumbled.

Kaemada smiled slowly, still looking at the Kamalti. Elisabei shivered. It was spooky.

Eian translated as she spoke. "They share everything. Everything. But because we all agree before we—I mean, they—act, they do not change their minds so quickly and easily as you are used to, Reinan."

"Still, it's probably best not to take chances." Elisabei frowned at Kaemada, but it was too dark to do much down in the tunnel. Hopefully the condition didn't worsen. She wasn't sure she could fix mind-sickness.

Fear washed over Kaemada's face and bearing in a wave. "My brother, my friends! The Collective heard them. They're in trouble. The tunnel leads to a chasm." She shook her head abruptly. "The Kamalti bring travellers—like you, Elisabei—to the cage at the end of the tunnel and drop them off. They haul the cage back to the top so the Collective cannot escape."

"I don't remember any of this," Elisabei argued.

"The Collective reads the memories of the travellers and sends them on to the city. Some try to escape. Many have climbed the chasm walls. They die. The Collective feels those deaths, the fear, the pain. The chasm terrifies them." She shuddered abruptly, dry-heaving. Eian, translating, looked pale.

Elisabei looked at Reinan. A cage that could be hauled to the top of a cliff? A chasm whose walls might be climbable? It sounded ominous, even if they didn't have a child and a woman of questionable mental wellness to deal with.

"We have to go up the chasm!" Kaemada said. "The enemy has our friends. You can show us the ways to fall in the chasm."

Elisabei shuddered at the way Kaemada drifted into speaking Traveller's, but in plural speech. "We don't want to fall, Kaemada!"

"There may be a way. We can guide you. You will show us," the woman continued.

Reinan exchanged another look with her, and Elisabei sighed, glancing back toward the city. It would be a death trap, as the guards would take their anger out on everyone they thought might be involved. Reinan could well find himself hunted. And yet, a tunnel past creepy psions that led to a chasm no one had managed to climb didn't sound any better.

Straightening his shoulders, Reinan tilted his head toward the tunnel and picked up his pack.

One way was as good as the other, she supposed. With a sigh, Elisabei grabbed her pack and followed. She let Kaemada lean on her for support while her son held her hand, leaving Reinan free in case they needed defense. They slid past the watchful psions, who turned as they went to keep them in view.

The tunnel ended at the bottom of a ravine. Directly in front of them was a smooth section of rock with a large metal box hanging far above them. Thick chains led from the top of it out of sight to the side of the chasm walls. She could see no way to get to it, though, and no chains dangled from it to the floor of the chasm.

Kaemada's weight grew heavier and the air grew stifling as Elisabei all but dragged her along. Kaemada began to startle at nothing, and Elisabei wondered if she was hallucinating again or if it was just their surroundings. Several times, the woman pointed at the chasm walls, naming people and indicating where they had started their climb as well as where they fell and died. Bones, fragments of tools, and other garbage littered the ground in large mounds. At one point, Kaemada let out a strangled sob and rested her hand on the skull of some canine animal at the edge of the cliff, weeping. Elisabei dragged her away from whatever hallucination had gripped her, ignoring her weak struggles. Twice, they were nearly hit as people above dumped buckets of refuse into the chasm.

Finally, Reinan stopped and stared up at the wall. "Here, the rock is good for climbing."

"Betah Eian?" Kaemada asked, looking doubtful. Her question needed no translating.

"We will use my shawls to tie him to my back," Elisabei said. "And Reinan can carry you."

An excited spark lit in the boy's brown eyes.

Kaemada protested, but Elisabei cut her off. "You're in no condition to climb. Be carried or stay here."

Thankfully, the woman didn't call her bluff. Kaemada nodded. "Tsíffrorse, Reinan. The Collective trusts you can find a way up. We have seen your memories."

Reinan's glare burned like fire, and he went very, very still.

Elisabei laid a hand on his arm. Her instincts screamed at her to put distance between them and this woman who knew too much and, apparently, was still connected to the psions that attacked them. The whole situation set her skin to crawling. And yet, she agreed with their assessment. If anyone could get them up the cliff walls, it would be Reinan.

Reinan abruptly lifted Eian and tied him to Elisabei's back, and Elisabei began to breathe again. Eian laughed and clung delightedly to her shoulders as Elisabei tied Kaemada to her husband's back with their length of rope. It was humiliating, she was sure, but how else were they all to get up the wall?

Elisabei started the climb, casting a worried look behind her at Reinan. She shook her head to herself and attended to the task before her. He'd better not slip.

The arduous climb was punctuated by Kaemada pointing out the places where previous climbers had fallen, stressing places where they got farther. Reinan went slowly in those areas, avoiding some altogether due to weak stone. Occasionally, they found tiny ledges where they stopped to rest and catch their breath. Elisabei avoided looking down, always keeping a firm hand on the rock wall, even while resting. She couldn't wait to be back on solid ground. But danger and hardship were no strangers to her—she wasn't going to let a rock wall beat her, even if her palms were slippery with sweat. Eian, for one, enjoyed himself immensely, and Elisabei had to remind him more than once to stop dancing about in the shawl sling for fear he might fall.

Slowly, slowly, bit by bit, they climbed. About halfway up, Kaemada ducked, clutching at Reinan and causing his hold on the rocks to slip. Looser stones nearby broke free to clatter down below them.

With clenched teeth, Reinan adjusted his grip, keeping his body close to the wall to recover.

"There's nothing there, Kaemada," Elisabei shouted. "Ignore it!"

They continued while Kaemada trembled, her eyes closed, and her head resting on Reinan's back. The silence was much preferable to the woman's ominous warnings of dangerous areas, however helpful they were.

They were resting again, about three quarters of the way up the wall, when the sound of singing came to their ears. A male voice muddied the words more often than not, but the tune was familiar. Kaemada straightened, looking around with wide eyes, her expression troubled.

"I hear it, too," Elisabei said, rubbing arms that felt utterly drained of strength. "The Preparation Song, is it not?"

Kaemada nodded, closing her eyes with a soft smile. Then she frowned.

"Why is it being sung here?" Eian translated for her.

Elisabei shook her head. "The question is, what do we do about it? Do we go toward it?"

"It's not my brother," Kaemada mused.

"The Kamalti did not seem very interested in our songs six winters ago," Elisabei said.

Kaemada nodded. "Maybe something has changed?"

Reinan rolled his shoulders and set his hands to the rocks again.

Elisabei sighed. "Might as well, I suppose."

They angled their approach, using the song as a guide, though their new direction led them through a difficult patch. Somehow they managed to reach the top. Clinging to the rocks, Elisabei peeked over the edge.

A narrow space extended between the chasm and a low wall that rose to about waist height. Beyond the wall, a massive pillar rose to the ceiling, big enough for ten houses in the City of the Lost. She couldn't see any Kamalti, but the song drifted from somewhere just past the wall. Beyond the pillar, towers of lights illuminated enormous buildings carved right out of the rock walls, with windows decorated by flowing curtains. Sharp-angled metal buildings sat on the side of the ravine, and the street beyond was paved with stone and lit with glowing orbs.

Nodding to the others, she hoisted herself up, keeping low to the ground due to equal parts stealth and fatigue. Reinan crawled up beside her, and she breathed a sigh of relief. Somehow, they had made it. She undid the knots, setting Kaemada and Eian free of their supports.

"I think it goes like this," a voice interrupted the singer. They froze. The voice came from beyond the wall as well, continuing with a corrected phrase. The first voice took over, muddling through the song.

Elisabei peeked over the wall. The singer stood with his back to them, raking smooth a circle of sand. Beyond him, near the base of the tower, another man stood painting at an easel. Farther walls stretched toward the pillar, creating an enclosed patch of rocky land. The humming man wore only a piece of white cloth wrapped around his waist, while the painter was clad in a gauzy robe trimmed at the edges with intricate embroidery.

"Now we know the way." Kaemada wilted immediately after speaking, blinking and rubbing her head.

The words were in Traveller's—it was the Collective speaking. A shiver crawled up Elisabei's spine.

The man with the rake turned toward them, rake raised, while the other lowered his paintbrush, mouth hanging open.

"Vefng, bring them inside, quickly!" the painter ordered.

Kaemada clutched at the shawl, grasping Eian's hand in her free hand. As Elisabei quickly considered their options, Kaemada pulled Eian close and dove over the low stone wall, gasping in pain. "Sheatedein!"

Guards. But why would the woman be running toward more faithless Kamalti? Elisabei crouched, scanning their environment with wide eyes. She didn't see any guards...

Elisabei groaned, glaring at Kaemada's back. Injured, hallucinating, and occasionally possessed by a Collective of psions. What a combination.

The man with the rake hurdled the wall, completely bypassing Kaemada and Eian to stand by the chasm's edge in a ready stance. It almost seemed a threat, but his back was to Elisabei and Reinan.

"The Scouts will be out—you cannot hide out here. Quickly!" the painter beckoned.

"Some here are not friends to Outsiders," the man with the rake—Vefng—said.

"Are you?" Elisabei asked pointedly.

The painter smiled. "My aunt has... Well, no matter. We must get you off the streets. Come inside."

"Why should we trust you?"

The man's smile seemed strained. "Trust me or do not. It is up to you."

Elisabei wavered, looking at Reinan, but he had no experience in Kamalti lands, and Kaemada was useless. The decision was hers. Six winters ago, the Kamalti had not used subterfuge—they'd simply found her off the trail, surrounded her, and marched her to a farce of a trial. The next thing she knew, she'd been in the City of the Lost. No traps—not like in the city. And could she really leave two helpless people behind? The Kamalti would send Kaemada right back to the city, where she would surely be killed.

The choice was clear. "Let's follow."

Keeping wary eyes on Vefng, Elisabei climbed over the low fence with Reinan. The painter escorted them all inside. Elisabei reluctantly put an arm around Kaemada to help her along. The woman's dress had a dark,

S. Kaeth

wet patch on her side, blood seeping through bandages to peek out the sliced fabric. She must have pulled her stitches.

As they stepped inside, the painter drew the gauzy curtains and beckoned them farther into the house. It was well-kept and larger than her and Reinan's home in the city, but not nearly so large as Elisabei had imagined. They entered a room filled with books—on shelves, stacked on tables, and lying haphazardly on the comfortable-looking chairs furnishing the room. So many things. She stared at the excess.

Their guide gave them a sheepish smile and began gathering up books in hasty, flustered motions. "Please excuse the mess. I was doing research."

Reinan hovered beside her, his face troubled. Only those in the palace had so many possessions. But they'd made their decision. Elisabei sat Kaemada down on one of the chairs while Reinan lingered near the door, ready to secure their escape.

Kaemada hissed in pain as Elisabei inspected one of her deeper cuts. Elisabei whipped out her needle and thread to restitch the wound. "Be still."

"Ameyitum." The strained apology came from gritted teeth.

Eian wandered the room, his face alight. Elisabei couldn't help but keep an eye on him—such curiosity didn't last long in the City of the Lost.

The boy picked up a book before the painter got to it and looked at the open page. He frowned. "Wrong."

"Eian, give that back to him," Kaemada said, stifling a groan as Elisabei tied off the thread and began to rebandage her. "Ameyitum."

"Stop apologizing," Elisabei said.

"Amey—" Kaemada forced a sheepish smile.

"It's wrong," the boy said, handing it to their host.

The young man hesitated, taking the book from Eian. He inspected it as if he'd never seen it before. "Wrong? This is a book of the history of this City. You read Kamalti?"

Elisabei watched the exchange, nerves prickling. Where had the other Kamalti man gone? She tied the bandage and stood, ready to escape if necessary.

Eian pointed at the page. "Here, it says:
Here where South meets East,
In the golden bowl of the towering ones,
The City of Tamarik shall rest,
Forever bathed in the light of the sun.
"It's wrong." The boy shrugged. "It should be 'Center meets East.'"

"You know the ancient City of Tamarik?" The man practically vibrated

276

with excitement. "I have been searching for references, looking for our origin."

Holding her side, Kaemada peeked at the page. A smile bloomed across her face. "It's so beautiful."

The man looked uncertain, but when Eian translated, his expression darkened instantly.

Eian tugged on Kaemada's sleeve. "Frown!"

The woman's brow wrinkled in confusion as she obeyed. "I meant no disrespect. I only commented on the beauty of the poetry of your people. It was meant to be an honor."

The man regarded her silently for a while after Eian translated.

Elisabei narrowed her eyes. What kind of people took offense to a compliment? The Kamalti were all mind-sick, and this man seemed as foolish a dreamer as Kaemada.

The stranger's tone took on a haughty note. "In the civilized world, one asks for items belonging to others with a smile and a compliment. So, for instance, should I decide I liked your boots and wanted them for myself, I would compliment them and smile."

"Oh!" Kaemada said. "I did not mean I wanted your book. We share much of what we have, but if we want something another has, we simply ask, straightforward."

Elisabei shifted her weight. The danger pressed on her from all directions. They shouldn't share information so freely with these people. It wasn't like they really cared. Who knew where the trap was?

"Ah, that is considered rude here."

Elisabei scowled. "Who are you, and why do you pretend to want to help us?"

"Ah, I am Tjodlik, of the Philosophers of the City of Hadr."

"T-jo-d-lik," Kaemada tried.

He smiled at her effort. "Tjodlik."

She tried again. "Tjodlik. It's nice to meet you. I'm Kaemada, and this is Eian."

Tjodlik tilted his head to the side as Eian chattered the translation. "I thought all Outsiders spoke the Traveller's Tongue. Why is it that you are not speaking the Traveller's Tongue, but this boy does?"

Vefng appeared in another doorway among the shelves, causing Reinan to whirl toward him. The man paused, his expression wary, carrying a tray with a bowl of water and a cloth. "To cleanse you from your journey. Shall I bring refreshments?"

"Just supper, please, Vefng. Thank you," Tjodlik said, and the other man bowed, set the tray on an end table, and left the room.

"Not all of us speak the Traveller's Tongue," Elisabei said before Kaemada could speak, willing her to be silent.

But the woman spoke anyway. "I injured my mind and appear to have lost my ability to speak the Traveller's Tongue—temporarily, I hope. I mean no offense."

Elisabei could physically stop the boy from translating, but who knew how that could be construed? And Kaemada would likely just be more difficult. It would shine a light on their weaknesses. She glared at the woman, who at least had the decency to look down, fidgeting with her hands.

Tjodlik cleared his throat. "Please, forgive my rudeness, but... you do not belong here."

And Kaemada spilled her soul yet again, the fool. "We're looking for my friends. I came with them here, to this city, almost six moons ago. Two women and a man, my brother, Taunos. The women are my friends, Ra'ael and Takiyah. They were supposed to be in the City of the Lost, but..."

Tjodlik stammered, astonishment all over his bearing. "Please, excuse me," he said, "Crystals and ships! Excuse my manners!"

He turned his back to them, hand raised to his chin. Clearing his throat, he spun back to face them and began again. "You must have been with the group my aunt has had dealings with. You were on the other side of the Great Divide. This is the City of Hadr. On the other side is the City of Codr. Your companions are still in Codr."

"How do we get there?" Kaemada asked.

"I can take you to Codr and help you find your friends, but we must keep a low profile until we get you over there. Outsiders are not supposed to be in our lands at all!"

Reinan grunted and Elisabei scowled. She didn't like relying on this stranger. And yet, wouldn't it have been easier to just call the guards on them right away? If the troublesome woman was going to spill all their information, well, Elisabei might as well ask for some help with her.

"This one needs healing." Elisabei motioned to Kaemada.

Tjodlik wavered. "The Doctors... I do not know which would be sympathetic."

"Do these Doctors of yours know much about sicknesses of the mind?" she asked.

"What do you mean?"

Elisabei shot Kaemada a glance, but the woman was already drawing breath to tell him everything. She cut in stiffly, "Her mind injuries. I believe she received them battling another psion. I have never treated a psion."

Tjodlik shook his head. "We have no psions here in the City."

"So, your Doctors will be of no use?"

"I am afraid not. I do apologize. I wish I could help."

"Elisabei, please stop worrying. When we find my brother, I'm sure he will know what to do," Kaemada said.

She snorted. "If your brother is half as good as you say, I cannot wait to meet him."

Their host pressed his hands together. "I will take you to him tomorrow. I hope you will get to see him before…"

"Before what?" Finally, some wariness crept into Kaemada's voice.

"I do not know enough details to say. Only that they have been serving some sort of punishment. There have been stirrings of discontent among the citizens of Codr." He cleared his throat. "Please, let me leave you to refresh yourselves. I will come to get you when supper is ready."

"Will the other man—Vefng—tell anyone about us?" Elisabei asked.

Tjodlik smiled. "Do not worry, please. Vefng is loyal. He has served me well as ebr."

"Ebr?" Kaemada's voice trembled with suppressed judgement.

Tjodlik nodded after Eian translated. "Yes. Vefng has only half a face left to serve before his sentence is complete. His repeated thieving prompted a sentence of ebrid, you see. After completing his sentence, he has opted to take a permanent, paid position in my household. I trust him completely. Now, please rest. I will return shortly."

He bowed slightly to them as he left the room, closing the door behind him. Elisabei gave Reinan a frank look. Everywhere they went, things were still the same. People set themselves above each other whenever they could. Not much surprised her these days.

Elisabei smiled a little, easily reading on Kaemada's expressive face how the woman was having trouble processing this. She would have to teach her a proper stoic face.

The thought surprised her. When had she begun expecting to spend time together rather than leaving at the first clear opportunity?

After a meal and some tea to soothe nightmares, they slept the sleep of the weary. In the morning, Vefng brought around a massive metal wagon with steam puffing out of a funnel at the front. No beasts drew it, and Elisabei stared in astonishment. Sitting behind a large wheel that stuck into the air, Vefng beckoned.

Elisabei gingerly followed Tjodlik and the others as they piled into the seats at the back of the wagon. Eian clapped his hands, and a smile sparked on Kaemada's face.

Elisabei shook her head. The woman was incurably optimistic.

Chapter Twenty-two

Ebr testimony is, by nature, faulty. Only when an ebr has regained citizenship status may he or she be allowed again to give testimony. The nobles in charge of the ebr must be held accountable for their ebr's actions. If the ebr runs away or the ebr's behavior is dangerous or exceedingly unruly, the noble may ask for a Running of the Ebrs. The ebr will run until exhaustion or death, depending on the judgement of the Caller.

—excerpt from the Kamalti City of Codr Code of Law

At the base of a massive tower, decorated at its crown by an enormous timepiece with its bronze gears visible as they worked, stood the three shackled ebrs. Stretching before them, the crowd jeered from behind two lines of thin ropes. The noise was deafening. Taunos and Ra'ael had tried to mentally pick the locks on their bonds, but their captors had made them drink the mind-numbing herbs. Takiyah had been forced to wear large metal gloves that went to her elbows.

Taunos swept his gaze across the mob. Several paces to the side, Dode argued with uniformed Scouts. The little family Taunos had helped feed stood near the back of the crowd, looking grieved and angry. He blinked in surprise; he'd never have expected them to be here. He turned his face away. He needed to be strong.

Closing his eyes, he allowed himself to take solace for a moment in memory. The scent of his beloved washed over him: medicinal herbs, spices, and the sharp tang of alcohol on her hands from disinfecting. He'd given up a life with her... for this. In his own way, he was as foolish as his sister had been. And what good now was the strength of his arms? What use was his protection? He had no way to get them out of this.

Answer's voice sounded sharply against the noise of the crowd. She stood with the Scouts by Dode, looking upset. Taunos strained his ears to listen.

"...not allowed according to the Law!" Answer was saying.

"We cannot cancel the Running," another Scout said. Taunos recognized him from one of Answer's many dinner parties—Bluff, he believed. "The Outsider attacked you in your own home. That offense cannot be left unaddressed. The Running must take place to restore the

Honor of all Scouts."

"And did killing a priest help the Honor of the Scouts?" snapped Dode.

Distress was evident on Answer's face. "Outsiders are not Kamalti. The Justices—"

That was surprising. Was she arguing for them or against them? He'd expected she would push for greater punishment, but something about the set of her shoulders, the look in her eyes, spoke of regret.

"The Caller says the Running will go on, Answer. Beware, lest you lose all status. Lady Dode, it would be a shame if you interfered. The spectacle it would cause if you forced Scouts to arrest you..." Bluff motioned to the guards beside Taunos.

Three guards stepped forward, snapping him back to more immediate concerns. Tension lined their movements as they removed the manacles from Taunos and Ra'ael but kept the collars on all three. Taunos reached out on either side of him and took Takiyah's gauntlet and Ra'ael's hand, squeezing as if to give them strength, holding his head high. He would not give in to the expectations of these Kamalti. He'd face this trial, whatever it was, with his pride and honor intact.

Rough hands grabbed at them, ripping their clothes from their bodies. The crack of a whip snapped above their heads and they jumped. Takiyah shuddered.

"Run," ordered one of the guards behind them.

The tip of the whip kissed Ra'ael's shoulder, and she jumped again, glancing up at Taunos as if for reassurance.

"Run," the guard shouted.

"Run," Taunos agreed, ushering them before him. The lashes came from behind, and he meant to take the brunt of that.

But as they ran, the crowd threw glass, beads, and rotten food at them, making the ground underfoot slippery in some places and sharp in others. The guards running behind them wore thick boots and kept a swift pace. If they outpaced them too much, they would tire quickly, and there was nowhere visible to escape to—crowds pressed around them, leaving only a narrow lane for them to run in and cutting off all avenues of escape.

Taunos slipped on fruit pulp and went down hard. Lashes from the whips rained down on him, unrelenting. Shielding his head with one hand, he picked himself back up and ran, blinking blood from his eyes.

They worked together, their focus grimly on the task of keeping one foot in front of the other. Taunos tried to use telekinesis to shield them, but the mental toll was too great, especially with his mind drugged. Takiyah and Ra'ael had been trained well. They moved in a tight V formation and kept pace grimly, focusing on avoiding rotten food and sharp glass.

They ran, and the course took a hard left, and they ran, and the course turned again to the left.

Ra'ael and Takiyah exchanged brief looks, and Taunos's heart sank. They were running a loop. When they reached the base of the clock tower once more, the guards behind them switched out for fresh guards, whipping them with renewed energy so they had to quicken their pace.

There was no way out.

They were on their third lap when Ra'ael's posture shifted. The rage and exhaustion and pain must have begun to take over, and the potion that stopped her from concentrating, that he'd been drugged with for all those moons, would also keep her from stopping the blood rage. He grabbed Takiyah's shoulder, pulling her out of Ra'ael's view. The guards behind them whipped them in a frenzy, but Ra'ael trampled off with a roar into the crowd, tossing people out of her path like so many pebbles.

The rain of lashes drove them onward and Taunos quickly lost sight of the warrior priestess. The crowd swallowed her, churning dangerously as some tried to escape, and others surged toward her.

There was nothing he could do to help. He had to run.

~

Kaemada peered at the gathered crowd as she and the others climbed out of the metal wagon in Codr. Exhaustion and pain slowed her, but Elisabei's pain-numbing tea and salves kept her upright at least. Elisabei had far greater medicinal knowledge than she did, and Kaemada was relieved to be able to relax in someone's care once again. But she couldn't truly relax until she got her brother and friends and they all walked free under the sun once more.

She followed close behind Tjodlik as the clamoring throng reluctantly parted for him. Angry voices surrounded them, and she held tight to Eian lest he be crushed in the crowd. Kaemada grimaced at the press of bodies all around her, struggling to breathe. Someone ran past and disappeared out of view before she could do more than glimpse them, but the masses stood still in expectation, alert to a loud, churning commotion a little way off.

"What's happening?" Kaemada asked Tjodlik through Eian's translations.

"They are Calling a Running of the Ebrs." His tone was grave. "It is the worst punishment an ebr can face apart from execution, although they are sometimes paired."

Anger churned in her belly. It did not seem right to have ebrs, much less to torture them so. But Tjodlik seemed a reasonable man, and he had an ebr. She had judged too quickly in the City of the Lost; she couldn't repeat that mistake here. And yet, some things were just wrong, weren't they?

She shook her head and squeezed Eian's hand. This didn't seem like a place for children to be, but events had brought Eian into many such situations in the past moons. Other children were scattered among the onlookers, and that didn't seem right either.

A murmur rippled through the crowd, and Tjodlik leaned down to inform her, "The ebrs are coming around again."

"Around? As in, they run a loop?" Elisabei asked.

Tjodlik nodded.

"How many times around do they run?" Kaemada asked.

"Until they can run no more."

Kaemada bit her lip, her heart low.

Takiyah lurched into view, Taunos flanking her. The sight hit her like a punch to the gut, worse than all of Theron's beatings. Taunos was completely bald, so for a moment, she did not recognize him, but the features and movements were clearly his. Their ragged breathing and unsteady pace spoke of exhaustion, and blood ran in rivulets down their bodies. Takiyah ran with a pronounced limp, one leg twisted, and there was an odd red scar on her bloodied face. Taunos barely winced when the whip came down on him, and Kaemada's stomach twisted. It was not bravado but exhaustion that kept him from reacting.

She quickly peeked at Elisabei's face, but the woman was staring with a clenched jaw. So, this was not a hallucination. This was real. Anger rushed through her, and she gripped the ends of the shawl Elisabei had given her until her fingers turned white.

Ra'ael was nowhere to be seen, but the crowd's commotion continued farther up the lane. Her skin prickled and shivers threatened—that was likely Ra'ael. How long had she been able to endure this torture before she had lost control? The Kamalti could never have prepared themselves for what they unleashed.

"Blood rage," she murmured, then spoke louder, turning to Elisabei. "My friend Ra'ael, she has the blood rage. She must have succumbed. Can you help her?"

"I think the crowd will take care of the danger. I will tend her wounds after she's unconscious, if I can," Elisabei said dryly.

"We'll need for stopping the mob," observed Reinan.

Takiyah's leg gave out. She crashed to the stone ground. Staggering, Taunos reached to help her up, but lashes rained down on both of them. Taunos hovered over Takiyah, shielding her, though it drove him to one knee.

It was too much.

A shout broke from her, and she pushed her way through the crowd. She caught glimpses of the cobblestones, of Takiyah struggling to rise, of Taunos slumping to the ground. Kaemada shoved through the last of the onlookers and raced onto the lane, snapping the flimsy ropes. The guard raised the whip, and Kaemada flung herself between him and her bruised and bloodied loved ones.

"No!" She raised her hand, pushing on the whip with her telekinesis, more on instinct than thought.

The whip faltered, her push blocking it from cracking. Crouching beside Taunos, she covered him with the cloak she had borrowed from Elisabei and Reinan and draped the shawl over Takiyah, who mumbled unintelligibly.

Tears streamed down Kaemada's face. So much torture. So much pain! She kissed her brother's forehead, aiming for a patch of unwounded skin among the rivulets of blood.

He grimaced, then stared. "Kaemada?"

The guard struck her, flinging her to the cobblestones. Pain blazed through her battered body, and Taunos bellowed in rage. She picked herself up and gestured peace to her brother, but this time kept her eyes on the guard.

"Stop this mind-sickness, please, I beg you!" Could he even understand her?

"Get out of the way," the guard growled.

Explosions sounded behind her. Shouts in the crowd drew the guard's attention for a moment.

"Do not hit them again. Surely this must be more than enough to atone for any slight," Kaemada said, hovering over her brother.

Taunos gripped her arm, trying to move her aside, but she ignored him, taking advantage of this rare moment when she was stronger than he.

A small hand touched her elbow. Eian stood beside her.

"Move aside," the guard ordered.

"Eian, go back to Elisabei," Kaemada urged him. She looked up at the guard. "Strike me if you must, but do not hurt the boy."

The clamor of the crowd began to die down, and Tjodlik stepped up next to her.

"I may as well give up on all pretense of observing tradition, since it is being so spectacularly disregarded." Tjodlik bowed to the guard, his voice pleasant. "Please, may I speak to the Scout in charge of this Running? It seems clear it has ended, at least for now, and I have need of words."

The guard scowled but lowered his whip. He motioned to another guard. "Run and get the Caller."

Taunos groaned as Kaemada knelt beside him again. He reached for her, his hand wavering, and she held it, her fingers entwining with his.

"You're alive," he breathed.

Tears pricked her eyes once more, and she struggled to tear off the awful gauntlets around Takiyah's hands. Her shaking hands and clumsy fingers made it difficult, and her frustration mounted to panic as Taunos and Takiyah both lay there, gasping for breath. Tjodlik reached over her, easily freeing the gauntlets, but blocked her hands when she went for the cruel collars on their necks.

"The collars must stay until the conclusion of the ceremonial punishment," he whispered.

She nodded. It was not all right, but she was too exhausted and in pain to argue.

"Tsífforse," she thanked him, holding Takiyah and Taunos's hands and trying to rein in her emotions.

She'd never thought they'd be in so much trouble. She was the one always getting in trouble. They could always handle whatever came.

Eian settled next to her, and her brother reached up with his other hand, brushing his cheek roughly with the back of his fingers. "Hello, little man."

With a grin, Eian took Taunos's hand in both of his and snuggled in.

Where was Ra'ael? How badly was she hurt? Kaemada turned, straining to see from her position. The crowd had opened up, forming a little semi-circle well away from a crumpled Ra'ael. Elisabei crouched over Ra'ael's body, her voice curt as she snapped orders. Was Elisabei setting up to tend to all the injured, not just Ra'ael? Kaemada smiled for just a moment. Dreamer, indeed.

Tjodlik stiffened where he stood. A wide-eyed woman approached. Her hand covered her mouth as she glanced at Taunos and Takiyah before she lifted her chin, snapping her gaze to Tjodlik. "Who wishes to speak to the Caller?"

Tjodlik frowned at her. "I do, but you do not carry the badge."

"I am the one who is in the way of you getting your wish."

"I am Tjodlik of Hadr. I am of the Philosophers."

She gave a brief nod. "What brings you here?"

"I came upon these who live Outside." He indicated Kaemada and her companions.

The woman's expression darkened as she looked at Kaemada. "This trouble all started with her."

Finally, Kaemada recognized her. One of the women guards who'd found them at the stairs and refused to answer her pleas about Eian. Lady Answer—Taunos had poked fun at her name.

Her brother surged upward, and Answer stumbled as she hastily retreated. But Taunos was too weak even to sit, and he fell back.

"You need to rest. Please." Kaemada trailed off, squeezing his hand.

Taunos opened his mouth to argue but slumped, his eyes closing. The back of Kaemada's neck prickled. What had happened to her brother, the hero of Torkae?

All throughout, Tjodlik kept his gaze on Answer. "They came to inquire about the welfare of their friends. I suppose it was a good thing they came, if only to say goodbye."

Her friends were unconscious, and Kaemada was not in much better shape. Her voice shook with anger. "They need healing."

"Speak the Traveller's Tongue, by the Crystals!" Answer snapped.

"They need healing," she tried again, wincing as Eian repeated her words.

"Healing is not allowed."

"Not always," Tjodlik said. "There is room for mercy, should the Caller of the Running choose. You are not him. But it would go better if you were supportive."

Answer jutted her chin at Taunos's unconscious form. "He was my ebr. He attacked me to get asylum for the other one."

Wrath emanated from her like a physical thing, though guilt lurked in her eyes and horror lined her face. Kaemada watched her carefully.

"The Running was for a failed asylum attempt?" Tjodlik nodded thoughtfully. "I see. That makes sense."

"It does?" asked Kaemada.

"Yes." He looked at Answer. "My sympathies. It is always a great dishonor for one's ebr to seek asylum. But surely you can see how one may question how appalling the treatment was for you to cover it up in such a way."

Answer opened and closed her mouth in outrage, then finally found her words. "There was no appalling treatment! I treated him well, and he took advantage of that!"

"Of course," Tjodlik soothed, his tone dripping with skepticism.

Eyes burning with humiliation, Answer swept up what remained of her broken dignity. "I will ask the Caller for an audience for you."

As Answer walked away, Kaemada spoke in a low voice to Tjodlik. "Was it necessary to so embarrass her? Will it go worse for us now?"

Eian chattered away his translation, and Tjodlik replied, "We cannot choose for others where they lie, and Answer had chosen her camp. I, therefore, found it necessary to back her down, whatever the cost to her pride."

Chapter Twenty-three

Zegmohv, how fare your machines? These wondrous gifts, our legacy from the Takanis, are breaking down! We are loath to dismantle them, for our knowledge is insufficient to even begin to understand their inner workings.
-scrap of a letter from Doctor Kimtan of the City of Zhabik to Doctor Zegmohv of Codr

The Healing Hall was a large room full of lights and clean, plain beds, and devoid of any warmth, comfort, or hominess. How did they expect people to heal without the solace of community and the safety of home? Kaemada ran her thumb across the back of Ra'ael's hand over and over while Eian ran around with two Kamalti boys, playing with a ball. If only she could speak to her friend—Ra'ael always knew what to do. There was no way for Kaemada to help here, especially when she couldn't even trust her own senses. The side of Taunos's bed had turned into a snake and tried to bite her not long after they got everyone settled, and she'd nearly fallen into another bed when she'd jumped back to avoid it. Heat burned in her cheeks just remembering the incident. Even worse was the idleness. She was in no shape to help her brother and her friends, even after all they'd been through.

An elderly woman entered the Hall, and Tjodlik leapt up and went to her, clasping her hands. "Aunt Dode!"

"Ah, Tjodlik, what a pleasant surprise. Have you been cataloguing the disgrace of our City?"

Tjodlik looked down, muttering something, but Dode smiled, patting his shoulder. "No matter. We have done this to ourselves."

The boys ran past, stopping beside Taunos, their chatter lifting some of the oppressive gloom. "This is Taunos. He's my tachírmahkae," Eian said, pride in his voice as his fingers tapped Taunos's shoulder. Taunos did not wake up, and Kaemada's heart sank lower.

The older Kamalti boy nodded, taking the hand of the man with the wounded leg who sat nearby. "He fed my father and I. We were there, at the Running. Father tried to help."

"Thank you," Kaemada said, catching the man's eye.

Her voice must have carried her gratitude, for the man smiled and gave her a nod. "The Caller of the Running will put up a fight, but so will we. We saw what happened at the chapel."

She returned his smile and pointed to herself. "Kaemada."

"I am Rikr. You know, you Outsiders are not the monsters I had thought you would be."

Dode and Tjodlik approached, and Dode stroked Ra'ael's cheek with tender fingers.

Kaemada stared, struck with surprise, and ducked her head. She'd thought far better of the Kamalti than they were. Instead of legends, they were just people, like her own people, who had condemned the captives of the City of the Lost through inattention and lack of care.

Her voice grated when she spoke. "Why do you send people to the City of the Lost, to live in permanent imprisonment?"

Confusion lit in their eyes, and Kaemada remembered they couldn't understand her. She clenched her fist, looking down at Ra'ael. She couldn't even communicate alone.

Carrying rolls of bandages she'd found on a shelf, Elisabei paused nearby, repeating her question with her arms folded. Kaemada looked up at her, hoping her gratitude showed on her face.

Rikr blinked. "Permanent..."

Slack-jawed, Tjodlik shook his head. "Travellers who trespass on our lands are lost—typically, that is. They do not intend to trespass. So, we bring those who are lost to the City of the same name. The City of the Lost."

"You're trying to help." Horror filled Kaemada's whisper.

A scowl twisted Elisabei's face. "If I had known that's where you would send me, I would have objected. Firmly. The City of the Lost is where the worst criminals go to live out their days. They have lost the right to join in Rinaryn culture and we have lost them. That's the reason for the name."

Tjodlik bowed his head, covering his face in one hand. "It is easy to overlook details when you are set on ignoring one another."

"We have done much harm," Dode mused, holding Ra'ael's hand. "May we be worthy of making amends."

A scream burst out of Takiyah as she woke, flailing. Kaemada threw her arms around her, holding her until her shuddering had passed. One of the Doctors approached with a cup of water, but Takiyah eyed the Doctor with clear distrust until Kaemada took the drink for her, giving it to her friend once the Doctor walked away with a dismissive sniff.

Takiyah glared at the Doctor's back a while longer and then drained the metal cup in one long gulp. She wiped her mouth with the back of her hand, then grabbed Kaemada's hand. "Why are they healing us?"

"You must be healed for judgement," Tjodlik said.

"That's ridiculous," Takiyah spat. She looked around, her green eyes hard and narrowed, and paused at Elisabei. "And why are you helping them?"

Elisabei plucked the cup out of her hand. "I'm not going to just sit here. I know herbs, and I can stitch people up well enough—and those stuffy Doctors can benefit from some watching."

A smile cracked on Takiyah's face, and she nodded once as Elisabei walked away.

"It provides time," Dode said, straightening her shoulders. "And with time, we can put things in motion. Do not give up yet."

Kaemada met her gaze and nodded. It was so much like Elisabei's saying: where there's life, there's hope. As Takiyah's shuddering ceased, her eyes grew drowsy, and she laid back down, clutching Kaemada's hand until slumber loosened her grip. Kaemada pulled the blanket up to her shoulders, smoothing it out.

Hoping to soothe her, hoping she'd hear her, hoping for some measure of comfort, Kaemada hummed the Discovery of Daevin.

"That sounds very much like a traditional Kamalti tune," Tjodlik said.

Rikr joined in, and soon songs turned to stories. Eian sat on Kaemada's lap happily trading tales with the others, many of which held striking similarities between Rinaryn and Kamalti versions. It was almost like at home, except for the surroundings, except for the wounds they each bore. They needed to go home.

They were trapped here, deep in the city, and far from the stairs. They needed to get out, away from people who would make them captives, who would torture them. Not through the City of the Lost—she was never going back there again. Her brother and friends were in no condition to travel, and certainly not to fight. Neither was she, she had to admit.

But the similar stories and songs spoke of a possible connection, and Kaemada snatched for it. Everyone only wanted safety. The Kamalti tried to achieve it by wrapping themselves in order, while the people of the City of the Lost sought ugliness.

At home, sometimes, there would be trouble with a different kaetal. Perhaps it made sense to think of the Kamalti as another kaetal, one long lost to them. In that case, she'd need to talk to their Saimahkae to get her family, her friends, to safety, but the Kamalti didn't seem to have one. So who could she reach out to, and how?

In the morning, Dode led a river of other Kamalti, all dressed in their finery, into the room. "And now, the culprits must look on the damage they have wrought. Witness the depths of pain and misery to which you have stooped!"

Some of those in the crowd pushed others farther into the room, anger in their bearing, while others slunk forward, looking sullen or guilty. Answer was among those escorted in, and Kaemada got to her unsteady feet. No more harm would come to her friends. She wouldn't allow it.

"Priest killers." Rikr also stood, his weight on his good leg.

"The Outsiders tried to claim asylum!" shouted one of the finely clothed men.

She resisted the urge to shrink from the hatred in his gaze.

Rikr jabbed a finger toward Kaemada while shouting at the cluster of Kamalti. "They have done less damage than you nobles have! Killing a priest? May the gods have no mercy on those who care nothing for them."

Kaemada stepped away from the jabbing finger carefully, skin prickling with danger. Was this real, or yet another hallucination? The others were unconscious, and she could not lean on their strength.

A woman in the plainer clothes of the poor joined in, eyes narrowed on the nobles. "You used holy Gifts against the house of the gods. Have you no decency? Those Gifts should be stripped from you as a penalty."

"How dare you speak to us that way?" said one of the nobles. "We rule this City."

"Only on our backs!"

There was a division here, just as there had been in the City of the Lost. The rich in their finery, and the rest of the people just trying to survive.

"How is that one alive, anyway? Did she not fall into the chasm?" another noble asked, pointing at Kaemada.

She pulled her shawl tight around her shoulders. "The Collective caught me."

Tjodlik positioned himself nearby, his composure at odds with her worry. "I remind you, no harm may come to them until the Justices convene."

"As Scouts are meant to keep order, I do hope you intend to address this appalling lack of order and legality among your own," Dode said with a smile that spoke of danger.

Kaemada's gaze flicked back and forth between the sides. So much danger lurked here, so much darkness and pain. But there was light, too. Those standing up for them like Rikr, Tjodlik, and Dode, even the Kamalti children playing with Eian. And in the City of the Lost, when she'd been so out of her depth, when cruelty and kindness had been the opposite of what she'd expected, Elisabei and Reinan had helped her, twice.

Several of the Kamalti seemed to have no issue with them, and trading stories and songs last night had been somewhat enjoyable, even given their circumstances. It was the nobles who were more likely to scoff.

It was them she had to convince.

She scanned the nobles—mostly Scouts, Dode told her. They were an argumentative group: Dode and her comrades argued with Justices over legality while disgraced Scouts sat stiff and sullen. Answer often remained silent, shifting uncomfortably. Guilt and shame filled her face as she stared at Taunos's bed. The woman's eyes met hers, and all expression shut down, smoothed away to a hard mask and glinting eyes.

A shudder crawled up Kaemada's spine. Anyone but her. But apparently, Answer had power, and despite her role in the torment inflicted on the others, Answer's eyes held the remorse that Theron's eyes had lacked. She had failed to reach Theron, but if she could bring Answer to their side, with Dode's allies as well, perhaps they had a chance.

Taunos stirred, and Answer stood, stalking out of the Hall.

Kaemada's heart leapt as her brother winced and opened his eyes, then struggled to sit up.

"Will you lay down?" Elisabei snapped at him from Ra'ael's bedside. She gave Kaemada a sharp look as if she were at fault. "I can see the family resemblance. Both of you seem to want more work for me."

Kaemada smiled, squeezing his hand. "Her tongue may be sharp, but she's a good healer."

A soft groan escaped Taunos as he lay back down. "I will take your word for it."

"How do you feel?" Her voice came out in a whisper, for she feared the answer.

"Thirsty." He grimaced.

"Give him this," one of the Kamalti Doctors said, pouring liquid into a cup and handing it to an assistant. The assistant offered the drink to Taunos.

Elisabei faced them, hands on her hips. "And what's this?"

"It will relax them and subdue their magic, for the safety of us all."

The glower on Elisabei's face was fit to match a raging thunderstorm. "No wonder they're not waking up! How often have you been slipping them these?"

"I do not want to be drugged," Taunos growled. "I have spent the last six moons drugged against my will, and I have a craving for untainted drink."

Tears pricked at Kaemada's eyes. Was that why Takiyah had fallen back asleep so quickly? She ducked her head. At least Takiyah was awake now, eyeing the Doctor warily from her bed.

Glaring at the Doctor, Elisabei handed Taunos a water pouch, and he drank greedily.

After handing it back, Taunos gripped Kaemada's hand in both of his. "I knew it. I knew you were alive."

She squeezed his hands again.

Takiyah leaned over, drawing Kaemada's attention toward a commotion near Ra'ael's stretcher. "Kae, what's Eian doing?"

"What?"

Many of the nobles had left the room. The Kamalti Doctors and Elisabei were arguing, gesturing wildly as their fight escalated. Eian stood near them, babbling away.

"Listen," Takiyah said.

"…know how to use it," one of the Doctors was saying. "The machines take many circulations for even Kamalti to master."

"It's too complicated for you," said Eian.

"You're not going near her!" Elisabei snapped.

"I do not trust you," said Eian.

"She is our patient. Where have you trained?"

"This is my territory," said Eian.

"Life, in all its harshness," Elisabei shot back.

"Experience taught me," said Eian.

Takiyah turned to Kaemada. "He's translating."

Kaemada shook her head. "But there's no need for that. They can understand each other!"

Takiyah frowned. "Listen to your son, Kaemada. It may be needless, but he's translating what everyone knows is truly behind their words."

How could she not have seen? "He… he read Kamalti writing. Only he said the book was wrong, but how could he know? And he seems to have some inkling of Kamalti customs—he told me to frown when I gave Tjodlik a compliment. And somehow, he opened doors into the mountain…"

"There is probably another explanation." Taunos's voice was weary, his eyes closed. "Is he telepathic?"

"I have tested him many times. He has no psionic abilities of any kind."

"Perhaps he's hiding them?" Takiyah asked.

Kaemada gave her a frank look. "How much control can a boy with only four summers have?"

"I would ask you."

Kaemada shook her head. "Maybe this is something new. Why did we not see it before?"

Taunos chuckled, then grimaced as the chuckle turned into a cough. Kaemada quickly turned to him with water, which he sipped, then waved away with a grateful smile. "How much chance has he had to be absorbed in a conversation between two different cultures?"

Takiyah nodded. "If Eian had never gotten lost, we might never have known. But what does it mean?"

"They seem about to come to blows over there, cha'atanahn," Taunos broke in, his eyes still closed.

Grateful for the distraction, she turned. Reinan stood behind his wife with his arms crossed while her arms moved sharply, accentuating her words. The conversation had devolved to thinly veiled insults, with Eian in the middle.

"Shareil, shareil!" Kaemada stepped, stumbling a bit, between them with arms raised, close to Eian in case she had to whisk him out of harm's way.

"Kanae, kanae!" Eian repeated, folding his arms over his chest.

Kaemada marveled at him. Of course Takiyah would notice it—she was always paying attention to the details.

"Not until they back down! Nae shareil!" Stubbornness radiated from the set of Elisabei's shoulders.

"This is our home and our land and our equipment! We will not take orders from savages!" bellowed one of the Kamalti.

Everyone began shouting at once, striving to be heard despite Kaemada's efforts to calm them. Pushing forward, one of the younger healers slipped and knocked a machine off the cart. It clattered to the floor with a clang, loud in the sudden silence as the Kamalti stopped to stare.

"...you better than me!" Elisabei finished her rant.

"You novice!" A Kamalti Doctor rounded on the younger man.

"My sincerest apologies!" He bowed his head and retreated. "I, I, I will pay..."

"You will pay for this? Do you know how precious it is? It is an invaluable piece of equipment!" The Doctor's raised voice echoed across the Hall.

"I heard peace and quiet are good for healing. Apparently, there's a different opinion among our healers here," Taunos remarked lightly to Takiyah.

Takiyah's whisper carried. "Kaemada has not said a word of the Traveller's Tongue. And she's usually the one careful not to offend."

Apprehension flooded Kaemada, and she swallowed hard. *Show no weakness, show no damage,* her internal voice screamed. She had no Tannevar to help steady her, to add to her senses, to be strong together.

"I will ask her about it. Why would she risk offense?"

Takiyah snorted. "She will not tell you."

Kaemada shook herself, focusing on the matter at hand. She would deal with Taunos and Takiyah later. Hopefully, much later. She gestured to the machine. "What is it?"

"Nothing you would understand," the Doctor snapped. "It is advanced healing equipment."

"Perhaps not," admitted Kaemada as Eian translated for her. "But Takiyah is good with metal things. Could it hurt for her to take a look? After all, it's already broken."

"Do not let her. Either she will sabotage it, or she will steal our secrets," another Doctor broke in anxiously.

Elisabei glowered. "If she sabotaged it then it would be no good for healing. Why would Takiyah destroy a machine that could save Ra'ael?"

The Doctor stared at her in fury, but before he could reply, the senior Doctor said, "I see no harm in letting her look. There are none with the skills to repair it, and if its secrets cannot be fully cracked by Kamalti scientists, I highly doubt a savage will glean any from it. It will keep her out of the way."

Takiyah raised her eyebrows, but he seemed not to notice.

"Is it necessary?" Elisabei asked.

"The machine enhances the body's natural healing properties, significantly shortening healing time and reducing the risk of death," the novice said, eager to show off. His superiors glared at him for his troubles.

The crisis appeared to be over for now. Kaemada sank into her chair by Taunos's cot as the Kamalti reverently set the machine before Takiyah. Eian crawled up beside the metal box, looking on with bright eyes and occasionally pointing to things. Takiyah bent over it intently, now and then murmuring an instruction to Eian.

Takiyah indicated a part of the machine. "This powers it?"

With surprise evident on his face, the Kamalti Doctor nodded.

She traced something inside, tilting her head to see it at different angles. "This does not run on steam like many of your machines."

Grudging respect seeped into the Doctor's tone. "This is more ancient." He leaned down by her to join in her inspection. "Is this your magic, understanding machines?"

Takiyah furrowed her brow at him but didn't answer, instead continuing her inspection. The three of them huddled together, their voices falling to a murmur as Takiyah occasionally pointed to something or asked questions.

Perhaps it was a start. But there were still so many dangers. She didn't want to think about that. Kaemada turned to Taunos. "Are you in any pain?"

He waved away her concern. "It's fine. It reminds me I'm alive."

"You're bald."

"I was an ebr to Answer's family, and they thought my hair unseemly. I was required to shave it." His eyes glinted as he grinned. "Maybe I will get some peace from being pressured to court, unless there are very many women who like bald heads."

Her brother's irrepressible good humor put her at ease, but her smile died as a tailosae climbed onto Taunos's head, and began grooming its fur. She rubbed her eyes and tried to ignore it, making an effort to joke. "Or maybe you will find you're even more desirable."

"Oh, Eloí's light, let it not be so!" He shifted to look at her. "Kaemada, are you all right? Why are you not speaking the Traveller's Tongue? What is that you're wearing?" He plucked at her shawl as he interrogated her.

Kaemada shook her head. Everything they'd been through while she'd languished in the palace, wondering when they were coming for her... She did not trust her voice around the lump in her throat. "It's a shawl. They wear it in the City of the Lost—the people who live outside the palace, that is."

Concern edged Taunos's tone. "Kaemada, what's wrong?"

"Nothing." Kaemada snapped. There couldn't be a tailosae grinning at her.

Taunos frowned in annoyance. "Clearly, it's not nothing. You're wounded, you're jumpy, and you're only speaking Rinaryn. I do not see Tannevar... My deepest sympathies, sister."

Kaemada shook her head.

"Are those handprints around your neck?" He struggled to sit up again. "Who hurt you, little sister?"

"It's nothing! Do not hurt yourself." Kaemada pushed him back down, shrugging the shawl higher up to cover her neck.

"It clearly isn't nothing, Kaemada."

"Please," Kaemada whispered, trembling. She wrapped her shawl tightly around herself and steadfastly ignored her brother and the tailosae. His sympathy would be too much to bear, especially in the face of all they'd been through. There was no Tannevar there to keep her steady, only the pieces left of him in her song. Broken, like her.

She shut her eyes, clinging to those pieces. Her friends and her brother deserved to know they couldn't trust her. She couldn't trust herself. Her shoulders were stiff as stone and the words came out reluctantly. "I keep seeing things that aren't there. And I'm worried. For all of you. For Ra'ael."

Ra'ael's ragged breathing joined the murmur of Takiyah's voice, but Taunos sat silently, his hand warm around hers.

Kaemada kept her eyes closed, kept herself stiff to be strong. She could do this. She had to. She needed to make the connections, just as she would with another kaetal. But she didn't know how *this* kaetal worked, and the City of the Lost had taught her that jumping in blindly to help often hurt, instead.

Kaemada opened her eyes. There was Dode, turning away from conversation with a noble by the door and walking back toward Ra'ael. She cleared her throat. "Dode, may I ask your thoughts on something?"

The elderly Kamalti didn't answer, and Kaemada looked down at her hands, shoulders slumping.

"Cha'atanahn, you're still speaking Rinaryn," Taunos said.

She grimaced. Ah, yes. Yet another weakness.

"Would you like me to translate?" Taunos squeezed her hand.

Kaemada fixed him with a fierce look. "If you say my words, not yours."

His eyes held apprehension, but he smiled. "Of course, little sister. Are you all right?"

She clenched her jaw, managing a jerky nod.

By the way he raised his eyebrows at her, he saw through her lie, but he called out to Dode instead of questioning her further. "Dode, my sister would like to ask your thoughts."

Dode's browridge raised in surprise as she approached. "Of course. How may I help?"

"Thank you for all you have done. I wish to reach out, to help change your people's views of my people."

Taunos grinned at her as he translated.

Locking eyes with her brother, Kaemada continued. "I thought I might start with Answer."

Anger and ferocity swept the grin from her brother's face, but though his misgivings were clear on his face, he translated faithfully.

Dode's voice was calm. "There is a chance you could get past her pride and offense. If so, that might help tip things in the desired direction."

Tugging on her shawl as if that would help her maintain her composure, Kaemada nodded. "How would I set up a meeting with her to soothe ruffled feathers?"

"Ruffled feathers?"

"To calm any hurt feelings. Like her wounded pride."

"Ah, I see. An honorable sentiment."

"Is there a specific way your people apologize?"

Taunos interrupted. "You do not need to apologize, little sister."

"It will not be the first time I have apologized for my brother." Her smile softened as his expression became troubled.

He sighed, his voice strained as he spoke. "Just be careful. I just got you back. Please, Dode, make certain nothing happens to my sister."

Dode nodded. "You will not use words, for to verbalize such emotions would be crude and vulgar. Instead, you will give gifts of crystals, a much more refined method of communication. Each crystal has a specific meaning, so you will need to buy certain colors and shapes."

"You will need money," Taunos prompted. "Our people do not use money."

Dode waved a hand. "I will provide it for you."

Kaemada hesitated, searching her unusual features. "Is it a good idea?"

Dode's smile broadened. "It is. I will set up the meeting and have Tjodlik take you to buy crystals in the morning." She patted her hand and then stood.

One of the Scouts standing guard by the door scowled at Dode as she approached. "The Outsiders may not roam our City. They have caused quite enough chaos, Philosopher Dode."

Dode scoffed. "One would have to be blind not to see! But at least our chapels are safe from them."

The Scout stiffened. "If they had not been in the chapel, it would not have been torn down."

"At last, you admit your anti-civic attitude."

The Scout scowled. "Your attack on the Scouts will not succeed, Lady Dode."

Dode raised her browridge again. "Your lawlessness will not succeed, Scout." She stalked out.

Kaemada turned to her brother, forcing a smile she didn't really feel.

She covered him with a blanket as he laid down, her hand still caught in his. Connected.

Connecting with the Kamalti where there was already so much enmity, so much bad blood... Fear and self-doubt still paralyzed her, and yet, she couldn't stand to do nothing. She had to do whatever she could—even small deeds—to bring a little brightness to their song, to turn the Kamalti toward peace.

Where there was a potential connection, she could build a true one. She'd done it enough at home, mediating between disagreements. She just had to be careful not to repeat her mistakes.

They needed the goodwill of the Kamalti to go home. Even more, her people as a whole needed the Kamalti. They had technology and weapons that could help keep her people safe from the Darks. They had resources, and the fighters among them were good—she well remembered fighting them. But the Kamalti needed them, too—their freedom, their flexibility, their casual peace, the open air and broad spaces. They just didn't know it yet.

~

Be still, be quiet. Sleep. You are broken. We will fix you. We will come for you. We will stay. It will all stay the same. Nothing changes. The broken will be fixed. We have learned much. The ways of warfare, the value of liberty. Be still. We will fix you.

She sat up with a jolt, wincing as pain flooded her. The memory of the dream dissipated like morning mist.

"My apologies." Tjodlik's expression was surprised and contrite as he stood before her. "I did not mean to startle you."

She smiled as Eian opened his eyes and stretched from where he'd been sleeping next to her.

"It's fine, do not worry." Her mind felt much more clear this morning. It didn't even bother her too much when Eian translated for her.

"My aunt says you wish to buy crystals for Answer?"

Kaemada nodded. "Yes, are you ready now?"

Tjodlik nodded.

"Kaemada," Taunos interrupted from the bed beside her. "Tell me truthfully. Are you feeling all right?"

She put on a confident smile and hoped he wouldn't see through it. At least her words were true. "I see nothing that isn't truly there."

Though clearly worried, Taunos said nothing more against her plan.

"Please can I come? I want to see more!" Eian clutched at her hand.

"Acha'iyih, I do not know if it would be safe."

"I'm bored." He pouted.

"I will keep you both safe," Tjodlik said. "The presence of a noble affords much protection."

Kaemada scanned the room. Elisabei was busy with Ra'ael, and Takiyah and Taunos could barely move. Ice squeezed her heart at the thought of leaving Eian with strangers. What if something happening to him? There was Reinan, but all she could see was Theron and the guards of the City. She fought down a shudder. No. At the moment, she was the most mobile. She swallowed hard, searching Tjodlik's face, remembering the deference given to Dode even by those who argued with her.

"Are you sure?" Kaemada asked. She'd need someone to translate for her, it was true. So when Tjodlik nodded, she gave in, to Eian's excitement.

As Tjodlik pointed out the sights and patiently humored Eian's questions, Kaemada watched the people—common Kamalti people, just trying to go on with their lives. Their sky was stone instead of blue, and their air was clogged with smoke instead of filled with life. Some looked at them askance, but most ignored them. Occasionally someone would call out a greeting to Tjodlik or give them a friendly nod. Not so different, under the trappings, from her own people.

Just as in the City of the Lost, they didn't need Kaemada to save them. Perhaps, she could help them help themselves, just as her mother had tried to do with the Darks. She could never convince all Kamalti and Rinaryn to work together. That had been a naïve dream. Even this city was likely too much. But to convince individuals? That, she could do. First, she had to understand them.

They entered a little shop that sold beautiful crystals of various colors and designs as well as little metal boxes. Tjodlik indicated each crystal, explaining what it meant, but very quickly Kaemada's head swam with all the details. A squat green pyramid meant envy, but a tall green pyramid signified hope and aspiration, and a tall blue pyramid stood for longing, and so on. Some of the crystals shimmered and danced before her eyes, and she placed her hand on the table to keep herself steady. She tugged her shawl more closely around herself as if that would ground her. Thankfully, no full-fledged hallucinations formed.

"This is a very complicated system of communicating." Kaemada stared around her, bewildered. "Please, will you help me pick them out? I do not wish my ignorance to negatively affect my message."

Tjodlik shook his head after Eian translated. "It simply is not done.

These feelings cannot properly be expressed in words. It is quite rude and, well, uncivilized."

"But how am I to learn this system so quickly? You grew up learning it. I'm, as you say, an Outsider. There must be room for a little flexibility."

"It would not be proper. But here. First, think of what you want to say."

"I want to express my apologies for any wounds, physical or otherwise, Answer may have felt, and my hope for friendship."

Tjodlik frowned, vexed as the words came out of her mouth, even though he could not have understood because Eian did not translate. Instead, her son ran through the store, gathering several crystals. With a wave, she cautioned Tjodlik to stop and watch. The storekeeper scowled at them and crossed his arms as he waited, staring at Tjodlik.

"Do not worry," Tjodlik said. "All will be paid for."

The storekeeper nodded, but his arms remained crossed, and his stare continued until Eian returned to Kaemada with a variety of crystals predominantly in blue and yellow.

"That was fun!" he proclaimed.

Kaemada tousled his hair. "You're full of surprises, acha'iyih."

"How did he do that? I thought your people were not familiar with the Crystal Language," Tjodlik said.

A laugh burst from her, surprising her, and she ruffled Eian's curls. "He's very special."

"You will need a box for those."

Kaemada nodded and picked out a small wooden box that reminded her of home while Tjodlik paid the relieved shopkeeper. As Kaemada followed Tjodlik out of the store, she thanked him profusely for his help.

Tjodlik smiled at her. "I wish you and your friends all the best of luck. It would be a shame to lose this opportunity to once more learn from each other."

Chapter Twenty-four

What can we do about the Outsiders? They trample through our City and then depend upon our charity for healing. The common people are beginning to support them, no doubt stirred up by that troublemaker, Lady Dode. We should seal up the entrances and bar Scouts from the Outside to prevent further encounters. The cost alone makes me shudder.

-personal letter in the City of Codr

"Why will she not just say what's wrong?" Taunos grumbled.

Kaemada's secrecy over her injuries had been needling him ever since she'd found them again. He'd missed her, grieved for her. And now, impossibly, he had her back, alive. Except she wouldn't allow him to help.

Takiyah snorted, reaching into the machine to twist something. "She does not tell you a lot of things."

"She should not have to carry this alone. Isn't that why there's a kaetal?"

"We cannot help if she does not let us. You know that. But at least we're here." There was a slight edge to the last word.

His shoulders tensed. He'd travelled a lot, yes, by necessity. And by necessity, he'd never explained his absences. But being away from the kaetal didn't mean he didn't care. "I'm only away trying to keep you and the rest of the kaetal safe."

"Well, it obviously isn't working," Takiyah returned, green eyes flashing.

"You do not know—I'm trying—I know I have done much good." He raked his hand over his head, frustrated that he couldn't tell her. Not even now.

"And you do not know you could not do more good at home." She frowned. "Taunos… Are you running?"

"How can you ask me that?" Taunos struggled to his feet. Of all people, Takiyah was implying he was a coward?

"All right, that's enough, both of you," Elisabei snapped. "Back in bed with you. And back to your work. Stop talking to each other. There has been enough pain and suffering without you two poking at each other with big sticks disguised as words."

Taunos scrutinized Kaemada as she trailed back into the Hall behind Tjodlik and an exuberant Eian. Exhaustion dragged at her features, and she slid down the wall to the floor, closing her eyes. The wooden box she carried lay to one side of her. Had anything gone wrong out there? Why did she look so worn? Frustration rose like a tide in him. He wasn't in any shape to have watched over her like he should have.

Stifling a groan, Taunos hobbled over and sank down next to her. His injuries burned, protesting the movement. With a wince, he held his side until he was settled. This was important. Something terrible had happened while he'd been a captive, and he hadn't been there for her. His heart ached that he still couldn't be there for her, that she kept pushing him away.

"Elisabei will not be happy you're out of bed," Kaemada said.

A snort broke from him. "Ah, yes, I have been so concerned about her happiness with me."

The corners of her mouth tugged upward.

Heartened, he plunged ahead, keeping his tone casual, as if he'd just returned from any journey. "What have you been doing the last six moons?"

Her shoulders hunched and her head ducked. He sought calm composure, steadying his breathing. For so long, he had kept the worst details of his journeys from her, cherishing her undying optimism. She was the starlight in the darkness the realms inflicted on him, and someone had dimmed her brightness. Stretching out the more injured of his legs, he rubbed at the bandaging. When he glanced back, Kaemada was watching him.

He raised his eyebrows. "Shall I go first?"

She dropped her gaze, and so he began, playing up his exploits and the few good times while glossing over as much of the bad as possible. It was easy, the typical way he related his adventures to her, although this particular one carried more creative license than most of his other adventures. When he ended, she gave him a frank look, clearly seeing through his fabrications.

"I never meant for you to get hurt," she whispered. "Any of you. Ameyitum. Saiameyitum."

Taunos put a grin on his face. "Ah, cha'atanahn, if you take all the blame, what will the rest of us have? Please share."

A smile pulled at her mouth, and his grin became real.

The smile faded as her summer blue eyes, now dark and troubled, avoided his gaze. "I do not want to talk about it because that would make it real. Would make me face it. And I do not want to. But my dreams torment me anyway. Whatever I wish, it was real."

Taunos nodded, unraveling a bit of bandaging on his leg so he could braid it. Elisabei would no doubt have strong words for him later, but it was worth it. What he was seeing in his sister's responses… too much attention would shut her down again.

She spoke, in whispers almost too quiet for him to hear and in louder tones quaking with outrage, of the City of the Lost. Careful to keep his attention on the braiding, he shoved down the pain and rage her story stirred in him.

"I was angry at you for a long time," she said. "Ameyitum. I did not realize… Every choice I made revealed more danger. When you tell your stories, there's a thrill in your voice, an eagerness to overcome such insurmountable odds. But me… I felt only fear and my unworthiness."

That was ridiculous. "You're not unworthy."

"I am—I always have been. For so long, I have tried to avoid shaming you. I drag Ra'ael and Takiyah down with my weaknesses, and you, too."

Where was this coming from? How long had she thought like this, that she was somehow weak? Did she have no idea of her own strength? "Never, Kaemada. You never shame me."

"I could not even deal with Tikatae on my own. How was I supposed to face something like the City of the Lost?"

"Kaemada, listen to me. You were the only one who saw good in Tikatae. It matters not that I never saw it. You did, and I love you for that."

"Tikatae—I could see—I wish you understood," she floundered. "And I saw the same in Theron."

"I do not need to understand. I know. You see beauty where others see only filth. Your strength is shared with those you love. Your heart gets you in trouble, but I hope it always stays so big."

"I'm your weakness." She turned to him, her eyes flashing. "Even now, you never think of the trouble I have caused."

"You are not weak."

"You see? I'm a blind spot for you, one place in the realms where you can see no wrong."

"And what's so bad about that?" he demanded.

"Because of me, Eian experienced things no child ever should. What if I have damaged him?"

He shook his head, unable to keep quiet. "You have taken Eian into the wilderness on many occasions. Every Rinaryn mother does. The mountains are perilous, but he's not the first child to be lost, even when there is a kaetal watching. You had no way of knowing he would enter the mountain."

"I killed a man." It was a whisper, tears shimmering in her eyes. "I have killed before. Darks. But this—he wasn't physically attacking me. I killed him for crimes he hadn't committed yet."

"Your lives were in danger. That was the king's doing, and as far as I'm concerned, you were right to do it."

Anguish filled Kaemada's voice. "I have caused too much suffering, seen too much. The psions in the City were murdered because I revealed who they were. Tannevar…"

The need to fix it, to end her pain, drove him to interrupt her. "Cha'atanahn, listen. Life is full of hard choices. The living is in making them to the best of our ability. Sometimes we choose right, sometimes we choose wrong. We make the best choices we can at any point in time. The rest is up to Eloí."

Tremors wracked her small frame. "I'm showing everyone a false face. I'm pretending I'm still the woman I was before all this, the woman who shuts out all the injuries and pretends that everything is normal, that everything can be happy again. The real woman is shattered like broken shards lying scattered on the ground, and nothing can ever fix her."

"A broken pot, once mended, carries the story and love of the mending," Taunos reminded her.

Fury burst from her with startling ferocity. "But I'm not mended, and no one can ever mend me."

He dropped the half-braided bandaging. Where was this anger coming from? He'd always protected her, even from harsh reality. The scene reframed for him. Perhaps that was the problem. He'd complained that his people lifted him up too high, never realizing he did the same to his sister. Here he was, soothing her hurts, wiping them away. Again. His sister felt weak and was trying very hard to appear strong, while he always expected her to be there with a smile for him. It turned her brittle.

He'd always altered his stories to protect her even from that danger. He didn't do that with his beloved. Oh, he altered his stories, yes, but not to protect her. He respected her too much for that. Did he afford his sister the same respect?

"Kaemada—"

"How can one broken pot fix another? I'm not yours to save."

Taunos winced. "I'm sorry, little sister."

She shook her head. "Ameyitum. I should have told you sooner. It's too easy to lean on you. It's not fair to you."

Biting back the pain, he wrapped an arm around her shoulders and gently drew her close.

Kaemada stiffened, pulling away. "I do not want to hurt you."

"Nor do I ever want to hurt you again. I do not like seeing you in pain. I never realized how you saw it."

She relaxed, pillowing her head on his shoulder. Her tears wet his shirt, but his tension eased as he held her.

He smiled a bit—she'd done that on purpose, no doubt. Offering peace after her words. She was right; she didn't need him to save her. She just needed him there. None of them would ever be the same, but that was all right. His family was alive. This was why he risked everything travelling the realms. This was what was important.

~

Answer fumed as she strode through the streets. Her meeting with the leader of her section of Scouts had been a disaster. He'd dismissed her project proposal—a system to catalogue all the new steam-powered machinery—out of hand, with barely any consideration.

"Really, Answer," he had said. "Are you a Philosopher, to archive and debate, or are you a Scout? Come back with a more appropriate idea, should you have one."

The snub resulted from the Running of the Ebrs; she was certain of it. Why trust her with anything? She'd lost control of her ebr, and as a result, the reputation of the Scouts was being smeared. Bluff ran his mouth, spreading the word that she'd questioned the Running in the first place. Even that was turned against her as the Scouts closed ranks. Either one was wholly loyal to the Scouts, or one was an enemy.

And now, she had a summons from the Philosopher she least wanted to see. What could Dode possibly want? She had been able to refuse the summons of the Outsider five days ago, but to refuse Dode's summons would shame her family for bad manners. Her peers already openly mocked her for the events of the past few days. When her parents returned from Glinr, they would undoubtedly be disappointed in her. She didn't need more shame.

As she approached the guards standing outside the Hall, Answer forced herself to assume a demure smile. There was no need for them to see how upset she was. Words flew all too swiftly. She even gave the guards a little nod as she passed.

S. Kaeth

Her ebr Taunos was there, no doubt unlearning all she had struggled to teach him now that he was once again among his own backward kind. Thick bandages padded his legs from his feet all the way to his knees, and the rest of him was more bandage than not.

She winced. He had saved her life multiple times. She'd threatened war, and even then he hadn't really hurt her—only her dignity, being tied up like that. But driven by her own humiliation, she'd nearly allowed him to be killed. Somehow, she'd lost control of events. She'd only meant to stop him from escaping, but the mob tore down a chapel, and a priest was dead, and Dode was leading the Philosophers in denouncing the Scouts, and she hadn't been able to stop the Running, and... She yanked her gaze away from Taunos and her own guilt.

The tall red-haired ebr was also up and about, fiddling with a healing machine. The black-haired ebr lay on a cot, still unconscious and tended to by an Outsider and a Kamalti Doctor. Answer frowned, but the Justices did want the ebrs to be presentable as soon as possible, and surely the Doctor could keep the Outsider from making mistakes. One way or another, the Outsiders would soon no longer be her problem. Perhaps she could forget this whole thing and get on with her life. Her reputation, and that of the Scouts as a whole, had to still be salvageable, didn't it?

Manic giggles rang out, grabbing her attention with the complete disregard for decorum. A little boy launched himself at Taunos regardless of the bandages, and her ebr caught him. As if he were a player on a stage, Taunos rolled backward in defeat while the boy lifted his arms in victory.

The healer from the Outside scolded him in caustic tones, something about mending broken bones, and the red-haired former ebr laughed. "Taunos has an aversion to caution."

"And what if you two hit a machine?" scolded the healer.

"Takiyah looks bored. She needs something to do." Taunos grinned.

Taunos's sister laughed, fiddling with a quaint piece of cloth over her shoulders. Answer eyed the fabric. These Outsiders were not civilized—she couldn't expect their taste to be refined. Near her, a large Outsider man sat at a table, mixing powders and liquids. No one seemed to be supervising him, but again, the Doctor surely could handle it.

There was no sign of Dode. Answer reined in her temper.

"Answer." Taunos straightened, seeing her. "What brings you here?"

"Where is Lady Dode?"

"Dode?"

"The Lady Dode," Answer said, stressing her title and frowning at Taunos's lack of manners. "Do not forget your place."

Taunos gave her that impossible grin. "I'm no longer your ebr, Answer. Do *you* forget?"

His sister hushed him, and amazingly, Taunos turned back around, though he gave Answer a stern look. He'd never been so obedient for her. Wrapping her shawl around herself, the sister approached, her steps stiff and limping. In her hands, she carried a little wooden box.

Answer hesitated. She could leave, but if Dode was merely running late, Answer would appear hasty or perhaps even afraid of these people. That would never do. She straightened her posture and stood her ground.

With a smile, the Outsider held out the box, chattering away something in Rinaryn.

There was little choice. Answer accepted it, refusing to marvel openly at the beauty of the wood. "You should speak the Traveller's Tongue if you intend for me to understand you."

"She cannot," Taunos began, and his sister spun around and snapped at him. Whatever she said, Taunos turned away and took the little boy to the opposite end of the Hall with the Outsider man and his mixing. Relief filled Answer despite herself.

Kaemada turned back to Answer and crudely gestured toward a small table near the wall on which sat a pot, satchels of tea leaves, and two plain mugs. The motions were too big, too sweeping, but the meaning was clear. Once again, Answer found herself trapped by etiquette, and she sat, bracing for an uncomfortable time. Ignoring a summons was one thing— she could claim she was too busy—but to decline refreshment while waiting around would be ever so rude.

Smiling again, Kaemada gestured for her to open the box.

Surprise filled her as the light reflected off several gleaming crystals nestled inside. Kaemada was prattling away at her, and Answer made her tone severe. "These crystals are meant to be read in silence."

Kaemada settled back, her hands clasped in her lap and embarrassment on her face.

Answer returned her attention to the crystals, taking more time than strictly necessary to read them. A part of her enjoyed watching Kaemada squirm. But the crystals spoke clearly of apologies, atonement for past wrongs, desire for new beginnings, and hope for friendship.

"Who tutored you?" Answer finally asked, unable to keep the appreciation from her voice. The crystals were lovely and perfect, and the wooden box would have been expensive.

"Tjodlik."

Answer nodded, recognizing Dode's nephew's name. She stressed his title. "Lord Tjodlik tutored you well."

With yet another smile, Kaemada babbled something, and Answer frowned. Undaunted, Kaemada tried again, this time adding abundant gestures.

It left Answer to guess aloud, like a child. "Your... Heart? Your heart... Smile? Happy. Your heart is happy. Glad. You are glad... I... Heart? Emotion... Smile... Like! You are glad I like them."

Nodding, Kaemada beamed.

It was contagious, and a smile tugged at Answer's mouth, which she suppressed. She cast a self-conscious glance around the room. "This is an absurd way of communicating."

The woman gestured again, this time without speaking. "Me... You... You? Me, you. Me and you! You and I... Building? Pushing... Working! You and I working... Together?"

Again, the smile and nod.

"Well, yes, this does involve some working together, but it is no less absurd or inefficient!"

A shrug answered her. Kaemada gestured to where the Kamalti Doctor and the red-haired ebr were working on the machine. She first pointed with a single, ungracious finger before catching herself and using her whole hand to gesture, as was proper.

Answer shook her head, refusing to give words to the scene. Yes, Outsiders and Kamalti were working together here in the Healing Hall, but it would never continue. The Outsiders had misstepped badly, and the Scouts would never forgive them. Answer had to stand with the Scouts or risk losing everything. Besides, the Outsiders were violent and terrifying and uncivilized. Especially if one believed the stories. It was the Outsiders who had broken their vows first. No relationship could last between the two races.

Kaemada fidgeted a moment and then gestured to the tea with a questioning look on her face.

Answer nodded, keeping an eye on the herbs. Would this woman try to drug her? She herself had drugged Kaemada's brother, but that had been necessary. The Outsider swept a white packet of tea toward herself— that would be leaves mixed with pain-numbing herbs—and slid a satchel of plain leaves over to Answer. It appeared to be standard and untampered with, so she put it in her cup. With a grimace, Kaemada hefted the pot of hot water and poured the water over the tea leaves to steep.

Eyes narrowing slightly, Answer considered the woman quietly.

Kaemada had arrived during the Running of the Ebrs, a Running called because of Answer's wrath toward this woman's brother. A brother she was apparently very close to. And yet, Kaemada called Answer here to apologize to her?

Uncertain how to handle the thought, she asked, "Do you know where the Lady Dode is?"

Kaemada shook her head.

With a frown, Answer looked over the room, stiffening when she found Taunos watching her.

Kaemada babbled something. The woman's gestures were easy to read this time.

"He will stay over there, far from here," Answer said, and the Outsider nodded.

"Why do you care about my comfort, to send your brother away? Or are you simply making certain a fight does not break out? Because I assure you, a proper lady does not get into a fistfight."

To her surprise, Kaemada laughed, leaving Answer to wonder if she were being mocked. Laughter echoed across the room as well—Taunos was throwing rolls of bandages at the red-headed ebr, who taunted him with playful insults. They both subsided when the Outsider healer snapped at them, enlisting Taunos's help to turn the black-haired ebr to avoid bedsores.

How could she reconcile the gentleness and carefree joy of her ebr here with the violence, petty annoyances, and constant small rebellions she'd lived with over the last few faces? It seemed hardly possible this was the same man. She glanced at Kaemada quickly, just a flick of her eyes, to find Kaemada watching as well, a fond smile on her face.

"Is this for show?" Answer turned on Kaemada.

With a puzzled look, Kaemada shook her head.

"This is how he normally is?" Answer asked.

Kaemada began gesturing again.

Answer sighed. "This truly is a ridiculous way to communicate."

The woman called out something, and the little boy ran over, while Taunos frowned, making no effort to hide his surveillance.

Answer watched the little boy cautiously as he waved at her with a big smile. Kaemada indicated him and said, "Eian."

Then she babbled something and gestured, but it was the boy who spoke in proper Traveller's. "Do you mind if he translates for me? I mean no offense."

Caught off-guard, Answer nodded. "Go ahead."

A smile brightened her whole face as she tousled the boy's brown curls. "You're right that it's awkward speaking without words. But I did not wish you to be uncomfortable while waiting."

"Why do you care about my comfort?" Answer asked again, narrowing her eyes.

"You're a person," Kaemada said, as if that was an answer in itself. "What made you choose to be a Scout?"

The question threw her. "I wanted to see the Outside. For that, I had to become a Scout."

The woman tilted her head. "No one else goes outside?"

"Of course not! Only Scouts, and only those who train for it. It would be terrible if just anyone went Outside—anything could happen."

"Can anyone join the Scouts?"

Where were all these questions coming from? Pride forced the words out, even as she watched Kaemada's face, looking for the trap. "Only noble families, of course, but any noble can choose to be a Scout, Philosopher, or Justice."

Another tilt of her head answered her, and confusion showed plainly on Kaemada's face. "What if a noble wanted to be a painter or a Storyteller?"

"Well, that would be absurd. Impossible. Painting is a hobby. Only commoners view it as a profession."

"Oh. How does one become a noble or a commoner?"

Answer scoffed. "One is born into their status—one cannot become something else. The commoners take up their parents' jobs unless they are fortunate enough to be fostered by someone with a profession they are more suited to. But nobles are given the choice of what they want to devote their lives to."

Kaemada's gaze went far away, and she smiled.

"What?"

"Ah. The last time I was in my kaetal, among my people—it seems so long ago. I was upset that I could not be what I wanted to be, but it turns out I had more freedom than you."

Answer's eyes narrowed, her composure fracturing. "What do you mean?"

Her hand indicated her companions. "Any of us can choose whatever task we want to do, and it can change day-to-day, even."

There was something open and vulnerable and humble about the injured woman being translated by a little boy. Answer didn't feel the need to protect herself as she normally did in conversations. No rivals waited to pull her down or take her place. She found herself opening up, talking far more freely than she was used to doing. After all, in a few days, it wouldn't matter what Kaemada thought of her.

"How does that even function if everyone changes their minds?" Answer asked.

"We all work together, or we won't survive. People tend to concentrate on the tasks they're good at. My frustration over my talents being frowned upon by the others seems small now."

"But there is no order there! How do you function without basic order, without the safety of the Scouts keeping that order?"

A smile answered her. "Perhaps one day, if we put aside our fear and anger, we can find out. My people would benefit from so much of your knowledge."

"Yes, all the benefit would be yours."

Kaemada tilted her head again. "Much, yes, especially if you helped us defend against the Darks. But I see ways we could help you, too. The air here is choked with smoke, and you have no room. There is no sun or wind or dirt here, no great expanses of trees or grasses. We could trade with each other, become friends once more, just as Elisabei and your Doctor have been learning from each other's knowledge. Just as Tannevar and I supported each other."

"Impossible."

"Unlikely, perhaps, but then, that's why we dream, isn't it? To have the courage to reach for the unlikely."

It was absurd. The entire situation was.

"Would you help me learn more about your etiquette here?" Kaemada asked. "I would like to avoid further misunderstandings, further resentments. Nothing like the Running can happen again."

Answer clenched her teeth on her agreement. The Running had been a terrible idea, and if she'd only been able to stop it... If she'd not acted on her own humiliation, but instead spoken to Taunos like a person... She'd considered him unreasonable, but her own unreasonable actions had led to this, and her guilt lay heavy on her shoulders every time she saw his bandages.

But tutoring the sister would be entirely inappropriate. Answer resolved to give Kaemada a book on the subject, surprised at herself.

Had she leapt to a conclusion about these people at their first meeting? Fondness for the boy poured off Kaemada in every interaction, and guilt stabbed at Answer as she remembered the terror in the woman's voice when they'd first met.

"Each of us has stories we tell ourselves about who we are," Kaemada said, looking at Eian as he translated for her. "But sometimes the stories are not accurate. Sometimes they're too small."

"What do you mean?" Answer asked.

Dode finally entered the Healing Hall, and Answer tensed. She needed to finish this conversation so she could catch Dode.

"Please, do not let your society make you smaller than you are. And I will do the same. By putting aside the requirements placed on us by those who wish to contain us, we could each do great good for our people."

Answer nodded slowly, her thoughts going to her meeting with the Scouting leader. She barely noticed as Kaemada and the little boy left, feeling mystified. Dode took the now-empty chair, and Answer straightened, pushing thoughts of the strange Kaemada out of her head.

"Not quite what you expected, hmm?" Dode asked.

Answer withdrew behind her aloof facade, closing up her emotions again. "Lady Dode, you certainly kept me waiting."

"Ah, yes, I apologize for that. My plan required that I be late."

Her plan? She'd been played. Answer rose to her feet. "You worked together to set this up?"

Dode laughed, remaining seated. "No, dear, I worked alone to set this up. I knew she bought you the crystals in good faith, and that you refused to meet her. That is as far as the scheming went. Tell me, are you happy now that you refused meeting sooner?"

"What did you want to meet with me about, Lady Dode?" Answer kept her tone curt.

"I wanted to check if these Outsiders' belongings might be brought to them. The Hall is going to get quite... fragrant... with all the unwashed clothing," Dode said.

Answer frowned, then nodded. "I will make an inquiry."

"I also wondered if the Scouts are going to pay for the repairs to the chapel." The elderly woman smiled at her.

That was a strike too many against her, and her heart still felt too vulnerable, too unguarded, after opening up to Kaemada. Answer drew herself up and took a deep breath to calm herself and keep her composure. "Lady Dode, good day to you."

Chapter Twenty-five

There are many differences between dreamwalking and telepathy. When using telepathy, any reach out of one's mind provides a hole another can use to enter that mind, and any information you consciously acknowledge is easily gleaned by the other. Secrets, knowledge, plans—every thought is available to the owner of the mind the psion is in. With dreamwalking, that knowledge can be better kept to oneself, at least for a few moments. However, dreamwalking is lethal if the psion cannot return to their body and makes it impossible for the psion to pay any attention to the outside environment.

-notes from Kaemada Sierso, psion

Ra'ael sat up and rubbed the grit from her eyes. Kaemada cried out in her sleep and Takiyah murmured, each battling their nightmares. Moving with care, Ra'ael got out of bed, wiggling her feet on the stone floor. It was eerie to sleep slung above the ground, and even more unnatural sleeping above hard, unforgiving stone. She still hadn't gotten used to it and longed for her simple sleeping mats laid on good dirt. After a cautious stretch for healing wounds, she headed for the table at the side wall to make more calming tea.

It had been five days since she'd awakened, five days since she'd learned the Kamalti were healing them only to judge them. It was disgusting. Dode assured her she was doing everything she could to "help her fellows come to their senses," as she said. In the meantime, they had each gone through several rounds with the miraculous Kamalti healing machine. It was similar to being healed by Rinaryn healers back home, although Ra'ael would have much preferred those old, familiar ways. Regardless of the method, their bodies were each nearly whole again.

But the machine, just as with the healers, could only soothe physical hurts. Takiyah and Kaemada each bore deep wounds to their spirits, and Ra'ael had taken charge as soon as she'd regained mobility. Chants, Kamalti teas, and sacred stories were all she could do without the sacred herbs to burn or the proper leaves for teas, but she trusted the spirits that those would be enough. This was her realm, and Taunos eagerly followed her lead, grateful for something to do, she guessed.

It probably would have been better for them all if Answer had stayed away, but the woman insisted on coming often for little meetings. Supposedly Answer came to speak to Dode, but she spent much of her time talking with Kaemada instead. Seeing Answer couldn't be good for Takiyah and Taunos's spirits, not so soon after all they had been through. It was bad enough that they'd only been given Kamalti clothing to wear, not their own.

Elisabei glanced over at her as Ra'ael moved but continued her hushed conversation with the Kamalti Doctor. A respect had bloomed between those two. Even the healer's husband, on Kaemada's urging, had begun opening up to Taunos while he fiddled with the strange powders he liked to mix. She smiled a little, shaking her head. Kaemada had also managed to get a group of Kamalti coming regularly for story-swapping nights! Kaemada was like a force of nature newly awakened. She'd always been mild-mannered until backed into a corner, and whatever had happened in the City of the Lost must have been quite the corner, because Ra'ael was still waiting for the ripples to fade.

She typically stayed well out of the way as Kaemada meddled, talking with one group of Kamalti after another, apparently striving to build some sort of understanding. They were all changed. Nothing could go back to the way it had been. They would have to figure out this new way of being and whether the Kamalti would be part of it.

They couldn't be, though. At least, not until there was justice for Takiyah's torture.

Judgement hung over them, but Ra'ael scoffed at the idea. The Kamalti held no true authority over them, even considering their captivity. Between visits with Dode, Ra'ael conferred with Taunos, preparing several contingency plans, just in case. They would not be caught unawares again. Takiyah's eyes sparked with suspicion every time she looked at a Kamalti, even Dode, even the Doctor who thanked her for repairing the healing machine.

Humming the ancient Torkaema's Lament, Ra'ael tapped a separate rhythm with each hand while she waited for the water to heat. Taunos joined in a moment later with a third rhythm and a harmony. No surprise there—he'd always been a light sleeper. When he was home, she often tried to sneak past him in the mornings without waking him. She rarely succeeded.

She glanced at Elisabei and Reinan. They seemed unaffected by the rituals, but surely they would need comfort from traumas, too. So as Reinan stood from his work at the side table and wandered over to his wife, she offered them a nod, continuing her humming and forgiving them for not adding their voices.

"What do you do when words fail, when there are no more songs to be sung, and the dancers are sleeping?" she sang as she poured hot water into cups to steep the tea. She lifted the tray, letting go of both rhythms, and smiled at Taunos as he added in another.

Takiyah and Kaemada woke to the rich, slow tones washing over them, just as she'd intended. Torkaema's farewell to Naran was a perfect encapsulation of loss and uncertainty. It was her favorite to help people work through trauma—something the Dark attacks had given her plenty of experience with. In the song, Naran never came down from the Holy Mountains, and so far, neither had they. She handed each a cup of tea as they sat up, cautioning Eian to take care with his, as it was hot.

Song complete, Ra'ael continued with a morning ritual to ease the waking minds of the others. She turned her face to the east, closing her eyes as if she could feel the warmth of the rising sun by force of will alone. "I give thanks for the sunrise."

"I give thanks for us all being together," Taunos said, giving her a look as he sipped his tea. She smiled at him, grateful he was playing along.

"I give thanks for you all being alive." It was the same gratitude Kaemada had expressed each morning since Ra'ael began this ritual, but Ra'ael let it go, for it sounded heartfelt.

Takiyah was silent, as she tended to be, and Eian took over for her. "I give thanks for secrets found."

A smile brightened Kaemada's face and she tousled his hair.

Takiyah finally stirred and straightened. "I want to go home."

Ra'ael opened her mouth to speak, but Takiyah abruptly stood, setting aside her cup and limping to the side room where the latrines were. Her limp remained even after multiple times in the machine. She would have it all her life, along with the scars from her branding. Ra'ael only hoped her spirit didn't have similarly permanent wounds. She glanced at Taunos, who gestured peace. There was comfort in letting go of her antagonism toward him.

With her smile melted away like morning mist, Kaemada hunched over her tea, staring into its depths.

"Kae. What is it?" Ra'ael refused to allow wallowing.

Kaemada huddled into a ball, but she responded without further prodding, which was an improvement. "I can still smell the burning, feel the flames. I dreamed all night the city was burning."

"They have done us much injury, but little sister, burning the city?" Taunos eyed her the way Takiyah eyed broken machines. "That does not sound like you."

"It's not my wish! I had no desire for such thoughts."

"Perhaps the spirits are telling you something," Ra'ael said.

"An opportunity to take advantage of?" Taunos asked.

"Or a chance to avert disaster?" Ra'ael mused, nodding to Takiyah as she returned.

"Plans," Eian said.

Takiyah's gaze flashed to Eian. "Plans?"

The boy looked at her solemnly without elaborating. Kaemada plucked at her shawl, her expression growing darker.

Sipping her tea, Elisabei joined them. "Can psions not unintentionally pick up on others' thoughts?"

"It's forbidden," Kaemada cried.

"Taboo," said Eian.

Ra'ael shook her head. "All this stress would weaken your mental walls, Kaemada."

Kaemada nodded slowly, and Ra'ael continued, "If the sender also had heightened emotions, it would stand to reason that these plans could bypass your mental defenses, especially while you're asleep."

Taunos nodded. "Good point, but why share their plans in advance? And we haven't met any psions, so who's the sender?"

"We met Kamalti psions." Elisabei's tone made the hair on the back of Ra'ael's neck rise.

Kaemada nodded. "They live on the outskirts in a community of their own. Somehow they caught me when I fell."

"But why warn us? Why send their plans to Kaemada?" Ra'ael asked.

"Maybe they think she would be on their side." Takiyah hesitated, then lowered her gaze and muttered, "I'm not entirely against it, I must say."

Taunos shrugged. "After what they did to us, who could blame you?"

"Why not just find out?" Elisabei interrupted.

"What?" Ra'ael asked.

"Instead of speculating, why doesn't she simply ask them why? They don't seem to have the typical Rinaryn taboo against touching another's mind."

"That does not mean I may trespass." Arms wrapped around herself, Kaemada looked frightened and fragile.

"Who would it hurt?" Taunos asked.

"The rules are there for a reason," Ra'ael argued.

"Seems silly for having a person with such abilities and the community for saying, 'You have a great gift—now never use it,'" Reinan rumbled.

"That's not how it is." Ra'ael clenched her fists, glaring at Reinan.

"Really?" Taunos asked. "It seems to me Reinan has a point."

"Whose side are you on?" Ra'ael turned on him. Taunos and Reinan had been spending a lot of time together in the last few days.

Taunos raised his hands in appeasement. "You must admit, it's rather strange that our culture is more accepting of your blood rage than our psionic abilities."

"The rules are there for the protection of all," Ra'ael said. "You know our history. If your memory needs a refresher, I will happily give it."

"No," Kaemada breathed, opening her eyes. "It was a mistake."

"Come up with an original argue—" Taunos halted mid-sentence and turned to his sister. "What was a mistake?"

"They're not used to shielding their thoughts from others who may eavesdrop." She flushed with shame. "I really did not mean to hear."

"Shareil, cha'atanahn, you're not on trial here."

"Why are they planning to burn the city?" Ra'ael asked. She wouldn't toss out such useful information, even if Kaemada's actions were ill-advised.

"More importantly, when?" Takiyah asked.

The color drained from Kaemada's face. "Oh no. What have I done?"

"When?" Takiyah insisted.

The doors burst open and the senior Doctor rushed in, all decorum abandoned. "Move, move, move, we must escape."

Screams and shouts echoed from outside. The building shuddered around them. The Doctor grabbed the healing machine, cradling it in his arms as he dashed out of the Healing Hall ahead of them.

"I think that's our answer," Ra'ael said.

"Move, move, outside now!" Taunos urged, repeating the words of the Doctor.

Ra'ael quickly led her people onto the streets, glancing back to make sure everyone was following. Taunos held Eian in one arm and guided Kaemada ahead of him with the other. Elisabei and Takiyah clustered in the middle, carrying bags of supplies, and Reinan hefted his bag of newly prepared Boom and brought up the end of their ragged little group.

Smoke rose above the buildings in their neat rows, and the crash of stone striking stone rang out nearby. People screamed and raced past, while the sounds of slaughter echoed in the wide streets, creating a horrifying cacophony.

"Is this truly happening?" Horror filled Kaemada's face. "The psions are coming. They said… they said I taught them the ways of warfare, the value of liberty. They come for revenge."

Enormous blocks of stone, each as tall as a person, soared in an arc before crashing through the city. The massive columns that held up the cavern ceiling and doubled as residences shivered with the impact, dust rising from them. People filled the stairs and lifts on the outside of the columns, packed together. One unlucky side was struck directly, and the stone sheared off the entire lift, then rotated and clipped the stairs, wrenching them away from the building. Screams, punctuated by the thud of more stones, filled the air.

The higher levels, where the smoke rose from the machines of the rich, were inhabited by the poor, and the stairs downward became death traps as panic mounted and people were trampled.

"It's our chance to get out," Elisabei said.

Takiyah nodded, her eyes hard.

Ra'ael turned stair-ward. She could just see the stairs chiseled into the side of the cavern. Her eyes swept Detr-ward. Dode's house was just up the street, near the base of one of those columns. How would Dode survive this? She had enemies and they might take advantage of such chaos to gain their revenge on her. Ra'ael chewed on her lip, rubbing her sweating palms on her too-slick Kamalti clothes. She had to put her duty to her own people first. They needed her most.

Kaemada's voice quavered. "'We are powerful. We are strong. We're not subject to their judgement of our worth!' That's what I told them. And now this!"

"Oh, cha'atanahn," Taunos groaned.

Ra'ael shook her head. "You cannot take the guilt for everything others do. Let them take responsibility for their own actions. There are many more Kamalti than us—it's folly to assume we would make any difference."

Mind made up, she led the way through the streets, trying to avoid the sounds of violence. They darted behind the gelatin shop, around the square of glassmakers, only to be confronted by the blaze that had been the cluster of papermakers. Next to it, the flames licked at the copyists' garden. Ra'ael backed up as another stone crashed into the ground two blocks behind them, obliterating the once-impeccably straight street and tossing debris into the air. Angry shouts and shrieks of pain came from the section of papermakers' shops.

She coughed, struggling to breathe through the dust and smoke. The elegance of the Kamalti's clean lines was turning to rubble. Another stone whistled through the air, and this time she saw its origins—the chasm. The boulder crashed against another pillar, and figures fell screaming from the stairs which were ripped from their anchors. The psions must be throwing rocks at the city, working together in vast numbers to lift such heavy weights. How many were there? She trembled with the need to fight, but they needed a way out, not a battle. Not with Eian with them, and with Takiyah and Kaemada so vulnerable. She reoriented herself. They'd have to pass close to one of the columns with residences—assuming the street remained clear.

"We have to help them," Kaemada shouted over the noise.

"It would be wrong to stay and die." Takiyah's features grew hard and she continued limping toward the stairs.

"Rinaryn do not stand by and let others suffer. We cannot just let them die!"

"They're not Rinaryn," Ra'ael shouted.

"No, but we are." Kaemada wrenched herself free from Taunos's grasp.

"I'm not staying," Takiyah snarled.

"Eian cannot stay either," Kaemada said, pushing her brother forward. "Go, get out, get him home safely. Get Takiyah home safely, too."

"We're all getting out safely," Taunos started.

"No. The best way to keep Eian safe is for me to stay. If I can turn the psions away or delay them long enough, you can escape with him. But I cannot leave these people—children, elderly, people who cannot fight—to die when I put them in danger. I witnessed too much pain and did too little in the palace. I cannot bear to do nothing again."

Ra'ael shook her head. Kaemada was the heart of them all, but there were times when the mind needed to rule over the heart. As much as she wished they could help, the risk was too great. How many hits could the pillars take before the ceiling collapsed on them all? Sometimes not everyone could win.

"I'm the only one who can do this. And I'm doing it." Tears streamed down Kaemada's face as she kissed Eian, who began to cry. Then she embraced her brother. "Go. Please, keep him safe. But go!"

Leave Kaemada behind? Another rock crashed against another column, and the air filled with screams. No. She couldn't. And Takiyah couldn't last much longer. They were her responsibility.

There was a way to take care of them all. A way that went against all their laws. She swallowed hard, grabbing Kaemada's arm to impress her words on her. "Kaemada, listen to me. Do what you need to do, but your body is coming with us."

Eyes wide, Kaemada nodded. Another impact resounded, knocking them off their feet. Leaping back up, Ra'ael glanced at the chasm. The bridge to Hadr was gone. Figures, small in the distance, lined the Hadr side, and Ra'ael squinted. Crossbows. They fired in volleys, yet still, a flood of ragged Kamalti surged over the lip of the chasm, whipping smaller stones ahead of them at the trapped and injured. The distance was too far—Codr was cut off from help.

Her people had to come first, she reminded herself. First and greatest, she was priestess. So why did her heart feel so heavy? She prayed for Dode's safety and pushed forward, winding between the locksmiths' and the jewelers' blocks. Takiyah jogged beside her with a lurching but determined stride, hands flexed and ready to release her flames. Taunos carried his sister, who had apparently lost no time dreamwalking, while Eian trotted at his side. Elisabei and Reinan brought up the rear.

The air was thick with smoke and dust, choking her. The cavern's ceiling collected the smoke, forcing the poor who lived higher above ground level to spill from the limited protection of their homes in search of air they could breathe. The stairs began to screech and buckle beneath their burdens.

They turned the corner of one of the columns. One of the lifts had stuck, packed beyond capacity with desperate refugees. Young and old, trapped in a metal box swinging helplessly many paces above the ground. Bedraggled Kamalti lurched up the switchback staircase attached to the column, making their way toward the stranded lift.

Ra'ael had never expected to wish for the arrival of the Scouts, but she found herself angry that they weren't here to help. She gritted her teeth. Takiyah and Eian had to remain her priority.

More ragged Kamalti came down the street toward them, some with smooth gaits, others shuffling along. Ra'ael spun around but the thick press of bodies clogged the streets behind them. They were surrounded.

~

Kaemada hurled her mind from her body. Her brother's song surrounded her body as he caught her, carrying her. She reached out to him. *There's a chance I'm not strong enough. There are so many minds... I might be lost in the Collective.*

You're on psion duty, little sister. Protect our minds; I will keep your body safe. Then come back to us.

Taunos would try to be the hero and sacrifice himself to get them out. But not this time—she wouldn't let him. He deserved the very brightest of stories. All four of them did.

Now to seek out the Collective. Her mind swayed without an anchor, without Tannevar. But she didn't need to find the psions. They found her, crashing over her like a waterfall.

She embraced them. Ripples of surprise and suspicion moved through their shared mind. They had expected her to fight them, to act the warrior again, as she had spent so long trying to do, chasing a dream that had died the night Tikatae stabbed her in the knee.

She leapt on their confusion. *Stop this mind-sickness!*

Mind-sickness? This is not madness, but sanity. No longer will we be relegated to the darkness. Join us in our glory.

There is no glory here, only slaughter. It's mind-sickness.

The vermin Above deserve no less for casting us Below. We will not return Below! We will die first.

Your anger is right. But there are innocents here—my friends, my brother, my son. I will not let you hurt them.

They are lesser. They are weak. You cannot truly be friends with them.

No! You think the other Kamalti will stand for this? They will seek revenge. You will all be destroyed.

Not if we destroy them first. You are one of us. Why are you doing this? Why do you attack your own?

Around her, several psions stopped, falling to the ground, and their presence in her mind became stronger, more physical. She stared around her. They were dreamwalking?

Laughter rippled around her. *Yes, your dreamwalking, as you call it, is not a unique ability.*

I have never met anyone else who could do it. Kaemada retreated a little.

It takes telepathy and telekinesis—not an unusual combination.

It's unusual in Rinara.

Your people are broken. Psionics should be much more common.

Kaemada shook herself mentally. *Please! This isn't what I meant. You're Kamalti, whatever you might say. These are your own people you're hurting.*

They do not have the Gift. They are not ours.

They're people! What of the others thrown away with you, those who do not have the Gift?

They are of us. Of us, and lesser.

Lesser, you say? Lesser, as the Kamalti think of you? A society of status, just like those you focus your hatred on? Kaemada poured out what she'd learned of Kamalti society from her talks with Answer, displaying it for them. *How can you say you're different from those who mistreated you?*

They are not innocent.

Neither are you. Who are you to pass judgement?

Anger roiled in them, magnifying through the massive Collective at their back and seeping into Kaemada's song. They immersed her in the suffering they'd endured. Sleeping in filth, eating garbage, never having enough. It echoed the lives of those in the City of the Lost.

Maybe that was what defined people: the mistakes they hid away and tried to ignore, the pain they caused without meaning. She saw it again and again: in the City of the Lost, with the Kamalti, even her own people.

No, people were more than their mistakes. They were always more than their mistakes. But attacking in vengeance would not make anything right. The king of the City of the Lost had thought it worth it. The Collective was just as wrong as he had been. Nothing was worth the cost of terrorizing others.

Your hands are not clean, either. The Collective surrounded her with the moment she killed the king.

That's why I'm asking you not to do this. Because I know what you will lose. She indicated the battleground around them in the dreamscape. *This isn't justice. This is vengeance. You do not care who you hurt as long as they hurt.*

Songs all around her were silenced, people who died simply because the Collective couldn't lash out directly at what had actually hurt them—the society they'd been born into. Just as Takiyah distrusted all Kamalti, not only those who hurt her. And she understood this, the pain of it. It poured from Takiyah's song into the dreamscape, from the songs of the Collective.

All are complicit in the treatment we have suffered. They see and do not speak out. They do not stop it.

All? Even children like Eian?

The Precious Vessel. Let go. We will be sure he is safe. We will deliver you all safely to the Outside.

The Collective knew precisely what she wanted. How could she refuse, especially when their words rang with truth? She'd risked everything for him, and now, there was a chance to be free of this mountain. No more fighting. Eian was only one child, but he was hers. All she had to do was let go.

Her mind drifted. She could let go.

The Collective reeled with her, she realized. She was losing herself in the Collective again. She forced herself to focus. *Do you not see? You can show those who wronged you that they were wrong. You can show them what it really means to be noble. If you continue to do battle like this, they will argue they were right, that you're an enemy and too dangerous to live. You cannot fight hate with hate. Do you not see the foolishness of this?*

We cannot stop. We are too vulnerable here. We must continue until we can show the Above a strength not to be toyed with!

She was vulnerable. She'd known she might be sucked into the Collective. Ra'ael had sent her anyway.

Wrath. They'd sent her where she would fail.

No! Taunos had always protected her, but now he was relying on her. They all were. That was respect.

She drew herself inward. *I am my father's daughter. And I am my mother's daughter. And I am Galod's student.* Laughter bubbled out of her. *And that's what he has been trying to get me to understand for so long.*

Her thoughts cleared slowly, like a fog lifting, the pull of the Collective fading as she defined herself apart from them and drew herself out of the tossing ocean of their existence.

She was Kaemada Sierso, a psion, and she would not let this continue.

Reaching out, she picked up the panic of the people around them, on the stairs, in the lifts, running from the flames and their nightmares. She streamed it at the Collective, flooding them with the pain and terror they were causing. Discord erupted through their song in the dreamscape.

No song stands alone, she shouted at them. *We build our songs from those who we surround ourselves with, inspired by the stories of those who have gone before us. We build our stories from theirs. And you need to know what you're destroying.*

The revulsion and uncertainty of the Collective thrummed through her. Still, stubbornness wove through their song. *We have been separate from them for so long. What care we for their pain?*

The songs of the people rang out in the dreamscape, blending into one great song. In some places, the song swelled, louder than the individuals. Songs streamed toward the haven of these patches of brilliance, and she wasn't surprised to see her friends there, fighting, the music of their souls loud and bright.

And her own song, still with themes from Tannevar woven into it, as it always would be. Pieces of her had died with him, and fragments of him still lived in her.

We all sprang from tiny pieces of the greater song of Elot's creation. How can we justify ending other parts of the song to strengthen our own? Your separation is that of the harsh winters, but the growing season has come, and the kaetal can come together again, each bringing their piece of the central fires to make the kaetal whole once more. Only the separation has been long—lifetimes long.

Just like the separation between Kamalti and Rinaryn.

Participation, rhythm, tune, words. The Kamalti and the Rinaryn had to work together, for all their safety, including that of the psions. Without that communal rhythm, without the joining of their songs, Eian would be in danger again from vengeance seekers from either side. So would her friends. The psions, in their search for vengeance, were jeopardizing all of those lives, including their own. All she'd been trying to build. Anger flared in her, even though she understood. How could she not, when she was so connected to the Collective? She drove her song into theirs, carrying with her the echoes of the tunes of their victims.

It is time it ends.

~

Answer held her head high, striding quickly along at the center of the double columns of apprentice-Scouts. She was *not* running. Scouts were prepared for conflict from either tunnel into the cavern—from one of the other City-states—or for intrusions from the Outside. Apparently, no one had given thought to the monsters of the chasm.

The first priority of the Scouts was to get the Justices and Philosophers to safety. They'd secured the Hall of Scouts first, for the embarrassment would prove politically fatal should the sharp-edged building be taken by the creatures. Every failure on their part would be scrutinized in agonizing detail for the foreseeable future. They had to be perfect. They'd spread out from there, securing all the metal buildings first, and then branching out to contain the threat. But they were so very outnumbered. The latest estimates at the Hall were of eight hundred attackers.

She'd longed to stay in the Hall of Scouts, where it was safe, but every able-bodied combat-focused Scout was out fighting. That left her to rescue noble families, with trainees as a guard. They had five families to collect that had been cut off in the confusion of the initial attack.

They are safe. They are safe. She repeated it over and over to herself as a litany. They would be far enough from the chasm. The creatures couldn't have penetrated so far, could they have? She stamped down on the part of her that wished Taunos were here to protect her. She didn't need the Outsiders, couldn't be seen with them any longer. It would ruin her social standing if anyone thought she sympathized with them.

Is that what she was? An Outsider-sympathizer? Her mother would die of shame.

Screams and shouts, the ring of metal, and the crash of stone as buildings collapsed all filled her ears. She couldn't shut them out, and by the time they had collected two of the families, her nerves were strained to breaking. The trainees startled at the sounds of clashes, of voices shouting or crying for help. The Scouts were on their way, Answer told herself, pressing her lips tightly together. If she showed her fear, the trainees would surely panic, and the nobles they'd gathered would lose faith in her. If they distrusted her, she'd have no control over them.

"Lady Answer." The boy at the front turned. The entire group stopped with him.

"What?" Fear, and the fear of it being known she was afraid, made Answer terse.

"Lady, it sounds like there is fighting ahead. Shall we go stair-ward?"

"That would be better than chasm-ward or ahead toward the fighting." Answer made a mental note to praise the boy in front of his superiors to make up for her tone. She tried to shake out her jittery hands.

"Are the Crystal Rooms working?" That was Lord Jath, tottering on the arm of his equally elderly wife.

"Yes, my lord," she said. "The Scouts have made certain the Hall of Scouts remained safe."

"Well, do not preen for fulfilling the bare minimum of your obligations," Lord Jath snapped.

Answer averted her eyes, only to realize the boy was watching with a little smirk on his face. Well, then. Maybe she wouldn't congratulate the disrespectful trainee. "Let us continue."

If she survived this, she would keep her head down and work hard until she rose high enough that no one would dare disrespect her in public. That, at least, would please her family and the Scouts. The best thing for her would be to forget the Outsiders like a bad dream.

The boy straightened, nodded, and turned them stair-ward.

Ten blocks from Crystal Square, the fighting boiled out into their street. A flood of people streamed toward them in various states of dishevelment. Behind them came misshapen monsters with cruel smiles. Kamalti. The monsters were Kamalti.

She'd known it, of course. The monsters came from the chasm, where those with magic and deformities were sent. But to look into their eyes and see a person... she tightened her fists and stiffened her back to avoid shivering. What could these creatures possibly want?

Aware of the noble's judgemental eyes, Answer ordered the boys to form up closely around them in the shelter of a shop and directed the refugees to the Square. Where were the Scouts? Only three were visible, running toward them with torn uniforms and bloodied daggers and cudgels. They were too far away! The creatures driving the citizens of Codr forward would be on them in moments. What could she do?

The refugees swarmed past them, and there at the end was a familiar face. Taunos, bloody yet again, stumbling and gasping with fatigue. He carried Kaemada's body while the other Rinaryn man carried the blood-raged woman, battered yet again. The sight made her heart lurch—when had she become almost fond of the Outsiders? It must have been all those talks. They were not who she'd thought they were. The Outsiders were all there—even that little boy, keeping to the middle of their group just as she was keeping to the middle of hers.

She straightened, throwing her shoulders back. She was a Scout! She would not suffer these creatures to destroy her beautiful City. She would stand for order against the chaos, and that included not letting the Outsiders escape while her City burned. And yet, and yet... She'd misjudged the Outsiders—all of her people had. Was it possible her people had brought this disaster on themselves, too?

The press of her group joining the others in their dash for safety nearly swept her off her feet. She looked—really looked this time—at the situation. The red-haired ebr—Takiyah—tossed a glass and metal ball behind her toward the attacking creatures from the chasm, and moments later, the ball erupted. The Rinaryn healer followed it up with another. Some of the creatures pressed forward from the other side, nearly overwhelming them. Taunos, still carrying Kaemada, leapt toward them, spinning as he drove them back with kicks and punches, impossibly holding the line. In the turmoil of the crowd, two Scouts worked their way toward the back, taking up stations to either side of the Outsiders, firing crossbows at their attackers. This rag-tag group formed the rearguard, protecting the people of Codr in their flight to safety.

The Outsiders were helping her people and paying dearly for it.

She shouldn't have expected anything else. Irritating as Taunos was, he'd consistently rescued her from danger, while she'd drugged and berated him. Kaemada had shown remarkable compassion and curiosity for a savage. More compassion than Answer had shown.

"Lead them to the Hall of Scouts," she shouted to her trainees, breaking out of the safety of the middle. This was a terrible idea, logic told her. This was not the way to gain status and power.

Perhaps tonight logic could sleep a little. Survival had to be more important than status and power, didn't it?

Tremors betrayed her, her legs like liquid as she joined the Outsiders at the back of the cluster of refugees. The chasm creatures pressed in, and Answer held her hand out to Takiyah. "I wish to help."

Takiyah gave her a suspicious glance.

Answer pressed her lips together for a moment, then tried again. "I can throw just as well."

"No, you cannot—we're out." The Rinaryn healer wadded up the empty bag as Takiyah tossed the last ball.

Answer refused to show her disappointment. Why had Fate caused the two Outsiders who were most friendly to be unconscious and unable to speak for her? Still, she must do her duty and bring the people of the City safely to the Hall. Tonight, that included the Outsiders.

"We're not going back to captivity," Taunos gasped as they retreated. He staggered, his left leg buckling before he recovered.

"Things will get bad soon. We're almost out of ways to distract them," Takiyah said.

"Are they dead?" Answer asked, glancing at the two unconscious women. The last time Taunos's sister had been thought dead, Ra'ael had tried to kill her.

"Dead?" Taunos shook his head, keeping up their careful retreat. "Ra'ael saved many of your people before going down. Kaemada is fighting the psions."

"It does not seem she did very well."

"Mind to mind."

"Magic!" The objection burst from her before she could stop it.

Taunos turned a withering look on her.

A cold grin broke on Takiyah's face. "We can stop using our magic to protect you, since it bothers you so much."

Answer opened her mouth to say something contrite, something that would appropriately apologize, but nothing came. They were acting like Scouts, saving her people, and she was behaving ungratefully. And yet, the other Scouts would see only enemies when they looked at the Outsiders.

A great wave of water loomed above them. Impossible. There was no significant source of open water nearby. Screams rose around her. Citizens scattered, and Answer nearly lost her footing. Terror chilled her.

"To the Hall of Scouts!" she shouted, stooping to help an older woman who'd been knocked down. She looked up, but the wall of water was gone as suddenly as it had appeared. She shivered. Magic.

"No, it's a trap!" the healer shouted. "They're causing us to see things."

Lord Jath, beside her, glared at them. "The Hall of Scouts is safe, you said. What are you playing at?"

"She's right. Run your prey into a trap—always a good trick for hunters," Taunos said.

"We are close to the Hall of Scouts. We will all be safe there," Answer tried.

Takiyah sneered. "You will all be safe there."

Answer chewed on her lip. She deserved that. "You have no reason to trust me, but you will never get out at this rate. You carry too many casualties."

"I will not go back!" Takiyah whipped around, and Answer stepped backward before she could stop herself. She looked behind them, beyond the refugees. There it was. The Hall of Scouts. They would make it.

"No. I will speak for you." Answer shook her head, committing herself. She looked at Taunos. "You saved me because I needed saving. Now you are in need of saving. Let me help you."

Stones whipped toward them from the stair-ward direction. She fell, tossed backward by the impact. Blood slicked her hands. Screams sounded all around, and someone stepped on her leg, sending pain bursting up her shin. She struggled upright. The creatures were upon them. She gasped for breath that wouldn't come. This was how she would die.

But she was not their first target.

The healer was the first to crumple, crying out in pain. Ra'ael convulsed, and then Taunos staggered. Answer hauled on his arm, swinging him toward the Hall of Scouts, and shoved him hard. "Go!"

She turned, grabbing Takiyah, who grabbed the Rinaryn healer. The two Scouts dragged the healer's husband toward the Hall along with her. Everyone else was inside. Pain gripped her like a vice around her skull, squeezing her to mush as she crossed the threshold. She slapped the glass pane by the doors. The doors of the Hall of the Scouts glided shut. With another desperate slap on the glass, the doors hissed, sealing them in.

The pain vanished. Answer sagged, clutching light-headed at the wall. At least she was not the only one. Others who had been gripped by the magic of those creatures drooped in relief as well.

"Thank the gods!" Zhedr breathed, slumping to the floor. It looked very ignoble, but at the moment, she did not blame him. Surprise and gratitude filled her to see him.

"You overstep yourself!" Lord Jath scolded her.

"You cannot offer them sanctuary. Leave them outside with the other magic users, I say!" Lady Ebez said.

Perhaps monsters were everywhere, not so clearly defined as us and them.

"They stay in partial payment for their heroic deeds," Answer said, trying to ignore the tremors rising in her. She controlled her breathing, determined to stay calm.

"They saved three Scouts who were with me," said Zhedr.

Other voices murmured agreements, mostly from the common people. Stories began to flow of the Outsiders' heroism, and Answer sighed, grateful for the backup.

"How did you know the Hall would block their magic?" Zhedr asked.

"I did not," she confessed in a whisper. Beyond him, Kaemada thrashed near the wall, while the others who'd been under attack now lay still. Taunos held her with gritted teeth, trying to still her flailing limbs.

"What is happening?" Answer asked, stepping toward them despite herself.

Taunos shook his head. "She warned me they were so many, she might lose herself. And moving her, I may have done her damage. I do not know."

Kaemada sat up so suddenly her forehead collided with Taunos's, knocking him backward. "Non-psions must pay. Lifetimes of mistreatment, and we will show—" She gagged, collapsed, and Taunos struggled to hold her again.

Answer blinked. The words were in Traveller's. The woman hadn't spoken a word of Traveller's since… since the chasm.

"You see?" Lord Jath shouted. "You cannot trust a magic-user."

"E orashyi," Kaemada screamed. "Líumkoom e orashyi!"

Answer stepped backward. It was like a horror one might see at the amphitheater. Except there, after the story was done, one could go home and laugh off the fear. This… this was different. She'd thrown her word behind these Outsiders. Had she made a fatal error?

"Taunos! Tachí, ozaseiwi. Abothe."

Taunos's jaw clenched as he held his raving sister. A wide circle of open space stretched around them as the citizens of Codr made their way farther into the hallway, away from the Outsiders. The Scouts stood near the door, catching their breaths and looking on warily. Answer twisted her bracelet uncertainly. These displays of magic would only undo any good she'd done them, but how to stop them?

"What barrier? Drop what barrier?" Taunos asked.

"Die! Burn the City. Burn the vermin clean. Ah! E orashyi. Líumkoom e orashyi! Ozaseiwi!"

"Does this building block magic?" Takiyah asked.

"I-it must." Answer lifted her chin, forcing herself to meet those piercing green eyes.

"The barrier," Kaemada's child said. He stood by the wall behind Taunos.

"The pain of the psions' attack stopped when I shut us in here," Answer realized.

Takiyah nodded. "More precisely, it weakened when the doors closed and stopped when you did something to the wall."

"You cannot share the secrets of the Scouts," warned one of the Scouts standing by the door.

Answer fixed him with a glare as she stepped to the door, pressing the pane. The doors hissed as they unlocked, and Kaemada fell limp.

The Scout glowered at her. "If the monsters breach the door, it will be your fault."

"I outrank you. Do you really want to go against me?" she asked. "Without the help of these Outsiders, you would be outside the doors as well."

"You cannot trust magic users."

But she did. Somehow, she did. She looked at Takiyah, then at Taunos, his sister laying limp in his arms. "How is she?"

He shook his head, looking lost. "I do not know."

"What matters most is making sure nothing gets through those doors." Takiyah got to her feet, limping over to stand beside Answer and the Scouts guarding the door. She glared at Answer. "I would rather fight alongside anyone else, I think. But I will fight. And then I want to go home."

The trainees ushered the nobles farther into the Hall. Great thumps slammed against the doors, and Answer jumped, but the doors held.

"They should not be here!" Lord Jath repeated, gesturing at the Outsiders. "Throw them out with the other magic-users!"

Takiyah turned and stared at him, pointing at the refugees littering the hallways. "Remember this, you coward. None of you would be here without us."

Something slammed against the doors again and Lord Jath flinched. Takiyah merely turned back to the door. Stomach in knots, heart hammering against her ribs, Answer stared at her. How could she remain so calm? Grumbling loudly, Lord Jath retreated deeper into the interior, where it was safer. A part of Answer longed to follow him, but down the hallway, her supervisor scowled at her, arms folded.

She needed documentation. It was the only way to keep any status after going so drastically against protocol. Without support for her decision on record, she'd be stuck with all the worst jobs and lowest pay, only nominally a Scout.

Fingers trembling, Answer opened the panel in the wall and grabbed a crystal and recorder. Commoners sprawled on the once spotless floor, weeping or groaning or just sitting and staring. The Rinaryn healer moved among them, having traded her exploding bottles for needle, thread, and bandages. With a steadying breath, Answer followed, gathering the stories of the refugees onto the crystal.

Zhedr passed around cups and a jug of water. Taunos missed the cup Zhedr handed him, and it clattered to the ground.

Answer gaped. "Are you all right?"

"Headache. Overuse of my magic," Taunos said, stressing the last word slightly with a grin. The City was under attack, and Taunos was still needling her, even while mopping up the water that had spilled on his sister. Answer shook her head, oddly comforted by the familiarity.

"He will be able to see again when the headache calms down," Takiyah said, still facing the door. "If we live that long."

"Here, let me." Zhedr pressed the cup into Taunos's free hand and then dribbled some water into Kaemada's mouth. "You know, if you hadn't rescued me—"

Testimony from other nobles would mean more than just the tales of the commoners. She winced, knowing how Kaemada would frown at that, but it was the way society worked.

"Wait!" Answer held out the recorder, her eyes boring into Zhedr's. "Will you pledge your support for them on record?"

"Of course."

All that long night, Takiyah and the Scouts guarded the door while Answer and Zhedr gathered testimonies and pledges of support. Throughout the night, reports came in from the Scouts still fighting outside, and the work was a good distraction from the worry. More and more reports came of the creatures simply stopping, staring at nothing or falling to the ground. Finally, they turned in a flood and swarmed back to their chasm like one enormous creature.

They had beaten back the monsters.

Takiyah limped to where Eian crouched near the wall. They huddled close to where Taunos slumped, eyes closed, his sister limp in his arms, and where Ra'ael lay, unconscious on the floor. Magic had saved them all, even those who would have left the Outsiders to die.

Maybe magic didn't make one dangerous. And maybe monsters didn't always look like monsters.

Chapter Twenty-six

The dwarves broke through first, hacking their way through the stone of the mountain to evict our people from their homes. They came wreathed in flame, and fires everywhere obeyed them. They were joined, though thankfully in few numbers, by elves of like height, who came with lightning from the Outside, harnessed and trained to their bidding. Among them darted child-sized gnomes, and death was in their fingers.

-fragment of a Kamalti children's tale

Answer rested her hand on Obedr's arm as they swept into the Grand Council Chambers, already abuzz from the Codr nobility crowding the room. There were only a few empty spaces left on the benches—all the prime spots had been claimed, of course. She'd taken too much time preparing that morning, but every detail had to be perfect.

The Detr-ward tunnel had caved in during the attack, and her brother and parents were cut off from the City. That left Answer as the sole voice for her family, casting her family's vote, at least until the rocks were cleared and the tunnel reopened. She'd agonized over whom to pair herself with for the entry, finally deciding on Obedr. Not only was he a good family friend, but his confident, jovial demeanor would mask her nerves. It didn't hurt that he was a powerful man from an influential family, either. It would be good to remind the other nobles of the friendship between their two families. Especially given what she planned to do.

They headed toward the stairs, and Answer fixed a pleasant expression on her face as they made their way through the throng. She nodded to each of the Lords and Ladies of the Scouts, the Philosophers, and the Justices they passed. Zhedr, seated beside his father among the other Justices, caught her eye and smiled at her. Her smile grew of its own accord and her face heated. Would she see him at Epiphany's dinner party tonight?

She cleared her throat, disciplining her thoughts. This meeting was important. The decision reached today could very well change the Future for their entire race. She nodded gracious greetings until Obedr paused to greet an old friend. Her entrance was done, and if she made small talk, her nerves would surely show, so she continued up the shallow steps. She spied an open bench and claimed it just as the massive doors were opened on the other side of the chambers. Conversation quickly died down as ten smartly dressed Scouts escorted the Outsiders in and sat them on a bench before the table for the Justices, facing the crowd of Kamalti nobles.

Answer's stomach churned. Her mother may never forgive her, and her career might never recover. Was she strong enough to see this folly through? She could lose all remaining status among the Scouts. And yet these Outsiders, after everything they'd endured, forwent the chance to escape and instead lent aid to a City that was not their own. She'd seen the aftermath. She knew what it had cost them.

Again and again, the Outsiders had saved her life, while few of her own people would have shed tears—not real tears, anyway—had she met an early demise. They had saved countless Kamalti and never asked her to save them. And yet, how could she not?

And yet, how could she?

Doubts clawed at her. What if she was wrong? What if they came back with an invasion force? What if there was not enough support from the other nobles and she looked like a silly child, enamored with the savages? Answer smoothed her dress and clasped her hands in her lap, hoping to assume a demure front.

She drew in a deep breath and let it out slowly, feeling her cheeks heat. She would not leave without casting her family's vote. This was her chance to do something significant, something worthwhile. She shook her head slightly. Before the meeting, Ketrik had had the nerve to remind her that the family's Honor depended on her actions. Even her mother had sent a message by crystal ordering her to press for execution. Only her father seemed to trust her to do what was best. Fury simmered below the surface of her mask of calm. No, she would not waste this Opportunity.

She relaxed her shoulders and tried not to watch the Outsiders too much. The healing machines had made them presentable, but they bore guarded expressions, except for Kaemada, who slumped against Taunos and Ra'ael as if it was too difficult to sit straight herself.

The Justices filed in and stood behind the table. Ringing a crystal, the head Justice, Lord Tokl, brought the meeting to order. "We are here today to determine whether these Outsiders before us shall be granted life and allowed to leave and rejoin their world, or if they should face death. Much has happened since the arrival of the Outsiders. All things must be taken into consideration."

Tokl's tone was foreboding, and Answer shifted uncomfortably.

Throughout the room, various nobles rose to claim a chance to speak, and one by one, the Justices called them forward for testimony. Answer remained seated, for she was not sure she could handle standing and waiting for so long without trembling. If she showed her nerves, it might ruin everything. Already, too many Scouts dismissed her as foolish and immature, as a youth with flights of fancy who had more say than was good for her. She held tightly to her calm, wishing it would extend to the core of her.

Throughout the long morning, arguments were made both for and against the Outsiders. The Hall bore witness countless times to the dangers of the Outsiders and the assertion that they were a violent enemy. However, the Hall also repeatedly heard that the Kamalti had done similar damage, and the things the Outsiders had done as ebrs were no more than typical crimes the Kamalti themselves committed against each other. They were far from acts of war, the supporters of the Outsiders argued.

The Doctors testified that the Outsiders had apparently taken care to avoid killing, aside from Ra'ael's blood rage. The senior Doctor testified of Takiyah's help fixing the healing machine and Elisabei's help with herbal remedies. Dode spoke eloquently, as always, smiling broadly at Ra'ael for all to see. If only Answer could be so confident, so immune to what others thought of her. Some nobles relayed stories from the common people in their columns, stories of how the Outsiders had risked their lives when they could have escaped.

Old Lord Jintrem wheezed as he spoke. "The Outsiders saved countless lives when they fought the psions. I would not want to face the likes of them in battle, but only be by their side."

Prodigy, heir to his family's Fortune and Honor, shouted out, "Who knows but that they arranged it all?"

Answer smiled as the cocky young man was swiftly silenced and brought back to order by his father. She'd always found his arrogance to be insufferable.

Finally, Justice Tokl fixed his rheumy eyes on Answer. "Lady Answer, have you anything to say for your family?"

Answer rose, keeping her focus on Justice Tokl. She took a deep breath. All the arguments her mother and father would have made had already been made. Her own arguments had been made, too. Couldn't she just... do nothing? She could avoid going against her mother's wishes, against the majority of the Scouts.

She clasped her hands together, her gaze drawn to the Outsiders, to the people she'd just begun to get to know. Yes, they were terrifying with their magic and their chaos, yet how could she call them savages? No. She would not repay them with more faithlessness.

Answer swallowed hard, returning her gaze to the Justices. "Every point that could be made has been, I am certain. I do have on crystal the names of several nobles who pledged their support to the Outsiders' freedom, and I myself bore witness to their acts of heroism. I heard firsthand the accounts of several nobles and other citizens whom these Outsiders rescued from the onslaught. I urge the Justices to consider: if these heroes are savages, what, then, are we?"

Obedr leaned over to whisper, "Not safe, not smart, my dear. Attacking our own? You have ended your career."

Answer forced a smile at him and stepped forward, descending the stairs until an apprentice Justice reached her to take the crystal. The boy sped away as she returned to her seat, and when Justice Kethik received it, he gave her a nod. It was done.

Justice Tokl rose and rang the crystal again. "All testimony has been received. The Council will now retire to ponder our decision. We will reconvene at the ringing of the crystal."

Answer glided alongside Obedr again through the milling throng as he escorted her out of the Grand Council Chambers. It was out of her hands. Somehow, the Outsiders had gained more support than she had thought they might. Had they needed her assistance? Silence would have been safer. Would Opportunities fade from her in the coming faces, all her striving to prove herself for naught? She shook her head to clear her thoughts, smiled at Obedr, and excused herself to think alone, losing herself among the crowd before he could object.

The crowd thinned as she left the building behind and wandered the square. Soon enough, she found herself near the ancient statue there, drawn to the fierce features carved in stone. Three people, all with strikingly different characteristics, and none of them Kamalti. A tall, stern man with broad shoulders stood, his arm outstretched, while beside him, turned to face slightly toward him, stood a slender woman nearly as tall with wild hair and pointed ears, her hands raised to the sky. Before them stood a diminutive man with a wrinkled face, his head bent over some contraption he held in his hands.

"What is this?"

Answer gave a start. She disciplined herself to composure. It was just Kaemada standing next to her, also pondering the statue. The boy stood beside her, translating again, and Taunos and Takiyah were walking toward them. Answer nodded to the two Scouts following the Outsiders.

"It is a statue to the Three Allied Races," Answer said, willing herself not to shudder. "The dwarves, the elves, the gnomes."

Eian echoed, "The Ifreesian, the Stormseekers, and the Kelm."

Kaemada turned to the boy as if his nonsense had meaning.

Answer shook her head. "Their names have been lost to the ages. They left the area—"

"Island."

"—when we were but infant races." Answer fixed the mannerless boy with a stern gaze.

"How did you find out about them to erect a statue?" Kaemada wondered as the others joined them.

Answer drew herself up. "We remembered. We have artwork depicting these vile creatures. The dwarves and their allies assaulted our mountains, trying to force through to destroy us. We beat them back—with the help of the Takanis, they say—and have preserved their memory. If ever they return, we will recognize them and we will crush them!"

Kaemada retreated a careful step, and Answer bit her lip before composing herself once more. She hated the Three Races. The stories had given her nightmares as a child. As she grew older, she'd sought out knowledge of them, refusing to let fear rule her.

Takiyah stepped forward, inspecting the statues. She stopped, staring at the tall man with the outstretched arm, his palm upturned. "Is this one holding a flame in his hand?"

Answer nodded. "The dwarf."

"Ifreesian," Eian inserted.

Dwarves were supposed to be short, and they were supposed to be myths. But the word had always been applied to the tall man of the statues.

"Little sister, are you all right?" Taunos stood behind Kaemada.

Answer eyed him. His "little sister" had fought off a horde of psions. She doubted Kaemada needed his hovering presence.

Kaemada nodded, her gaze distant as the boy chattered away useless translations. "I understood the psions, but I still fought them. I worry, will I ever be free of the shadows of them in my mind?"

Answer shook her head. "You will fight them off again if need be. I have learned much in the past days—you Outsiders are not to be underestimated."

~

A chime echoed through the metal building and into the square outside, summoning all onlookers to return and witness the Justices' decision. Taunos led the way with a grin as the ever-present Scouts escorted them to their bench. He refused to go to judgement already defeated.

Finally, the Chief Justice emerged. "We must take pains to preserve our way of life. However, this way of life did not rise in seclusion, but in cooperation. Therefore, it is our decision to let the Outsiders return to their world."

A murmur ran through the crowd. Eian jumped up and down, and Kaemada flung her arms around each of them in turn, beaming. Taunos held her tight, hope rising in him for the first time in a long time. Freedom. Home was so close, and perhaps he'd finally be able to get them there. Nothing else mattered—no tricks of the Kamalti, no twisting of justice, nothing, so long as they could leave.

The Justice raised his hands for quiet. "Further, we will entertain the notion of resuming relations with the outside world, but only on a trial basis with a limited scope. We have much to discuss amongst ourselves, especially in regard to the old agreement. Do we continue to send the lost travellers to this "City of the Lost," even taking into account the information these Outsiders have provided us? If not, what new solution must we find? These questions will be a high priority in the next Council meetings. Perhaps, in time, we will return to our arrangement of old and walk under the sun—or we may continue our solitude and our order. So shall it be."

He stepped down, and the air filled with thousands of voices raised in conversation. A messenger wound his way through the throng to them, bowing. "The Justices extend their congratulations and their apologies for the difficult time you have had."

That was an understatement. Now was a time to be civil, though, even if that meant rolling over falsehoods and stretched truth. Taunos would continue to smile and nod until they were safe under the open sky, away from the traps and stifling pride of the Kamalti.

"Thank you," Taunos said. "You have our gratitude for the wise and just ruling."

"Follow me to the mountain entrance. Your people gather again for the festival above. You will please give this message to your leaders so we may move into the Future." The messenger handed a sealed letter to Taunos. "These are instructions for your leaders to contact ours."

Dode embraced Ra'ael warmly. "I am pleased I had the opportunity to

340

know you. Farewell."

Ra'ael smiled, gripping her arms. "Thank you, Dode. Please, watch out for yourself. Walk in peace."

At least one of them had avoided a terrible experience these last six moons.

As if his thoughts had summoned her, Answer approached along with three uniformed Scouts wearing stern expressions. Taunos stiffened. It was far too eerie a reminder of their first encounter. But Answer smiled, and the guards returned their packs and weapons.

"Thank you!" Kaemada smiled at Answer, reclaiming her pack.

Answer raised her browridge, her bearing stiff. "It seems evident you people will find weapons whenever and wherever needed."

Taunos happily armed himself, chuckling when his sister picked up his old cloak and grinned at Eian, wrapping it around him and squeezing him with joy. He indicated them with his head, looking at Answer. "You see? Old things."

"Someone I once knew told me your people are a lovable sort of mad, if I let myself."

"You should listen to that person. He sounds wise." Taunos grinned, pleased to see Answer flicker a smile in return. He was reluctant to hope much would change, especially so close to freedom. But she had spoken for them. That was a taste of change, at least. Not enough, but it was a start.

"I have not completely forgiven you," Answer said, her tone wry. "But then, I suppose you probably have not completely forgiven me. Let this be a new beginning, shall we?"

Taunos bowed with an exaggerated flourish. "My lady, I'm pleased to meet you. I am Taunos. Or, as my mother used to say when angry with me —"

"—which was at least twice a day—" Takiyah quipped.

"Adeion Denvin Firerel Taunos Sierso."

"By the Ships, you people have long names!"

Ra'ael muttered something about the superiority of proper Rinaryn names.

"It is a pleasure, Adeio... whatever it was. Taunos. I am Answer."

Laughter burst from him, amusement relaxing stiff muscles as Answer struggled to hide a smile, then finally gave in to it.

Regaining her composure, she nodded stiffly to them. "Farewell."

Grinning, he nodded to her, and then she was behind him, and freedom was ahead as he ushered the others on.

Once more, they strode through the city accompanied by guards. This time, Rikr and his son ran alongside for a time, whooping. A smattering of cheers sounded from others here and there through the crowd. Not everyone was happy with the verdict—there were several scowls, shouts of derision, and even some rotten food thrown at them—but it was a great deal better than their first parade had been. Some likely blamed them for the attack from the Collective, even though Kaemada's psionic battle with them had helped turn them back from the city. But none of that mattered. Taunos's heart rose as the doors grew closer. He cared nothing for Answer's people making amends—nothing could make up for what they did to Takiyah. All that mattered was finally going home.

They walked up the long stairs to a set of doors, where the Kamalti hastily donned goggles. Once through the doors, their guards scrunched under their layers of clothing, pulling their hats down low. The spring wind had a biting edge to it, but Taunos couldn't resist stretching a bit, enjoying the wide-open spaces and the feel of the sun on his skin. Finally. Beside him, Kaemada beamed, looking more alive than she had in a long time, clutching Eian's hand. Taunos stayed close to the Scouts, noting Reinan did the same. There was still danger so long as the Scouts were there.

The Scouts guided them down a faint trail, nearly invisible among the boulders and slabs of stone. After a time, their guides stopped and pointed down one path. "This way leads to the City of the Lost." Then they indicated another path. "This way leads to Talahn Valley, where your people gather twice each circulation."

Kaemada smiled at them. "Thank you for your help."

Taunos translated and bowed easily, happy to provide them that courtesy now that they were out of the Kamalti's domain. The Scouts bowed in return and hurried away, back to the safety of their mountains.

Watching them go, Taunos drew in a deep breath. He let it go along with the tension that had strung tight along his shoulders and back.

"Will you come and celebrate the Feast with us?" Kaemada asked Elisabei.

Elisabei laughed. "They did not need me for six winters. I do not need them, either."

"Oh, Elisabei," Kaemada started, but Elisabei cut her off.

"No, there is no place for Reinan there, for Reinan was born in the City of the Lost. And where there is no place for my husband, there is no place for me. We would only be considered Fallen. We will return to the city to make something from the ruins of the last king."

"The Angels," Kaemada said. "And the guards. Be careful."

"It will be dangerous," Taunos said.

"What in life worth having isn't?" Elisabei replied.

True words, though he'd be happy to stay away from danger for at least a few days. Taunos smiled, nodding.

"The Elders will not like it. You will have to select a Storyteller and Great Mother and join the Council of Elders officially," Ra'ael said.

Elisabei laughed. "I rather think we might be independent. After all, are we not Fallen?"

Ra'ael frowned, but Elisabei continued. "Besides, there's much rebuilding to do. We may as well get started."

Taunos clasped arms with Reinan. "Go well," he said.

The big man smiled and returned the farewell warmly. Taunos realized how much he would miss them. Still, his heart lifted in anticipation of finally being back among his people. Maybe they could put all this behind them. Just in time to endure the posturing and fit-throwing the Elders would display before allowing them back home.

Chapter Twenty-seven

The Rinaryn Council of Elders is comprised of 57 men, one from each village in Rinara. Most of the Elders are Storytellers, for the Storytellers are often regarded as the most knowledgeable men. On occasion, a man is deemed wiser even than his village Storyteller and so joins the Council.

Council affairs can be chaotic things, as Elders can interrupt at any time for clarifying questions, often backtracking or jumping forward in the narrative as they do so. After testimony or discussion of a problem, the Elders separate into groups by region. The regions discuss and argue amongst themselves until they come to a unanimous agreement. The regions then come together around the fire for discussion, comments, and a final decision.

—journal excerpt

Ra'ael twirled in a circle, her hands in the air. They were free! And as soon as they got home, everything would be all right again. They could figure out the future together, like always. Taunos's laughter only made her smile broaden. But Takiyah's face remained impassive, focused, and Ra'ael's grin faded. Taunos, Kaemada, and Takiyah especially would need help to make it through the upcoming moons after all they'd been through. Ra'ael would have to make sure the kaetal enveloped them as much as possible to avoid them withdrawing completely into mind-sickness.

Kaemada stumbled down the path, her arms wrapped tightly around a squirming Eian. She was clearly exhausted.

"Kaemada, you need a rest." Ra'ael reached out for the boy, but Kaemada withdrew.

She shook her head, refusing to meet Ra'ael's gaze. Like Takiyah, she was focused on her goal.

"Kaemada, let Eian down," Ra'ael said.

"No. I will never again take him from the kaetal alone." She shifted him in her arms, almost clinging to the boy.

Ra'ael grabbed her arm, stepping in front of her to stop her forward momentum. "Rinaryn mothers take their children alone into the wild all the time. Just maybe not on sacred journeys."

Kaemada's lips were pressed into a thin, flat line as she shook her head. "Never again."

"You're not alone, Kaemada." Ra'ael took her arms, gently peeling them away from Eian and setting him on the ground. She knelt in front of him. "Never, never leave the trail. Do you hear me? You stay with us at all times."

The boy nodded, and Ra'ael turned her attention back to her friend. Kaemada had wrapped her arms around herself, shivering as if freezing. Her face was taut with worry, her eyes locked on Eian as if she were afraid something would snatch him away, and they'd begin the last six moons all over again.

Ra'ael's heart ached for her, and she took her hands. "Kaemada, we got him back. He's safe, and soon we will be with the kaetal again. You no longer have to worry. He's safe."

Tears filled Kaemada's eyes and she shivered even more violently.

Ra'ael sighed. Kaemada's anxiety was perfectly understandable. She'd lost the song. But Ra'ael was priestess—she could keep the song for her until Kaemada was ready to join in again.

Forcing a smile, Ra'ael tried for levity. "Remember when all we had to worry about was the Elders murmuring against Galod?"

"Wait, the Elders were? Not just people in general?" Taunos raised his eyebrows, which were just beginning to grow again.

"Against all Galod's students, really." Takiyah kicked a rock.

"Seems so long ago." Ra'ael shrugged, moving them along. Taunos appeared lost in thought, and Takiyah and Kaemada trudged along, silent and distant once more. She chewed on her lip. She, by herself, could not bring peace to their spirits. She needed the help of Torkae's priests, Saimahkae, and Storyteller.

Still, she couldn't let them suffer alone. She linked arms with Kaemada and Taunos, nudging Taunos when he didn't immediately get the hint. He linked up with Takiyah, and Eian skipped along just ahead of them. As they walked, Ra'ael began the journey songs in time with the beat of their steps on the trail, and Taunos joined in after a few steps. She grinned. She could get used to working with him.

Eventually, the trail dipped, descending into the sacred valley. It was one of three trails from the mountains that ended up here. The noise of the festivities hit them before they saw the green of the valley itself. The rhythm of the drums and rattles, the clapping and stomping, and the pipes, horns, and whistles filled the air. Cheers and conversation and recitation joined the music of the instruments in a festive spirit.

The Seeker Tree stood in the middle of the valley, as it always had, its white bark and silver leaves unchanged summer after summer. It was as old as legend, tall and straight and ageless. Around it stood five basins of water, one for each region of Rinara. Floating candles, all ablaze, crowded the water, honoring the memory of those who had passed over the rim of the sky.

The grass of the valley was littered with tents, and wagons displayed various goods to trade from one kaetal to another. Open areas were decorated with ribbons and banners, and a foot race was just finishing, won by a young man from Dragonmoor, judging by the pattern of his armband. Around the edges, young hopefuls vied to impress masters for apprenticeships. Musicians wandered from one camp to another, performing for each kaetal.

By the time their feet hit the grass of the valley, optimism had filled Ra'ael. They had survived terrible, cruel things and had come out on the other side. The air of celebration was so vibrant that the past six moons seemed like only a bad dream.

First Kaemada, then Taunos, slowed and stopped.

Ra'ael frowned at them, eager to rejoin their people. "What's wrong?" she asked, as Eian tugged at her hand.

Kaemada shook her head. "They're not happy to see us."

"They're not expecting us," Ra'ael soothed.

Taunos shook his head as well. "They're not just surprised. They're wary."

"Three psions and the daughter of Torkae's leaders," Takiyah said, looking at Ra'ael with concern in her eyes. Kaemada held her weight on the balls of her feet as if she were considering running.

Ra'ael looked over the faces of her people. A sinking feeling snatched at her. They were right. This was going to be trouble. What had she really expected? They'd left the trail.

She straightened her shoulders. Torkae had faced trouble before, and they had always faced it together. The Elders may be unforgiving, but the Storyteller and Saimahkae would stand behind them. Teros... Teros could be made to see reason, and then he could help quell rumors and whisperings. They could still make it through this.

Takiyah broke into a run as soon as they saw the Storyteller and Saimahkae in the camp of Torkae, and Ra'ael let Eian lead her onward. Takiyah was caught up in the embrace of her parents, weeping with joy. Maeren reached out and pulled each of them into an embrace, peppering them with kisses.

"We thought the worst," the Storyteller said as he kissed their foreheads. "What happened to your face, my dear?"

"I missed you!" Takiyah's whisper was fierce.

"Six moons! Six moons and no word." Maeren released Taunos from her embrace and seized Eian.

The Storyteller cleared his throat, taking a step back. "The Council will want to see you as soon as possible."

Taunos nodded. "We have things that need discussing as well."

"Until then, say nothing to anyone," the Storyteller said.

"What's wrong?" Ra'ael asked. "Have the murmurings grown while we were away?"

Maeren sighed, then gave them a strained smile. She patted Takiyah's hand, having released the last of them from her embrace. "All will be made clear in time, my dears."

Taunos scowled, but at least he didn't say anything. The Storyteller embraced Takiyah again and smiled at them. "I will convene the Council. You will be called when we're ready."

Ra'ael nodded, her unease growing as Maeren ushered them over to the side of the valley, away from others. None of the kaetalyn came to greet them, and indeed, Talaera turned her back when she saw them. Others looked at them with suspicion, worry, confusion, or a mixture of the three.

All too soon, Maeren held her hand out to Eian. "Come with me, little one." Her gaze turned firm as she looked at Ra'ael. "You four must stay here for a time."

Unease twisted her stomach as Maeren followed Eian, who scampered away ahead of her into the camp of Torkae. A wordless moan escaped Kaemada, and she reached out for her son. Ra'ael embraced her, holding tightly and murmuring soothing words to her until Kaemada finally sat back, crumpling. Takiyah's face looked cut from stone, like a Kamalti statue.

"This is ridiculous." Rage heated Taunos's quiet voice. "We deserve to know what's going on and why we're set apart."

He started forward, but Ra'ael grabbed his arm. "Be patient. We will follow tradition. We will follow instructions, and we will hold to the course of honor."

Taunos shook his head. "No. Trouble is brewing."

"No need to throw sticks at a toelfa," Ra'ael said. "The Elders were chosen for a reason. They deserve to be heard."

Taunos opened his mouth to argue, and she cut him off. "And then—and then, Taunos—then we will tell our tale."

He turned away, frustrated. Takiyah held her staff in both hands, still statuesque. Kaemada had slumped to the ground and was staring at Eian, who sat not far off, enthralled by a storytelling contest.

"He loves the stories," Kaemada whispered.

"He does," Ra'ael agreed. The sense of foreboding grew within her. Eian was allowed back into the kaetal while they were not. Such a separation paralleled the separation for a Fallen—no one could be Fallen until they had gone on their yah.

She shook her head at herself. That couldn't be. The Elders would never overreact so greatly.

"I only wanted to help." Kaemada's voice broke. "I tried to keep him safe, but I brought only danger on all of us."

Ra'ael snatched her shoulders. "Listen to me. Stop taking responsibility that does not belong to you. You made mistakes—we all did. Beating yourself up will not help anyone."

Kaemada bowed her head, and Ra'ael sat beside her and held her for a while.

Words leaked from Kaemada little by little in painful tides. "I'm afraid I can no longer trust my senses. From the hallucinations. And the Collective. Three times they were in my head. And they took me over, Ra'ael. I carry pieces of them. I fought them, and it was like fighting myself. And through it all... I miss Tannevar. I'm missing such a huge part of me, and I have no way of being safe with psionics now. Every door is closed to me."

Ra'ael frowned, trying to think of something to say. Frustratingly, the perfect words did not come, leaving her to just hold her friend.

A wrestling contest started and was won before finally a young man approached. "The Council is ready for you."

The Elder's messenger led them to the large tent near the Seeker Tree. The flaps making up the door of the tent were swept back for them by two young men who remained outside. Before them, seated on mats, were the Elders.

Ra'ael bowed her head in respect and greeting, as did the other three. She offered brief, tight smiles to the Elders from Heartwood, who were most likely to be sympathetic. Kaemada gripped the ends of that shawl she'd taken to wearing until her knuckles turned white, and Ra'ael winced. She should have made sure Kaemada removed that before entering—it made her stand out.

"Ah, thank you for coming," one of the Elders said as he rose. "I'm Teryn, of the kaetal of Elyra in the region Mountainhold. We wish to discuss, with you, the Darks. Of all Rinaryn, you Siersos, in particular, have perhaps had the most experience with them."

Teryn of Mountainhold. The messenger six moons ago, the one who had been so hostile to Galod and his students, had been from Tseril in Dragonmoor. Dragonmoor kaetaln and Mountainhold kaetaln often supported each other in disputes. But why by all the spirits were they wondering about the Darks? Odd as it was, she hadn't thought of the Darks in moons.

"How can I help?" Kaemada asked.

One of the Elders frowned. "Kaemada Sierso, you will please use the Traveller's Tongue so we can all focus on your story."

"Saiameyitum. I have lost my ability to speak Traveller's."

"How is this possible?" asked another.

Ra'ael watched the faces of the Elders. This breach of protocol—not speaking Traveller's—would be a mark against them.

"It's true," Taunos stepped in. "My sister has been through much in the last few moons."

"Speak Rinaryn, then, but enunciate please! You of Heartwood tend to sing your words a little too much, making them muddy and hard for old ears to understand," admonished the Elder.

"We have waited to have this conversation for six moons," grumbled one Elder.

"We thought we might never speak of this at all when they disappeared," replied another Elder.

Ra'ael hid a wince. Hopefully, they didn't dwell on that.

Teryn motioned to the other Elders for patience, eyes remaining on Ra'ael, Kaemada, Takiyah, and Taunos. "Please, tell us of the events of the night six moons ago when the Darks attacked Torkae."

Holding herself still, Ra'ael searched the faces of the Elders as the Council asked question after question, drawing forth the story together with Kaemada. It was refreshing to be back in such a cooperative justice system with its continual back and forth in its search for truth, rather than the Kamalti Justices and their long-winded speeches.

It was also disturbing. As the Elders questioned, a pattern developed, a set up for some strategy. They spent far too long dwelling on Tikatae and Galod. So much had happened since then. As Kaemada described the attack on Torkae and Tikatae's death, the Elders inquired why they had not expected Tikatae to be behind the attack from the beginning. Ra'ael's skin prickled.

Taunos stepped forward. "Elders, please, if I may interrupt."

"No, no, Taunos Sierso. You're not interrupting. We have questions for you as well. Where did you train to hone your ranging skills?"

Suspicion lined Taunos's face. "In Heartwood, in the forest outside my kaetal of Torkae, with Galod."

"Like your sister?"

"And many others."

Ra'ael tapped her fingers on her leg, the sense of danger strengthening. They were being targeted for some reason, and it seemed to be wrapped up in the Dark attack and Galod.

"You're widely considered to be the most capable ranger of our time," Teryn said.

Taunos did not reply, letting the flattery or compliment, whatever it may be, fall flat.

Teryn leaned forward. "Why is it, when his home continues to be struck by attack after attack, that the finest ranger in all of Rinara cannot be found to protect his own kaetal?"

Ra'ael darted a look at Taunos. She'd asked the same question, accusing him so many times in the past. There was a hint of something— was that pleading?—in his eyes as he looked at the Heartwood Elders. She blinked. Was it was her imagination, or had several of the Heartwood Elders given him a firm but subtle shake of the head? What was going on there?

Taunos raised his chin. "I have chosen offense as the best defense for my home. As you're aware, I have travelled the realms these past summers, disrupting plans of the Darks and thwarting them where I may."

"But some attacks get through, regardless," Teryn said.

Taunos spread his arms. "I'm merely a man, like you."

Ra'ael narrowed her eyes. Was he challenging the Elders?

Dark attacks. Galod's students. They were implying Taunos was in league with the Darks. That thought went far beyond skepticism for his chosen task. It hit Ra'ael like a fist in the gut, and she eyed the Elders. What had happened while they were away?

Teryn tilted his head. "Given what Kaemada described, would you have been caught as unaware during this latest attack on your kaetal, had your places been switched?"

Taunos's expression grew stormy. "I may as easily ask that of one of you. No man knows what he may or may not know, do, or think until he's in that very same position."

"The answer is a simple yes or no. Do you think you would have been caught as unaware?"

Taunos narrowed his eyes and clenched his jaw, crossing his arms over his chest.

Ra'ael chewed on the inside of her lip. Please, please let his irreverence not bring down more trouble on their heads!

The Elders directed further questions to Kaemada. "Why is it, after so many atrocities, that you did not end the life of Tikatae? You battled him many times, and it wouldn't have been held against you in the heat of battle."

Kaemada shook her head. "There was no need for his life. This last attack was the only time it was him or me. He targeted Eian. Every other time, there was another way out, and if there's a way out without killing, I prefer that way."

"Even at the cost of your kaetal suffering repeated attacks?"

"As I have said, I do what I can to help protect my kaetal and all Rinaryn. The consequences for Tikatae's choices rest on his own head." Kaemada's voice quavered. Her certainty in basic truths had eroded over the last six moons.

"Why are we talking of Dark attacks when we have much more pressing matters to discuss?" Taunos interrupted. "We must speak to you about the Kamalti."

The Elders ignored him. "And yet your choice to allow a man to live whom you know continually chooses violence, that choice is on your own head, yes?"

Kaemada clenched her jaw, choosing her brother's former silence.

"That choice is on your own heads, Elders," Taunos spat.

The Elders alone could decide upon a sentence of death, but Taunos was taking a terrible risk, confronting the Elders in this way. Ra'ael shivered in the face of Taunos's rage.

One of the Elders leaned forward. "Kaemada Sierso. How did you feel about Tikatae? Did you hate him?"

She hesitated. "I was angry. Afraid, too. But I also knew he was in great pain after so much loss. I pitied him. How could I hate him?"

Ra'ael reeled. She wanted to stop the flow of time, roll it backward, and keep Kaemada from saying those words that would fuel this vendetta. Taunos, accused of working with the Darks, and now Kaemada, not hating the man she most should. Ra'ael and Takiyah would be next, accused of being Dark-touched. Accused of betraying their people. She'd expected punishment for breaking the laws, but the direction the Elders were going chilled her. How could these wise men even think they were Dark-touched?

"And Taunos, do you share this view?" an Elder asked.

"No. I hated him." Taunos considered Kaemada for a moment. "But then, my heart leans more toward my father's, while Kaemada, I think, has always had my mother's heart."

Ra'ael's stomach twisted. Taunos had done too little, too late, she feared, though she didn't know what else he could have done but bring up their mother. It was a desperate bid for honor. He had to know it wasn't likely to work.

Strangling the shawl, Kaemada broke in. "Whatever you may think of my actions, good can come of the events of the last six moons. This could be the beginning of a new friendship with the Kamalti!"

"This obsession with the Kamalti is really quite unusual!" objected another of the Elders.

A different Elder spoke up. "The Sierso family in Torkae once boasted ten children. Now, the only surviving Siersos are a ranger who cannot be found to defend his home, a psion overwhelmingly incompetent in her ability to think ahead and perceive dangers, and a dragonbonded who hasn't been seen or heard from for ten summers!"

The siblings' expressions became remarkably similar through the Elder's rant, their eyes fiery and features set in stubborn silence. Even their fists were clenched at their sides in the same way. Ra'ael didn't blame them. Their entire family was under attack, and there was nothing they could do about it.

"You know I love my people. I have only ever wanted to help," Kaemada said.

"If you're going to accuse me of something, accuse me straight on," growled Taunos at the same time.

Zeroun rose. "When Kaemada was injured, she refused healing for herself until all others in our kaetal were healed."

"Storyteller Zeroun, you may be too close to see clearly," Storyteller Teryn said.

"It is indeed convenient. If she had been healed, there would have been no cause for her to take this ill-conceived pegasus ride and then disappear for six moons," observed an Elder.

Ra'ael winced. How could they think this was evidence?

"Even if you doubt my heart, the people should not suffer for it!" Kaemada broke in. "We have an opportunity to discuss with you, about the Kamalti!"

"So you keep prattling on about, distracting from the real, serious matters at hand." An Elder fixed them with a stern look.

Another Elder flapped his hand at her as if to make her words disappear. "Potential smokescreens and matters of loyalty aside, it's still clear to me that there's a sickness in the Sierso line. Wasn't their mother a friend to the Darks?"

"She made herself an ambassador to them, believing that with communication, peace was possible!" Taunos growled.

"And they killed her for her efforts."

Kaemada clutched her brother's arm as if ready to hold him back. Ra'ael clenched her fists. It would do no good to attack an Elder, much less the entire Council. Taunos had to see that. But this wrath he was showing... it seemed clear there was more going on than she could see.

"She died believing she was doing Eloí's work. You cannot fault her for that," Taunos shouted.

Silence filled the tent briefly, and when the next Elder spoke, the tone became a little calmer. "So it is. You may believe that, yet I cannot help but wonder if some small seed of Darkness did not make its way in and destroy your family. Why was your family hit harder than anyone else? And again, and again, with Tikatae turning on you and coming at you repeatedly. These events are unprecedented. For the only three Siersos surviving to all lead lives so radically different from normal kaetal life... I must say, I find it hard to believe this is a coincidence."

"It may not be coincidence, but that does not mean there is anything nefarious going on," Taunos said.

"Your influence is. I cannot tell you how many young people I have heard speaking of their desire to travel to other lands and communicate with outsiders. And your unnatural preoccupation with the Kamalti cannot be allowed to endanger the lives of our young Rinaryn who might also become so... curious. Look, now we have four from Torkae overly interested in the Kamalti, when before we had only one."

Here it was. Ra'ael straightened her shoulders, preparing for the attack.

"If you would only listen, we could have a relationship with the Kamalti," Kaemada cried.

Another Elder spoke with an accusing tone. "This curiosity might be acceptable if it weren't so dangerous. Only last summer, several young people of Dragonmoor formed an elite band of rangers, modeling these four before us. They even call themselves the Siersan. Five have already lost their lives to their stunts and dreams. It's folly to allow this to continue. We have lost enough young people to this... influence!"

"Not to mention this so-called coincidence, whereby four of Galod's greatest students are all now standing before us! Perhaps, to root out this

Darkness, we should be looking at him," argued one of the Elders.

"He's not one of us," remarked Storyteller Taān. "He's not Rinaryn."

"Why are we talking about Darks?" Taunos exploded.

Storyteller Zeroun spoke up. "We must discuss this issue of the Kamalti."

"Storyteller Zeroun, you are too close. If this Dark seed has perpetuated, it has infected the entire family. Regardless of if that is so or not, this family is without the normal healthy structure of a Rinaryn family."

Another Elder waved the words away. "Who is to say they even saw Kamalti? Everyone knows the Kamalti are a myth. But six moons alone, without the watchful eye of Elders? That would have given them plenty of time."

"Time for what?" Ra'ael objected.

"It's clear to me that these tragedies were a warning." Storyteller Taān's booming voice drowned her words. "If Eloí had been pleased with those who stand before us, would they not have protected them in all their power? For the boy to be lost at all is a clear sign of their displeasure toward the Sierso family."

"If you look at the larger picture," another Elder spoke, "you can see that the decimation of Torkae and the repeated Dark attacks are further signs of Eloí's grace leaving the kaetal. The most reasonable explanation is the actions of this family."

Ra'ael's lip curled before she could stop herself. Looking at events as signs of the spirits' grace was faulty; it was impossible to tell the difference between a punishment and a test. Such theological nonsense drove a rift between her and Torkae's head priest, Teros.

"If they're infected with Darkness, Dark would call to Dark and explain why their kaetal continually is attacked while these before us manage to survive. Indeed, they could arrange it so they look like heroes."

"We haven't arranged anything! What is this?" Ra'ael asked, her fists clenched at her sides.

"Storyteller Zeroun has been able to lead the rest of the kaetalyn in light and grace, but for those who will not be led, doom falls on their own heads."

Storyteller Zeroun spoke up. "How do we know the trials faced by Torkae are not simply tests? This is all interpretation."

"The spirits allow for true interpretation of events!"

Ra'ael glanced to the side at Taunos, Takiyah, and Kaemada. All were trembling, but at least they were holding themselves together. Takiyah's jaw was clenched, her gaze steady on her father's face. That would make it very difficult for Storyteller Zeroun to do his job.

The other Elders paused in their arguments, and then Teryn gestured to the four of them dismissively. "Continue with your story."

They spoke of their time under the mountain, and Kaemada spoke of the horrors of the City of the Lost, pleading with them that a new system of punishment must be found and getting somewhat off-topic before Ra'ael got them back on track. They spoke of the wonders they had seen, the crystals and the healing machines, and the way the Kamalti grew food without the light of the sun. They spoke of what they had endured and how their fortunes had changed. Finally, they discussed the possibility of a new alliance with the Kamalti.

"I do not have to tell you how this could change our way of life for the better. In the old days, when the Kamalti were our close friends, both peoples thrived," Taunos said.

One of the Elders scowled. "That was also the time when we lived in cities and fought one another in bloody, needless wars. Surely you do not propose a return to those times."

"A friendship with the Kamalti does not mean a return to those times. It could mean less danger going to and from Feasts, and help in times of need," Kaemada said. "They could help against the Darks."

"They have much knowledge to offer us as well," Ra'ael said.

"They could help the Darks against us," one of the Elders said.

Another demanded, "What is the meaning of this, the loosing of the Fallen from the City of the Lost? Who gave you the authority to make such a decision, with drastic effects for all Rinaryn?"

Kaemada hung her head. "This was my doing if it was the doing of any of us. But Elders, please understand, many of those condemned to the City of the Lost were innocent of wrongdoing. They were born there or brought there by the Kamalti."

An Elder shook his head. "You have spun a tale in which actions that seemed small took on a life of their own, and the effects were far greater than you could imagine."

"Are you responsible for the Dark attacks recently on kaetaln in Mountainhold?" asked Teryn.

"What attacks?" Kaemada stared.

"While you lived in Torkae, that kaetal was attacked more than any others. Then you left and they had rest! But in the last moon, while you were in the mountains unseen, the kaetaln closest to the mountains have been attacked repeatedly. Is this mere chance?"

Ra'ael exchanged glances with the others, but they looked just as puzzled and outraged as she felt.

"For a Rinaryn to orchestrate an attack on a Rinaryn kaetal is appalling! This family has been touched by Darkness. It's like a plague, spreading wildly, and must be cut out," growled an Elder.

"Following in the footsteps of a man she just admitted to understanding and sympathizing with," shouted another Elder.

"This is absurd!" Taunos raged.

"Do not pretend your innocence. Not only have you as well as admitted to it, your warriors proudly proclaim your name," declared one of the Elders.

"What?" Kaemada squeaked, eyes widening.

"The Darks yell 'Kaemada! Kaemada!' as they loot and plunder."

The attacks had happened in the last moon before the Feast. Ra'ael wracked her mind to come up with an explanation, but only one came to mind. The City of the Lost.

"They take supplies with them?" Taunos stepped forward, his bearing severe.

"Did you not order them to?" challenged one of the Elders.

"Most of the Elders accusing us are from Mountainhold," Takiyah whispered under her breath.

Ra'ael nodded. And they dared to suggest Storyteller Zeroun was too close to the situation.

Together, Storytellers Teryn and Zeroun calmed the Elders down enough to have a bit of order.

Teryn looked at Ra'ael, his gaze sharp. "Ra'ael Tsrian, you're a priestess, correct?"

"Yes, Elder. I'm pleased to do what service I may for my people."

"What does a priestess do? What are you charged with?"

"As you well know, a priestess assists with the rituals and the ceremonies. I help to make sure they're timed and performed appropriately. I help encourage my fellow kaetalyn in their spiritual paths when they stumble. I uphold the laws, traditions, and customs of Rinaryn life."

Taunos sighed, rubbing his face with his hands. Too late, Ra'ael realized she'd stepped into a trap.

"And where is it written to blast your way into the Holy Mountains, using your powers wantonly?"

She hung her head. "It's not. It's forbidden to leave the path."

"And forbidden to use your powers except in dire emergencies, too—a fact which you all seem to have forgotten. What brazen acts you have committed!"

"We had an honorable goal—to save Eian," Takiyah pointed out.

"A direct violation of our ways, encouraged by one who is supposed to uphold our laws."

"We cannot overlook the way you repeatedly broke our laws. This behavior would never be tolerated in kaetal life, and it most certainly cannot be ignored on the sacred journey," said one of the calmer Elders.

"It may be that some Dark influence has grown in you four, possibly planted by your teacher. Why else would you so blatantly ignore tradition and wreak such havoc on Rinaryn society, taking the lives of innocents?" shouted one of the Elders from Mountainhold.

"It will take us some time to ponder all this and discuss it with one another. Please remain here at the Seeker Tree until we have reached a decision. But," Teryn continued as they turned to leave, stopping them in their tracks. They turned back slowly. "Do not make contact with the other Rinaryn. We need to decide where you stand before we may welcome you back from your travels."

The tent erupted as each of the wise men made his points and counterpoints and strove to be heard.

Ra'ael had never seen the Council or any of the Elders so loud and chaotic. She shivered again. Her steps trailed behind Taunos's stalking gait as they made their way to the Seeker Tree.

"I do not understand," Takiyah said quietly. "They cannot truly think we're behind this. Father is so angry. I have never seen him this angry before. He did not reference a single story!"

"How could they say those things?" Taunos hissed, anger and frustration and resentment pouring off him. "How can they speak those lies about us?"

Kaemada studied the grass beneath her feet, lighted gently by the sun sinking toward the peaks. "They're afraid. It's easier when you have someone to blame for your fear."

Ra'ael made a shushing motion. "We do not need them to add charges of psionic use against them," she whispered.

Though the sun was quite warm, Kaemada wrapped her arms around herself. "Something's wrong with the Council of Elders."

Ra'ael nodded. "I know. Could the Darks be influencing the Council somehow?"

Kaemada walked away from them a few paces, staring toward the camp of Torkae. "At least Eian is with Maeren and does not have to see this."

"The troublesome Sierso line," Taunos grumbled under his breath, beginning to pace.

Kaemada shook her head. "I do not care about that, but whatever they do with us, they should reach out to the City of the Lost at the very least. They're in such need." Looking at Takiyah, she continued, "Besides, they seem the most angry with Taunos and me. They will likely forgive you."

"You would be devastated if you were banished. You wouldn't be able to see Eian," Takiyah pointed out.

"They had charges against us all specifically except you, Takiyah," Ra'ael pointed out.

"Surely they will overlook it. We were trying to save Eian." Kaemada twisted her fingers together. "We did nothing wrong."

"Why would the raiders be shouting your name?" Taunos asked.

Drooping miserably, Kaemada shook her head.

"The City of the Lost. They must have broken through the wall," Ra'ael guessed.

Taunos nodded thoughtfully.

"I would think they would consider all the help you two have given over the summers," growled Takiyah. "Of course you're not associated with the Darks."

"Taunos leaves for moons at a time, and Kaemada said she did not hate Tikatae," Ra'ael pointed out. "Today, that's as good as admitting they're Dark-touched."

"That's not right. Tikatae was hard not to hate." Takiyah looked at Kaemada. "I would have said impossible, but proof against that is standing before us. But even so, when has an absence of hate ever been proof of being Dark-touched?"

"Because something is wrong with the Council," Taunos said.

Ra'ael shook her head. Yes, some of the Elders had apparently misplaced their wisdom, but not all of them. Storyteller Zeroun was fighting for them. Even if the Council went wrong, the Great Mothers were there as a check on that sort of thing. The Rinaryn system couldn't be destroyed so easily, could it?

"Maybe we could take Eian with us if we were banished," Kaemada ventured.

Ra'ael frowned. "That wouldn't be fair to him. He wouldn't have a kaetal, freedom to grow, and all the traditions. The nighttime fires."

"We could be his kaetal. A small kaetal, but still. We could have nightly fires, and sing the songs and dance and tell the stories," Kaemada said.

"No," Ra'ael replied firmly. "A child needs the greatness of a kaetal to thrive."

Kaemada sighed, sinking into the grass. After a moment, Ra'ael wrapped her arms around her.

The music of the pipes and drums drifted through the valley, a counterpoint to the heated voices of the Elders behind them.

Chapter Twenty-eight

There must be agreement between at least 38 of the 57 Elders, and the decision must be in line with the laws and values of the Rinaryn people as interpreted by the Council of the Great Mothers, or no declaration can be made. If the Elders cannot agree by sundown, they break for the night and resume in the morning. No issue may be discussed for more than three days. By the end of the third day, a final vote is taken, and if there is agreement, the judgement will stand. Otherwise, it will be tossed out.

—journal excerpt

As the sun sank toward the horizon, the arguments coming from the Elders' tent only grew in intensity. Kaemada placed her hand against the smooth white bark of the Seeker Tree, then leaned her forehead against it. Memories and images from the Collective flooded her, fragments and impressions left behind from their merging. The sense of distance troubled her: distance from the others, from the problems of the future. From herself, even.

"Do you ever wonder if the old legends are true? I mean, was there really an Ancient Man, and is this really the last place his feet touched the ground?" Ra'ael murmured beside her.

Kaemada smiled a bit. "I'm not sure the truth of it matters so much. I think the belief matters more, and what's done with such belief. Does it bring us together or divide us? Does it cause love or hate?"

"There is far too much hatred and fear in the air," Taunos said.

"I cannot blame them. Their homes have been attacked," Kaemada whispered. Just like that, the detachment vanished, and her sorrows and guilt piled on her, burying her.

"For the sake of all things good, Kaemada, be less understanding," Takiyah snapped.

"Stop making excuses for everyone." Ra'ael turned the fire in her gaze on the tent of the Elders. "How could they think Galod is Dark-touched?"

"He's very unusual," Kaemada said, and Ra'ael scowled at her. Kaemada frowned. Had that been making excuses?

"He also keeps many secrets." Taunos's expression darkened.

Takiyah shrugged. "Maybe it's as simple as the fact that he's not

Rinaryn."

"They said as much," Ra'ael agreed.

Kaemada sank back to the ground. If the Elders were against non-Rinaryn like the Collective were against non-psions and like the Kamalti were against outsiders, things were even worse than she feared. And Takiyah—what would that mean for her? The messenger six moons ago had antagonized her, and it appeared fears had only grown since then. Kaemada trailed her fingers through the thick grass. How could she save her friends and brother from more suffering on her account?

The Elders broke for the night, many of them looking angry and the rest looking exhausted. Storyteller Zeroun's shoulders were stooped as he collected them, and he leaned heavily on his cane. They followed him silently, for it was forbidden to question an Elder during a Council, even if they were in recess. No one wanted to make things worse.

When they reached the place where they'd waited before, Zeroun kissed them each on the forehead. He started with Takiyah, holding her a long time and whispering to her.

When he made his way to Kaemada, he murmured, "Lína's daughter, have faith. Torkae will not easily lose you."

He left them with a lump aching in Kaemada's throat and tears threatening to spill out every time she swallowed.

Maeren came with a basket full of delicious sweetened breads, fresh fruit, smoked meat, and greens. Her smile was grieved as she looked at them. "I have heard what happened to you. The other Great Mothers and I have been discussing the issue, but I fear we're as divided as the Elders. We will be certain their decision is just, of course, but aside from that... You four have riled emotions."

"How is Eian?" Kaemada held her arms around herself, feeling as if she couldn't let go.

"He's well, never fear. He has been pestering Soren for more riddles. With the spirits' help, you will be reunited soon."

"Saimahkae, the Council. Something seems wrong with them," Ra'ael said.

"So say all those accused, unfortunately. Never fear. The Storyteller and I are watchful." Maeren embraced each of them, bidding Takiyah keep her chin up, and returned to Torkae's camp.

The sky lit up with falling stars, and the music of the ancient songs filled the air, echoing the sound of the starfall. Ra'ael led them in their participation. The powerful, sonorous tones lifted Kaemada's spirits a bit, but the touch of lightness on her heart drowned in guilt as soon as she felt it. Despair crushed her once more. The traditional tunes ended, and the entertainment began—the music of the pipes and the drums, the singing and the dancing. Kaemada forced a smile to keep the others from worrying about her. The familiar rituals at once comforted and saddened her, for they could not partake. At last, they fell asleep under the falling stars.

In the morning, they woke as the sun's first rays peeked over the ridge of mountains surrounding them. They waited all that day under the Seeker Tree, listening to the faint sound of the Elders arguing. Occasionally, Ra'ael or Takiyah would grumble about how the Elders seemed to be dismissing all the things that had happened in the past six moons while still apparently taking their word that their story was true. True, and yet it might not matter, something that especially rankled Takiyah. But what could they do about it? Kaemada wished she knew a way to ease her friends' pain.

Games and contests played out in front of them, and Taunos watched intently, his fingers twitching and fidgeting. Kaemada grieved for her brother. He should be out there, joining in the contests he loved so much.

After a woman from Dragonmoor won an archery competition, Ra'ael leapt to her feet. "I'm tired of waiting."

She snatched up her sword and dagger and stared at Taunos. He grinned, grabbing his own blade, and she ran at him, both releasing their pent up frustrations through the sparring. Kaemada couldn't help but smile—at last, they were seeing what one another needed and meeting that need rather than holding each other to impossible standards.

Takiyah took the next turn sparring with Taunos, but he went easy on her until she scolded him. "How am I to learn my new limits with this leg unless I push those limits?"

He grinned and threw her five times before she figured out how to guard against it. As Ra'ael and Takiyah joined up together against her brother, Kaemada almost relaxed into the familiar sounds of sparring. Almost. There was no familiar laughter from Taunos—only a short laugh now and then at a particularly good maneuver—and the faces of the people passing by showed their disapproval.

Once the sparring settled and all three of them sank onto the grass once more to rest, Ra'ael asked Taunos, "If you're always away to help us, what have you learned that's useful?"

With a groan, Taunos collapsed on his back. "Will you ever stop pestering me, Wildling?"

"It will prove you're not running," Takiyah observed.

Taunos put his hand to his heart as if she had stabbed him a mortal wound. He turned to look at Kaemada. "Do you, too, doubt me?"

She smiled. "Never, brother. But I think it's fair to answer their questions."

Groaning again, Taunos sat back up. "You will not like the answer."

Ra'ael looked up to the heavens, as she did when impatient.

"I have learned much of the Darks. They're not some fantastical race that came out of nightmares to frighten and kill. They're called by many names, though ours is the simplest. 'Darks.' Ooooo!" His tone became mocking.

Eyes blazing, Ra'ael shoved him hard. "Do you dare mock your own people even while the Elders sit not a stone's throw away, deciding our future?"

Taunos raised his hands. "Shareil. I meant no sincere disrespect, only pointing out how silly a name we have given these people, once you think about it."

"You should be more careful," Takiyah said. "The Elders already think you're Dark-touched."

Beneath his jovial demeanor, strain showed in Taunos's eyes and the lines of his mouth. Kaemada frowned. These accusations wounded him deeply. Something had happened to him in the Council... something the rest of them couldn't understand.

"I have given much and will continue to give much to keep you safe from those people," Taunos said.

"You call those monsters people?" Ra'ael snapped.

"They are people, Wildling. And they're far more advanced than we are."

Takiyah scoffed. "If that's so, then why do they not simply wipe us from the land and erase our story?"

"Because they do not care about us. All those attacks, all those raids? They do not want anything. Why attack us? The answer is simple. We're practice."

Ra'ael frowned. "What do you mean?"

"I mean all those 'monsters' that we have fought for ages realmwalk in and realmwalk out of our land. They destroy and kill but never steal, and they're always young."

"That's why you asked about the recent raids, confirming that they took supplies," Takiyah said.

Taunos nodded. "Darks are not behind the recent attacks. They care nothing for supplies. It makes more sense that the people of the City of the Lost began raiding now that they're free.

"The Darks have an enemy, a real enemy. I do not know much about them yet. But I know that the Darks send their young warriors to us to get a taste of battle, to try out techniques and strategies, and to let their young prove themselves before going on to fight their true enemy." Taunos looked at them severely.

Kaemada shivered. Glancing at her friends, she saw the same shock and horror she felt. They were target practice for these people? What sort of dangerous foe must the Darks have? Pain gleamed in Taunos's eyes. Of course he would wish he could have spared them the knowledge. All those secrets. He shouldn't need to keep so many secrets.

"Against their true might, their real warriors, we would have no chance." Taunos's stern tone drove his point home.

Takiyah shook her head. "What about their enemy? Could we not ally with them?"

"I think we're in trouble enough for making unauthorized alliances," Ra'ael muttered.

Taunos shook his head, looking grim. "The enemy of our enemy isn't necessarily our friend."

"You should tell the Elders all you have found—hold back no secrets from them," Ra'ael hissed, leaning forward. "Your secrets are dooming us."

He shook his head again. "I meet with the Heartwood Council regularly when I return from travels. If they do not see, nothing I can say will convince them."

"Tell everyone else, then," Takiyah suggested. "Do not leave it up to the Elders."

Ra'ael shot her a dangerous look.

Taunos sighed, rubbing his face with both hands. Kaemada put her hand on his shoulder. He looked so... defeated. "The Heartwood Council swore me to secrecy. I should not be telling you even this much. That's why I have not said anything, why I had no defense for these accusations. The Heartwood Council should forgive us. They can get the others to see reason, but only if I follow their rules. If not... Well, do you really think the other Elders will believe me?"

He raised his eyes skyward. "On my travels, I have learned something else. Rinara, our land, is protected by something that has been carefully set up over centuries. Without that protection, we would all die."

"What is it?" Kaemada asked.

"Secrecy," Taunos said. "Nothing is as important as keeping this land safe, and that means secret. Nothing."

Kaemada sat considering her brother's expression carefully for a moment, the pain and grief he tried to hide. "What's her name?"

His expression flashed to annoyance, and he buried his head in his hands. Kaemada winced. He'd likely meant to keep that to himself.

Taunos spoke through his fingers. "Amanah. Amanah Teek."

"What happened?"

He shook his head. "I could not promise her my complete loyalty. She knew I had secrets. Secrets more important than her."

"Ameyitum."

He shook away her sympathy. "I would give anything to keep you and this land safe."

"What else can you tell us?" Takiyah asked.

He sighed again, finally lifting his head. His face was too composed, his voice carefully level, and his pain tore at Kaemada's heart. "I was getting close to discovering the Darks' homeland. They're raiders on many realms. I found a library, a land where knowledge is highly valued, a land that suffers magic raiders. But they do not let just anyone into the library. So I became a guard for them, the quickest way to work my way inside." He shook his head. "I went where they sent me, fought who they told me to," he broke into a humorless chuckle, "to avoid being accused of treason."

He took a deep breath and rubbed his face again. Kaemada sat still as stone, fearing to break his composure, and it seemed her friends held their breaths as well. He looked at Takiyah, then at Ra'ael. "I fought people I have no quarrel with, took wounds for battles I had no stake in, and lost for no gain. And then," he chuckled again. "I cannot read their language. All that knowledge, and I needed someone to translate it for me."

They sat in silence for a long time, letting it all sink in. The rest of the day, their conversations were muted. Ra'ael and Takiyah treated Taunos with great respect, as if trying to make up for doubting him, but that only irritated him. It seemed he wanted things to go back to the way they were, but after all they'd endured, how could anything be the same again?

~

"When is the next Summer of Mercy?" Kaemada asked.

The third day spun by slowly, leaving her in an agony of worry. At the end of the day, the Elders would make their decision, and Kaemada was thoroughly weary of waiting while other people judged her. They all knew the penalty for that which they were accused of.

"This is a Summer of Mercy, so the next would be in seven summers," Ra'ael replied. "But the soonest appeal could be made in one summer, remember."

"But who would put in a request for appeal?" Taunos asked. "Some of the Elders seem to have a vendetta against my family. Someone would have to stand up for us."

Kaemada's forehead creased with worry. "If we're banished, how will I speak? Am I speaking the Traveller's Tongue yet?"

Ra'ael shook her head.

"It matters not, cha'atanahn. I will translate for you," Taunos said.

Takiyah huffed out a breath, her eyes red and watering, though no tears fell. "This is fruitless!"

Finally, the flaps of the tent were drawn back, and the Council filed out looking grim, followed by a subdued group of Great Mothers. Ra'ael leapt to her feet to face them, but Kaemada found her feet with trepidation, as if this moment could be avoided. She couldn't shake the sense of unease that had settled over her. Her mind kept returning to the people of the City of the Lost, failed by the Rinaryn justice system and the Kamalti both.

An Elder played a haunting note on a pipe, the mournful sound filling the valley and drawing the attention of the Rinaryn gathered there. From across the grassy spaces, Rinaryn gathered with expectant faces. Catching sight of Eian holding Maeren's hand, Kaemada swallowed hard. The Storyteller of Torkae steadfastly avoided Takiyah's worried gaze, his face lined with tension and fatigue. The Elders who were the Keepers of the Law conferred briefly among themselves as they exited the tent, and then went silent.

"This judgement will be given inside the Council Tent," one of the Keepers of the Law announced.

The ever-spinning flow of time seemed to stop. Kaemada darted a look at Ra'ael, whose wide eyes echoed the force of emotion stealing breath from her belly. Verdicts were always pronounced for all to hear, out in the open, in sight of the spirits and Eloí. Feeling numb, adrift from reality, she followed the Elders and Great Mothers and the others inside the tent. Eian waved at her with a grin as he came along, holding Maeren's hand, but Kaemada couldn't muster up a smile in return.

"We were called together to discuss the judgement of the four gathered here: Taunos Sierso, Kaemada Sierso, Ra'ael Tsrian, and Takiyah Tiros, as well as the child Eian Sierso. The crimes of the accused include Dark-touching, as evidenced by their refusal to adequately defend the kaetal of Torkae against the man Tikatae Kiente and the Darks.

Additionally, they showed a repeated unwillingness to end the danger posed by Tikatae or submit him for judgement to the Council. They are accused of mind-invasion. Kaemada Sierso has admitted to willfully using her psionic abilities to invade the minds of others, causing harm and even death. There is no evidence that this was necessary, and Taunos, Ra'ael, and Takiyah admit to being accessory to this woeful lack of common decency.

"They have even committed crimes never before conceived of. They freed the dangerous Fallen in the City of the Lost, who were sent there for the protection of the Rinaryn people. They willfully entered into negotiations and relations with the Kamalti without first consulting the Council, or indeed, any Council, for advice and approval. They nearly started a war through their arrogance and blatant disregard for tradition and the law. These crimes are so heinous, they have never before been considered, and there is no appropriate punishment for them."

Kaemada reached out for Ra'ael's hand on her left and Taunos's hand on her right. She held tightly to them as if they were a link to sanity, willing them courage.

"Furthermore, there is the tragic neglect and endangering of Eian, their charge, throughout these many mishaps and ill-conceived misadventures. The boy, Eian, is charged with mischief resulting in bodily harm."

Kaemada started forward to defend her son, but Ra'ael and Taunos pulled her back and held her fast. Her gaze went to him, her sweet boy, who smiled around him. There was no way he understood what was happening.

"After careful deliberation, we find the appropriate punishments for the four adults here accused would be so severe, death would come long before justice was carried out. We have decided after much consideration to show mercy."

Kaemada breathed a sigh of relief. Mercy. Her knees felt weak and her head grew dizzy. Was the nightmare finally over?

The Elder went on. "Though these four accused threw away their lives, we shall grant them mercy and let them keep their lives. However, they shall be banished. At no time while they still draw breath shall they enter a Rinaryn kaetal."

Cold seeped into her bones. It couldn't be. They were Fallen?

"Furthermore, the Storyteller of their kaetal, this troubled kaetal of Torkae, will no longer be a part of this Council. He has shown an appalling lack of leadership in allowing the hermit stranger Galod to live near his kaetal and corrupt these four so completely. That lack of leadership has continued such that these four would show complete disregard for tradition and law—yes, even a priestess of his kaetal! Torkae must have a new Storyteller. Zeroun will diminish and be simply him, with no place on any Council, and no place of any authority."

Kaemada couldn't breathe. She caught Storyteller Zeroun's eyes for a moment before he looked away, calm but sorrowful. This was not how it was supposed to be.

"Zeroun wasn't alone in his lack of leadership, for he should have been helped by his wife, who was the Saimahkae of the kaetal of Torkae. As such, Maeren will no longer be the Great Mother. She will also diminish and never again hold any position of authority, and no place on any Council."

Beside her, Takiyah trembled. Kaemada abandoned caution and manners and flung her arms around her while Takiyah dissolved into sobs.

The Great Mothers murmured as Maeren and Zeroun stepped away from the ruling bodies that had expelled them, somehow holding on to their dignity. Kaemada caught Maeren's gaze for a moment, just as she had Zeroun's. Her Saimahkae gave her a small, brief smile, so swift it might have been a hallucination. Kaemada reeled. What had happened here? How had their punishment flowed onto their Storyteller and Saimahkae?

"As for the boy, Eian, we have decided to show him mercy as well. He was adopted by the accused Kaemada Sierso, and there he received his corruption from those who should have helped him. There will be no punishment for Eian, nor will the banishment of Kaemada confer on Eian any of the customary dishonor. Instead, he will be given a new family in a new kaetal far from his old, corrupted influences. We will hope the damage isn't too extensive.

"Henceforth, the names of Taunos Sierso, Kaemada Sierso, Takiyah Tiros, and Ra'ael Tsrian are not to be spoken. Unthinkable crimes call for unthinkable punishments. They're not to be remembered, and it shall be as if they never were."

The ground rose up and hit her knees. Kaemada and Takiyah clutched each other in the dirt. No chance for appeal. All they had done had been for their people, and now they were to be purged from their song. Kaemada stared at Eian, every moment suddenly treasured beyond measure. He would forget her after adjusting to a new life. He would forget them all.

One of the Elders followed Kaemada's gaze to Eian and tore Eian from Maeren's hold. He took him out of the tent while the boy, confused and frightened, shouted and fought.

"Eian!" Kaemada screamed, reaching out for him.

Takiyah held tightly to her, and as Eian disappeared, Kaemada collapsed against her, her heart aching.

"Let the sentence be carried out immediately. Send these who are Fallen away and let them make haste out of our lands. Let the boy who was Eian be given a new name with his new home in his new kaetal, and let there stand guards over him for the remainder of the festival to protect him from any more atrocities," another Elder said, looking down his nose at them.

Kaemada clung to Takiyah. How could she trust that Eian would be loved and well cared for after the Council had so recently betrayed them?

"We need to move." Her brother's urgent voice seemed far away. "Get up. On your feet!"

She couldn't move, couldn't think. Strong arms lifted her, and the world swirled around her. What was real anymore? What was trustworthy? What could she hold onto? There was nothing, only churning confusion and cutting betrayal.

Kaemada stared, uncomprehending, at the faces of people as they rushed past. People she loved, people she'd thought loved her. The face that mattered most, she never saw. Eian. She would never see him again.

Impossibly, the three greatest heroes of Torkae ran beside her, fleeing with her. No more honor for them—they were Fallen.

Thank you for reading!

If you have a spare moment, please leave an honest review. Reviews are the best way to help other readers find books they'll enjoy, and they make an enormous difference for independent authors especially! If you want to help support your favorite authors, telling others about them and asking your local library to stock their books are among the best ways to do so. Thank you so much!

Don't forget to stay in touch to get free books like Prelude Cycle as well as more exclusive content, including bonus short stories not available anywhere else: Simply go to skaeth.com and subscribe to the newsletter!

A REFERENCE OF TERMS AND PEOPLE

As you've (repeatedly) suggested, Lenatis, I include a guide to the many different individuals and reference terms peculiar to their people to which I refer.

The People

Kaemada Sierso - a psion who has access to powers of both telepathy and telekinesis. This allows her to bond tightly to animals, as well as to dreamwalk. She is one of my pupils.

Ra'ael Tsrian - has the blood rage, causing her to go on a rampage during battles, and telekinesis. She is also one of my pupils.

Takiyah Tiros - the adopted daughter of the leaders of Torkae. She is not Rinaryn, though I do not know what race she is, and can shoot flames from her wrists. Another of my pupils.

Tannevar - Kaemada's bonded companion, a young wolf.

Taunos Sierso - Hero of Torkae, and my star pupil, as well as Kaemada's brother. He is powerful in telekinesis and can realmwalk.

Tikatae - a villager of Torkae who was banished and now enjoys tormenting the village.

Answer - a young noble Kamalti from the city of Codr, of the Scouts.

Dode - an elderly noble Kamalti from the city of Codr, of the Philosophers.

Elisabei - a healer from the City of the Lost and part of a rebellion

Reinan - an explosives expert from the City of the Lost and part of a rebellion

Tjodlik - a young noble Kamalti from the city of Hadr, of the Philosophers. Nephew to Dode.

Terms

Rinaryn - a native people of the land of Rinara. The Rinaryns themselves are less than extraordinary. They are bipeds, a little smaller on average than humans, and a great deal lighter in build (I expect they have hollow bones). They have round faces and brown skin and their hair tends to be black or brown, although children can have golden-blond hair which often darkens as they age. Their eyes are typically brown but can also be blue or grey.

kaetal - the semi-permanent villages the Rinaryns live in. They will abandon the kaetaln (plural of "kaetal") for each Feast of Starfall, as well as during harsh winters, and then come back together for spring or after the Feasts. When they leave the kaetal for the twice-yearly Feasts, they will dismantle each hut and refashion them into sledges or use them as firewood for the journey. Whenever the kaetal is broken apart, the Great Mother is responsible for keeping the flame of the central fires alight until all the people return.

ehreideikae - Lit: "one who watches/knows" - The Rinaryns call them "priestesses" and "priests" but they are in fact more akin to what we would consider therapists and counselors. While they do lead religious ceremonies for the kaetal, they spend most of their time soothing social fractures and tending to the mental health of the kaetalyn. Religious duties do not occur with the regularity we've noted elsewhere, for each Rinaryn is responsible for practicing their faith alone in the best way they see fit.

yah - the coming of age ritual of the Rinaryn people. At around puberty, when the family of a youngster and the elders of his kaetal (including the Storyteller and Saimahkae) have judged them able to succeed, the young Rinaryn will set off on their own to live alone off the land with no help for one month. Typically youngsters are sent out several at a time, so the kaetal can celebrate success all together (or mourn, If disaster strikes). A Rinaryn is not considered an adult until they pass their yah.

aeneshenon - winged Rinaryns. Very rarely, some Rinaryns are born with wings, creating six limbs instead of four. These are given much honor, and amazingly enough the wings are functional, allowing brief bursts of flight. According to their legends, when the Rinaryns were created, all had wings.

tailosae - a Rinaryn primate well known in the forests of Heartwood and Life Valley. Large eyes, prehensile tails, and a fruit-based diet are the main characteristics of this social primate species.

tserwora - a large, venomous lizard in Rinara. They dig large dens which they are extremely territorial of. The venom in a tserwora bite can kill a Rinaryn, and there is also the risk of infection.

zeriy - a large canine in Rinara who prefers the grasslands. They have long legs and are known for speed. Sometimes tamed as pets.

toelfa - a large feline in Rinara who lives in the forests. They have a curled ruff around their necks and a long tail with a venomous barb at the end. The venom is enough to kill small animals, but will merely wound and sicken a Rinaryn.

Saimahkae - lit: Great Mother. The highest ranking woman of a Rinaryn kaetal. Her responsibility is to keep the kaetal functioning day to day, attending to social matters and helping to ease any disputes.

Kamalti - a native people of Rinara who live only in the Holy Mountains. The Kamalti are said to live under the Holy Mountains, and at first I thought they were probably dwarves. However, the mountain range is also infested with dragons, making the existence of a dwarven kingdom unlikely (and making it difficult to properly investigate the matter). I find it most likely that the Kamalti grew as an idea from the fact that the journey is treacherous and rife with dangers, as a sort of childhood monster to keep their young in line.

Darks - an ancient enemy of the Rinaryns. These people send their young raiders to the Rinaryns, possibly through the use of realmwalking, for I have not detected the presence of technomancy (though of course the limitations of the atmosphere mean I cannot rule that possibility out.) They bear iron weapons and leather armor, painted black, and tend to wear black, as they attack at night almost exclusively. They never take land, or seem to want any resources, really. I suspect the raiders are sent to give them a taste for battle, a taste for blood. (Yes, as you've reminded me, I have not intervened.)

Torkae - a small kaetal in the region of Heartwood, in the northeastern quadrant of the island nation of Rinara.

Heartwood - a region in the northeast of Rinara

The Angels - a creature who hunts by song, stunning their prey so they can feed. These interest me a great deal and I hope to learn more of their function soon.

The City of the Lost - an ancient city where the Rinaryns send their banished people, "Fallen". This is the last remaining city in Rinara. It is said the gate is guarded by great statues which annihilate any large creature moving outward from the city, effectively making it a prison. I have not been able to confirm, as no Rinaryn will answer me as to the location of the city, and my explorations have thus far been fruitless.

Codr - a Kamalti city

Hadr - a Kamalti city

Anathel and Tharahel - the Rinaryn names for the two moons of the planet. The moons are of similar size, in a co-orbital configuration around the planet. This creates extremely dangerous tidal effects, which no doubt contributes to the Rinaryns not being a seafaring people.

tsífíorse - Rinaryn for "thank you"
ameyitum - Rinaryn for "forgive me"

shareil - lit: "peace"

Betah teimelei - a polite Rinaryn greeting, often shortened to simply "Betah"

acha'iyih - a term of endearment. Lit: "dear little one"

cha'atanahn - Taunos's pet name for his sister, basically meaning "abundance of heart/life"

nanovah - a Rinaryn word basically meaning "Forget about it"

ACKNOWLEDGEMENTS

This book has been the work of many years, and I could not have produced it without the help and support of so very many people. As always, I stand on the shoulders of giants. I am so grateful for the advice, support, and encouragement from my writing community and my family and friends.

To my husband, my rock, thanks for being so amazing. You're consistently there for me when I need you. You're the best alpha reader a writer could ever have, and then you read things again once I think I've got them polished. I believe you read this story three or four times? Thank you for your steadiness through my nerves and waffling and stubbornness.

To my children, you are so understanding and supportive: asking questions, helping out around the house, and giving me your thoughts. I wish the world for you and love to see you creating your own stories, breaking past the limits others might place on you!

Thanks to my family for encouraging my love of stories, science, and fantasy.

To Alex, thank you for all the hours worldbuilding and magic system building when we were younger. It's been lovely to use the role-playing system we created as the underpinnings to my stories, even tucked away out of sight as it is. All that time spent building the classes, lore, and mechanics are still being used!

My amazing critique partners, I can't say enough good about you. R. Lee Fryar, you have an amazing gift to see right to the heart of my stories and my characters and you never hesitant to point me on the path when I stray. Thanks to you for helping my characters shine with their whole hearts. And for Ariana Townsend, you *got* Kaemada in a deeply internal way and joined R. in continuing to encourage me to dig into her. Not only that, but you copy edited this whole giant manuscript for me, and I cannot thank you enough for your care and attention to the details of all the rules I had laid out. Thanks to the two of you, this story is the best I can make it, and I love its polish!

To my writing groups, the Inklings, the Parliament of Pens, Quillhaven, and the Writer In Motion groups, thank you for providing such community and encouragement. I have my tribe and I'm so thankful for it! You're all amazing.

Special thanks to Rosie, Pancake, Moxie, Honey, and Zelda.

To my fantastic beta, gamma, and omega readers, for all your feedback and questions and insights: Liza Tucker, Becky O'Connor, Billy Brinkley, Laura Kehoe, Autumn, Michael Chatfield, Jeremy Nelson, Amy Brown, Timothy, Agnes S., Mist, E.P. Larrson, 🚀, Jerusha Renee, Carrot, KJ Harrowick, Peach Hurtado, Catherine Bloom, and Ysabelle Suarez.

To Jeni Chappelle and Maria Tureaud for your constant support and generous editing advice. Thank you for the motivation you so freely give the writers around you.

To KJ Harrowick and Melissa Koberlein for your launching advice and pointers, and to Misti Wolanski for your grammar tutorials: an enormous thank you from the bottom of my heart! Thanks as well to Whitney Hill for marketing advice and Ben Gartner for support!

To my phenomenal cover artist, Dave Brasgalla. I can't tell you how amazing it is to see my ideas made real in the form of your gorgeous paintings. I could spend days just staring at these amazing pieces of art, just as I hope my readers can get lost in my words.

To Michael J Sullivan, for your writing and marketing advice. I'm amazed and humbled by your generosity and hope I succeed in continuing to pay it forward.

And of course, if no one read my works, things would be more boring (but I'd still be writing!) Thank you for giving me the opportunity to spirit you away to another world for a few hours/days.

ABOUT THE AUTHOR

Ever since a college professor told S. Kaeth she'd have to eventually focus on just one thing, she's been dead set on proving him wrong.

From charging through the wilderness, wrangling alligators and snapping turtles, trapping and counting moles, or supervising prairie burns for college credits to doing research and training frogs, lizards, and a lungfish, she treats life as an adventure. She traded hikes, natural history interpretation boating tours, and creature encounters for the slightly-less-exotic-but-no-less-fun mammal training about the same time she began to get serious about her writing craft.

You can find her teaching herself languages and lesser-known fiber crafts, hiking, or playing Capoeira when she's not practicing the fine art of weaving a tale.

OTHER BOOKS BY S. KAETH

Continue the series with:

Let Loose The Fallen (Book Two of Children of the Nexus)

The priestess searches for her faith.
The fire-wielder wrestles with her past.
The psion dreams of peace.
And the hero is torn between his heart and his duty.

While grief scatters the four protectors to the winds, outside forces write history according to their own whims. The fate of the Rinaryns lies twined with that of the boy, Eian, caught in a tug of war the heroes are unaware of.

But the evidence lies waiting for Taunos and the others to see, if only they can move past their betrayal.

(Continue reading for the first chapter of Let Loose the Fallen)

Or, read standalone books by S. Kaeth set in the same world:

Windward

When dragons fight, mountains weep.
Dragonbonded Palon and her partner, the dragon Windward, are

renowned for their flying skill among the dragons and dragonbondeds who make up their family. Palon's days are filled with everything she loves, especially riding the wind. Even being tasked with teaching their way of life to Tebah, a newly bonded teenager, can't bring her down too much.

But when treasures from the dragons' hordes are found in Palon's collection, her idyllic life comes crashing down. Framed, she battles to find the truth, to prove her innocence, while her every move is cast as further evidence against her. As if that wasn't enough, her teenage charge's increasingly dangerous behavior puts them both at risk. Tebah's suspicion, homesickness, and defiance would be frustrating enough even if Palon wasn't in the spotlight, with a rival smearing her name at every turn. Dragon tempers shorten, and challenges and disputes shake the ground.

Windward and Palon must find a way to clear her name while also keeping a teenager who hates her and everything about dragon life safe, before their community turns completely against them or vigilante justice succeeds.

Beneath the Gods' Tree

Amanah knows all-too-well the dangers of catching the attention of the upper class of Arruk. Using her position as a guard to steal secrets of healing and help other lower class people means she must remain unnoticed, working from the shadows.

Fellow guard Taunos is boisterous, laughing, larger than life-and always around. He attracts attention as easily as breathing, which makes being associated with him dangerous. Better to stay far away, regardless of her attraction to him and his easy calm.

But when Amanah inadvertently insults a magistrate, she must flee the city to avoid his vengeance. She takes a last-minute job escorting a pair of noblemen to another town-a job Taunos is also hired for.

As she spends more time with Taunos, his confident charm draws her in, especially when he uncovers her dream of becoming a healer and offers to help make it a reality. Taunos sees her as no one else has, even when she's doing her best to be invisible. But opening herself to romance might be as dangerous as the wildlife and bandits they face in the wilderness.

Yet as the end of her mission looms, she's not sure she can resist the draw of Taunos and of pursuing her dreams, even if it means drawing the ire of those in power.

(This book takes place about three years before Between Starfalls, a little after Prelude Cycle)

Read on for a sample of the continuing adventure:
Let Loose the Fallen (Children of the Nexus Book Two)

~

Aetha
Chapter One

When the psions broke through the wall of the City of the Lost, they thought it was freedom. How could they predict the terror to come? The Angels came far sooner than they were expected, feasting on those who had only run for freedom. For a chance at life, not mere existence. The Angels gorged themselves for many nights, not even dragging their prey away with them. The survivors made no effort to properly lay the dead to rest, for it was far too dangerous. They huddled in their city, called it the Angels' Feast, and spoke of it only in hushed tones. Even more terrible, with the hole in the wall, the Angels were able to glide through the streets each night, hunting for their prey.

—account of Kaemada Sierso, psion

"Please, little sister, you have to eat." Taunos's strained voice trembled in the close air.

Kaemada stared at the wall, mechanically opening her mouth when he bumped her lips with the spoon. She held the gruel in her mouth without chewing, and the moments stretched long like a thread tugged to breaking. Finally, her throat bobbed as she swallowed. Her eyes never changed their direction, her face wan and expressionless. His sister was dying, little by little, right in front of him, and he could not save her.

Taunos sucked in a harsh breath. His heart was encased in ice, his chest too tight. It took all of his control to help her finish her meal—only half a bowl, even less than last time. Dark smudges had grown beneath her puffy, bloodshot eyes, and she was losing her muscled physique, wasting away.

He paused when she refused to open her mouth. The spoon bumped her lips again as his hand trembled. She didn't respond. He might as well not be there. There was no use forcing her—he had tried that before, and the meal had just run out of her mouth, down her chin, and onto her clothes. He would not damage her dignity further.

He cleared his throat, wiping her mouth gently with a rag. Sitting back, Taunos finished her meal. Just as always, her mind was elsewhere. Hatred for his own Elders burned in him, for they had dealt the final, mortal blow to his sister when they ripped her son from her, after all they had been through to see him safe. She'd been in a daze as they fled: he, his sister, and her two best friends, all four banished from Rinaryn society in an unconscionable act by those who were supposed to be wise. They'd wandered, while the hunting songs of the Angels had driven them ever closer to the City of the Lost. And then, they'd discovered what littered the plain beyond the hole in the wall of the city. Bodies, scattered like so much refuse. How many had joined the escape? How many had survived the Angels' Feast, as it was now known?

Kaemada hadn't spoken a word or moved on her own since, and he knew she blamed herself.

Footsteps scuffed on the dirt outside. Guards? Others who lived in the city, looking for trouble? Taunos leaped to his feet in a ready stance, facing the doorway, bowl in one hand and spoon in the other.

Takiyah and Ra'ael pulled open the poorly-made door and swept aside the tattered rag that hung in the doorway to patch the holes between the shoddily fitting slats.

Takiyah paused for a moment, smirking at Taunos as he relaxed, then limped past him to set down her armful of bread. Ra'ael followed, depositing the food on a blanket stretched on the dirt floor. Both were dealing with their banishment in their own ways—poorly, and with bad tempers. Ignoring them lest politeness spark further trouble, Taunos wiped the bowl and spoon clean and set them to the side then prowled the length of the tiny house. It was too small—this wasn't helping his sister either. This whole city was surely hindering Kaemada's recovery, with all the memories it must bring. It had been a mistake to come here, even though it was the only shelter—so they'd thought—from the Angels' nightly hunting. Even if desperation to survive had driven them to this place of nightmares. He needed freedom. He couldn't stand the quiet, the inactivity.

"How was the market?" Taunos asked, forcing levity into his tone. He'd demanded there be only optimism in the house. Kaemada's song was currently deciding whether or not this world, this story, held too much pain to continue the cycle or not. He meant to weight her on the side of life as much as he possibly could, whatever the cost.

Takiyah dropped her words into the silence. "I'm leaving."

Shock and anger choked him, leaving Taunos to glare at her.

"Me too," Ra'ael said.

How could they even think it? Didn't he know them at all? Taunos stared at them. "You cannot!"

"I'm Fallen, remember? I can do whatever I'd like." Takiyah crossed her arms, her gaze level but unyielding. "I was kind enough to bring food back before leaving."

"Tinker—"

"Takiyah," she corrected him. "We cannot go back to the way it was before."

"What about Kaemada?" He glanced at her. They had to stay together. Everything would fall apart without them. Kaemada was on the edge as it was, and if she died…

Takiyah shook her head. "I cannot help her. All of us have tried. Besides, when I needed to leave, to escape the Kamalti, she stopped to help them. Our enemies, and she needed to risk us to give them aid."

"She was torn between aiding you and aiding the innocent." Taunos's eyes narrowed. How could she not see this? "She wanted a way to do both. And still, she would have chosen you, and you know it."

"That's the point, Taunos. It took her time to decide. I would have chosen her in an instant. There would have been no choice."

"Please." He cast a glance behind him. Eloí's light, hopefully she hadn't heard. How many wounds could a song take before it just stopped?

"This is not a discussion, Taunos." Takiyah's voice was flat, fully without sympathy. "I'm not asking permission. I'm doing you the courtesy of informing you."

"And you?" Taunos asked, looking at Ra'ael. How could they both abandon Kaemada? How was he supposed to help his sister on his own when she needed help with everything, as if she were an infant once again?

"This is not what the spirits intended." Ra'ael's voice was soft, as it always was these days. No more fire, no more passion. She had died inside just as surely as Kaemada had. "I thought this would be the path laid out for us, being Fallen and coming to the city of Fallen. But no—we are still functioning as a miniature kaetal. You, telling stories nightly—"

"I'm not a Storyteller," he cut in.

Ra'ael shook her head. "Even so. We must embrace this new path."

Takiyah snorted. "Embrace being Fallen?"

"This is what the spirits desire."

The heat of her inner fires raged in Takiyah's voice. "And my torture, did they desire this, too? When I was beaten and branded and my leg broken to prevent further escape attempts? I should accept this all as the will of the spirits?"

Ra'ael grimaced, staring at the wall instead of them. "I do not know anymore. We are Fallen. I only know I have to find the spirits' will, to discover the laws that will let me hear the song of the spirits once again. We cannot combat the Elders. We must find our new path as Fallen."

Taunos pressed his hands to his face, dragging his fingers down his skin. This was foolish. He tried to keep his voice low, and it came out more as a growl than anything else. "What of the plan for the next storm? Even if you make it past the guards, they will increase patrols if they see you. You will destroy the plans—tens and tens of people, Kaemada included, whose bid for freedom will be thwarted due to your selfishness."

Takiyah spun on him, her green eyes ablaze as she stared down at him from her height.

Taunos stood his ground, returning her fire with that of his own.

Her mouth twisted before she spoke, hissing the words sharp as knives. "I will wait until then. But Taunos, do not *ever* call me selfish again."

"With your plan, I'm unlikely to ever see you again," Taunos returned.

She turned away, her shoulders and back stiff. Moments spun past, and then she shook her head, pushing past him to lurch out the door.

Taunos watched her go, clenching his jaw so as not to grind his teeth.

"I'm going scouting. I will stay nearby so you can get some rest," Ra'ael said.

While Kaemada was near motionless during the day, at night fits took her, such that they had to gag her and hold her down. Even so, her fits were violent enough that none of the three had to sing the counter song to the Angels. The Angels could be right outside their door, clawing at the flimsy wood, and still the power of the Angels' song would be disrupted by Kaemada's screaming, babbling nonsense. None of them had even felt the pull since coming here almost a moon ago.

Even so, the missed sleep wore on him. Taunos nodded wearily, hoping his gratitude showed. And then Ra'ael, too, was gone, and Taunos was left alone again with his catatonic sister.

Blowing out a sigh, he moistened a rag from the water jug and washed Kaemada's face, arms, and hands for her and then picked up the comb. Her curls tangled quickly without care, and this was another thing she was not able to do for herself.

"Do not listen to them, little sister," he whispered. "They do love you, just as I do. Their anger and hurt has simply blinded them for a while."

He held a handful of her hair in his fist, working out the tangles from the ends and moving upwards toward the top of her hair. As he worked, he talked, hoping she could hear him, wherever her mind was.

"Remember, life is not only pain, little sister. There is love and beauty, too. Remember listening for the starsong and climbing the great bluffs of Heartwood? Walks in the forest with the summer sun dappling the ground through the leaves?"

He worked in silence for a while, thinking, and then finally began the story of Kalei and the fae, working his way through the tangles as he spoke, hoping that being reminded of Kalei's trials would help Kaemada come back to them. Once the tangles were free, he braided her dark honey hair to help reduce the knotting. It wasn't as nice a job as Ra'ael or Takiyah would have done, but it would do. But both story and chores had to end eventually, and even extending them didn't bring Kaemada back. She still sat, staring at nothing, heedless of his failure, his ineptitude. He couldn't save her from this.

"Lay down, cha'atanahn," he said, gently guiding her down on her side. He covered her with his old cloak, tucking the top under her chin, and then swept his hand downward over her eyes. "Close your eyes. Rest, little sister. Rest."

Two steps away, he laid down in front of the door and tried to think of a plan before sleep took his exhausted mind.

When he woke, feeling as if there was sand in his eyes, Kaemada's eyes were still open, staring through him. It had been too much to hope. She only shut her eyes during her fits. He rose, groaning and stretching, as Takiyah came in. She limped heavily on the leg that had been broken during their captivity, and Taunos turned his gaze away from her so as not to provoke another outburst.

He paused by the door. "I'm going out for a bit. Are you all right to stay with her?"

"The guards are everywhere out there. Something is wrong."

Taunos clenched his jaw. More problems. "Are you going to watch

Kaemada?"

"Yes, Taunos, stop fussing."

"I'm not fussing, I'm—"

"Just go."

Taunos pressed his lips together for a bit, but Takiyah ignored him, taking off her boots and setting them in her corner. He turned, trying to quell his concerns, and cast a last glance at his sister. She stared at the wall, still laying on her side. He hesitated, wondering if he should leave her like that.

"Go!" Takiyah rounded on him, flicking her hands at him as if he were a swarm of spirits'-teeth.

Taunos frowned at her but went.

Outside, clouds had gathered, dark and ominous. The narrow streets were even more gloomy than usual. Even so, a small amount of relief spun through him, loosening his shoulders. It was better than being confined indoors, even if he was trapped under a dome in a ruthless city. Soon, he would feel the wind on his face, and perhaps that would bring Kaemada back. All he had left were fraying hopes for the impossible.

It was too dangerous to bring Kaemada outside—the guards still hunted for her, the psion who had killed their king. The restriction grated on him, for he knew how his sister loved the outdoors. They'd had so few days to spend together in recent summers, but always outside: deep in the forest or climbing the bluffs, racing along the trees or diving into waterfalls. How many storms had they watched together? A slight breeze gusted by, hailing a stronger wind outside the city. Lightning flashed in the boiling clouds, and thunder drummed. Taunos glanced up as rain poured down, spattering off the mysterious dome that covered the city, sliding off its curved surface, except where the rain found the holes in the dome, falling to water the crops planted below.

They'd been waiting for a storm strong enough to keep the Angels from hunting. This one might be exactly what they were waiting for.

A pair of guards jogged past.

Taunos ducked his head and hunched his shoulders. He quickened his pace once they had gone, but even so, he'd barely made progress before another pair came running down the opposite direction. What was going on?

He watched them go, pressing his back against the mud wall of a house to avoid being trampled. They turned a corner, and he crept after them, the hairs on the back of his neck prickling. The guards were always dangerous, always ready to cut you down for the slightest inconvenience, but now, something had changed.

Takiyah was right, as she all too often was.

The dim alleys were littered with filth, and Taunos covered his mouth and nose with his sleeve, trying to avoid breathing the worst of it. Soon, he reminded himself. Soon, he could return to open skies and wide spaces, fresh air and clean water to wash in. It looked like tonight would be the night, given the flashes of lightning.

A clash of metal rang out ahead of him, and he paused. Hardly anyone in the City of the Lost had metal except for the guards—it was one of the many things they hoarded to set themselves apart.

He crept forward then ducked back as a guard tumbled past his tiny alley. The few people who were out scurried away, casting panicked looks over their shoulders as they distanced themselves from the battle. The guard rose to his feet and launched himself at another, and Taunos retreated further into the shadows of the alley.

The guards were fighting each other? Why?

More important, should they take the chance given them by the storm to leave or wait until after the chaos of the guards fighting, lest they be discovered?

Taunos shook his head as a crash of thunder overhead rumbled. Though the guards fighting spoke of danger for any innocents caught in their path, they had to take the chance. Who knew when the next night storm would be? They'd just have to hope that the chaos of the guards fighting would work in their favor.

If they didn't take the chance of the storm, they'd have to sneak out some morning with the other laborers working in the new fields beyond the wall and then make their escape. Even though Kaemada had killed the king, not enough had changed for the City of the Lost. The guards had kept the city a prison, despite the fact that there was a way out now. It allowed them to keep the power, the control over those they considered less-than, especially since they forced the city folk to take shifts working the fields outside the walls. Always under supervision, of course, lest anyone run.

If they tried to escape that way, fewer people would succeed, and at much more risk.

No, tonight it was. It had to be.

The guards were used to spending the nights safe in their houses of stone, away from the threat of the Angels, so if their internal fighting didn't keep them from habit, the night would be clear. And if not, at least they were distracted.

He hurried through the muck toward home, sliding on filth around corners. If they left immediately, they'd be able to get farther before the next threat from the Angels, perhaps even making it out of their range altogether.

"Taunos." Elisabei wandered down the street next to her husband Reinan, who held a pot.

All too aware that unfriendly eyes might be watching, Taunos smiled as if at ease and gestured at the house that confined them. "Elisabei. Reinan. Come in."

Elisabei frowned at their door. "You need a new door, if you can find it. The Angels'll get through soon."

Taunos nodded, keeping up pretenses just as she was. Deep gouges in the wood bore the mark of Angels' fingers, digging at the door to gain access. Their house was near the wall and therefore was targeted more often by Angels, but at least the door faced away from the hole in the wall, sheltering them a little. He opened the battered door and ushered them in, quickly shutting it behind him.

He immediately wanted to escape. The room was far too close with so many people inside. Takiyah was folding their rags, while next to her, Ra'ael chopped vegetables. Kaemada lay in the corner like a child's forgotten doll, while Reinan placed the pot by Takiyah's fire. Ra'ael lifted the lid, and her face lit up with a smile.

"Broth!"

"Do not get too excited. The bones were three days old. It'll be weak," Elisabei warned.

As Ra'ael poured some of the grain and vegetables she and Takiyah had purchased that morning from the market into the broth, Taunos knelt by his sister and gently pulled her arms, sitting her up. He sat next to her, slinging an arm around her shoulders while she stared past Takiyah.

"Any idea why the guards are fighting?" he asked Takiyah.

She raised her eyebrows. "They're fighting?"

Taunos nodded.

Reinan frowned, his heavy eyebrows furrowing. "That's no good."

"I saw it myself," he said then dropped his voice to a murmur. "We need to escape tonight, in the storm."

"The guards never fight among themselves," Elisabei said, then softly, "It'll be dangerous though, with the guards fighting. If they continue, we might be seen."

Taunos smiled. "A necessary risk. Is everything ready?"

"They fight among themselves when there is a dispute over rule,"

Reinan rumbled, covering Taunos's whisper, though Elisabei nodded to him.

"What does that mean for tonight?" Takiyah asked.

"Not much different," Elisabei whispered. "Stay far away from them. Get to the walls and run."

"When was the last time they fought?" Takiyah's gaze was intense, but Reinan only shook his head. The muscled, barrel-chested Resistance leader who pretended to be a simple cobbler had been born in the city.

Taunos's arm tightened around his sister. Without her, they never would have met, never would have been connected. In fact, Kaemada was the thread tying all of them together—himself to Ra'ael and Takiyah, Takiyah and Ra'ael to each other, the three of them all to Elisabei and Reinan, and then to the Resistance. One thread couldn't hold cloth together though, especially if such cloth wanted to tear.

He dropped a kiss on the top of her head, whispering to her, "Hang on, little sister. Only a little longer, cha'atanahn. Only a little longer."

"Since we're leaving at night, we will have a problem." Takiyah nodded at Kaemada.

"We have to." Taunos tightened his hold further, as if he could guard his unresponsive sister from implications. She was in trouble, not trouble itself.

"I know. But you know as well as I do what happens."

Taunos nodded. His sister's fits took her nearly every night, as soon as her eyes shut. He bent to murmur in her ear, needing to believe some part of her could hear him. "We're leaving soon, under cover of night. Hang on, please, little sister. We will need quiet."

"We might need to tie her up more tightly than normal," Ra'ael said.

Taunos's gaze flicked to Kaemada's raw, bruised wrists, where she had injured herself during past fits.

"And gag her thoroughly," Takiyah said.

"Not too tightly or she'll suffocate," Elisabei cautioned.

"It has to be done." Taunos clenched his jaw. He looked at Elisabei. "When?"

"As soon as it's full dark."

They ate, keeping up a murmur of conversation as if this night was no different than any other. The lie of routine was crucial to their survival, and as such, the four had hosted Elisabei and Reinan often, especially as their house was bigger than the couple's. It had all been planned, ever since their arrival in the city.

And now, escape was finally almost upon them. Taunos felt almost as if he were vibrating with enthusiasm as he helped his sister eat then use the latrine pit. And then, with the sky darkening even further, they laid Kaemada down and began to bind her tightly with ropes and scraps of fabric tied over their blankets. In very little time, she was cocooned in tight strips of cloth, staring sightlessly at the ceiling. Taunos placed the bite stick in her mouth and tied the gags, using a couple extra layers to muffle her as much as possible under Elisabei's wincing guidance.

Kaemada did not resist—she never did. It would have been better if she did.

"Watch her to be sure she continues to draw breath," Elisabei said.

He nodded, pushing his worries away in favor of focusing on the escape at hand. The risk needed to be taken for the chance of success.

Taunos swept his cloak over his shoulders and made sure his daggers were in easy reach. Ra'ael grabbed the bag of their supplies, and just like that, they were ready. He caught Reinan's eye, and the big man glanced at Kaemada and then at Taunos meaningfully. Knowing Reinan, he likely had a contingency plan. Taunos would have to carry Kaemada.

He settled her over his shoulder as gently as he could. Following Reinan, he ducked out of the house, leaving the door open. After all, there was no longer any need to close it.

They ran through the empty streets, Taunos trying to joggle Kaemada as little as possible. In the City of the Lost, no one lingered longer than they needed on the streets at the best of times. With the guards fighting, it was just plain stupid to be where someone could see you. No one would be expecting them.

They cut through an alley and down another street then a quick turn to the right, meeting up with another small group, silent and wide-eyed. Winding their way toward the gaping hole in the wall, more and more groups joined theirs until they were a mass of people, fighters scattered among those who could not fight.

Clashing metal rang out to their left. Elisabei veered away, but their group had grown bulky, and many were too slow in seeking hiding places. Several guards spilled through an alley into the street they'd just turned onto, and more fighting could be heard on the main road behind them.

One of the guards shouted, "Stop!"

The guard fighting him didn't seem to notice them though. "Theron, you maggot, get back here!"

Taunos's blood ran cold. Theron. Was that *the* Theron? He stepped forward, intent on the thoroughfare, where several guards ringed in two combatants, both in the leather armor the guards wore. Both were bleeding from several wounds and panting from exertion.

"Does my life annoy you, *King* Kunos?" taunted one of the guards. "A constant reminder of your failures?"

"My failures?" scoffed the other. "You're the one who let that woman get out of hand. You're the one who failed to control a psion and keep her from killing your king. You're the one who let them escape. I may have failed thus far in escorting you to your death, but that is a far cry from being beaten by a woman!"

Taunos's gaze fixed on the guard who must be Theron. It didn't matter who the other guard was. Theron didn't know it yet, but Taunos's meeting with him had been long overdue, and he intended to repay Theron for all the horrors he'd put Kaemada through the first time she'd been in the city.

"Taunos!" Ra'ael hissed.

Reluctantly, he turned away, shifting Kaemada on his shoulder. First, he needed to get her to safety. His reckoning with Theron could wait a while longer. He fled down the street toward the wall.

A sharp, wild laughter sounded behind him as Taunos hurried to rejoin the end of the group. They were pouring out of the hole in the gates now. Ra'ael and Takiyah were both near the end, and Reinan was running back toward him, his face fierce.

"Down!" Reinan shouted, and Taunos obeyed instantly, flinging himself to the street, his arms stretched forward to cushion his sister's head.

She stiffened and thrashed, catching him in the chin with her knees and knocking his vision white. A terrible keening came from her throat. That was no good. It'd attract the guards. A knife protruded from the wall of the house in front of them—if he hadn't ducked, it would have lodged in his back. He spun around to look for whoever had thrown the blade.

Theron barreled toward him, teeth bared and another dagger glinting in his hand.

Muffled shouting came through Kaemada's gag, and she writhed around Taunos's feet, nearly tripping him. He leaped forward to find clear footing.

Theron drew another dagger in his free hand, his eyes intent on Kaemada. "She never should have come back. Get out of the way."

"She's my sister." After all Theron had put her through, he might as well know who was getting Kaemada's revenge.

Theron paused for a moment and then grinned, the expression full of menace.

And then Reinan darted past Taunos and hit Theron, the bigger man slamming the younger to the ground. Taunos hesitated. The need to join the fight, the thrill of the challenge, thrummed through him. And this was Theron, his sister's tormentor! This altercation had been long in coming.

And yet, Reinan was risking his life to give Taunos a chance to get Kaemada to safety. That was the whole point of tonight, after all.

The conflict within him raged as wildly as Reinan's battle with Theron, but Taunos turned, sheathing his daggers and wrestling Kaemada back over his shoulder. Even bound tightly, she still squirmed with all her might, and it took most of his concentration just to avoid being taken down by his own little sister. He charged down the road to the hole in the wall, darting through a few paces behind Ra'ael and Takiyah, at the rear of the bulk of the Resistance. The glory of rain showered down on him, drenching him with cold and turning the ground sodden under his feet. Taunos kept watch while the last stragglers streamed by.

Whatever internal power struggle had sparked the guards' fighting kept them distracted. Reinan was charging toward him yet again, and Taunos watched for bows. The guard from before had Theron in a headlock, and they spun wildly as Theron tried to twist free while keeping his head intact. Reinan tugged on Taunos's sleeve just as Theron rammed his dagger into his opponent's chest. Taunos turned, sprinting through the hole in the wall.

Theron's words chased Taunos out of the city. "I am King Theron! Enjoy your freedom for now, cowards, but I'll burn the Resistance like a blight. All who shelter psions will share their death! Especially that psion Kaemada!"

Taunos ran, falling in alongside Reinan once he got up as much speed as he could with his sister thrashing about on his shoulder. Without Reinan, he wouldn't have made it. He needed to do better. With Ra'ael and Takiyah's plans to leave, he'd have to keep his sister safe on his own.

He ran as fast as he could manage until they were past the fields. There was no pursuit right now, but they were far from safe. He settled for a distance-eating lope at a pace he could sustain while carrying his sister, rather than sprinting.

"Stupid, back there," Reinan scolded, steadying Kaemada when she nearly fell off his shoulder. "You could have killed us, your sister included, with that childish stunt. You cannot improvise like that when others are depending on you for sticking for the plan."

Taunos nodded. It had been stupid, and he'd known it. Again, the giant of a man made him feel small, with so much to learn. "My thanks for your help."

He drank in lungfuls of sweet, rain-filled air. The flat landscape was disorienting in the dark between flashes of lightning, and the rain made it even harder to see, but Taunos loved it. His shirt was slicked to him, his cloak drenched and pulling at his shoulders, and his boots squished with every step, but they were free. They were free.

"The Resistance set up near a stand of trees that way." Reinan indicated the direction with his head, and Taunos angled that way. "Most of a day's run."

"I cannot—ow!"

Kaemada jerked, twisted, and kneed him in the head, screeching as she did so. Taunos shifted her again and ran on.

"These fits, they have not gotten better?"

"I'm surprised the fit did not begin sooner, honestly." Taunos panted between phrases. "Normally, she would have been thrashing about the time we left the house. It's fortunate she hung on as long as she did."

"We don't have much for helping."

"I hope, being free and away from that city, with all the memories, she will come back to us."

"You and your sister," snorted Reinan. "All hopes."

Taunos raised his eyebrows at the older man, but the dark likely hid his expression. They ran on, saving strength for the long journey ahead.

They'd left the fields far behind and reached the first hill before Taunos noticed that his sister had gone suddenly, prematurely, calm. He shifted her to his other shoulder, but his senses nagged him. Something was wrong. He glanced back, but no one was pursuing. He stopped, and Reinan paused near him, drawing in deep draughts of air.

Taunos laid Kaemada on the ground, tilting her head to the side to avoid the rain drowning her, and knelt beside her. She lay too still. Fingers clumsy, he removed her gags and the bite stick to listen. She wasn't breathing.

"Eloí's light and spirits around us!" he swore. "Kaemada, you listen to me, little sister. You are not allowed to cross the rim of the sky, do you hear me? You are not allowed to die!" He tilted her head back and breathed for her then slammed his fist onto her chest.

She jerked but then lay still again.

"We're free, little sister. You cannot die now, not when we just got free!" Again he breathed for her and again punched her.

"You will break her bones," Reinan said.

"A healer I knew once taught me this."

"Beating up dead people?"

"She's not dead yet."

But Reinan had a point, and after breathing for her another couple times, Taunos placed his hand on her chest and pressed sharply with his telekinesis, hoping that would accomplish the same thing. Several repetitions later, with Reinan standing sentry, Kaemada jerked halfway upright, drawing in a long, haggard breath. Bound as she was, she soon fell back to the ground and lay there breathing, blinking at the rain falling into her eyes.

Taunos collapsed over her, laughing with relief. "Thank you, little sister. Thank you for listening."

Reinan quirked his eyebrows. "I need for trying beating up dead people more often. Time for going."

Reinan gathered up Kaemada in his arms, for which Taunos was grateful, as he was exhausted. She looked so small, curled up against the big man's chest, her eyes still open. She was calm again, even though she was staring off into the horizon. They ran, then walked, then ran again, gaining ground on Elisabei and the larger group as the second moon crested the horizon, providing only a sliver of a crescent for light.

"I'm not sure why tonight is different, but I'm thankful. Typically, her fits last longer."

"And typically you do not beat her?"

"I really wish you would choose a different word."

Reinan shrugged, trudging along with his long-limbed gait. "It may be my ignorance of psions, having rarely interacted with them before her, but it seems that—well, maybe you know better."

"What, Reinan? I value your input."

"Well, it seems I have seen her thrash like that before."

"In the city."

"No, before. Will you listen? Under the mountain, too, when she was fighting the psions."

It was true. Taunos had seen it, too, and it was so obvious now that it was pointed out. Taunos felt ten times the fool. "How could I not see that?"

Reinan chuckled. "Sometimes it takes someone looking in from the outside for seeing truly. I lived in the city near fifty winters, and yet your sister immediately saw we could do more with the Resistance than just annoy the king. She killed the king and gave us an opportunity. Elisabei and I are grateful for her since. I'm glad for enlightening her foolish older brother in payment."

~

Thank you for reading.

The story continues in Let Loose The Fallen (Book Two of Children of the Nexus)!

www.ingramcontent.com/pod-product-compliance
Lightning Source LLC
Chambersburg PA
CBHW031152050726
47495CB00019B/1522